HUES OF SEOUL

HUES OF SEOUL

Mystery and Suspense
In
Today's Korea

Charles T. Mitchell

Hues of Seoul: Mystery and Suspense in Today's Korea

Copyright © 2021, Charles T. Mitchell

www.charlestmitchell.com

ISBN: 978-1-7334881-2-9
Library of Congress Control Number: 2021902130

Washington, D.C.
Published in the United States of America

*

DEDICATED TO

Elena Kim-Mitchell

CONTENTS

Prologue   i

1   Bridge of No Return   1

2   The K-Pop Princess and The Mountain   33

3   An Angel of Hongdae   91

4   The Fishmonger of Incheon   121

5   The Letter Writer of Insa-dong   159

6   Mapo, Bridge of Sighs   191

7   God Kimchi of New York   233

8   Jeju Island Enlightening   283

Epilogue   321

PROLOGUE

As the far horizon summoned the Korean peninsula's afternoon sun, countless trees, swaying in the autumn wind, cast legions of misshapen, twisted shadows, forming silent, rippling waves of serpentine processions, many of which slowly marched up the western slopes of Seoul's picturesque, parkland draped Mount Namsan. The blustery wind was wildly stirring the tall pines, broad oaks, and graceful maples, while kicking up a colorful mix of fallen needles and leaves, tossing random twigs, and disturbing the hair and attire of the post-lunch hikers scattered amongst the shifting shadows along the various trails. Conjured up during the weeks following Chuseok, that national holiday when Koreans everywhere celebrated family and, ostensibly, the yearly harvest thanksgiving, real and simulated, the strong fall wind held only a hint of the deep chill of the coming winter. For centuries, the centrally located mountain, formerly Mokmyeoksan, with its fortress walls, garrisons of soldiers, and string of fiery signal beacons, had served as a time-tested barrier to a hostile, outside world, securing the people and traditions of old Korea, until physical barriers were no longer strong enough to hold back more modern invaders. The proud mountain had then suffered for many decades, before, eventually, coming to serve as an inspirational monument to freedom and as a beacon of hope for a people setting their own course in the modern era. Yet, even in the midst of the gleaming, ultra-modern city of Seoul, many older traditions still thrived, with Namsan acting as a familiar torch light for those wanting to harken back to an older order. Maybe not on the stages with the K-pop stars, nor in the boardrooms of the corporate chaebols, nor in the classrooms of the top high schools and universities, nor in the high-rise apartments of the rich and middle-class alike, nor in the streamlined lifestyles of its youth. But, gliding below the surface, just around that blind turn, a few steps over that small hill, and in the evening shadows of the old city gates, an essence of old Seoul still lingered, quietly resisting the press of the modern era, while biding its time, silently dreaming how the old ways, while probably lost, might linger a bit longer, before fading into and, one day, out of, the memory of the peninsula's people.

Not far from Namsan's old city wall path, about a third or so of the way up a stepped trail bordering mostly tall, firm pines mixed with stands of poplar, oak, and maple trees, one particular visitor walked alone, leaning slightly against the fall wind. Dressed in black jeans and a dark blue shirt, covered by a darker blue sweater and a charcoal windbreaker, the visitor, obviously not a local from his foreign appearance, had paused, just beyond a curve in the old city wall, to determine the simplest path to ascend to the famous plaza at the top of the mountain. In previous visits, the windblown visitor had taken the cable car near Myeongdong, out of a sense of adventure, and to avoid the endless steps of the long, winding trails to the top. However, in order to think through some tough issues with a critical project, the visitor had chosen to hike to the top over unfamiliar trails, hence his caution over which path to take. Since the hour was well after lunch, most mid-day visitors to the park had already made it to the top, or had split off from the trails and had found quaint little spots for outdoor respites, even with the wind, so there were no large crowds to follow.

The autumn temperatures, for a brief couple of days, had been unusually mild, allowing romantic couples, old retired folks, and escaped office workers to linger under a blue sky accented by passing puffs of white clouds, while enjoying the early autumn vibrant yellows, reds, oranges, and browns against a backdrop of green pines and fir trees. A few hikers had already been up to the mountain early and were descending. The visitor, in an attempt to gauge which route was the most opportune, had carefully noted the routes of several small groups, and of several single hikers, returning from the summit to head back down into the anonymous steel, glass, and concrete of contemporary Seoul. As was the custom, several of the younger hikers greeted the visitor with the polite formality of quick bows, since he was obviously older than the youthful office workers and students. The visitor, in turn, received nods of acknowledgement of his own polite greetings from older hikers. However, for most of the visitor's trek up Namsan, he was the only soul visible on long stretches of one of the winding, western trails.

After gazing over the seemingly endless steps of the path leading upwards, while averting his eyes from the signs cautioning hikers to remain on the designated trails, the visitor cast about looking for what might be a shortcut, hoping to bypass one of the wide twists in the main trail ahead. Spotting a likely candidate that crossed a heavily shaded stand of trees, he hesitated for a split second, but, spurred on by a brief blast of colder air, he then stepped away from the official route to walk along the branch path, faintly etched into the ground. As he walked, the visitor marveled at the silence and serenity of the newly discovered path, with most of the sounds from the city below resolving to a low, barely discernable murmur, all but drowned out by the rustle and sweep of swirling leaves, bird calls, and swaying tree limbs.

Just as the visitor was about halfway between where he had deviated from the main trail and where he would return to the same trail higher up, he spotted a rather large, orange tabby cat, battle worn and tough-looking, sniffing the ground near a dense stand of older trees. Surprised that such a usually skittish, urban outdoor cat was not running away at his approach, the visitor slowed his stride to try to see what, in those trees, might interest the feline mind.

Suddenly, without warning, and with shocking speed, the cat jumped backwards on all fours and then, twisting its body in mid-air, spun around and dashed off to disappear down the mountain, passing the visitor without so much as a sideways glance. The visitor chuckled at the cat's odd antics, and then continued on the path, only to be hailed by a voice, its owner unseen.

"Excuse me, young man. I hope you are well. Have you, I say, have you…the time?" a gravelly, older voice, with a hard to place accent, abruptly asked from the shadow of the copse of older trees the cat had just abandoned in frenzied retreat.

Surprised at the sudden appearance of anyone on the isolated shortcut, the visitor squinted into the trees to try to get a better look at the speaker.

"Why, yes, I do. Let me just look at my watch," the visitor absently responded, amused that some old fellow had called him 'young.'

Mildly distracted by the tabby cat's retreat and the surprise appearance of another hiker, the visitor paused, checked his watch, and then looked back to the cavernous space in the trees. But, he was denied a peek at the owner of the voice as the sky suddenly had become overcast, dimming the already sparse light cast into the thicket of old growth trees.

"Excellent…," the disembodied voice answered, as a previously unseen break in the trees suddenly revealed what appeared to be a low bench, hewn from the living rock of the mountain, just inside the stand of trees. "Please, good sir, would you like to have a seat? Maybe a brief rest?"

Peering into the dimness of the small clearing with the stone bench, the visitor was curious as to why a trail hut, which he assumed was beyond the bench, would be tucked away from the main path. He took a small step before stopping himself and replying.

"I'm sorry, grandfather," the visitor called in a strong, if foreign voice, using the general honorific for addressing an older man in Korea. "I thought you meant the hour, not spending time."

"Oh, humor my aged self for a fleeting moment, young man. I've only to ask a question of a fellow traveler," the voice answered, its pitch abruptly lowering, losing much of its harshness. "Yet, if you must, carry on up to the summit, then, if you've no poet's curiosity."

Squinting, again, into the stand of old, massively tall trees, bunched oddly close together at that turn in the shortcut, the visitor actually considered entertaining the old guy's questions and resting for a few minutes, given that he still had, he thought, about half-way to go to the top.

Looking back down to the main trail, which turned and disappeared only a couple of dozen meters below, the visitor saw no other hikers, locals or tourists. Looking up the trail, a group of young high school or college kids, who had passed him just after he had left the main trail, was still visible, but would soon fade from view around another turn.

"Alas, youth's eternal optimism," the still detached voice called, a certain longing seeming to drift over to the visitor. "Those little ones, too self-absorbed to have heard my call, will be quite tired by the time they reach the top."

"I'm sure they would have taken your offer of a brief rest, had they heard your invitation, sir," the visitor quipped to the voice, then immediately regretted trying to banter with the fellow, knowing such would only delay him further.

"Ah, yes. I had been distracted by more…more pressing matters when they were approaching," the voice replied, sounding smoother and more distant than before, as if receding into the tunnel of trees. "Enjoy your stroll, young man."

For the briefest of moments, the visitor saw, or thought he saw, the voice's owner, who appeared to be a tall, thin, older man, wearing a traditional, blue-grey Hanbok, and a traditional 'gat,' a black, horsehair hat worn by the upper classes in days gone by. Intrigued by the imagery, the visitor then stepped toward the fellow and, in doing so, passed an unmarked, but defined threshold of the small grove beside that less traveled path.

Stepping into what he thought was the outer courtyard of a trail hut, usually found in the far mountains for hikers to rest, attend to bodily needs, and maybe find water, the visitor was surprised when the little enclave seemed only to hold the stone bench and a few other boulders, with the entire area surrounded by a tight stand of towering trees. Looking into the darker spaces at the rear of the copse, the visitor could see a long, rectangular shape, but no details. Beyond the shape, the visitor heard rustlings, like the sounds a cat or a small dog would make when looking for a quick refuge after being surprised, no doubt by the visitor's sudden appearance.

Looking back to the stone bench, the visitor saw a thin, bony hand extend out of the grey, no, now darker cloth of the Hanbok, and tap the stone top of the bench three times, creating an intriguing ringing sound from the stone.

Bong…Bong…Ta-Bong!

The unusually clear, nearly temple bell quality of the stone's sounds drew the visitor in, and, truly interested at that point, he stepped fully into the embrace of the trees, unaware that, behind him, an unseen hand seemed to move the trees closer together, shutting off any exit through the entrance the visitor had just stepped through.

Abruptly, the blurred image of the scholar slipped away into the rear of the enclave, causing the visitor to pull his eyes from the attraction of the sounding-stone bench. Sensing something amiss, he then turned to step back out of the trees. Puzzled at the closeness of the trees, he sought the break through which he had just stepped, but to no avail. In fact, he felt, bizarrely, that the trees were actually crowding into him and pushing him back toward the bench.

Fighting to stay frozen to his spot, yet unable to push back against the crowding tree trunks and branches, the visitor finally yielded and allowed the trees to force him to the bench, where he stood, his legs pressed against the cold stone, looking around for the owner of the voice, ready to talk or even, if necessary, fight his way out of the odd cul-de-sac, even though a quick glance revealed no other breaks large enough for him to squeeze through between the trees.

Breathing.

Raspy, almost consumptive breathing was all the visitor could hear for nearly a full minute, not the smooth, level breathing of the fading scholar from before, or even the first gravelly voice. The breathing had a forced quality, bringing up long ago memories for the visitor of a sad, far too full cancer ward, where such sounds had often preceded a patient's demise.

Shaking off the old memories, and finally fed up with the game, the visitor pushed against the trees, but they seemed to simply draw even closer the more he resisted, eventually pushing him back again, to finally sit on the cold, grey and white stone of the bench, where he dropped his small backpack and took out his phone.

"Okay, sir, whoever you are, I've had enough of this, whatever it is. I'm calling the rangers to…," the visitor began, then cut his challenge short when he saw his phone was unresponsive and quite dead. "How? It has a nearly full charge!"

Suddenly, from the lower part of the small, oval enclosure, which was naturally slanted up a bit toward the summit, a low growling sound drew the visitor's full attention. Trying to stand, but, again, pushed back by overhanging branches, the visitor looked around for something to use as a weapon, but found that the only thing he could use would be his flimsy backpack. Grabbing the pack, he prepared himself for whatever might jump out of the shadows.

Slowly, from deep within the murkiness of the narrow, dark spaces between the gnarled and twisted trees at the back of the enclave, a murky, flowing form emerged, like thick smoke from a pile of poorly burning wet moss.

Wet moss?

When had he ever seen moss burning, the visitor wondered? He then squinted against the darkness to try to better discern the emerging figure.

After several seconds, a tall, wraith-like man, or man-thing, emerged from what the visitor felt was the very wood of the closely spaced trees. The creature, for creature was the word that first came to the visitor's mind, was tall, but slouched over, bringing the thing's grisly face, a pasty mass of jumbled muscles, pockmarks, open sores, and bits of hairy moles tossed in for added revulsion, down to its sunken chest. The creature's hair, half hidden by a frayed cowl of some rough, dirty cloth, was black and stringy, with all manner of leaves, vines, and twigs embedded in it.

Moving, the visitor realized with a shock. The detritus in the thing's hair appeared to be moving, as if the vines were growing, twisting around themselves.

The creature's body was clothed in the same rough material as the half-cowl, a dark, dirty patchwork of drab, sack-like cloth loosely sewn together with some sort of heavy, yellowed thread or thin twine. Far from the elegance of the earlier Hanbok, the habit enveloping the tall figure spoke more to a sad beggar than to an educated official. At the thing's feet, the visitor could see neither shoe nor boot, but only blackened, root-trailing stumps peeping out from under the long, dark slacks or gown, where shod feet would have resided on most men, or hooves on beasts.

Alarm finally sounded in the visitor's head as the creature fully emerged and leaned in to stare into the surprised man's wide eyes. The visitor recoiled and involuntarily let out a shout.

"Hey! Can anybody hear me? Hey! In here. Behind the trees. At the bench! Hey! Can...any...body...?" the visitor called, but then fell silent as he watched a small group pass unaffected, just beyond the trees that had trapped him with the creature.

"Yes, dear boy, they can not, do not hear you. Or, rather, they, in their selfish little worlds, choose not to hear the cries of the lost and forlorn," the man-thing said in a raspy, fluid voice, as he, or it, slid next to the visitor on the bench, causing the visitor to move to the far edge, gripping his pack for some level of protection from what he surmised was some sort of socially outcast hermit or maybe a homeless old degenerate with major hygiene issues.

"What is it you want?" the visitor demanded of the creature, hoping his voice carried enough menace to influence the mound of vile flesh and rags.

"Why, child, I'm going to eat you, of course," the creature said in an unhurried, matter-of-fact way, causing the visitor to suddenly look more puzzled than frightened.

Struck by the bizarrely casual nature of the creature's declaration, the visitor took a moment to collect his thoughts, assess where he stood, and then replied, using what he hoped was a commanding voice.

"Seriously? In this day and age? Plucking passerby for an afternoon snack? What? I suppose you also can fly? And can shape shift?" the visitor, deciding his host was a wayward hermit, asked in the most sarcastic voice he could muster, given the circumstances, which he was having trouble believing.

"Fly? Fly! Oh, were I able to fly! I'd not be here, that's for certain, boy," the creature replied, allowing its diseased tongue to slide across the boils and lesions that passed for a mouth.

"What? Leave here? Why? You've obviously got a never-ending supply of unsuspecting prey tromping by your den here on the way to the Namsan Tower," the visitor quipped, employing a tactic of engaging in conversation as he tried to figure out how to break out of the encircling trees.

Sniff. Sniff.

The creature had leaned over the bench and, pushing back its greasy strands of hair and writhing twigs hanging over its bleak, black and yellow eyes, it sniffed its guest for several seconds, nearly unnerving the visitor.

"Yes. Nicely fit. Some fat. Enough to flavor the rest, you have. Days to prepare you, no need. Just a quick drop into the pot," the creature cooed in a distinctly different, odd, singsong voice as it continued to sniff the visitor.

Suddenly, the creature recoiled, slapping at its gruesome face with its thin, yellowed hands, as if trying to bat away a bad smell.

"You're not...awful smell...not of the peninsula's people," the creature suddenly coughed between swipes at its own face. "What's this other stench? I've known it. Before. Long before. Too many now in Joseon are, the same. Ilbon? Japanese? Yes? No. You are not Japanese. No Japanese blood."

The creature then hesitantly leaned back and sat apart at the opposite end of the bench, seemingly lost in thought and ignoring the man with the odd scent. Its hands no longer were trying to wave off the visitor's odor, but were resting at the beast's sides.

After a bit, the creature then turned back to the reluctant guest, extending its black and purple tongue to slide along its lower, festering lip.

"Jungguk? Chinese? No. Not from over the mountains. More over the seas?" the creature said, a semblance or spark of understanding slowly creeping onto its cratered face, using its tongue almost as a snake would, as it appeared to sample the air near the visitor. "Wait? Yes, over the seas? Ports and strange foods, I taste. Too much meat, your people eat. Drink spirits too much."

The creature then seemed to again withdraw into deep thought, causing the visitor, who had endured the creature's antics with clenched teeth, to finally express his agitation.

"American! Miguk saram, that's what you...you smell!" the visitor burst out, angry at the odd dance they were playing, yet suddenly proud of declaring his heritage, especially if he was to have his life threatened by some maniac on the side of what should have been peaceful, historic, even romantic Namsan.

"Miguk, American, like the soldiers from before? Tough, they were. Only a few remain. Full of self-importance and good deeds they believed in, for a time," the creature mused, its voice falling back to the language of the earlier scholar. "Far shores bring far ideas, yes?"

The visitor, confused as to what the creature was mumbling on about, simply nodded, letting his veiled eyes dart about the enclave as he did so, hoping to find a way out, while he assessed how to overpower his odd host.

"American? But, your scent. It has overlapping layers. They hide your...your savory essence, like the covering of a mirror. Very, very local," the creature mused, but only briefly.

"But, we can't be too discriminating, boy. You'll just have to do," the creature finally said, looking back toward the visitor. "Part of me wonders why you are on my mountain, but, I shy from asking, for my slipping memories tell me, your kind tend to talk, and talk, and talk."

"My wife is first generation. From California. Yes, I must have a confusing...aroma?" the visitor blurted out, both angry at letting himself fall in with the addled hermit, and desperate to take a wild shot at throwing out something, anything that might keep the old crazy talking a little longer.

The creature, drawn out of its reverie by the visitor's anger, slid closer, its tongue making tiny flicks at the visitor as the creature spoke, its voice and speech as odd as its appearance.

"Confusing? Not entirely unknown, if confusing," the creature continued, waving its thin, rag-covered arms at the passing hikers just beyond the trees. "Different bloods, so many have, yet, so few know, or want to know. Taste only a few pure Hanguk, Korean, now. More in the old days, my uncles and cousins tell me. Wait? Why climb my mountain if you are not of this place? Rare is the outsider who graces these old stones."

The visitor, surprised that small groups were wandering by when he had been nearly alone for most of his trek, thought for a moment and, betting on the creature's already demonstrated curiosity, answered with another challenge, hoping to distract the beast further.

"Why? Are we suddenly not tasty enough? Is my flesh too outcast for your sensitive palate? Too waeguk? Too foreign?" the visitor demanded in mock affront, hoping to keep the creature talking, while trying to recall a more formal Korean term for being ostracized than 'wangtta,' outcast.

"Aiyee!"

Suddenly, the creature stood its full height of over two meters and began to howl an unearthly lament, which shook the very trees around them until even more autumn leaves rained down from frightened branches. Outside, on the far trail, several hikers pulled their jackets closer at a sudden blast of colder air coming from the group of trees.

Swinging its long arms all about as it stomped and howled, the creature struck out blindly, shocking the visitor when the tough bark of old trees was ripped by the man-thing's raking, talon-like fingernails. The visitor was further stunned when the creature slapped the top of one of the small boulders just beyond the bench, sheering off a good chunk of the boulder's top.

The visitor, realizing his quip might have just sealed his fate, was frozen to his spot as the creature stomped from one end of the tree-bounded enclosure to the next.

Strong. Immensely strong, the visitor realized, partially repressing his thoughts of overpowering the lunatic and forcing it to release its accidental captive. His part-time hopkido classes years ago would be no match for someone with such brutish strength, the visitor conceded, wondering if the creature was a mad refugee from some elite fighting force.

As the surreal host stomped, bits of its tattered clothing and other, more grotesque debris fell to the leaf covered, stony ground. Even though the visitor wanted to close his eyes and wish himself away, he couldn't help but to stare in horror as the bits that fell off the creature seemed to wriggle into the rocky ground itself, under the leaves, and disappear.

"Outcast! You? You dare lament your sad little fate? You? A mere child? Bah! No more than a third of a human's cycle, can you be. You know nothing of being outcast!" the creature cried more to the trees than to the visitor, who tried to remain as immobile as possible.

"You're not one! You're not...not the other! That's what both sides said. Both! No one wanted the...the different one! The one not pure! Not those majestic giants of my...what do you call it...sire's side! Not the clever uncles and cousins of my mother's kind!" the creature howled, and then, throwing its bony, misshapen, yet deadly hands to the heavens, collapsed onto the ground at the edge of the small enclave, its chest heaving heavily.

Shocked at his captor's sudden crumbling in dramatic despair, the visitor's mind raced to try to come up with something to delay whatever fate the lunatic had in store for him. For the visitor firmly believed he had encountered a classic social outcast, a pariah, possibly a serial killer, lurking at the fringes of a society that had somehow not only disowned the beast, but had chosen to ignore him and his evil deeds.

Him?

The man, for he had ceased to think of himself as a visitor, but as a man desperately aware of his mortality, suddenly realized he had stopped thinking of the creature as an 'it' and had begun to think of it as a 'him.' The visitor, the man, then shook his head quite vigorously, in hopes of dislodging such sympathetic thoughts.

Turning slowly to look on the nearby mass of heaving rags and rancid flesh, the man again assessed his ability to overcome the lunatic and force it to release him.

No, those hammers of its fists would make short work of him, the man realized, and redirected his mental energies to pursue a line of conversation that would keep the creature from beginning its evening meal, or whatever ritual might be in store for its reluctant guest.

"Well, that's a coincidence. You're a mixed kid, too? Like my children?" the man asked, trying to keep his voice level and his stomach from churning at the stench rising from the creature's being so close.

For one full minute, the pile of rags and squirming flesh continued to quiver, its heavy breathing uneven and almost asthmatic. Then, just as the man had decided he'd try to climb one of the trees to attempt to escape that way, the pile rose up and confronted the man, its dark, black and yellow eyes only inches from the man's defiant face.

"Mixed? Mixed kid? Mixed…kid. Interesting. Interesting words," hissed the creature. "Mixed up. Clever. Clever words, boy."

Turning away from the man, the creature slid over to the far back of the enclave and, pushing back some dead branches, revealed that the rectangle the visitor had seen was an old firebox, an agungi, something the guest had only seen in the traditional folk village museums. Sitting on top of the low-slung, iron stove or buttumak of the firebox was the largest cook pot the man had ever seen. It, too, had an ancient, well-worn look. A gamasot, made in the older style of cast bronze, but with a heavy iron lid, which could create a high-pressure type of cooking, even long ago. Some large portion of the cook pot was embedded in the top of the buttumak, but a good meter or more was visible on top.

Fortunately, the man noted, the firebox was dark and cold, showing no fire had burned there in some time. He watched as the dark creature fussed about, seeming more like an old ajumma, lady, than some mythical beast.

Mythical!

The man sat bolt upright.

That's it! The dirty fellow, the man realized, whatever beggar life he had led, thought of himself as some old fairy tale creature and probably justified his psychotic behavior using a mix of superstitions. But, which ones?

The man racked his brain for what knowledge he had of Korean folklore, or even Chinese or Japanese mythical beasts, goblins, and fairies, wondering which the creature fancied itself to be.

"Ah, found it," the creature hissed, and showed the man an old tinderbox, the kind used to start fires decades before. "Now I will show you who is truly outcast."

"Outcast? Why are you outcast? Aren't you just a rather socially removed hermit? Not much to ostracize there," the man said as he stood up, standing as straight as he could, to allow him some advantage of height against the hunched over creature.

Turning, the creature eyed the man from behind greasy strands of dirty hair and vines, and, placing the tinderbox beside the massive pot, slid back to stand by the bench and slowly nodded to the man.

"One would think, young man. One would think. Wondered, I have, what being a normal hermit would be like," the creature said with an almost wistful tone, but that would be madness, the man thought, as he attempted a reply.

"So, what kind of hermit might you...?" the man began, but was cut off by the creature's sudden shout and rambling chatter.

"Neither side wanted the odd one!" the creature howled, bits of foam and other splatter hitting the man's chest. "My, what do you call them? The sire? They said I was not...I was not pure enough to return to the fjords and mountains of my sire's homeland. Cast out, my mother's side, took me in, they did, at first. Thinking that my sire's side would bring riches and many fat, sleeping children from their silken beds in Seongbuk-dong. Alas, the brothers' war had ended and, after a time, many far away humans returned to their homelands. My sire and his kind had to return to the cold lands with their humans. Later, my sire, angered that his kin had left us, tried to have an ally sneak me, and my mother, aboard a ship, but that ship was sunk by an evil water spirit angry at the ship's master for ignoring the old rites. I think I swam ashore, can't fully remember. Lived alone for a time. Found my way back home, but was no longer wanted. With the sire and his gang gone, the local cousins knew they would not be getting the wee children any longer, for which they had traded a few souls, sinew, and skulls. Pushed me away. None of the clans would take me. Pushed me nearly back into the sea, they did."

The creature then fell silent, only the sounds of its asthmatic breathing filling the small enclave.

The man gleaned the few bits of background that the creature shared and formed a few tentative thoughts.

"You're a, I would guess, you're a troll, then? Maybe an ogre?" the man asked, his face going a little ashen at the thought that he might actually be in the company of a deranged man who thought of himself as a Scandinavian spirit, a robber of cradles and consumer of travelers.

Suddenly, the creature clapped its hands, the sharp sound bouncing around the enclosure.

Almost immediately, from the small, dark, in-between spaces in the trees beyond the firebox, little children, at least the man saw them as children, emerged carrying kindling wood and ondol charcoal fuel, the traditional charcoal briquettes used for cooking and old-style, under floor heating. Four total little creatures. Maybe boys. Maybe little girls. Their rags were as pitiful as the creature's, but the children were definitely children, and probably not of the creature's issue.

The little helpers stuffed the kindling into the firebox and added a few pieces of the charcoal, placing the majority of the black bricks to the side.

Another small one, with large, sad eyes, and a slightly cleaner face, as if the poor creature had just tried to rub the grime off its thin cheeks, walked over to the bench. Hesitantly, with its reddened eyes full of suspicion, the half-clean little one placed a small bowl of what looked like spiced nuts and rice crackers close to the writer's backpack.

The little ones then all retreated and disappeared back into the trees just beyond the makeshift kitchen, each one looking over its shoulder with large, hungry, red-rimmed eyes at the guest as the wee creatures popped back into the dark spaces. The half-clean one wasn't quick enough for his, or her, master, who kicked out, just missing the little one's head as it scurried back to the trees.

Smiling at the retreating children, its face a jumble of renewed horror, the creature stepped back to pick up the tinderbox.

"Wait. Really? You're going to tease me with only half the story?" the man called, still standing, but feeling his knees weaken at the sight of the kindling and charcoal, and the stomach turning image of the hungry, if brief, stares of the ravenous little ones.

Placing the tinderbox back on the ledge, the man-thing, for the human captive had yet to agree to the creature's story of being anything else, turned and, briefly, seemed to be the old scholar again, so that the man rubbed his eyes, wondering what tricks the creature was playing. The creature then stepped back to the bench and sat, patting the top of the bench for the man to sit as well.

Hesitantly, one eye on the tinderbox and one eye on the vile face before him, the man slowly resumed his seat a meter from the creature.

"Heard the tales from the locals, you have? Goblin? A good word. Dokkaebi? More accurate. Encompasses more variety," the creature said, its voice clear for some odd reason. "Troll? Ogre? Night spirit? I always was proud of my sire's side. Not as much my mother's side. Especially after they left me on that beach, after our first try. Not too far from here. I ate crawling, dirty crabs until I hated them. Roamed the old Chemulpo area. Sometimes sat behind the youths camping on the low hills, listening to their ghost stories. More than once I'd slide into one of them and scare the entire lot off my beach. Then, one day, many seasons later, my mother appeared. She had run away. Defying her clan, she was going to take me to my sire. She said the stars were right, and had found another boat we were to haunt all picked out. It was a ferry. Was to take us around the small sea. There she was going to have her Japanese relatives, living there, but not Japanese, help us find another boat. A bigger boat. The ferry had plenty of human families for us to haunt and to keep us fed, so we were on our way."

The creature then fell silent for some time.

"What happened?" the man asked, to ensure the creature didn't wander back to the firebox, wondering if the beast's narrative would eventually connect all the disconnected threads.

"The ferry, loaded with many humans, for sure. Too many. And too much, what do you say, cargo? After an angry set of waves, sent by the big, swirling winds, the ferry wobbled, leaned to one side and, then, in a blink, sank. Yes, a second ship tried to drown me," the creature answered, its voice detached, morose. "It didn't get me, but, this time, my mother did not climb out of the sea. I learned years later that salty sea water doesn't mix well with certain domestic dokkaebi."

"How did you come to this mountain?" the man asked, trying to keep the creature talking and away from the firebox and cook pot.

"This mountain?" the creature looked confused, then continued. "No one wanted it. After a second period of lost cycles, that time on the shores of Jeju, under thrall to the fishing goblins, and then finding a haven near Busan, I made the long journey back to my mother's family, feeding on the meager leavings of cursed cousins along the way. I tried to find a hole or cave near my mother's family, but they ran me off. I tried up in Bukhansan, but it was full of wood spirits and, others, and they didn't want me, now an orphan, around."

"Why not?" the man asked, taking breaths in short sips to reduce the stench coming off his host.

"Growing bigger, I was," the creature replied, raising its head fully in an odd show of vanity. "Slowly getting bigger than the pure spirits and goblins. But, not quite as big as the Norse trolls or ogres. I was stuck in between. But, still too big to fit into most places that the local goblins use for hiding. Not that they wanted me around. Too big and clumsy, they would say. But, only behind my back. Too afraid to speak to my face."

"I can see that. But, why here and not some more secure tunnel or maybe even stay by the beach?" the man asked, throwing anything into the conversation to distract the creature.

"This, the mountain, still teemed with Japanese ghouls and lesser spirits, trapped here after one of the old wars," the beast answered. "They were mostly weak and abandoned by their own. Dismal lot. After eating a few of them, they all ran, almost, all ran. A few still linger in the dark places."

"Wait! Enough of this! I'm a goblin-troll-ogre, whatever you said, not a human fool!" the creature snapped. "I know you want to keep me talking so I don't start the fire. Well, I'm the troll-goblin, goblin-ogre, and you're the dinner, so my nature forces me to return to the fire."

"But, wait!" the man called as the pile of rags moved to stand. "You're neither goblin, nor troll, nor ogre, nor…whatever. You are unique. You're the only you. You have probably made your own rules for you. Why stick to rules of those who disowned you? Why continue to pay them tribute? Give them credit for who you are? You should make your own rules."

"Cutting out and discarding the tongues of chatty suppers, that will be my first rule," the creature responded, with something different behind its yellowed eyes.

Humor?

The man couldn't believe it, but he detected that the creature was trying to make a joke, even if a bit ghoulish.

Humor? How to continue in that vein, the man wondered, rummaging about in his mind for a retort.

"Discarding? Better to grease the tongues with soy sauce and garlic for a tasty bite," the man offered. "Wrapped in sesame leaves."

"No. Sesame oil, and green onions," the creature countered, then looked at the man expectantly.

"Kimchi and rice. Roll it up…in seaweed," the man answered, curling his own tongue in a loop.

Suddenly, from somewhere deep inside the pile of rags and bones, the man heard what he thought was the beginning of a chuckle. Frantically, the man mentally grasped at another idea and blurted it out before the seed of that chuckle died down.

"Pickled jerk tongue! That would be the tastiest morsel," the man slurred, pretending his tongue had already been removed for the appetizer.

The chuckle in the beast's chest slowly grew. Then, with little warning, burst forth as a full belly laugh from deep within the creature.

"Haw, haw! Haw, haw, haw!" the creature bellowed, again shaking the trees around them. "Pickled jerk! Haw, haw!"

For a full minute after the creature's laughter had subsided, the two sat on the stone bench in silence. Only the sounds of the late afternoon birds could be heard, but at a distance. Far below, the sound of traffic entering and exiting the tunnel floated up faintly to their stand of trees. Above, the cheerful sounds of friends out for the evening could be heard passing on the far trail, as the man wryly noted no other hikers were taking the shortcut that had led him to his possible doom.

"It has been many seasons, boy, ere I've uttered such sounds," the creature finally said into the growing mustiness of the enclosed space.

"Even the tiny ones are shocked and scared by such sounds coming from their master."

The creature waved its left arm toward the dark spaces behind the firebox where the dirty tops of the child-things' faces could be seen looking out in bewilderment. The creature picked up some sticks and tossed them in the direction of the little helpers, scattering them back into the trees.

Suddenly, the creature lunged at the man and, instead of sinking its rotting teeth into the man's neck, it grabbed the man's backpack and quickly dumped out the contents. Brushing most to the side, the creature picked up a notebook, and commented.

"Ah. Paper. No talismans that I see, though. Good. This will help the fire burn earlier and faster," the creature said with some relish, flipping through the printed pages, back to front.

"No! Anything but that!" cried the man, standing and stepping toward the creature. "Roast me. Skewer me. Cook me. Whatever. But, don't burn my…please don't burn my book. It has my hand written notes."

"Book? This is your…book?" the creature asked, sniffing at the pages. "What do these little bugs and squiggles say? They are not the old tongue."

"Stories."

"Stories? About what? Human fools?" the creature demanded, squinting at the apparently unfamiliar English words and turning the notebook sideways and upside down, seemingly unable to decipher the text. "And, why are you carrying this?"

"The café. Just above. At the tower. To edit. I like to go somewhere with a lot of people to edit the final version," the man said, inching closer to the creature with the wild idea of grabbing the notebook and tossing it out of the trees into the path of future passerby.

"Ed…it?" the creature asked, dragging its pockmarked hands across the pages, leaving ghastly streaks of black and green ooze.

"Correct any mistakes. Add new ideas. Delete wordy passages. Edit…editor," the man said in a rushed, almost panicked voice, standing so close to the creature that its stench was nearly unbearable, but wanting to seize the book. "What one does before publishing."

"Foolish boy, I know what is a book, it is. Why here? And not back where your sire is from?" the creature demanded, a new anger rising in its voice. "You can move about freely, untethered. Why here and not, wherever there is?

"The stories are about here. About this place. The people. Their spirit. The…," the man replied, then paused and, with an idea forming, corrected himself as a better plan came to him. "Fairies and myths."

"What? No goblins and ogres?" the creature growled, its yellowed eyes squinting to mere slits. "Are we not worthy of your flimsy pages?"

The creature then tossed the notebook onto the pile of charcoal and, crossing to the old stove, reached, yet again, for the tinderbox. The man, desperate to save his work even if he must perish, stepped forward to confront the creature.

"They forget, you know. The humans out there," the man said, leaning into the creature and pointing to a young couple that he could just see between the trees. "Over time. They forget the fairies and the goblins. And the trolls. The ogres fade into the stones of the mountains. The wood sprites and brownies cease their dancing. The dokkaebi grow listless and lose their humor. Once they all forget, what happens to you?"

The creature grumbled for a few breaths and then paused, a strange look crossing its hideous face. Its black and yellow eyes opened wider and its diseased lips pulled back over rotting, yet sharp, green and yellow teeth. Its head lolled to the left and, looking sideways, its eyes stared at the man, the writer of tales, with renewed interest.

"Yes? Go on?" the creature hissed, draping its right hand, boils and all, over the man's left shoulder, bits of wriggly things falling onto the man's jacket.

"Yes. Memories fade. Old people die," the man stuttered, trying to hit on an angle that would further delay his fate. "Why, I bet you haven't had a gold tooth in ages come through here. All the young people have perfect teeth, or they get those ceramic caps. You certainly can't melt those down into pretty chains and rings, can you?"

"Why would I want to melt down teeth for rings and such? Do I look like a magpie? Or a gutter trade dokkaebi?" the creature retorted, but continued to stare sideways at the man.

"Have you noticed a number of your mother's kin fading away?" the man asked, taking a wild gamble that the creature, or lunatic man, was a true loner and didn't have much contact with the world around him.

"Fading away…? Yes…yes, I have heard little these many seasons from the local goblins and spirits. Odd. Yes, faded away, they have," the creature repeated, shifting its weight to better stare at the man. "How do you…you, not of the peninsula, know this?"

The man took a quick breath and forced his gurgling stomach to calm down, lest the stench cause him to heave his breakfast all over his captor.

"It's only natural. If you and your kin are forgotten and no one is around to believe in you any longer, what is there to tell you that you even exist? Who will mourn you when…what old women will wail for you, when you are gone, if no one knows you are there?" the man replied, pushing leaves into a pile in front of the creature.

"See that pile of leaves? If you had not seen the trees earlier, to you they are simply temporary cushions on a hard, rocky earth. In a few weeks, they will be gone. As if they were never there," the man said, allowing his voice to become more melodic and, he hoped, more convincing.

The creature pushed at the pile of leaves with its left stump, scattering the pile across the ground. It then looked up to the autumn colors mixed in with the green overhead and, the man hoped, was maybe thinking about the fleeting lives of the trees' leaves. The creature then looked back to the ground and then to the man, slowly nodding its understanding.

"If…forget, they do, then no more, I am?" the creature asked, its voice distant and hollow, falling back into its earlier singsong.

The man nodded, biting his tongue as he really wanted to say 'especially if you keep eating all your witnesses,' but the man didn't want to remind the creature of the evening meal.

"If no more, can't prove to my mother's kin that I'm as good as any goblin, or dokkaebi, As good as any cousin," the creature declared, then continued, its speech shifting between the singsong of a simple mind and the complexity of a scholar. "If I'm gone, I can never find that unsinkable boat to carry me to my ancestor's fjords, where I must be laid to rest to reach my sire's burial mounds. A drifting, stinking ghoul, I would be?"

The creature's voice trailed off, its face showing something of a lost vision, as it let its own image of a drifting wraith with no direction slowly sink in.

"Such a shame, fading away like that. Why, when I first stepped into this glen, I could swear I saw nothing but trees and mid-day fog when you first spoke," the man said with sincerity, since it was the truth. "Even now, your image and shape seem to waver now and again."

The creature then stood, and, while watching the man, stepped over and picked up the notebook, its back cover blackened by the dust from the charcoal. The creature held it as if considering whether to tear out a page and stuff it into the firebox, or throw the entire book into the pile waiting for the starter flames.

"How long does it take to pen these tales, human?" the creature suddenly asked.

"How long? Why, it depends on a number of elements…," the man began, but was cut off by the creature.

"How long, human? Don't banter with me!" the creature roared, so loudly that small whines of fear could be heard coming from the rear of the enclave, where the little helpers had disappeared to.

"A few days for some. Weeks for others. The entire work…maybe six months to a year," the man replied.

"How long in seasons? Hot, rainy, cold, mild. How long?" the creature asked, holding the notebook next to the firebox.

"Seasons? The entire work, two seasons, maybe three. One story, less," the man answered.

"One story?" the creature asked, turning the book to the front, instead of the back, to look at and sniff the first pages, stopping at the contents page.

"One story? By seasons? Maybe...one third of a season, maybe faster," the man replied, his eyes widening at the creature's continued sniffing of the pages.

The creature then stepped away from the firebox and abruptly flung the notebook at the man, who caught it, smudging some of the charcoal dust on his jacket, leaving a large black spot under his right arm.

"Humans and spirits. What are these tales, human? Where do you steal them? Do you kill in these tales? Do you eat your kind's flesh as its fat drops, sizzling hot, into the fire?" the creature asked, a new, more dangerous level of excitement in its voice. "Do frightened babes cry for their mums, human?"

His stomach flipping over from the sudden, numbing interest by the creature, the man was briefly at a loss for words. Staring at his captor, he forced his mind to ignore the bile rising in his stomach at the creature's sudden excitement.

"Why these tales you scribble, fool?" the creature then asked, letting its revolting tongue slide left to right on the word 'fool.'

"Why? Why to examine the human...to examine how the world works," the man replied, overly cautious as to how he should answer. "How people react...how characters react in certain...how...lives, in spite of obstacles and trials, continue."

"But, why?" the creature spat at the visitor. "Gold, maybe the humans throw at your tales? Paint the fat humans like the high portraits, as they sit among their swilling thralls, do you, human?"

"Yes, some of it is for money, but it is more to get the stories out," the man replied, his writer's ire building at the creature's disdain. "To entertain, to raise questions, to bring to light the good...and the bad in man."

"Have my cousins in these, do you, human?" the creature snapped. "Do you tell lies, human, or do you tell the real tale?"

"I don't understand...?" the man replied, wondering what trap the creature was setting.

"Lies, human. Lies that you weak creatures control your miserable, short, pasty little lives," the creature hissed, losing its singsong voice for a voice more guttural. "No more than the bugs that crawl through my open wounds, human, do your brethren control their own."

"Well, yes, there are influences beyond anyone's control," the man answered. "But, the earmark of a man, at least a wise man, is how he, or she, controls the response to those...those uncontrollable elements thrown his, or her, way."

"Where are these tales? In your sire's land? Why do you...editor...why go to Namsan for a foreign tale, human?" the creature asked, a certain slyness evident in its voice that had not been there before.

"The tales are of…as I have said, the tales are of here, my host," the man answered, being cautious in what he said after hearing a note of deceit in the beast's question.

"Here…? Where is…here? My mountain? My village that has grown beyond the old river just there? My old kingdom, grown new and nearly unrecognizable? My peninsula, torn asunder by you foolish humans?" the creature cooed, its voice an inviting trap, drawing the man in. "Where…is…here?"

The man, fully aware that the creature was baiting him into some sort of terrible admission that would instantly justify the beast's lighting of the cook fire, considered lying to the beast. Yet, something in the back of the man's skull kept telling him to just tell the flat truth. And, if the beast pounced, throw the book over the dark top of the trees and meet his fate.

"They are stories of lives, over the years, of this land. More the people and some of their trials and triumphs," the man replied, steeling his stomach for the return of the creature's hungry little helpers. "With some of the beliefs, some of the legends, or myths, that can drive them to…well, stories of life, good and bad."

A gleam of triumph crept into the creature's veiled eyes as it replied.

"How do you, a fool human from another shore, a shore far, far away, tell tales of my peninsula? My…my prey? My cousins? How, dear little boy, can you be so bold?" the creature asked, its right hand swinging back and forth like a scythe preparing to slash the wheat that was the captive's neck.

"I observe, vile beast of the mountains and conqueror of oceans," the man replied, keeping his voice steady. "I see, I listen, I even experience. I talk, others talk. I love. I hate. I walk away. I run toward. At some point, I write it down."

"True, these tales are, boy?" the beast asked, its right hand scythe slowing a bit.

"True in my mind's eye. In one's imagination, anything is possible," the man replied.

For a long span of several breaths, the creature simply stood staring at the man, its right hand scythe swinging slowly, ever so slowly, thought the man, almost like the pendulum of a great clock. Or, the double-headed axe of a medieval executioner.

"A story, tell me," the creature abruptly demanded, breaking into the man's wandering thoughts as he tried to dream up more retorts to the beast's questions. "Of my land I wish to hear how you have mangled my prey's lives, stolen their secrets, whispered to their dying gods. I wish, boy, to hear you carve your words on my own fading mind, so I can better enjoy my after dinner wine."

Waving aside another clump of brush to reveal a carved stone table and stone chair or stool in the shadows, the creature swirled around to stare at the confused man.

"Tell you...?" the man haltingly began, his stomach bile again rising into his throat, choking off his words as he wondered if he should read the draft manuscript, or if he should try to craft new tales that would appeal to such an amoral, mindless, death-bringing devil.

"Yes. I demand, I request, a story. One story. One moment of respite from the cook pot. I had a rather portly solicitor a half-moon ago and am not quite at the famished point. Tell me a tale of your spirits and humans," the creature repeated as it settled into the stone chair, resting its arm on the table next to what looked like a large, of all things, beer stein, streaked with black ooze and bits of what looked like matted hair. "Tell you, I will, after, if you are spewing lies. Maybe let the little ones nibble at each lie...?"

The man continued to stare at the creature, which seemed to have transformed into an old man waiting for afternoon tea at some club in Mayfair, instead of a reeking mass of worn and diseased flesh. Shaking his head to rid it of the false imagery, the man forced the bile in his throat back down into his gut and, thinking quickly, if not clearly, given the stench of the creature, the closeness of the small enclave, and the nagging presence of the hungry little ones spying from the dark nooks, he decided making a deal with the creature was the better path, versus trying to fight his way out. Even though the beast appeared frail and brittle, the man knew, by instinct and by the earlier evidence, that the creature could crack the man over its knee like an egg over bibimbap, if the creature were so inclined.

"Why, yes, of course. A tale for time. Maybe, many tales for more time...? Well, it's a bit dark in here," the man replied, his mind racing, wondering which of the stories he should read to both capture the creature's interest and have his captor allow the man to read other tales, or if he needed to create new tales on the fly.

"Shall I light the fire?" the creature asked in another poor attempt at humor.

"What? Fire? Oh, no. No need. That street lamp just outside there should do. That faint light streaming through the top of the trees. Yes, that will do nicely," the man said in rapid succession, hoping to divert the creature from the man's blunder about the light. "I know the stories, of course, but just need to see the words to ensure you are getting your...your time's worth."

Turning to the book, the man gave the creature a long look and then, controlling his voice and trying to stay calm, called to his captor.

"Shall I introduce the tale or, dive right in?" the man asked, flipping open the notebook and finding the first chapter, which he had decided would be the best approach, as he was not certain the creature had been telling the truth when it said it couldn't read the text.

"Just tell. You decide if you need to introduce. I decide if the tale is worthy of an outsider to my land…and worthy of the delay in my dinner," the creature replied, leaning back into its chair, but keeping its black and yellow eyes trained on the reading man. "And, human, I may not know the scribbling on your pages, but I can count. And, smell, I can. Smell lies, we creatures of your nightmare, can. Smell fear, everywhere, we can. Smell distrust and deceit, our favorite snacks, they are. Yes, count I can, human. Know you and your tales are stories, I do. My cousins lurk in the folds of your book, there, even if you are too stupid to see them, human. I will listen for them. Disappoint, my little ones will feast early. Entertain, we may let them only nip at your fingers…."

Clearing his throat, the man, still worried about which of the stories might appeal to the beast, wondered again if he should just start at the beginning, and work his way through the book, thereby enticing his ghoulish host to delay until the entire draft had been read through. Such an approach would depend on the man's ability to convince the creature to want to hear more.

Since the creature did not appear to be able to read English, the man decided he could add to the tales on the fly, if needed, making up additional stories once the manuscript's content had been depleted. Even if the beast had counted the number of stories from the contents page, the man was hoping that the beast had no concept of the length of a story, or that some tales may be made up of several chapters.

Enough! The man shouted to himself in his mind. Overthinking as usual, he cautioned himself. Just tell the tale, he told himself, as he stole a glance at the creature, and allowed his gaze to drift to the darkened trees behind, and the waiting little ones.

Scanning the table of contents, the man, the writer of half-imaginary, half-real tales, trapped in a small stand of trees, somewhere on the side of a westward trail heading up to the summit of Mount Namsan, with either a true goblin of traditional lore, but of a mixed heritage, or a crazed lunatic, serial killer from the underbelly of Seoul, decided to wing it, hoping he could gather more insights while he related the first tale. He was determined to draw out as much information, regardless of how bizarre or unbelievable, to help him craft whatever approach worked, at any given minute, through any means necessary.

Whatever the creature was, fairytale monster or lunatic maniac, didn't really matter at that moment to the writer, only living through the tale he was about to read was what mattered. And, if he could keep reading, the writer wondered how many tales he could relate before the monster lunatic became bored and started the fire under that hideously huge cook pot.

"Right, let's simply start at the beginning. Sir? I haven't a name to call you?" the writer asked, pausing. "I'm called…."

"No names," the creature declared from the shadows, cutting off the writer. "Uncomfortable, I find, eating things I know the name of, if I have conversed with them on an equal...on some level of discourse."

The creature then chuckled at its little joke and waved for its guest to continue with the reading.

His approach reinforced by the beast's morbid humor, the writer turned to the book's first tale, a story of wretchedness and mysterious loss, hoping the creature might relate, and then maybe soften the beast's resolve to eat early. Fortunately, given the range of superstitions in human society, each of the tales, for the most part, had a hint of old lore, so the writer hoped the creature would find its own cousins, as it called them, lurking in the 'folds of the book' as it had said.

Whether he'd be able to convince the creature that men and women did, indeed, have sway over their lives, was probably a moot point. Yet, the hidden journalist in every writer would still ensure those threads were highlighted, regardless of his final path, up to the plaza and the cafés, or down into the ancient cook pot.

Ultimately, the writer acknowledged, his game was to convince the beast to delay the writer's demise, not only for the evening's meal, but also for some years to come, facilitating the reluctant guest's release from the dungeon-like enclave. Exactly how to do that remained just out of the writer's grasp, but, the longer he was able to tell his tales, the more time he'd have to fashion an argument that would convince the twisted mind of the creature that not eating the writer was in the creature's best self-interest.

And, of course, keep the little ones from nibbling away at his vulnerable extremities, the writer emphasized in his mind.

"Please, sir, let's think back a few years. Before the great plague that ravaged these lands, and those around the world. Before the change of...well, a few years, many cycles, before today," the writer began, settling in on the stone bench so he could see both the creature and the two routes the little ones had to take to reach him, their meal.

"Step a few dozen kilometers into the hills and valleys north of Seoul, to that no man's land that has lain as an open wound, a tragic scar across the peninsula for so many seasons, so many cycles. Even your own cousins, right? They are probably torn apart by the decades of exile beyond that winding border? Let's start our journey there, this afternoon. Think back to what you know of the border, the fearless soldiers, the endless barbed wire fences, the minefields, the lonely outposts. What could be lonelier than a bridge falling into woeful, wretched disrepair? A bridge of such import. A bridge of such renown. Forgotten and discarded. Yes, let's drift up there on the southerly winds for a few minutes, and take a quick peek just beneath the surface of daily military routine and control. Yes, just a quick peek."

1

BRIDGE OF NO RETURN

North-northwest of Mount Namsan, about as far as an advanced artillery shell's range, a bleak section of the long, open wound of the no man's land that splits the two halves of the peninsula quietly hosts an old river, the Sachon. Not a raging river, nor a particularly long river, but a river that has played a critical role in the history of the Korean peninsula. While that river deserves its own treatment, this tale is about an old bridge that spans that lonely, isolated river running through the forbidden zone. The old bridge is a desolate, soulless place, bereft of any of those traditional, humanizing touches given to similar loyal structures that safely support men and women, or less fortunate beasts of burden, on their lives' many layered journeys. Scarred, naked concrete, laced with rotting iron, covered in twisted, near-dead vines, littered with dry, brittle leaves, and random bits of detritus blown in from both the north and the south, are the tattered patches on the heavy coat that woeful structure has been doomed to wear. A rough, pitted road surface, faded to dirty charcoal over the decades, challenges a few hardy weeds to eek out short, nearly companionless lives. Now and then, a rare wild animal dares to scurry across its deserted expanse, risking exposure for convenience. For the bridge, its days of hosting multitudes of people rushing to and fro, always too busy to pause and speak to the bridge, or even notice the structure under their rushing feet, had long passed into shadowed memory. The bridge had done its noble service for years, especially at the end of the last major conflict that had raged across the hilly, once heavily forested land. Yet, while built to be a path between here and there, and, sometimes, back again, the sad structure had lost its calling from disuse and neglect. From the time a cave dwelling ancestor first dropped a log across ancient waters to make his

1

miserable cave life a little easier, a bridge's duty had been to serve quietly, silently, without complaint. The lonesome bridge over the Sachon was no different, and would serve, if given a chance, as long as someone took care of its structural wants and if the river did not decide to rebel and, aided by some monstrous deluge, push the bridge down and scatter its aging debris all the way down to the Han River and beyond.

All bridges have scuff marks from sandals, shoes, or boots, track marks from wheels or tires, stains of oil, sweat, and blood, scratches left by those who had to drag their goods across, and, once in a while, hopeful markings of still innocent children who frolicked on, over, and under such intriguing playgrounds. Maybe a child caught his or her first fish in the shadow of that bridge? Maybe a young man proposed to his one true love when the bridge was new? Maybe soldiers, bonded in the hell of battle, swore oaths of fealty to one another on that now silent passageway?

What, if anything, did the forlorn bridge over the Sachon still recall?

The old bridge, even in its desolate state, did continue to harbor faint, very faint, memories of long ago.

Echoes of a time before.

A time of hope and promise, crushed by a time of suspicion and division.

Of an unresolved, brutal conflict of brothers clashing with brothers, fresh on the heels of a decades-long subjugation by outsiders.

Of the ebb and flow of forces from both sides attempting to gain the ultimate advantage.

Of vainglorious advances and withering retreats.

Of a forced stalemate, leaving hundreds of thousands dead.

Of countless, tortured souls deciding, in a life-changing moment of dark confusion, which way to cross, forever wedded to one side or the other.

After the last war, other than a few short outbursts of brutality, the bridge had only a decades-long, running memory of a barricaded, unused, and unloved passage, a remnant and silent reminder of what should have been a long forgotten conflict, given mankind's ability to create new wars to scare away the memories of those that had come before. Other than the occasional, wayward wildlife, no one had crossed that forlorn bridge in those decades.

Yet, even through the bridge's darkest decades, with little use other than as shelter for a few wandering animals, and a place for the opposing sides to glare at one another on respective national holidays, life, or something like life, continued to dwell within the bridge's protective, if crumbling expanse.

Woven into the murky darkness of the bramble of overgrown brush and twisted, dwarfish trees, littered with a confused jumble of old, rusting military gear that bordered and barricaded both sides of the languid river's banks under the bridge, were two accidental habitats which could easily invoke the days of those aforementioned, early cave dwelling ancestors.

Over the decades, since the time when the bridge had decided the fate of so many, two dark dens, reeking of the most foul stenches that would cause even the toughest soldier to swoon, had been hiding deep within the underbelly of the bridge's supports, on both sides of the slowly moving river. So dark were these pitiless gouges in the river banks that the light of day not only never reached into the depths of the dens, but they were so dark that the river betrayed no reflection of the dens nor of their contents to anyone on either bank above looking at the river's surface below the pitiful expanse.

If a boat were to venture by, which was highly unlikely due to the rocks, decaying military barriers, and drifting forest debris along that stretch of the river, the two dens would still be hidden from even the most experienced of scouts by the tortured twists of forbidding brambles and impenetrable darkness.

Such dens were where one would expect cruel night beasts or burrowing river rats to dwell, or any manner of spiders, snakes, bats, or other blood curdling denizens of the night. Yet, even those seeds of children's nightmares avoided the areas of the two dens, a nod to the skin crawling fear those dens had evoked over the years.

So, just who, or what, occupied those two pools of despair beneath that decaying bridge of disrepair?

Unfortunately, as mankind often fails to learn from the mistakes of those before, he also tends to lose the collective knowledge and wisdom of the ancient ones, forgetting much of what has been handed down in the never-ending pursuit of the new. Consequently, the true origins of just who the two occupants of the dens were had been lost, if it had ever been known, to any other than the occupants themselves, and they were, as you will soon see, ill prepared to offer any enlightenment as to their miserable origins.

A few old tales, albeit discounted by learned authorities, hinted at witches from the days of Joseon, or, even farther back, dim stories of deserted, devotee-bereft forest and mountain demons left over from days of living in mud huts, under grass roofs. Other ideas, from travelers out of the north, held that they were the cast off mistakes of secret work of unspeakable experiments, manufactured in horrific camps in the north to be unleashed one day to devour those south of the bridge. Others, especially local villagers, unsullied by urban concerns, would chant old songs, often ignorant of their meaning, but convinced that the songs kept the bridge's hidden horrors at bay, even though the villagers never got closer than the barbwire barriers of the no man's land, choosing to err on the side of caution, even at a distance, rather than worry about esoteric intellectual arguments.

Whatever the true origins of the two hidden dens' occupants, all one must accept is that something wicked, yet ill-defined, dwelled in darkness and secrecy beneath the old bridge, waiting.

Of particular interest, even if the crumbling concrete and rusting steel of the bridge itself were mutely indifferent if humans ever returned, the two who inhabited the shadowy dens, one on each side of the bridge's underbelly, did indeed, on the contrary, care if the humans returned. In fact, if the wretched beasts residing in that murky gloom had had souls and a priest to minister to them, they also would have prayed vigorously for the regular return of humans to the bridge.

Sadly, the two below did not, by any apparent evidence, have souls, nor had there ever been evidence of an accidental priest or shaman in their miserable midst. So, they were doomed to ponder their grim lot in life with the innocent dimness of the few wits they had residing in the cobwebbed recesses of their simple minds. Some scholars, from the old days, might have argued that the two did not even have minds, but simply the reptilian type of brain that reacts and charges at its environment over the slightest sign of prey, danger, or weaker entities.

Yet, even the most jaded of men, such as those rare few who had had the misfortune to actually meet the two residents, no doubt would acknowledge that the den's inhabitants had some manner of mind. For, the two had the command of rudimentary speech, and, as everyone knows, if you talk, you must be able to think, even if only a wee bit, and in foggy lurches. How many of us know someone who talks, and talks, and talks, yet shows no outward evidence of having much of a mind? Yes, we all know a few. And, if one can talk and think, might there be a soul lurking under that brutish, dullard exterior?

With no professor around to listen, interpret, and espouse on the two occupants, we will have to make do with what bits the wind carries over to us, augmented by the murmurings heard in local soldier bars and the juicier insights from the occasional well-oiled sergeant on leave in the nicer joints in Seoul. Granted, the gentle winds can carry the muted conversations only so far, which is why they are rarely heard beyond their respective sides of the dismal, deserted bridge, leading many to suspect a great deal of the backroom talk had been crafted over the years to elicit more beer, rather than give an accurate accounting.

Yet, once in a while, stronger winds, both from off the Manchurian Plain and from more sober soldiers, would blow a few of the bridge dwellers' secrets down to those who knew how to listen. When such winds were stronger, the muffled conversations would float up around the trees and shrubs near the bridge, causing the routine, conscript troops to create a long running game of who got to 'not' report the sounds, due to their superiors' displeasure over such unwelcome reports.

4

Some decades before, not long after the closing of the bridge as a result of the tragically murderous tree incident, sentries on both sides had repeatedly reported odd, conversation-like sounds to their superiors, only to be abruptly assigned to even more unforgiving posts deeper in the zone. For some unknown reason, probably because the sounds always subsided when sergeants or officers arrived to listen after seeing the reports, the higher up military brass had decided that the fickle winds and active imaginations of the dedicated, yet bored soldiers at the decaying bridge were the culprits. The top sergeants, one may assume independently on both sides of the river, had then banned anyone from filing official, unverified reports on the muffled, phantom conversations.

Consequently, when the rank and file heard what they thought were the conversations, they would quickly cover their ears, turn up their radios to drown out the sounds, or simply walk farther away to avoid both the wrath of their superiors and the far more reckless, odd pull of the tantalizing sounds.

That curious allure of the sounds, like a modern day version of Homer's long ago Sirens, did, however, on rare occasions, draw an unsuspecting soldier closer, for private, undisclosed, and certainly unauthorized investigation.

When a new recruit, eager to impress, heard the sounds and openly announced he would go looking for the source, the older hands would always try to pull him back, knocking the poor soul a few times on the back of the head, and telling the dazed newcomer that he was dreaming on the army's, pick the side, time. However, once in a while, an even more rare, woefully overzealous recruit would become disobediently eager to impress his superiors, and, of course, to seek any distraction to stem the pervasive boredom of garrison life. Even in the zone, manned by the nation's finest, ninety-nine point nine percent of daily life was wholly uneventful for the line soldiers, of both sides.

Such exercised curiosity would, inevitably, result either in the unfortunate disappearance of the inquisitive soldier, or in the green recruit's abandoning of his post and running home, even if hundreds of kilometers away. Many a young soldier had been retrieved and thrown in the brig for going AWOL (away without leave) after investigating those strange sounds under the bridge.

In the case of those few who simply did not return, their superiors, after waiting the usual twenty-four hours for those zealous, missing recruits to reappear, would invariably check the boxes for 'accidental' and 'landmine' with 'no remains found' and file the reports under 'routine,' knowing none of the officers would bother to read such.

Yet, not too long ago, just a week or so after Chuseok, when soldiers had returned from the loving embrace of their families to collide again with the boredom and booted grind of camp life, there was a rumored instance when two overeager soldiers, one on each side of the wistful bridge, allegedly had encounters with the dens, on the same day.

A very odd day, that day.

With the ban on routine communications between the two sides still very much in effect at the telling of this tale, we will, of course, focus on the account of the unfortunate fellow on the southern side of the bridge, with hopes of one day hearing the corroborating northern tale as well, while allowing for a bit of poetic license on the northern soldier's actions.

While the younger soldiers who had heard the rumors of that day were sworn to secrecy on pain of severe punishment, the sergeants were a bit more lenient with their own tongues and, relaxed of an evening at one of the few clubs near the zone which catered to a range of nationalities making up the forces on the southern side, the normally reticent military men spoke in hushed tones for only their foreign comrades to hear, all the while impressing upon their doubting audience to maintain the utmost secrecy, even though there was zero military or other apparent value to the story. The foreigners, themselves nicely mellowed by the local soju, agreed, fully expecting to remember nothing of the conversations the next day.

Yet, by way of one of those honorable military men, a former teacher of the author's, the tale did make its way out of the zone and into these pages, with, of course, exact dates and names obscured to protect our border guardians, critical bulwarks of the peninsula's stability and security.

On the auspicious day of the rare encounters, as fate would have it, a long negotiated agreement had resulted in the silencing of the incessantly blaring, monstrous loudspeakers, which usually blasted propaganda from both sides of the divide. Falling deathly quiet simultaneously, late in the afternoon, with dusk not too far away for the no man's land, the absence of the blaring speakers caused an unusual, and wholly welcomed, hush to fall over the land, like a warm embrace. Everyone was relieved, since the continuous noise played havoc on even the most well trained soldier's patience and good sense.

At the moment the loudspeakers were silenced, two young recruits were cautiously patrolling on opposite sides of the derelict bridge, keeping eyes trained on their counterpart across the slow moving river. Each soldier was abruptly introduced, for the first time in their few short weeks in the zone, to the otherworldly silence that naturally permeates the no man's land.

After the ringing of their ears, even with plugs, subsided from the mercifully silenced loudspeaker barrage, it was so eerily quiet that the two opposing recruits, who could each see the other on the opposite bank, simply stared at each other in disbelief at the rare, true silence.

Being true to their profession and to their respective national laws, neither soldier motioned, signaled, or otherwise attempted to communicate with the other, letting the very warlike image of the tall, no-nonsense stance of each young soldier convey their messages. They simply stood their separate ground in the silence, both wondering absently how long the blissful quiet would survive.

Yet, after only a few moments of welcome silence, the two recruits began to hear other sounds.

Birdcalls and animal chirps arose from the forests, the river, and the small glens around them. The wind swayed tree limbs and rustled the autumn leaves. Water trickled over rocks. A vehicle in the distant with a bad cylinder, on the north side, whined back to base. The hum and buzz of countless insects rounded out the sounds that rose up out of the zone's rare moment of silence.

Both soldiers, after staring at the other for what felt like the appropriate amount of staring time, and, being very careful not to show any signs of surprise to the other and to not provide any gestures or silent communications to the other, eventually turned away from their respective river banks to head back to their separate outposts for the late afternoon reports.

Suddenly, a low rumble of not quite intelligible murmurings caused both soldiers to stop dead in their respective tracks, swinging their weapons to the ready, heads cocked to catch more of the odd sounds.

Frowning, the soldier on the south bank tilted his head one way and then the other, all the while keeping an eye on his enemy across the river. Of course, the soldier on the north side also mimicked his enemy's gestures and searched for the source of the odd noise. While both were well aware of their respective sergeants' orders, as fate would also have it, that day both soldiers, from both sides, were of the curious type.

The southern military man, due to his well-educated and inquisitive nature, was always looking for the underlying causes of things, even in the blunt hierarchy of his mandatory military time. The northern military man, due to a small seed of inquisitiveness, but mainly due to an inner, nearly unconscious desire to delay his return to camp and to the routine abuse by his more senior comrades, was always looking for a distraction.

Both soldiers managed to locate the general direction of the sounds at the same time, and both slowly turned to look at the shadowy, bramble-covered under passages at each soldier's respective end of the desolate bridge. Dark and murky, even on a sunlit day, as evening bore down, the under passages were both black abysses promising severe and vile accidents for anyone foolish enough to investigate.

Unfortunately, national pride and individual zeal overtook each of our intrepid recruits, no doubt because each could see the other and, maybe, just maybe, did not want the opposing side's soldier to report that his counterpart on the opposite bank had shirked his duty, shown his tail feathers, and scurried back to the safety of base camp.

The sounds continued.

Both soldiers had heard, or imagined they had heard, muffled conversations coming from under the bridge. Both sides.

Yes, each soldier had heard louder sounds on his own side and then answering, softer sounds from the opposite side.

An obvious explanation, which occurred to both recruits, was that two or more deserters from the north, or south, were using the darkness and seclusion of the underside of the old, disused bridge to escape to the south, or north. Yes, for a fleeting moment, the two also considered that maybe, just maybe, the unseen culprits were trying to escape from the south into the north, but both quickly surmised that was ludicrous, as one misguided soul might try to dash to the north, but two or more as a group was highly unlikely.

Both soldiers each soon steeled themselves and, weapons at the ready, moved toward the sounds. The southern soldier used a small, bright beam of light from a device on his chest to show the way, while the north side soldier used a flickering light attached to his vintage rifle. Both stepped hesitantly down the steep, uneven slopes of their separate banks.

As the two were staring hard into the blackness of the under passages, both soldiers suddenly, without warning and without sound, disappeared into the bridge supports' dark, gloomy underbellies.

Silence.

Deathly silence.

No calls.

No commands.

No screams.

No shots fired.

Only silence from the two black abysses.

How many minutes or hours passed in the nothingness, neither of the two vanished soldiers could tell. At some point, they both were vaguely aware that they had fallen into a hole, or slipped into a fox's den, judging from the stench and cloying nature of the dank surroundings.

Yet, both also heard a confused mumbling, in some barely intelligible half-language, that seemed to be gurgling up close by in the semi-darkness.

While the language the two military men heard was little more than shreds of the common tongue on the peninsula, both slowly realized they could just, on the very edge of their minds, understand the low, guttural rumblings of their two, as yet to be revealed, hosts.

"What we have? Man-food?"

A wretched, slurred voice, full of gurgling and spittle, called from the northern bank to the southern bank.

"Yes, I think we have men. Men soldiers. Today."

A more coherent, less muddled voice had answered from the southern bank, with language a tad better structured than the much simpler utterances from the north.

Darker shapes within the blackness of the dens, the origin of each of the voices was barely discernable by their respective soldier. The two hosts, at least to the few unfortunates who had seen them, appeared to be close in age, although, over the years, the wretch of the north had faded into a shadow of his southern brother. The two were so simple that they were never heard using names for themselves, and, of course, did not use a proper name to call the other one.

Over time, the farmers in the south had bestowed the two disembodied voices with names to ease the telling of such tales. In a nod to how the river flowed more north-south at that point, the southern resident was labeled 'Namdong,' Southeast, and his even simpler brethren to the north was called 'Bukseo,' Northwest.

As the two beasts chatted, the two recruits were in frozen, trance-like states, somehow induced by the touch of their captors, or from some vile chemical brewed in the cesspit of the two lairs. Struck mute, they could still see and hear, and, as the seconds ticked by, even move a little, but not enough to aim and fire their weapons or to try to fight by hand. Helpless, the two military fellows could only listen, as if through cloudy water, to the odd conversation shouted between the two creatures. While the two hosts might have appeared to be shouting, the accidentally rich acoustics under the bridge allowed the two occupants of the secluded dens to actually use voices just above a whisper.

"What do? Chomp them?"

Bukseo, the wretch of the north, was always hungry. For over six decades, his cupboard had been nearly bare. When fewer and fewer unfortunate meals, more bones than flesh, had wandered too near in the early days, the pickings had been so slim that malnourishment had damaged the wretch's health, both of body and mind. Any morsel that happened to wander his way, whether it walked, crawled, slithered, or flew, he would consume without much thought as to what he was doing. Of the few soldiers or foraging farmers that had fallen his way in the interim decades, they had been so bereft of nutrition, mental and physical, that the wretch of the north had lost much of his ability to reason, or even speak coherently. Had the poor beast been alone, without his brother to the south, he would have wasted away into the dust of memories long before the two soldiers had happened along.

On the other hand, Namdong, the wretch of the south, while equally as hungry on most days as his benighted brother, had had much more substantial fare over the years, given that his southern prey had so much more to offer his discerning palate. Although his brother's addled mind was irreversibly damaged, the southern wretch would still share his catches with his less successful brother. Yet, while he needed to satiate his gut's constant hunger, the wretch of the south felt he desperately needed to exercise what little was left of his own mind.

As the years had stretched into decades and his only constant companion was a brother who could barely converse, Namdong had yearned for opportunities to keep his mind from going dark, just as his pitiful brother's had done. Consequently, while he also eventually ended up consuming whatever came his way, since that was his lot in life, he would always spend some time contemplating whether the meager morsel was worth the effort, allowing his starved mind to have some limited exercise. That day was no different.

"A moment, horribly fetid, ghoul brother of mine. A moment."

Now, insulting each other was a key part of the wretches' lifestyle. The blunt comments were not malicious, simply the only kind of comments they knew.

Looming over the soldier on his side of the river, the wretch of the south reached out with…?

Well, let's just call the appendage an arm with a hand for ease of understanding the beasts.

Namdong, the wretch of the south, reached out and stroked the top, side, and face of the southern soldier's head. Then, the beast's long, boil laden, slimy tongue, smelling of rotting teeth and putrid pus, rolled out of its black cavern of a mouth and slid back and forth over the recruit's face.

Across the narrow river, Bukseo, the wretch of the north, was also assessing his own prey, but making a much messier job of it, leaving large deposits of greenish-yellow mucus all over his captive's face, head, and uniform.

"Nearly empty, this one," the wretch of the south called out to his brother. "Not much of a meal, or even a satisfying snack. But, there is something there, just what?"

Namdong then stroked the left side of the recruit's neck and then leaned in for a closer look, large red eyes gleaming nearly black in reflection of the torchlight on the soldier's chest.

"Ah! This one has the mark of the string box. The western strings. Violin?" Namdong called out with a hint of excitement. "Maybe some meat here after all."

"This one. No play music. No read book. No study studies," Bukseo called. "Eats. Smells. Drinks. Gambles. Loses. Cheats. No meat at all."

The two beasts then ceased talking and commenced to utter a series of grunts and whistles, as if they were exhausted from the few moments of conversation and the large amount, for them, of thinking they had just done after being surprised by the soldiers.

The surprise visits had come during a time of long hunger for the two beasts. While small prey of the forest and river kept the sad misfits alive, barely, their true prey, their ultimate meals, which could shore up their miserable bodies for months on end, were the fatted humans who stumbled into their clutches only rarely those days.

Even though they did not keep an accounting, the northern wretch was not very accomplished at luring his prey into his den, often scaring them away before they were in peril of falling. The southern beast, on the other hand, was adept at dragging his few victims into his darkened den, even though his opportunities, due in large part to the better minds and physical conditions of his prey, were far fewer than his brother at the other end of the bridge.

All these thoughts drifted through the southern wretch's dirty skull, while the northern beast simply stared, empty-eyed, at the morsel before him.

After a bit, Namdong spoke, almost coherently.

"Surprised, toy boy, that I know the violin? I know many great things you puny ones do to stretch your minds, to gloat over me, and my brother across the unforgiving water. Buk? Janggu drums? Many a drum man has fallen into my lair with their meaty arms and thick legs," the wretch chuckled, letting his distended nostrils flare, causing dripping mucus to flap around his face.

"A few…what do you call…horns? Soft, those horn players. Minds very squishy, easy to drag clean," Namdong added.

"Buk? Drums? Drummer? Drumming…?" Bukseo called from the other side, repeating the sounds of drums, the only instrument he ever remembered longer than a few minutes, because he liked hitting things.

"No, vile stench of our deserting father's cursed loins, not drums. A small gayageum. Strings. Hard for these tiny hands to play, but play they do, right, boy?" Namdong said to the air around his hole, and not to the soldier.

The two recruits, still somewhat paralyzed, but beginning to feel movement in their limbs again, both, independently, wished to be fully frozen in place, for each had the urge to bend over and vomit in the worst way from the stench of the beasts' foul breaths, the gagging fog of the dens, and the mind searing creepiness of the beasts' diseased tongues. Yet, they held it in, both concluding that such an act would, no doubt, hasten their demise.

"Chomp?"

Bukseo asked as he wrapped large, greasy, mainly bony hands around the poor soldier's shoulders and pulled the frightened soldier toward Bukseo's cavernous mouth.

"Another moment, soulless spawn of swamp gas," Namdong cautioned.

"Let us think about this."

"Ugh!" grunted Bukseo, disappointed that his brother was delaying his meal, however meager. "Hungry!"

The odd thing was, the wretch of the north had always let his southern brother oversee their activities and had never thought to question such. So, he eased off on the soldier's shoulders and settled in for the inevitable wait while his brother thought about things beyond Bukseo's simpleton's grasp.

The beast of the north, not a deep thinker himself, or really any kind of thinker, had always begrudgingly allowed his brother to the south to take his time thinking through new situations. Of course, since the beast on the northern bank was quite empty-headed, every situation, regardless of the number of times it had happened, always seemed to be new to him. Even when his fog-draped, hollow mind sniffed or slithered a lumpy, infected tongue over something that seemed familiar, he inevitably deferred to his brother's usual call to pause and think.

On the southern bank, Namdong, after sliding his rough, elongated tongue once more over the southern soldier's already slimy face, settled back on his substantial haunches and, rocking side to side, began to talk more to himself than to his brother across the way. The beast's voice was muffled and full of ups and downs in volume, making it quite difficult for his captive to fully understand, given that the language was of an ancient sort and that the beast's language arts were somewhere below that of a stable hand of yesteryear.

"Where? Where are all the fat ones?" Namdong lamented, swaying his body to the north as he spoke. "Fat ones have been gone away many, many seasons. Too many to count."

The beast then ran his hands over the soldier's weapon, flicking at the bumps and angles, clicking the front sight with a yellowed nail. He then poked at the utility belt around the soldier's waist, seeing the small eggs with the strong noise.

"Ah, you carry the eggs that take life, not give. Good, good. There may be something…something here," Namdong said to himself and then raised his scratchy voice. "Pus filled bag of dung, this one carries the eggs of death. Does yours?"

"Eggs?" Bukseo, the sad wretch of the north, his mind clouding up fast, as it had already had too much thinking for one day, mumbled in confusion. "Eggs?"

"Look at his middle!" Namdong yelled, flinging all manner of debris from his rags as he turned to squint at the other soldier across the river.

"He has no middle, curse of my missing father!" Bukseo yelled back, fingering the utility belt of the northern soldier, which held very little and certainly no exploding eggs. "He is skin and bones. His middle is stuck to his back."

Bukseo then started to chuckle, thinking what he had said was somehow funny, but, as the thought and imagery fled his simple mind, his chuckle drizzled into a whine.

"Hungry! Bird eggs, even I would eat, older pool of my droppings," Bukseo called back, sticking his long, filthy fingers into the mouth of the soldier, as if looking for bugs that might have crawled inside.

"No eggs? Bad show. We could have thrown the eggs and started a big fight," Namdong said, shaking his large head in seeming disappointment.

The wretch of the south then grabbed his soldier by the throat and, looking at it sideways, howled a bloodcurdling cry that spoke of lost souls and fearful passages into an unforgiving underworld.

"Have we been so long without conflict that only these thin ones, void of any truly interesting flavors, are all that are left?" cried Namdong of the south, looking toward his brother. "What is our lot if we are to suffer these as our last resort? Is this our fate, to wallow in our own filth as these...these puny misfits dance above us? Do we travel to the far north, to be with our sad, mean-spirited country kin, to wander the bleak tunnels of the camps and deep mines, consuming as many of the tiny humans there, but never being satisfied?"

The sudden flash of eloquence by the southern ghoul shocked both soldiers as the beast turned his deformed head toward his side of the bridge.

"Or, do we risk going into the south, where new ideas and disbelief of the old ways batter us? Yet they still harbor the killing shamans, who might soon render us defeated, starved, and swept out of the threshold like most of our despicable brothers before us?" Namdong cried to the walls of his den.

Moving back, deeper into the swill of the dank shadows, the beast of the south continued his soliloquy.

"There are the ships. Yes. Ships have many dark, wet places. Tasty places...full of low beings that can fill our aching bellies. We could venture to new lands, follow the lost souls. But, salty water is dangerous, and so many of our dwindling kind have vanished in the pain of the salty spray cascading over the doomed decks, have they not?" Namdong asked of himself, swaying back and forth.

Suddenly, the tortured speaker of the southern den nearly sat on the southern soldier as the beast collapsed in a dramatic pile of sore-laden flesh and near hollow bones, as he held out his own skeletal hands to the north side.

"Oh, simpleton slime of a brother mine, what should we do?"

Shaking himself out of a near slumber, Bukseo, only vaguely accustomed to his brother's ravings, as Bukseo's short-term memory was only partly functioning and his long term was a muddled morass of confusing images, answered in his usual way.

"Chomp? Suck out brains? Now?"

For an answer, the wretch of the south absently reached over to his right into a dank, murky recess, grabbed a random bone, with blackened, rotted flesh from countless years gone by still clinging to the ghastly thing, and hurled it the thirty meters across the gap to where the grisly bone smacked the wretched Bukseo on the back of his boil infested, bulbous head.

"Hey? Why hurt...? Oh, chomp bone?"

Whereupon, Bukseo began to gnaw on his brother's discard, but on the stripped end, not the end with the rotten flesh. This puzzled the northern soldier, whose face was only inches from the gut-turning morsel which passed in an out of his torch's dim light as the beast sucked on the bone like a hapless child at its mother's breast.

"Let mother sooth you, rotting brother," Namdong called, his voice gurgling at the effort. "Should we throw these wretched, empty shells back in hopes that they might return one day full of hate and evil, after a few years of glorious war?"

"Let our long sacrificed, rotting mother sooth you, vile brother," Namdong continued, repeating his gruesome words. "Should we...? Yes, I think we throw these skinny, empty shells back, and wait for them and their many brothers to return for a good war, full of hate and evil, detesting their fellow man, abusing their women, betraying their brothers, selling their parents, and abandoning their beggared children. Yes, we'll snatch a few snakes and dumb fish, and let these skinny ones go."

"No! No! Want chomp! Need chomp!" Bukseo mumbled in between the slobbering of his noisy sucking of the discarded bone.

"Dismal spawn of that grisly witch you now enjoy, how can I make you see? Consuming these two empty souls burns more fat than we have to spare. Better to nurse our occasional innocent forest creature, pure and untainted in its primordial drive to survive, than try to drain even the most meager of ghastly nourishment from such nearly empty shells."

Namdong then looked hard into the eyes of the southern soldier, who had begun to feel more of his body's control return, but not enough to fight back. The soldier felt he could barely close his eyes, but something deep within him compelled him to allow the grim apparition of the horror before him look into his wide open eyes, deep into the soldiers bare soul.

"Weakness, I see in this one. Too young to know stark betrayal. Too foolish, still, to know hate for his enemies. Sees the world as a place of wonder and peace, this foolish one does. Yet, I also see the seeds of death, the early roots, tendrils of fear, which will grow stronger as the seasons turn. Empty now, of that black vengeance which feeds our darkest hunger, but will grow, this one will," Namdong nearly sang as he held his dripping eyes on the eyes of the southern soldier.

"Rotten brother of my defecation!" Bukseo shouted, uncharacteristically lucid for a few breaths as he interrupted Namdong's near trance. "This one knows hate and evil. Let own baby go hungry in winter so he be fit for army trials. Beats his juniors after cheats them."

"Scabby, seeping wound of a cur's inner thigh!" Namdong growled back. "Would he be tastier now, or a few years from now, once he is in a more powerful position and, therefore, can terrorize even more juniors?"

"Want chomp!' Bukseo declared and drew the northern soldier closer to his gaping mouth.

Faced with imminent death, or worse, the northern soldier finally found that his tongue was still attached, and worked. Although his voice was muddled and he wasn't sure he could use the old style correctly, the terrified soldier sputtered a few words.

"What did it say?" Namdong called, straining to listen to the odd words from the shaking man.

"Say eat the southern one. Share. Says the southern one is better fed," Bukseo answered, his grinning lips test tasting the northern soldier's bone thin arm, after forgetting about the aged bone he had been chewing.

"Hah!" answered Namdong, his momentary deep thinking replaced with an odd merriment. "It is a good tidbit, who wants to save skin and give away skin not his. Let's do contest."

Excited by the notion of a game, both Namdong and Bukseo then pushed their two victims a meter or so into the dark dens, blocking any attempt at escape. While not properly a game, Namdong, in order to maintain any level of mental stimulation, would often pit victims against one another, more in an attempt to see what they would do, rather than play to any real outcome.

"I will go first, as your skinny already spoke, although his mangled words hurt my ears," Namdong declared, leaning into his captive.

The southern soldier, who had yet to utter even a squeak, as he believed any show of weakness, like a frozen voice, would result in his immediate, and messy, consumption, regardless of what his captor had just babbled about releasing him and his northern counterpart. The well-trained soldier, was, however, listening to his body, waiting for the moment when the paralysis would wear off more completely, and, once in control of his mind, hands, and feet again, would attack. For the time being, the southern soldier let his rational mind retreat and be at ease, letting the surreal nature of the beast and its sibling settle into the front of his mind, preventing the seeds of insanity being planted, which was the only rational explanation for his predicament.

Poking the silent soldier in the chest, Namdong demanded the soldier defend himself against being volunteered by the northern soldier.

"Your skinny cousin offered you as a meal, little man. What say you?" Namdong asked, trying to make his voice more official, but only succeeding in sounding childish to his captive.

Staring at the beast, and then across the river, the southern soldier, feeling his limbs becoming more mobile and his stomach, while still trying to climb out his throat, was not sending signals to his bowels. Looking back to the beast, the soldier wondered how long he could keep the beast's interest as he waited for his body to be his again. Or, more cynically, how long could he drag out the inevitable?

Finally, the southern soldier, being a good and solid grandson to one set of surviving grandparents, began to present his case using nearly correct elements of the older tongue used by the beasts, all the while staving off his own creeping fear that lunacy might soon descend upon him, if he accepted that he was trapped in a cave, under a bridge, with…with something that viewed itself, and its evident sibling, as some sort of ghoul.

While the young southern soldier had no earthly idea what might sway the two beasts, or at least the one directly in front of him, he had recognized a few obvious traits of his jailer.

To wit, the two beasts appeared to be related somehow and, therefore, as brothers or cousins, would have the typical jealousies and rivalries the inhabitants of the peninsula were famous, or infamous, for. The beasts were also only concerned about feeding, and feeding well, given the southern one's obvious disdain to waste his energy on eating the inexperienced soldiers. Comforts, given the wretched state of their dens, and personal hygiene, given the obscene state of the beasts' bodies, were not interests of the creatures at all. In addition, their odd talk, drawing conclusions on the attitudes and even skills of the two captives, spoke to some primordial sensory ability to see beyond the physical. Somehow, at least the one that spoke more coherently, embodied traits of some of the myths the soldier recalled from childhood.

Searching far back in his memory, the southern soldier tried to call up stories from his grandfather and grandmother, but he only could remember nursery rhymes and fairy tales. None of the darker myths of Korean folklore were ever told to him and his brother and sister, so he came up blank trying to explain the two beasts.

Failing at mythology, the southern soldier had then looked around in the near darkness of the den, straining to find anything within his view that might help him shape his answer to the beast. Finally, just as the beast of the south poked the soldier's chest again, causing the little torchlight to bounce all around the cavern and over his hideous host, the young soldier noticed an oddity about the den that might help.

Very few actual bones, or evidence of slaughter.

Was the fearful beast more of a talker, than a diner, wondered the southern soldier? Was the creature more interested in its own mental prowess, than in having a meal?

Or, more likely, thought the southern soldier, am I just rationalizing because my mind can't accept being eaten, alive, by such a monster?

"Speak, or maybe I'll just toss you to my worthless sibling to the north and we can watch the two of you soldier boys fight it out as my vile sibling gnaws away at your tender extremities…?" Namdong laughed, yellow spittle oozing out of the left side of his grinning mouth.

"With the utmost respect, my lord of the dankest den," the southern soldier abruptly began, as he attempted a stiff bow, hoping to loosen the paralysis, while nearly shouting to his captor, in order that the beast to the north would hear, as well as the northern soldier, whom he hoped had brains enough to understand the southern soldier's eventual intent.

"As you, so wise and full of worldly awareness, and your…brother, to the north, so dull and full of clogged offal, have argued, we are but poor table fare for such discriminating diners," continued the southern soldier. "So, I would have to agree with you, over your ignoble brother, that a delay of several years would be wise. Even though he wants to dine on that skinny fellow who claims to be a soldier, but is just a bastard offspring of an evil moron to the north, your brother would be better served by waiting for another war, so he can hungrily devour the many fatted human calves who will fall into these waters at our victorious advance."

"Ha!" Namdong shouted, showering the soldier with bits of muck and slime. "See? See, my groveling slab of excrement? The smart one, this one of the violin, knows you well, and agrees with me!"

"Chomp him!" Bukseo shrieked from his den's gaping mouth, angry that the puny human dared to demean Bukseo in front of his sibling. "He just wants to run."

Now, the northern soldier, in spite of his limited education, malnutrition, and rigidly regimented life in the north, did have a healthy drive to survive, so joined in the southern soldier's scheme.

"Oh, blinding light of northern brilliance, I agree that you, fount of all river beast knowledge, and your brother, the sad simpleton in league with that slouching southerner who claims to be a toy soldier, are justified in wanting to consume a better class of victuals," the soldier called, trying to match the high language of his southern rival, but jumbling up the old tongue. "Yes, should wait, not for the stumbling advance of the southern clown army, but for the scores of miserable wretches who will be throwing themselves into the river to drown, rather than face death at the advance of our glorious army of righteousness."

Both soldiers then paused, briefly, to gauge how their respective beasts were absorbing the arguments, or not.

For Bukseo, the beast of the north, he was enjoying the tones of the northern soldier's speech, and, as his captive talked, became even angrier at the southern soldier for using such harsh language. Bukseo gurgled a throaty laugh each time his soldier demeaned Namdong, to the south.

Namdong, on the other hand, a little brighter than Bukseo, was aware that the two soldiers were trying to work together, but wasn't quite sure what their game was. Also, Namdong was even more susceptible to flattery than Bukseo, and he was quicker to anger if maligned, with that anger clouding his judgment.

"Callous ooze of my armpit's stench, don't let that skinny one call me such names!" Namdong called, distracted from his own captive.

"Beastly scab off of my filthy bottom," Bukseo called back, "he only speaks the truth. Your skinny one talks mean to me. Chomp him for being mean!"

"Oh great and strong beast of the southern terrors," the southern soldier shouted, trying to drown out the northern beast's taunts, "that one is pitiful, weak both in mind and body, withering away in his own filth, shaming you, his stalwart role model. He only wishes to satisfy his selfish, momentary hunger and, dare I say it, is not capable of capturing anything better than that miserable boy toy pretending to be a soldier. Of course he wants to chomp, as chomping is all his empty head can grasp. When did he last capture his own fat and juicy meal without help from his stronger and more cunning brother? When did he last offer you a share of his kill? When, I ask you, has your dear, wretched brother ever thrown you a morsel or two during the lean times?"

Slowly, as if a single thought was shaping itself in the dark and rarely used recesses of the two beasts' horrid minds, Namdong, moderately thinking beast of the south, showed growing realization in his yellow-rimmed, red-black eyes, while, at the same time, Bukseo, simple and sad beast of the north, turned his back on his prey and glared across the water at the southern soldier.

As if on cue, both beasts began to yell at each other, with Bukseo getting his words in first as his thinking limit was reached within a few seconds, while Namdong gave the thinking process an entire half-minute.

"Corrupt spawn!" Bukseo shouted, flinging gobs of mucus into the water in his fury, which some of the less discerning fish gobbled up. "You no feed me! I feed me. Look at my many bones and heads. Look at the floor of matted, rotted flesh from so many years of my own kills!"

Now, recall from earlier that the beast of the north had considerable problems with his memories, and, since he habitually was at a complete loss on events of the past, he would fabricate, often without even realizing he was doing so, his own version of past reality. Had the poor creature but squinted his feeble eyes and turned them to the interior of his den, he would have seen only a few thin bones from birds and snakes, a broken turtle shell, and, instead of the many heads he claimed, one squirrel skull perched on a small ledge over the creature's sleeping spot.

The beast of the south, on the other hand, had a nearly perfect, if sometimes fanciful, memory, a bit inflated by his warped visions of his own great feats in the past. Consequently, he was well aware of his decades of supporting his less mentally endowed sibling to the north, yet had always been accepting of his role. However, the sharp words of the southern soldier had awakened two elements long dormant in Namdong. Jealousy and envy.

"Maggot-ridden pus of a burst boil," shouted Namdong, raising himself up to his full height, towering over his captive and nearly hitting his deformed head on the underside of the bridge, "you would have perished in your own swill, gnawing at your own limbs, many, many seasons ago, if I hadn't sworn a blood oath to our despicable mother creature to take care of your worthless hide. Even as you were finishing her own steaming cesspool of diseased tripe, she demanded my vow to keep you from starving. And, this is how you thank me?"

With that last blunt retort, Namdong picked up a large stone and tossed it in the direction of the northern bank. Even angry, he did not want to actually harm his sibling, but just wanted to emphasize the debt that Bukseo owed Namdong.

Bukseo, his mind returning to its less lucid state, was beginning to forget what the northern soldier had just said, but did recall bits of it.

Bukseo did recall that he was angry at something, and that it had to do with his brother, but was now fuzzy on the details. So, true to how he handled his muddled memories, he simply made up something to fill in the conversation.

"If you won't let me chomp my skinny, then you no chomp your skinny," Bukseo yelled across the river as he spat black bile into the murky water.

Bukseo then scooped up the stone Namdong had just tossed randomly and, aiming for the southern soldier, threw the stone to land within half a meter of the soldier.

At Bukseo's attack, Namdong, worried that his dinner might be squashed before he could enjoy it, or release it for another day, grabbed the soldier and planted him a little farther from the den's mouth, amongst the brambles, in order to make it harder for Bukseo to hit him with a stone, for, after the first stone, Bukseo was looking for another to throw.

Namdong then grabbed a smaller stone and using his superior strength, threw it so accurately that he managed to knock down the northern soldier, albeit without actually hurting the man, only soiling his uniform further with the vile matting of the den's floor.

Bukseo, seeing his morsel was now in danger, grabbed the soldier and, mimicking his brother's actions, jammed the northern soldier into the brambles behind and above the den, somehow remembering from his youth that above the den, close to the bridge's underside, was safer from thrown projectiles, as they tended to hit the underside of the bridge and fall into the water.

Namdong, seeing his brother place his morsel in the safety of the area above the den, turned and shoved his own soldier into the similar location above Namdong's den.

Then, for some fifteen or twenty minutes, with late afternoon fast turning to evening, the two wretched beasts tossed insults and stones at the prey of the other, both nearly always missing.

For the soldiers, they were actually in worse positions as the areas above the dens were small and cramped and gave no opportunity to escape while the beasts where standing just to the side. Consequently, as the two beasts dueled, the southern soldier decided to add a little more fuel to the fires of jealousy.

Using the loudest voice he could muster, in the old language, speaking slowly, so that the beasts might better understand, the southern soldier yelled over to the northern soldier.

"Hey, stupid boy, see what you've done?" the southern soldier yelled at his counterpart, in a voice dripping with contempt for the two beasts. "Now they are going to kill us and not even eat us. We'll end up a bloody, unfit mash under this bridge that even the maggots will avoid, so that our rotting bodies will remain for years to remind our wandering souls that we met our sad fate at the hands of silly and selfish children who no longer can claim to be fierce beasts."

"So true!" shouted the northern soldier without delay, fear driving his survival skills and ability to immediately ascertain what his otherwise mortal enemy to the south was up to. "The only consolation for us and our wandering souls will be that people will come to realize these bratty children are not the fierce, disgusting beasts of legend, but merely bickering cubs unworthy of the fear of grown men. Children will come down here to play with their bones in less than ten years, I think."

"No, a mere five or six years!" the southern soldier added quickly, watching the two beasts as they began to throw smaller and smaller pebbles. "Yes, these two are nothing like the ones we have in the south. Why, there are a pair under the old Mapo Bridge that call down all manner of victims every week."

"Yes, we have an even more ferocious pair far north, on the river the Chinese call Yalu, who are so fat and well fed that they only need to eat a well-rounded smuggler once a decade," the northern soldier replied.

As the two soldiers continued to toss insults over the heads of the beasts, Namdong and Bukseo began to drop the smaller pebbles into the river and then, without fanfare, stopped throwing stones altogether and stood staring at each other across the water.

Finally, after some minutes of listening to the two soldiers lament their sad fate at the grubby hands of two creatures that the soldiers not only did not seem to fear, but seemed to actually pity, the two vile brothers ended their momentary feud, with Bukseo forgetting there ever had been a feud within moments of cessation.

Pity, however, was as a dagger to the proud beasts. Even Bukseo, the simpleton of the north, was struck to his miserable core by the puny soldiers' taunts. Namdong, with his vague sense of responsibility for his child-like sibling, coupled with his own overblown sense of self-worth, had long held the belief that mythical creatures who dwelt under bridges in dark, vile dens were to be feared and loathed, not pitied and coddled.

Why, in the old days, terrified villagers offered songs and sacrifices, not insults and pity, Namdong recalled in a moment of clarity.

His anger rising, especially as he watched how the evil words made his vile brother's shoulders slump in silent dejection, Namdong of the south shook his upraised, clenched fists at the northern soldier, then turned and did the same to his own captive, reawakening memories long buried, nearly forgotten.

"Weak? Pity? You two dogs feel pity?" Namdong's voice was low and dangerous as he moved toward the southern soldier, while his sibling watched and copied Namdong's actions. "Such as you have no right to look down at us, your betters!"

"Oh, great cesspool of ancient filth, I do not mock you!" the southern soldier shouted, pressing harder his strategy. "Nay, we cherish the spirits of the bridges and byways in my old village, heaping great respect on such ancient guardians. Yet, I only see the vile underbelly of two lowly grave robbers, not the proud bridge guardians of old. Why do you dwell in these dank holes, feeding on chance, when the world is full of greener fields and fatter catches?"

"Long we have fed on the flesh of much greater stock than your sorry carcasses," Namdong, letting his voice slowly rise to a roar, almost sang to his captive. "Promised greatness by…by those masters that came before, we were. Our lot was never to dwell in such darkness, but to lay claim to the vast countryside as we herded you cattle here and there. Yes, ours was to be a paradise. Close, we were. Very close. Then, the big war happened. Scattering so many masters that we cannot even count. Then the other, the last war, tore our brethren asunder."

Namdong waved his hands to mimic his kind being swept up and then separated by the last war.

"Our masters let us go our own way. No longer did they have the treasure to feed us, our kin, our mother. They condemned me and my

21

brother to…to choose. Follow brethren and head north, into the vast emptiness, or follow brethren south, into the gleaming cities and new ways. Our mother, she chose to do neither. She chose to wait, under this shelter. Yes, to wait until you humans and our masters returned, to continue to do battle, to feed our hollow stomachs and aching skulls. We've waited. Waited and waited. We continue to wait, violin boy, for the return of the great conflicts. The scream of men slipping into their hells, where we catch them as they fight us, the final adversary. Yes, you and your cousin across the way are pitiful stock to have come from such great warriors of old. When I think of the great captains of men that I have consumed, at the pinnacle of their short-lived glory, my stomach churns at the thought of downing such lowly cattle as the two of you. My brother, sad, mindless fool that he is, still deserves better than the dregs those to the north can supply!"

"Where is your mother?" the northern soldier shouted, causing Bukseo to slap the man so hard blood flew out of his mouth, which Bukseo quickly licked up.

"Silence, squirming bug!" Namdong called across the water. "Even my simple fool of a hollow brother will not allow our hideous mother's name to be spoken by the likes of you!"

Turning back to the southern soldier, Namdong stood, crookedly, and, staring into the soldier's eyes, spoke in a calmer, almost normal voice.

"Obedient, we were, violin boy," the southern wretch declared. "Stayed under this bridge. Many years of great feeding these dens afforded us. Yet, over time, fewer and fewer harvests of your kind were made. It was a slow change. So slow, we didn't see our mother wasting away. So slow, we missed the moment my dullard of a brother lost what little mind he had. Yet, obedient we were. Even when our vile beast of a mother creature fed us with her own diseased flesh during the hard times, we listened and we obeyed, violin boy. Now, we continue to wait."

Grabbing the soldier by the scuff of his neck, Namdong leaned in, licked the man's stone silent face, and, opening the diseased maw of his black and yellow mouth, slammed his rotted teeth into the soldier's left face cheek.

That ferocious bite, which the soldier had assumed would remove his head and a part of his left shoulder, only nipped over a triangular flap of flesh the size of a five-won coin, just below the man's left cheekbone.

After watching his sibling, Bukseo copied Namdong's attack and left a similar bloody mark. Yet, no flap of flesh could be seen hanging, as Bukseo, unlike his more cerebral brother, couldn't resist at least a small snack.

Namdong then seized the soldier by his shoulders and held the soldier's bleeding face next to his own, licking the blood, Namdong's own nod to a treat, as his red-black eyes searched the soldier's face.

"I taste…I taste some of the old ways in this one. Yes. He will come back. His curiosity demands it. Will we be here? Will we have fled north? Drifted south into the massive city?" Namdong asked, as he licked and let his eyes wander.

"This one tastes of revenge. Hate. Trickery. Will sell his one child one day, this one will," Bukseo called, his own tongue acting as a dressing over the wound in the soldier's face, draining the color out of the man's already pallid complexion. "Stab his boss in the back, one day, this skinny one will."

Bukseo continued to lick the wound and savor the northern soldier's blood. However, after several lingering tastes, the beast's own slime sealed the blood flow, causing the wretched creature to whimper, almost as a newborn in pain.

Namdong, hearing his brother's eerie cry, yelled over at the northern soldier.

"Boastful boy, be wary of playing with my cur of an unforgiving brother. I can still crush you if I desire. Or throw this skinny...this one over to you so the two of you can start a new war," Namdong called over his brother's whining.

"Oh, grandfather! Fathers of my fathers! Forgive me this wretched fate at the simple claws of these mindless beasts!" the southern soldier wailed, trying to signal to the northern soldier to copy him. "Grandmother! I know I disappoint you so, to end by the mangled, unclean paw of a sad little river beast. Even death by a wingless imugi, grandmother, would have been a nobler fate."

After shaking off his revulsion at the northern beast's taking a bite of his cheek, the northern soldier joined in the wailing laments of his southern adversary.

"Aiyee! I will not climb the mountain to join our glorious leaders, but will be flung into the cesspit to swim with the castoffs of our glorious society! Better to have been served to those southern dogs than have these...these country buffoons end my pitiful life! My apologies, great leaders!" the northern soldier cried, bowing continually to his imaginary role models.

For a number of minutes, both Namdong and Bukseo simply watched and listened as the two soldiers traded wailing insults about the creatures. Since both the soldiers had trouble with the old language, the two wretches were slow to grasp the full impact of what the two skinny morsels were saying.

Yet, after a particularly loud howl from the southern soldier, a small light seem to arise at the back of the southern beast's red-black eyes.

Namdong slowly rose to his full height and, waving at his brother to watch, the southern beast leaned over his wailing captive, opened the massive maw of his jaws and prepared to bite the soldier's head off in one snap.

"Chomp now?" Bukseo yelled, his excitement palatable as he mimicked his brother's move and stood over his own cowering soldier. "Chomp now and no more silly talk? No more telling bad tales?"

Just as both Namdong and Bukseo were about to dig into their respective meals, three small water deer, a mother and two fawns, decided the moss growing at the southern edge of the river was better fare than what they had been eating, and wandered down the bank to stand no more than a long stride from the beast of the south.

The bizarre incongruity of the passive, without fear animals grazing at the river's edge, just as the two beasts were about to savagely devour the soldiers, seemed to cause something in Namdong to click. Somewhere behind the southern beast's nearly dead eyes the southern soldier saw a ray of...of an idea and, maybe, for the soldier, a ray of hope.

Namdong suddenly threw his scabby right hand into the gaping hole of his mouth, as if using his own hand to stop the nearly automatic attack on the soldier.

"Wait! Stupid child! You have it!" Namdong yelled at his brother and, to ensure his brother heard him, picked up a sizable stone and threw it with great accuracy, hitting the simple beast on the side of his head, knocking him to the ground and cutting short Bukseo's attempted major bite of his captive's head.

"Bukseo, you foolish pool of...you stumbled into the answer!" Namdong called, causing his already dazed and confused brother to simply grunt in reply.

"They must talk!" Namdong called. "They must return and tell this tale! Word will flow to the masters! Our brethren will return! The wars will rage!"

Bukseo, his head clearing, did not like what his brother was proposing.

"Only one needed to tell a tale, cow fly's dung," Bukseo shot back, his mind, squarely focused on keeping his meal, was able to discern some minor logic in keeping only one of the captives alive.

"But they don't talk...the sides of the bridge...don't talk to each other," Namdong yelled. "They both must talk."

"How know they talk, scab on a...on a scab?" Bukseo yelled, his mind already hurting from too much thinking, and far too much talking.

"They will," Namdong replied, leaning menacingly over the southern captive.

For the next number of seemingly endless minutes, at least to the southern soldier, Namdong, using as descriptive a brush as he could with his limited vocabulary, outlined, well into sunset, how the two soldiers would, indeed, return to their respective camps and tell the tale.

The incentive?

Namdong outlined, through additional sensory licks of his captive's face and head, and with Bukseo doing the same to his soldier, how the two beasts would call upon their few night cousins, for whom wandering far and wide was easy, to slip into not only the soldiers' beds on some random, storm-thrashed night, but also into the homes, schools, and wee nurseries of their families and their few friends.

Namdong hammered into the two soldiers the stark reality that their actions, or, rather, inactions, would result in decades-long harassment of them and their kin, into seven generations, where each successive generation would curse the soldier who had condemned them.

Namdong then plucked off the bit of flesh covering the wound on the southern soldier's face and, looking at it hungrily, grabbed a small rock and, squishing the bloody side to the rock, tossed the small projectile to land at the feet of his brother. Bukseo, seeing the morsel, almost started to cry with joy, except he had never known joy, nor even knew how to shed tears. So, he simply licked the bit of mashed and dirty flesh from the stone and waved back at his sibling.

"Let your similar scars mark you, boy, and your cousin across the river," Namdong wheezed, his voice having grown hoarse from overuse.

The southern soldier, his body almost fully recovered, was shocked at the continual use of the word 'cousin' by the vile creature before him, allowing his disdain to show on his face.

"Yes, don't look surprised, violin boy. Many of you baby soldiers share far grandfathers, just as puny as you two. Let the marks on your faces forever remind you of your shared debt to my brother. Your debt to me," Namdong said quietly, more as if he were some disheveled schoolteacher at one of the lesser high schools in southern Seoul, one without a subway stop.

Curiously, the three small deer had not only continued to munch away at the edges of the river moss during Namdong's harangue, the mother also had only briefly looked in the direction of the southern soldier and, since generations of deer had had no enemies for as long as the bridge had stood vacant, she simply discounted the soldier as a non-threat and went back to eating. Watching the trusting creatures, the soldier felt that the three deer did not even see the beast ranting before him.

Finally, no doubt fearing any further delay would cause his weaker willed sibling to simply gobble down the northern soldier and ruin Namdong's scheme, Namdong stretched his left hand out, and, waving what seemed to be a tattered old fan that had been hidden in his rags, hissed out a dire warning, almost as a challenge.

"Fear us! Remember us! Fear us, as we dwell in these dank pits of despair, waiting for whatever fool stumbles our way. But, we will not be in want forever. Remember fools, you men live for war. Your own vile kings and princes betray one another, in a never-ending cycle! Fear us! For we live off the death screams and endless agony of such conflicts. Remember, you fight, we win! Such is the ageless order of this land! You and yours will be back!"

Spitting what looked like blood and yellow rot into the river, Namdong continued, his voice sounding as if it was tearing at the beast's throat.

"War will ravage the lands again! We will have many fat, evil, swollen soldiers, and those even more swollen by the valor of ignorance. We will drink the twisted minds of boys and men, and maybe a few tasty women, ravaged by a war they will fight, but never understand. We will grow stronger, bigger. Better to serve our masters when they return. We will be strong enough to leave our miserable lairs and venture into the cities. Back into the spaces between your sad little lives and your recurring nightmares. War is our friend. War will bring more food. More chomp for my simple brother!"

Yelling the last bit so that his brother's clouded mind would, hopefully, grasp the concept, Namdong shoved the tattered fan, or whatever it was, back into his rags and, without warning, lifted the southern soldier over his head.

Pausing briefly so that his brother could see and mimic his actions, Namdong, the wretched beast of the south, then turned and threw the southern soldier far up the riverbank, nearly to the road surface above. As part of the same movement, the beast reached over and, with blinding swiftness, dispatched the two offspring of the small mother deer.

So quick were Namdong's movements that the mother deer didn't notice the young ones missing for several chews of a patch of grain-like grass she had found. Once she had noticed, she looked around, did not see the two, bleated a call, and then scrambled up the bank in search of the two she would never find.

Namdong then shoved one of the small deer, its slim neck obviously broken, into a large hole at the side of his den, and turned back to look up the edge of the bank, where he could just see the legs of the soldier.

"Today, I will take my fast, miserable boy. Too much bounty and I may become weak and soft, a direr fate than my brother's exposed bones and sagging flesh holding up his empty skull," Namdong called from below to the soldier, who wasted no time in bolting from the edge of the bridge.

Namdong's last words, almost fully intelligible to the southern soldier, but still holding an edge of disbelief, drifted out of the murky den, pursuing the soldier in the night air as his head cleared more fully.

Bukseo, not quite grasping all that his sibling had uttered, but copying his wiser brother's moves, simply grabbed the northern soldier, nipped another small piece from the man's bloody face, and, tossing him up the bank as well, shouted after him.

"What my brother said! And, don't forget it!"

The northern soldier sailed out of the murky under passage to land nearly at the top of the bank near the crumbling asphalt of the bridge's road heading off to the north. Momentarily dazed, he looked around as if drunk, saw no pursuit and no counterpart on the southern bank, so then immediately scrambled up the remainder of the bank, jumped onto the road and ran without looking behind him, all the way to his base camp over two kilometers away. And, yes, for a foolish moment, the northern soldier considered running away, but that had never ended well for his comrades.

Namdong then tossed the slightly larger of the small deer over to his brother, its broken neck flopping hideously as Bukseo grabbed the meal and retreated into his den, the beastly sounds of his quenching his hunger too vile to describe.

Turning from the summarily dismissed soldiers, Namdong stood and stared at the pit that his brother had retreated into across the way, not speaking and making no gestures. Then, he slowly retreated to the inner darkness of his own respective den, waiting for deep sleep to quiet his rumbling belly and hurting head from his exhaustive efforts with the soldiers. Unlike his single-minded brother, the beast of the south preferred his deer to age a few days to help with the flavor.

Within mere moments, only Namdong's guttural snoring escaped in low tones from under the bridge, to mix with the fevered gnashing of his simple, but happy, brother of the north, with both noises weaving into the rich, evening forest sounds surrounding and embracing the dismal bridge.

The southern soldier, having felt full control of his body finally return to him as he had flown through the air, had immediately cushioned his fall by executing a nearly flawless Kuk Mu Kwan roll and stand maneuver. He had then run a few meters from the sloping embankment and had spun around, weapon at the ready, to face any threats from beneath the bridge, or from the other side of the demarcation line.

Silence.

Too dark to see back under the bridge.

Too dark to see his enemy's position, but the southern soldier did hear fast moving footfalls fading into the distance that told him the northern fellow had wasted no time in putting distance between himself and the bridge.

Wait. What's that rumbling, the southern soldier wondered?

Was the nightmare beast…sleeping? Yes, sleeping, the southern soldier realized, while still trying to fathom what had just happened.

The soldier then waited a few moments, motionless, expecting the unseen hand from earlier to reach up from the abyss and drag him back into that dank lair.

Nothing.

The soldier then backed slowly away from the bridge, being careful not to tread on the tree incident memorial, while remembering to bow his head in memory of those brave souls from years before. Pausing as he bowed, he wondered, but just briefly, if the two seemingly mythical beasts, or deranged sociopaths, had been hunched beneath the bridge during the incident, waiting for a random combatant to fall into their gaping maws.

The southern soldier then shook the thought out of his head, bowed again to his fallen brothers, and then headed back to base. While unseen to the southern soldier, his northern counterpart was, we can surmise, moving fast along the broken road to reach his own secondary headquarters to report, wondering how close to the truth he could safely venture.

No sounds other than the wind and a few lonesome bird calls could be heard from the bridge itself as the two previous captives hurried away. The rumblings of the southern beast had mixed into the background noises of the night, and the northern beast had quickly satiated its hunger, saving…well, saving certain succulent bits for nibbling on over the upcoming days and weeks.

The southern soldier reported promptly to his outpost and asked to speak to the duty sergeant. The northern soldier, who had considered running away right up until the moment he was spotted by his own checkpoint, undoubtedly also asked to see his superior, being careful to say nothing that could be overheard by his mistrustful comrades.

After the sergeants, on both sides of the bridge, had heard the tale from their respective recruits, both of the older, battle-tested ranking soldiers ordered more persuasive measures to double-check the recruits' tales.

The stories held.

Both sergeants then drew up sufficiently vague reports and had their respective soldiers sign oaths of secrecy.

In addition, the sergeants independently decided to end the recent agreement to silence the loudspeakers. The north turned their scratchy speakers back on first, spewing heavy doses of poorly crafted propaganda toward the south. A few minutes later, the south turned their speakers back on, blasting their counterparts with K-pop, traditional music, Korean Rock, American bands, and nationalized newscasts.

Deep down, even if neither of the sergeants wanted to fully admit the unbelievable presence of the elusive beasts under the crumbling bridge, they both undoubtedly wanted to ensure that the corrupting sounds of the wretched beasts' imagined conversations did not float up through the hills and over the mountains to lure more powerful and, therefore, tastier prey to the edge of the zone, and to the edge of war, or beyond.

The sergeant of the south filed his report under 'routine' daily happenings, admonished the reporting soldier to keep his wild story to himself or risk appropriately harsh discipline, and dismissed the confused soldier to quarters. We can imagine that the northern sergeant did the same.

The incident resolved, the southern sergeant then wandered over to the coffee hut. The old warrior decided, as he walked, that he would put the far too clever, too inquisitive, violin playing music star on tower watch next time, until the pop star's mandatory service time was complete.

Lightly scratching his weathered cheek, where an old, almost invisible, diamond shaped scar tended to act up at dusk, the sergeant of the south concluded that it would be better for all if the beasts, if they really were there, did not have too many well-educated, clever recruits to chew on.

No, no more poets, the sergeant decided, as he sipped his coffee and motioned for the rather slow, somewhat easily confused attendant to retrieve a lemon tart.

Looking at the grinning young recruit closely, the sergeant slowly smiled, asked the kid his name, and, after taking the lemon tart the kid awkwardly handed him, made a mental note to work on a transfer for the young food service recruit to bridge patrol.

Yes, the simpler, the better.

INTERLUDE I

Was the beast sleeping, the writer wondered?

Craning his neck to peer under the creature's cowl, the unfortunate captive tried to get a glimpse of the beast's yellowed, black-rimmed eyes through the tangle of hair, vines, and ghastly dregs. But, movement from the dark spaces beyond the stove caused the writer to jerk back and prepare himself to fight the little ones. He briefly wondered if he would be capable of smashing in the skulls of the child-things, even as they gnawed at his flesh.

"Fear, foolish boy, feeds the likes of the skittish little ones. And, many of my cousins. It's their nectar. Can send into a frenzy, yes," the creature mumbled from underneath its cowl. "Yet, they will not emerge until I deem it so. They, too, know fear."

Stretching its long, thin, yet powerful arms, the beast seemed to be shaking off its slumber as it stared at the writer.

"This tale of doomed brothers, are you certain of the river? Of the bridge?" the creature asked, its tongue flicking in and out of its mouth.

"Well, yes. That's where the story unfolds…," the writer began, but was waved silent by the beast's left hand.

"Another, boy. Another lost cousin resides under…well, let's just say along the wound across my peninsula, near the eastern sea," the creature offered, its voice calmer, less blunt. "I have not thought of him for many,

many cycles."

The creature arched its rag-draped back, like some oversized tomcat on the prowl, and continued.

"Mayhap your tale is my cousin's tale, just changed to confuse those who would go in search? Maybe try to exorcise? Maybe so the mudangs and baksu, those infernal shamans, can drag him and use his weakening powers as their own, human?" the creature asked, an accusatory tone bubbling up from the beast's throat.

"Why, no, I…the tale is something I put together from stories I had heard in the military, years ago," the writer responded, intrigued by the unexpected reaction of his captor. "What…who is this cousin you speak of?"

"You are clever, little human, to dredge up a tale of trolls. No, goblins, or maybe ghouls, to entice me to ask for more. Clever," the creature answered, ignoring the writer's question. "Long have I wondered if the big fighting my sire spoke of might return. Maybe my sire would return if his humans came back to a big fight? Yet, the big fights are a danger. Can fatten my brethren for a time, but can then starve."

The writer let his own silence linger, hoping the creature would say more, react more, and give the writer additional signs that the tale had impact and that the creature would want to hear another.

"Have you traveled into the dead zone, little man?" the creature suddenly asked, unfolding itself from the stone chair and table, and gliding over to the stove to nudge the pile of ondol charcoal bricks and bits of leftover kindling. "Have you heard the tortured singing of my cousins trapped in the in between spaces? Most have faded into the forests, or have become twisted rocks, starved of their rations of humans and souls. Long ago, human, my mother took me with her cousins to slip some trinkets off one of their own who was fading into stone, just to the rising sun of the place you speak of. Terrifying, it was, but my mother wanted me to know what happens if we let our hunger go too long."

"What did, what happened to her cousin?" the writer asked.

"We did not remain," the creature replied. "Only stripped the goblin of any usable ornaments. Some very, very old. One of the cousins, a bit of a ghoul, took one of his stone hands. As a prank. Amusing, to see the eyes wanting to scream, but the mouth half-frozen in stone, unable to cry out."

The creature then tapped on the edge of the cook pot with its talon-like nails and turned back to the writer.

"Maybe, little fool, you have more tales of my cousins in your scribbling?" the creature asked, its hand hovering over the fire-starter.

"More? Why, yes, there are several in the work with more mythical elements," the writer replied, trying to keep the eagerness out of his voice. "Shall I offer another?"

The creature was silent for a long moment. It then turned and seemed to glide, rather than walk, back to the bench, and sat down close to the writer. The creature then sniffed the writer several times and even darted its tongue out, catching the back of the writer's left ear.

Repressing a shudder at the oily, sandpaper texture of the beast's diseased tongue, the writer continued.

"The mountains, oh vile one, north of here, are they somewhere your cousins haunt?" the writer asked, trying to hold his breath against the stench. "Your singing stones of this bench and, maybe others in your sitting room here, bring to mind the tall granite peaks of the mountains surrounding the city, and all up and down the country. Maybe there are other singing stones from the old days tucked away there?"

"Mountains? Fool, even the smallest children know my cousins roamed the vast peaks. My cousins. Not many remain in the mountains. Many have been run off the cliffs by the legions of mudang women parading up and down, up and down," the creature said, shrinking away from the writer, as if trying to escape the writer's comment about the mountains. "Few are those remaining who can bring sound from the old stones, boy."

"I'm truly sorry to hear that," the writer replied. "I'm certain there would have been many interesting and horrific tales from such mountain dwellers."

"Enough chatter, boy!" the creature abruptly bellowed. "I've said too much. You will just steal my cousins' stories so those fools out there will throw coins at your books. Enough! No more questions! You just tell your tales, boy."

The writer, trying to keep his stomach level during the beast's outburst, was not sure he had heard correctly.

"Tell another story?" the writer asked, gripping the edges of his notebook.

"Quickly, before the moans of my little ones move me to give you to them raw!" the creature grumbled and then settled back into its mammoth stone chair.

The writer, acting quickly, glanced at the next tale in his notebook and, feeling confident the tale would stand, with only minor alteration, set the scene for his host and the banquet guests creeping about in the shadows.

"Right! Let's remove ourselves, then, to the mountains just north of the city, to one of those national parks that are so popular with the hikers on the weekend and with the ladies groups everyday," the writer stated, as he began to narrate the second tale, using his most dramatic voice in hopes of keeping the creature interested for more tales to come.

"Let's turn our attention to someone who, even in the midst of raging popularity, can be as lonesome as a forest troll, or as misunderstood as a woodland fairy. Let's walk with her as she stumbles into the old ways, and harkens back to the olden days of those misty mountains, when men prayed, and sacrificed, to other gods, and paid tribute to those sacred singing stones. Even though, as you know, much of that tradition has faded with time and lost memories. Yet, once in a long while, at the cusp of the season's change, when the air carries a certain flavor, and the right stars float about the morning sky, one may hear a rare enquiry echoing off those long quiet stones. If, and, only if, the questions are truly sincere, those old gods might choose to awaken, and, for the briefest moment, offer an answer. "

2

THE K-POP PRINCESS AND THE MOUNTAIN

Barely an hour due north of Mount Namsan's forested heart, after weaving through Seoul's steel, glass, and concrete, one arrives at Bukhansan National Park, looming large as a big brother park, watching over the city, her people, and their dreams like the stalwart guardians the mountains have been for millennia. While there are many other worthy mountain parks scattered around the city, Bukhansan, or Samgaksan, three-horned mountain, as many locals call it, is so close to the urban center and accessible by several subway lines and many buses, that it is a favorite destination for playing out the near manic obsession of the locals for hiking. The trails, steps, and rope lines are crushingly crowded on nearly all weekends and holidays. However, for those with rare schedule flexibility, there are special times that a few select hikers know when to head to the mountains for a less public experience. The cold days of early winter, when people are beginning to hide from the change in weather, and, of course, the bitter cold, middle of a Seoul winter, are ideal. Days that are superstitious will also cause many hikers to find recreation elsewhere. Days when the November rains come, or threaten to come, also reduce the number of visitors. On those late fall days, when the copious leaves and the abundant rain conspire to make the trails slippery and the ascents tedious, the rangers will selectively close the more difficult stretches of trails for the well-being of all, even the most ardent of hikers. The park service will even close entire mountains during particularly treacherous weather.

Just such a stormy event had occurred overnight, bringing a touch of uncertainty to Bukhansan's trails on a particularly brisk, yet fog shrouded, late fall, nearly early winter, morning. The mountain was not closed, but only a few groups of hardy older ladies, hell bent on ensuring they maintained their rigorous hiking schedule, were braving the cold, damp morning air. A few college students, possibly members of a track team, also could be seen warming up just inside the southeastern visitors' entrance to one of the less popular, steeper trails. Only a few couples, ranging in ages, were sprinkled along the trails in the early morning, with each couple no doubt trying to get in a good hike before starting their mid-week day in offices, or other work or school pursuits. Yes, it was a workday, after a strong autumn storm, which helped immensely in thinning out the more casual, mid-week hikers.

One young lady who had decided to brave the cold, the fog, the storm-dashed trails, and the uncertainty of closed trails, was, at that very moment, determinedly making her way, alone, through the maze of shops, apartment buildings, and offices toward that less popular entrance near the southeastern edge of the park.

The young visitor, not arriving via the subway nor by way of a bus or taxi, had had her chauffeured car drop her by the station so she could walk the few blocks to the trail entrance, thereby giving anyone who cared to notice the illusion that she had naturally come from the station or by bus, placing her in that assumed strata of the vast working class in Korea's economic caste system. She had also forbidden her driver, who had become a friend and ally over the years, from following her, in order for her to experience a couple of hours of rare, cherished freedom. Her manager thought she was sleeping in, an illusion she had strived to cultivate for those times when she just wanted to get away from it all and find some alone time, even in the midst of a possibly crowded hiking trail. While holiday trips to the mountains of Europe or the various coasts of the Mediterranean had given her a few days each year where she was truly unknown to other tourists, allowing her family to have as normal a holiday as possible, the young visitor still longed for her old walks among the hills and mountains above her former home.

As the slim young hiker passed through those jumbled blocks of mostly still closed shops and offices on the approach to the park, she could have easily passed for a high school or college student. Most likely Ewha, from her demeanor and her clothing. Maybe Yonsei, but she didn't have that rushed look one often associates with Yonsei's undergrads. Hongik? Chung-Ang? Possibly, from the detached, yet creative air emanating from her, as her eyes took in the beauty of even the grey, drab shops she passed. Probably not SNU, as the mountain was a bit far from the main campus for such a mid-week morning romp. Of course, she could have been a student at any number of the respected schools sprinkled about Seoul, or even from one of the solid schools in the provinces. She could also have been a shop girl, or an office assistant. Although her expensive, high-end hiking boots, well worn, but well-maintained, would have been better protected by someone who would have needed a month's wages to purchase such branded, exclusive footwear. No, not a shop girl.

Yet, even with her high-end boots and tailored clothing, in the cold of the morning mountain air, the young lady was anonymous, detached from any immediately recognizable association, something that she, sadly, could rarely experience. However, her young face, with her telltale beauty mole buried under makeup and covered with her jacket's fur lined hood, and with her soulful eyes protected by the trendiest sunglasses, continued to betray signs of worry and guarded expectation of discovery as she maneuvered the early morning carts, trucks, cars, motorbikes, and bicycles of the suburb's slowly awakening shopkeepers, workers, and residents.

The sudden opening of a window above a bakery shop caused the visitor to flinch and turn away, thinking the housewife had recognized her and was opening the window to get a better shot with her camera phone. While the delicious aroma of baked goods pulled at her, she hurried past the shop, her head down. A young child, playing with her younger brother on the steps of no doubt her parents' sundries shop, waved at the passing young woman, only to frown in puzzlement as the pretty young lady ignored her wave and hurried on, turning away from the child without responding. Even the walls of the buildings along the streets and alleys seemed, to the skittish visitor, to lean in and spy over her shoulder, hoping to catch a glimpse of her face so they could whisper to the alleys and shops ahead that she was coming.

Of particular concern to the shy visitor were the two newsstands that lay along her usual path. So, to reduce her exposure, she had decided to take a slightly different route, through an unknown, somewhat darkened alley, and had managed to miss the first newsstand, where the hawker was sharp-eyed and quick with loud, self-serving comments. She always had felt uncomfortable the few times she had gone that way, sensing the hawker's eyes trying to peel back her various disguises to discover her identity.

About two blocks on, as she approached the second news stall, which also sold a small variety of writing and paper products, she turned her face away from the familiar old woman who had sold the visitor the occasional fan magazine in the past, yet had never let on that she had ever recognized the visitor. As the girl passed, the old woman, her sight clouded long ago, relying more on her gut for recognition, paused and turned, wondering why the familiar clip of the girl's hurried step had not stopped as usual. Even though the girl's visits were few and far between, the old woman fondly recalled the girl's chatter and honest, if guarded, conversation when the young visitor had perused the fan magazines and a few tabloid headlines during visits in the past, always buying several and refusing the standard discount for multiples.

As the visitor hurried forward, she felt, with minor guilt, the nearly sightless eyes of the kind old woman on the back of her neck, even through her coat's thick hood. Unable to face all the glaring headlines the old woman was obliviously stacking in the news racks, the visitor called a fleeting, but respectful apology which drifted back to the old woman like a discarded bit of out-of-date newsprint.

Practical as ever, the old woman simply shrugged, waved briefly at the blur of the hurrying figure, and, turning back to her work, hummed along with one of the popular girl-band tunes playing over the well-worn, 1970's radio at the back of the news stall. Placing the latest tabloids prominently, the old woman scoffed at the bold lettering, doctored cover photos, and outlandish claims, but continued to place the scandal sheets where she knew the passing workers and visiting hikers would see them and stop to buy. No one, even those headed up to the mountain, the old woman knew, could resist a juicy headline, regardless of its truth.

The young visitor, still hoping she hadn't offended the nice old grandmother at the newsstand, finally broke free from the almost suffocating press of dingy grey buildings and shops leading up to the park's entrance. She hesitated at the wide crosswalk to the entrance, and turned her gaze up toward the mountain before her. A thin fog, with thicker patches here and there, blanketed much of the base of the park, giving her little to see other than hazy outlines and the tops of a few taller pine trees, some of the only green still remaining at that time of year.

Yet, on the very threshold of her rare escape, the young woman continued to hesitate, seeming to struggle with the decision to cross over to the wide plaza and enter the park. Skirting the newsstands and avoiding random gazes had rattled her resolve more than she had anticipated, so the visitor had begun to worry that other hikers, the other visitors around her, may have already read over the morning's tabloids, or, at that very moment, were reading the social media posts, or, worse, the anti-fan sites with their blind, mindlessly cruel, hive-like attacks on....

"Let's go!" an older, kindly voice called out, abruptly interrupting the young hiker's worried reflection.

Evidently, when the crossing signal had switched to 'walk,' a bookish older man, walking with a child that was probably his granddaughter, had loudly urged the bundled up little girl to cross, snapping the young woman out of her hand-wringing indecision and causing her to hurriedly follow the two across the street.

Once at the welcome plaza, the young visitor saw several hiking groups gathered near the ranger station, so realized she needed to quickly move on or risk being recognized. No doubt, several of those middle-aged women or those jocks in the other group would have been following the major news and, possibly, the tabloids and the fan sites, she convinced herself. Any one of them could be aiming a cell phone at that very minute, the visitor imagined, pulling her hood closer. She then sped up her pace, leaving the kindly grandfather and the child at the entrance, and tried to pass the hiking groups quickly and without being noticed.

Hurrying by one of the larger groups, a lively pod of highly fit, middle-aged ladies, the young woman kept her head bowed low and turned away in a show of respectful deference to her elders, and to ensure she maintained her anonymity. She also hoped her heavy clothes and sunglasses would shield her from prying eyes. Yet, even with her quick gait, one of the women, hair still a natural color, so on the younger edge of middle aged, noticed the well-dressed, quick-footed young woman, and hailed her with a morning hello, both just to be friendly, and to get the younger girl to turn around so the group could get a better look at her. The young visitor guessed that the woman had called out either from being naturally nosy, or, just as likely, from the perspective of some in the group having sons and so were always looking for just the right match, especially one who wore expensive, high-end hiking boots and stylish clothes, as did the hurrying young lady.

"Happy morning, to you, young sister," the woman called, half-cheerfully and half-inquisitively, waving her arm in a polite, 'come here,' palm down gesture.

Pausing briefly in mid-stride, the young woman half-bowed to the cheerful greeting and, hurrying forward, called back with a quick, scarf-muffled good morning to the beckoning woman in purple. The young hiker hoped that her slight discourtesy would ensure an uninterrupted beginning to her hike, and prevent identification.

The curious older hiker, smoothing her puffy, lavender hued, down coat with the hand she had just used to wave at the almost rude young girl, continued to watch the well-dressed youth for a bit, wondering who the strange, standoffish girl might be. Once the young lady's slim figure had faded into the fog that still shrouded the base of the mountain, the woman filed away a mental snapshot of the young lady's clothing, to include the expensive hiking boots, for recognition on the trail later, thinking she'd confront the young upstart on one of the narrower trails where the rude girl could not hurry away.

Quickly passing the various signs, warnings, and safety notices, the young hiker reached the base of the secondary trail she always took on her rare hikes, and breathed a silent sigh of relief, satisfied that she had walked the few blocks of shops and had entered one of the main Bukhansan trails without being noticed. Best of all, she mused, she had gained the trail without picking up one of those inevitable chatty types who self-volunteered to be a stranger's hiking partner. However, forever vigilant against clever snoopers, the youth looked back down the trail, just briefly, to ensure that the inquisitive woman in purple and her group were no longer interested in her.

The young hiker then turned her head to look up the mountain and drew in a deep breath of the damp, cool air. Without further delay, she struck out on the trail with a brisk and determined pace. Even for one with her diminutive stature, her strong, dancer's legs had a determined stride, so she made good time.

As she ascended the trail, the late fall, early morning air at the lower levels of the fog-shrouded mountain wrapped the slim young hiker in a chilly mist of her own breath, which danced about her porcelain face as she approached the branching trail leading to her favorite viewing spot high above and just outside of Seoul's slowly awakening downtown.

Fleece-lined, light grey slacks, layered white cotton blouse and cream colored cashmere sweater, covered by a heavy ski jacket, light pink with white accents, all worked together to keep the visitor warm, but not too warm. In contrast to her usual, darker, more subdued tones when out in the world with family or team, she had chosen the brighter outfit to help boost her troubled mood and as a nod to her best friend, who had urged her to splurge on the cheerful outfit some months before. Her face still obscured by the encircling hood of thick, faux sable, a nod to her friend's love of animals, she finally let herself breathe evenly and without effort after a climb of about a hundred meters, and a thousand mental kilometers from the worries of the city.

Of the few other hikers she passed, the young lady paid even less notice than she had given to the middle aged woman at the visitor plaza. A young couple rushed past her, nodding a greeting, but the young lady was too self-absorbed to notice. Neither did she notice an older couple who had paused to rest at the first courtesy bench, rushing by the two without the customary hello and 'excuse me and I have to rush' comments expected of the younger generation. The old couple, however, simply sighed at the young lady's lack of traditional manners, something becoming all too common, they thought, as the too skinny, in their minds, girl dashed past them without a greeting.

Being self-absorbed was, for better or worse, a usual trait of the young hiker. Over the previous few years, she had always had numerous handlers who not only ensured she was seen doing and saying the right thing in public, they would also speak for her as she moved about open places. Consequently, the young hiker's public persona, which she was desperately trying to keep hidden in her desire to remain anonymous during her small escape, still shone through as she climbed the trail. To the young, self-centered hiker, part of her felt she was the only visitor of importance on the mountain that morning, and she certainly did not have the time nor inclination to chat with strangers, even those who obviously shared her love of hiking. Her preoccupation over concern with the tabloids at the newsstands, her suspicions that random strangers were watching her, and her worry over the social media and fan sites were also weighing heavily on her escape, which caused her to be even less considerate of others around her once on her refuge of a mountain.

With the plaza far below her, the youth glanced back down the trail and to the city beyond, her eyes stinging from a sudden gust of wind rolling the fog up the trail. Pulling off one glove, she wiped the resultant tears from her eyes behind her sunglasses, turned back to the trail, slippery with wet leaves, and looked for the opening to the branch trail to her favorite spot, her secret den of solitude, her true escape from the cares of the city below.

Good, the young hiker thought, as she continued. No one was around.

Just as the young lady turned a blind corner near a major divergence of two separate paths, a more difficult one trailing off the main, more easily scaled trail, she was suddenly halted in her tracks by a dew covered barricade over the main trail.

Shocked, the young hiker leaned in and read a small sign directing hikers to use the alternate route to the top. A small map showed hikers the change and the few short steps to the alternate trail.

Closed?

The path to her escape diverted?

The young hiker's entire mood, which, while still a bit nervous from her solitary walk through the edges of the village, had been growing increasingly upbeat after evading recognition, and from being only a few minutes from her morning's destination, suddenly came crashing down as she considered the implications of the alternate route. From what she knew of the trails, the alternate route would lead her dead straight away from her intended destination.

Realizing that her entire morning scheme of evasive maneuvers would come to naught, that the entire plan, to escape for a couple of hours before she had to be back in the real world, a secret plan she had delayed for weeks until the events of the weekend had driven her to risk the outing, was about to be thwarted, the young hiker clenched her small, graceful hands into fists and thumped her legs in frustration.

Damn those magazines, the young hiker cursed in her mind, realizing that, once the tabloids, paper and online, had hit the stands that morning, her ability to escape for a few hours would be gone for months, possibly years to come. The fan sites and anti-fan sites were too clever to be duped once they began their endless vigils, after the news was widespread and the blame game kicked off. With the inevitable cutthroat competition between the news, pseudo-news, fan news, and anti-fan news, to name just a few, her movements would be dogged night and day, in country and outside.

The hike, her hike, the young woman lamented internally, was to be her sole respite before the storm of public opinion crashed against her fragile ship of engineered indifference. Even she, who had weathered her share, and more, of misdirected controversy in the past, would not be impervious to the impending shark fest of the entertainment world's instant news cycle's unquenchable appetite for any snippet of juicy information, whatever its truthfulness, she realized, her spirit slipping.

After a moment and a few deep breaths, the young hiker managed to control her mounting frustration and anger, while she also held back a few threatened tears. Tears that wanted to come, not over her own selfishness, but over her yearning to return to the place she and her dearest, truest friend had shared many years before. Before their roads in life had become more complicated. Before they had lost their youth. Before they had entered the surreal bubbles of their chosen careers.

No!

The word of refusal burst into the young woman's mind, causing her to stand dead still and listen to the mountain around her, straining to hear the footfalls of any others who might be near. Squinting through the fog, she also looked for any shapes that might be just beyond her sight, ready to discover her and confront her on her next, quite out of character, actions.

"No!"

The single word of desperate defiance then rushed forth from the young woman's angry lips, bouncing around the trail, ducking into the crevices, rebounding off the rocks and trees lining the path, and driving aloft nearby morning birds. Throwing her hands to her face, the young hiker couldn't believe she had shouted out loud.

Mentally weighing the needs of her emotional goal over her respect for and healthy fear of the rules, the young hiker, with that outburst of defiance, felt she was on the cusp of deciding the barrier was only a mere inconvenience, not a blockade to her determined progress, when she was surprised by a shrill voice, which seemed to answer her desperate cry.

"Carry on!" the aged voice called.

Looking quickly around, the young hiker wondered if she might have imagined the voice and its bold declaration to head up the trail and ignore the barriers. She had seen no one just seconds before, so was puzzled by the old voice.

Silence.

Shaking her head, and concluding she was imagining things, the young hiker again looked longingly at the upper trail, sensing the familiar path calling to her. Yet, with renewed doubt creeping in, feeling that her brief resolve was sinking lower, in spite of the encouragement from the imagined voice, she turned her feet to retrace her earlier, all too short, happier steps back to the plaza.

"Carry on, young one! There's no one about to see your momentary transgression," the voice called again, but was now attached to a rustic, older woman, dressed in grey-green, sporting heavy boots and using one of those older, twisted wooden walking sticks, browned and scarred with age, matching the rough skin and tanned face of its ancient owner, who wore her grey-streaked, black hair long, well below her bony shoulders.

Shocked into silence, the young hiker simply stared as the old woman walked, or, more accurately, hobbled over to the barricades. Where the old woman had been standing was a mystery to the young woman, but she quickly regained her composure once the old woman was within arm's length.

"Madam...Grandmother, I'm sorry. I did not see you there. Please forgive me for missing you," the youth began with a quick bow, but was waved off by the old woman's sunburnt and oddly muscular hands.

"Mustn't apologize, young one. Walking the old trails in the morning mist can confuse anyone," the old woman replied, her deep-set, black eyes searching the young hiker's half-hidden face, as if looking for some hint of recognition. "Alone, are you...? Yes? Are you going this way...?"

The old woman pointed up the blocked trail with her walking stick as she beckoned the young hiker with her left hand, yet did not attempt to touch the youth.

"I...yes, grandmother, thank you. I was going that way, but the trail is closed. Probably from the storm," the young hiker, her heart still heavy, slowly replied, half wondering how she could extract herself from the old woman's obvious chatty mood, and retreat back down the mountain.

"What? You're going to let a little something like a sign stop you? Why, if there were real dangers, wouldn't they have stretched a rope across and made the barriers sturdier?" the old woman asked, her voice dropping its earlier shrillness and becoming more melodic, more interesting to the youth.

"Grandmother, I don't want to disagree with you, but the barrier is quite definite," the young hiker answered, but with less conviction as the seed of nonconformity, that had been planted when she first had encountered the barricade, seemed to be growing, drawing strength from the old woman's sympathetic and urgent words.

"You go ahead, young one," the old woman cajoled, winking at the narrow gap between the barricades. "I'll watch for any authorities or walkers from below."

"What? You mean...just go around?" the young hiker asked, excitement growing in her voice, part of her mind relishing the thought of breaking the rules, yet another part holding her back, fated to retreat to the inevitability of her life beyond the mountain.

"Young one, how often do you get the trails to yourself? I've lived among these rocks...down in the village, of course...many, many years, and I know when they are dangerous. Trust me...dear," the old woman replied, a brief smile crossing her face as she continued to beckon for the young hiker to slip through the gap in the barricade. "Only a few steps, young one. You are so thin, you can easily make it through. A few steps to freedom and your own path."

Trust her, the young woman asked herself in her mind? The odd, older woman didn't seem as addled as the old sometimes were, nor did the old woman recognize the young hiker, so she's not some fan stalker, the youth decided. But, there was something that was too eager, too expectant about the old woman wanting her to ignore the detour, thought the young hiker.

"Do you think…is it…truly okay?" the young hiker hesitantly asked, her foot poised to step forward, even as a nagging doubt held her back.

"Of course, young one. Of course," the old woman replied, a brief, disturbing gleam in her dark eyes abruptly vanishing as the old woman quickly turned her wrinkled face toward the upper trail. "If you don't cross, then who knows what adventures you will have missed? What personal reflection you may have never done? What untold…? Yes, cross the barrier, young one."

Suddenly, the thought of crossing the barrier gripped the young hiker without mercy, ridding her of any hesitance. As she looked back down the trail, clearer now that the fog was beginning to thin in spots, she smiled when she saw that no other hikers were visible behind her.

Glancing around like a villain in a bad drama, the young hiker, eager to act before she lost her sudden resolve, held her breath, and then, following the old woman's insistent gestures, slipped through the narrow opening in the overlap of the barricades, her years of dance training allowing her to pass through without any effort.

"I did it! Amazing! Oh, can you make it through, grandmother?" the young hiker then asked, her breath coming fast, from both excitement and a little fear after breaking the rules and crossing the barrier.

"Me? Why, young one, would I love to join you? Are you sure you want a companion on your trek…?" the old woman asked, her voice sounding farther away and more ethereal to the young hiker now that the two were on opposite sides of the barricades.

"Companion? Why, I don't want to upset you, grandmother, but I did want to have a quiet walk," the youth answered, then fell silent as the old woman leaned against the barrier and then jumped back, as if the barrier had given the woman a shock.

"Ask me over, young one!" the old woman suddenly demanded, her voice changing back to its earlier shrillness. "You must ask me over!"

"Grandmother, I don't know what you mean…," the young hiker began, and, shocked at the old woman's sudden, blunt demand, stumbled backward and let her enquiry fade away.

A snarl? Hissing? What happened to the kind old lady, the youth wondered? Something akin to growing fright entered the young hiker's mind at the bizarre transformation of the kindly old woman.

"You...must...invite...me!" the old woman called, her face twisted into a grimace as her right hand thumped her walking stick against the hard ground beneath the barrier.

Suddenly, something deep inside the young hiker, something from her early childhood and her grandmother's kitchen, something she could not quite remember, sounded in the back of her skull. She felt she could hear her own grandmother urging the youth to abandon the old woman at the barrier and get away as quickly as she could.

"Invite...me!"

Turning away from the now raving old woman, and, forcing herself to not look back, even though she imagined the old woman's hot breath on her neck, the young hiker quickly sprinted up the trail to a bend. There she ducked behind a wide oak tree hanging over the trail near one of the first jumbles of large rocks.

Her heart beating quickly in her chest from both her flight from the old woman and from the real possibility of discovery by the authorities, the young hiker leaned out and stole a quick glance down the trail.

Gone.

The trail around the barrier was empty.

The old woman was nowhere to be seen.

Staring at the area around the barricades, the young hiker wondered, for a split second, if the old woman had gotten in front of her somehow. Looking quickly around, she saw that she was utterly alone. However, she did see a group of blurry bodies emerging from the lower fog and, hearing voices from one of the lady hiker groups, she quickly dived back behind the tree, and waited as the voices paused, groused about the unexpected barrier, and then obediently headed off on the alternate route.

Peeking through the brush at the edge of her temporary hideout, the young hiker watched the lady hikers in bright colors disappear around a blind curve. A small calico cat, one that had seen better days, then darted from the mist-covered rocks and followed the ladies.

Odd, thought the young hiker, that the old woman had not approached the hiker ladies. Maybe the old woman only wanted to deal with single hikers? Or, smaller groups?

Shrugging nervously, the young woman then took a moment to calm herself by the tree, finally getting her breathing under control. Once fully assured that the old woman was no longer nearby and that none of the lady hikers had seen her, she stepped back onto the officially forbidden trail to trek up to her special side path.

Just as she stepped beyond the shelter of the old oak, the young woman froze in place at what she saw before her.

A man.

Partially obscured by early morning shadows and a few wisps of fog, but definitely a man. Only a few meters beyond her former hiding place.

How had she missed him before, the young hiker wondered? And, for a deserted, barricaded trail, it certainly seemed to hold a lot of surprise tenants.

Fortunately, the man's back was to her, so the youth thought she could sneak back to the tree undetected. Yet, as she tried to quietly turn back to the shelter of the old oak, her boots crunched on a few twigs brought down by the previous night's storm, no doubt from the very oak that had just hidden her, betraying her presence to the stranger.

Cringing, the young hiker turned back to face the stranger, whom she then saw was some sort of official as his uniformed image partially emerged from the mist and shadows. Out on his rounds, no doubt, she thought, and would now investigate the crunching sound and the blatant criminal who had ignored the stern warning at the barricade below.

Why did I let that old woman push me into breaking the rules, the young hiker wondered? Sighing, she abandoned thoughts of escape and waited patiently for the official to spot her.

Yet, rather than being on the hunt for brazen trespassers, the old man, for the official was quite old, wearing what the young hiker recognized as the local ranger uniform, seemed to have been placing a sign to indicate there was some danger from fallen obstacles on the main trail above. Evidently, the young hiker surmised, the old ranger was placing secondary signs to ensure trespassers got the message multiple times, and his appearance before her was simply coincidental.

The young hiker, standing politely and resolutely to hear whatever harsh words the ranger might have, once he had spotted her, was not frightened of the consequences of her actions, but was sorely disappointed, crushed, actually, as her quiet escape haven lay only another dozen or so steps up and just off the main trail. She desperately needed to get to that place, she knew, not only for herself, but, more importantly, for the sake of her friend.

Maybe the old woman had detected that sense of urgency, the young hiker mused? Yet, why hadn't the old woman crossed the barriers, the youth also wondered?

The old ranger showed no surprise at the sudden appearance of the law breaking, yet politely bowing young lady hiker, and, without speaking, he only pointed to the sign she had assumed he had just placed, smiled, and, using hand gestures, indicated she needed to move back down to the alternate trail.

The ranger, instead of berating her as a villainous scofflaw, then tipped his hat, did a short bow, and began to turn away. Yet, the young hiker, her head lowered, but her eyes looking up, saw that something had caught the interest of the old ranger because he suddenly stopped, stood looking up to the far reaches of the mountain, let out a short grumble, more noise than anger, slowly shook his head, and then turned back.

Stepping closer to the young hiker, the old ranger, in a warm, kindly, deep voice, then added his verbal endorsement to the sensibility of the alternate trail, removing his hat as he spoke, in a curiously western gesture.

"You there, young lady, I'm sorry you are inconvenienced," the old ranger called, his voice quietly melodic, using the older, formal way of speaking. "However, the upper ridge trail has a number of fallen trees from that storm last night. The forest trail is quite pretty this time of year, even though the leaves have all mostly turned and fallen, given the winds we've had this week. The pines and firs are, of course, still vibrant. I'm sure you will enjoy it. And, it connects to the main trail near the closest summit, after all."

Smiling at the ranger's kind words, rather than the expected authoritative verbal thrashing, the young hiker nodded and gave a small bow of thanks to the old ranger, in spite of her utter disappointment. She then took a long, deep breath, turned to head to the alternate trail, but, unable to force her feet to move, she sighed heavily as she just stood and wondered if she should just go back down the mountain, avoid the old woman, dash by the other hikers, the newsstands, the shopkeepers, and the prying eyes, and just summon her car. Yet, she also thought that maybe she should follow the ranger's directions? While she would not be able to get to her private spot, her rare escape and much anticipated recharging might be partially fulfilled if she just did a quick hike up to one of the cats' lookouts, about two hundred meters farther. She and her friend had always loved the mountain's cats and few dogs, who, although skittish, were willing to pause and preen for a tasty handout. However, she still felt a deep emptiness in letting down her friend, causing even more confusing, internal conflict, as she stood, torn with indecision.

Fishing out her personal mobile phone, the latest version, of course, the young hiker stared at it, but was having trouble seeing the screen.

Tears?

For the briefest of moments, the young hiker's training tried to kick in as she initially worried about her makeup, but then stopped herself, and, slowly, removed her sunglasses. Looking around to ensure that no one, mainly the old ranger, was watching, she shoved her sunglasses into her coat pocket, pulled off both of her gloves, and quickly wiped her eyes.

Haltingly, with her shoulders sinking low in utter dejection and with tears still threatening to stain her Burberry scarf tucked inside her jacket, the obviously saddened young hiker turned away to head back down the trail to the exits, having decided to surrender to the futility of using anything but her friend's old trail and secret spot to ease the emptiness and despair that dragged at her heavy heart.

"Miss?"

The ranger's quiet, but forceful voice gently interrupted the young lady's mental and physical retreat from the mountain.

The young hiker slowly turned, keeping her eyes downcast, more to shield the involuntary tears than to demonstrate proper social decorum by keeping her eyes lowered to a strange man's, even an old man's, gaze.

"Young sister, are you okay? Can I radio someone to help you? There is usually a nurse at the station, even this early in the morning," the old ranger asked in a voice that spoke of a truly caring person, one who wanted nothing but to ensure the well being of whomever he met.

Afraid to immediately respond, the youth waited nearly half a minute to collect herself, brush her eyes, and attempt to put forward a façade of control.

"Sir, grandfather, thank you ever so much," the young hiker finally replied, her lyrical voice giving her words a musical, if melancholy air as they floated over to the old ranger. "I am...I am truly sorry to have concerned you. I am fine. Just fine. I should not have listened to the grandmother and passed the barrier. My apologies. I will just go...go back."

As her final words stammered out, the young hiker looked up at the old ranger's kind, square and solid face, and, for a brief moment, felt a strange rush of warmth and caring concern in his ancient gaze, a feeling she had not experienced in many, many years. Taking a small step forward, she found herself not wanting to part so quickly from the mountain, and, counter to her usual suspiciousness, wanting desperately to confide in the complete stranger before her.

If she could just tell someone, anyone, the young hiker told herself.

Yet, years of grooming within a structured studio life then took over. So the young hiker quickly suppressed her overflowing emotions, took a deep breath of the cold air, looked longingly beyond the ranger at the twist in the path above that led to her friend's favorite spot, and then turned to leave, mumbling a nearly inaudible, but deeply sincere 'thank you' to the ranger.

"Young lady, forgive me for being too intrusive. I certainly do not wish to pry," called the old man, his voice wrapping a gentle blanket of kind awareness around the departing young woman. "I think you must have a special place up this path? Maybe somewhere you go to 'get away from it all,' even if only for a few short, priceless moments?"

Stopping in her tracks, the young hiker slowly turned back to the old ranger, her face revealing a painful mix of both alarm and hope. Had he recognized her, she wondered?

Was he trying to get her to reveal her secret place?

Was he really a forest ranger...?

The young hiker shook off the last partial thought and then started to reply.

"Sir, I...," the youth began, unsure as to how to answer the old ranger, mainly because she had been trained to be suspicious of any unsolicited kindness over the years.

"Don't be alarmed," the old man continued, as if reading her thoughts. "We see many people up here who yearn for a few moments of escape from the pressures of the city, of school, of family, of career, of life. Many have a favorite spot for just such reflection."

"Sir, you are...are partly correct," the young hiker replied as she turned her phone over and over in her hands, mentally debating if she should just say goodbye and call her driver. "I do so love the little trail that feeds off the main one above the major bend, just visible in the distance over your shoulder."

Without turning around to look in the direction the young hiker mentioned, the old ranger smiled as he answered.

"I see," the old ranger replied, his voice soothing, almost therapeutic. "There are several short trails that feed off the main one just above there. Two go into the forest to connect with the alternate trail, but those are barricaded today. The third one...the third one is not so well known. Rarely used. Goes across bare rock, so there is no trail revealed. But, it ends up at the edge of the cliff, which can be quite dangerous in the wrong weather, or if you are distracted as you walk."

The young hiker's quick half-smile, at the mention of the old cliff trail, revealed the truth to the old ranger.

"So, young miss, it's the cliff path you seek," the old ranger stated, then turned and looked up the trail.

The old ranger then turned back to face the youth and leaned fully out of the shadows and mist while giving the young hiker a hard, full stare as he spoke.

"Sadly, miss, this side of the mountain has served as the Mapo Bridge for a few tragic souls over the years. Yours is not such a quest, I trust...?" the old ranger bluntly asked, letting his words hang over the young hiker like one of the grey clouds blanketing the side of the mountain across the valley.

The young hiker was shocked, wide-eyed, at the old man's almost accusatory implication. She then vigorously shook her head in convincing denial of any thoughts of self-harm.

The old ranger then slowly nodded, his steady gaze assessing the young lady hiker. He then walked around the warning sign and, stepping past the youth, looked down the mountain to the lower barricade.

"Young miss, you said something about the barricades and an old grandmother...?" the ranger asked, his voice probing, seeming to seek out something other than the young hiker breaking the rules.

"Sir, yes...yes, an elderly lady. She...I know now it was wrong of me, but she invited me to cross the barrier...she seemed...nice. At first," the young hiker replied in a rush, images of the old woman's twisted face causing the youth to frown.

The old ranger then spoke very carefully, his gaze never leaving the area of the barricades.

"Young miss, this is very important...," the ranger said, his voice so low that the young hiker had trouble hearing him. "Did you ask the old woman to follow you?"

"Follow me, sir? Why, she did...she asked me to invite her over the barrier, but then...then she seemed just too eager for me to ask, sir. So, I must apologize that I did not ask her, sir. There was something...something was not...," the young hiker replied, letting her explanation trail off as she ran out of rational reasons for her abandoning the old woman.

"Wise, young miss. Wise, for one...one so young," the old ranger stated cryptically as he stepped back to the sign and, motioning to the youth, indicated she should follow him up the main trail.

Confused, a bit suspicious, but mostly excited to be given the chance to stay inside the barricades, the young hiker slipped around the warning sign and ran after the old ranger, who was taking long, effortless strides straight up the trail.

As she caught up to the ranger, the young hiker was able to spend a minute looking him over. His uniform was old, of the same design as ones she had seen before, but definitely of older material. He was carrying his hat, so his bare head showed he was slightly balding with a mix of grey and white hair. A refreshing look, the young hiker thought, given the country's craze of one dyeing his or her hair at the first sign of a single grey hair.

The ranger was neither too tall, nor too short. A good height. He was neither thin nor fat, and, from the look of his hands and how his clothes hung fairly tightly to his frame, the old man was still muscular and probably quite strong.

The old man's face was kind, full of spirit, with his clear, hazel and brown eyes giving off a twinkle when he smiled, which he was doing at that moment, looking back to see that she was following. His slightly tanned skin showed no major wrinkles and his step was assured. While old, he did not exhibit any of the standard maladies other old people she knew tended to display at his age.

As the two neared the first major bend of the upper trail, the ranger turned to the young hiker, held up his finger to his lips to indicate silence, and then quickly dashed around the bend, disappearing behind a large, vertical slab of rock, bordered by large boulders, which concealed the upper trail from below.

The young hiker immediately copied the ranger and dashed up the trail.

She glanced back just before she passed behind the boulders and caught a glimpse of another group of lady hikers arriving at the far barricade.

After a few meters, the ranger eased his pace and then stopped all together.

"Young lady, I think the gentle ladies of the Purple Lake, as they call their club, did not see you."

"Yes, they were focused on the barrier, so were not looking up," the young hiker replied, realizing one of the lead hikers she had seen might have been the middle aged lady who had called to her in the plaza.

"Now, miss. I will walk with you to your side trail, but then I have to go above and ensure no one tries to return from the summit via this main trail. At least, until we reopen it later in the day."

"Oh, sir, I am so sorry," the young hiker replied, sincere concern in her voice, which sounded a bit alien to her own ear. "You are not going to get in trouble for letting me stay inside the barrier?"

"Trouble, miss?" the ranger replied absently, a little preoccupied with parting and getting to his next station. "No real danger. More of a precaution as we are having some important visitors tomorrow and need to ensure everything is in order. The fallen trees will be removed and the closure allows us to replace a couple of the older cable holds near the top of this trail and two on the side trails. Easier to close the trails today as we don't anticipate a lot of visitors. However, just in case…."

The elder ranger then pulled a small, official looking pad out of his left jacket pocket, flipped it open, and, using a small pen attached to the pad via a short wire, quickly wrote out a pass for the young hiker, mumbling to himself as he wrote.

"Friend of family…knows trails…knows safety training. You have had your mandatory trail safety training…?" the old ranger asked as he looked over the pad at the young woman, his eyes telling her that a lie would end their short relationship.

"Yes, sir. Just this summer. For a shoot. My manager insisted," the young woman quickly replied, somewhat proudly, since she had taken all the lessons and tests herself and had refused any help, but mentally kicked herself for slipping up by mentioning a manager and a photo shoot.

"Good," the old ranger replied.

Finishing the pass, the ranger began to tear the sheet from the pad when he suddenly stopped and laughed at himself for missing the obvious.

"Name?" the old ranger asked, his pen poised.

"Name…?" the young hiker repeated, slowly, wondering for a brief moment if she should give one of her three pseudonyms her manager had invented for her for hotels, restaurants, and the like.

"Yes, your name," the old ranger replied with slight impatience. "This is only a formality, in case another official stops you and asks why you are inside the barriers. I'm allowing you to do this because you are obviously aware of the trails, know the correct etiquette, and, from the way you handle overeager strangers, how to avoid any potential dangers."

"Sir, should I have invited the old woman to join me?" the young hiker asked, wondering why the ranger had used such an odd reference.

"Miss, these mountains are old. Very old. They have been homes to kings and hideouts for thieves. They have been the refuge of monks and safe harbor of highwaymen. Even in these more modern times, these mountains can attract...can attract those who have more selfish interests at heart," the old ranger replied, his voice distant and his eyes scanning the trails below. "You must have a good heart, young miss, to have avoided the old...to have passed without any real harm."

The young hiker, still a bit confused by the old ranger's words, simply nodded.

"Again? Your name, miss?" the ranger repeated.

"Yes, sir. Of course, sir," the young hiker replied, still debating with herself as to which name to give, while wondering about the ranger's reference to the strange woman.

"Lee, sir," the young hiker finally answered.

"Lee, Sir," the old man repeated as he started to write. "Interesting first name. I'd swear it sounds just like 'sir.' Which 'Lee?' And, how do you spell your first name?"

For the blink of an eye, the young hiker thought the ranger was being serious and had mistaken her politeness for her first name, but, when she saw his eyes twinkling and a small grin on his face, she realized he was joking with her. She burst out in a short, nervous laugh, and then told him which family name of Lee she was using, but continued to hesitate on her given name, fearful he would immediately recognize her and her valiant attempt at being anonymous would evaporate.

The old ranger, sensing the young hiker was hesitant, smoothed over her fears.

"Okay, Miss S. Lee," the ranger mumbled as he finished the pass, his eyes twinkling.

Smiling more broadly, the ranger, nodding to the young hiker, finished the entry, tore the bright yellow paper off the pad, and held it up to show to the young hiker.

"There, you have it, miss," the old ranger declared with a mock flourish. "The pass, and, for a couple of hours at least, total freedom from the crush of crowds. A treasured few moments in a city and country where both the elite and the most common of her citizens yearn for privacy, and, where such yearning must truly weigh heavily on those more in the public spotlight."

"Sir, thank you. Thank you so much, sir," the youth began, and, deciding to be fully honest with the kind, old ranger, began to tell him more. "Sir, my real name is…."

Still gripping the pass, the ranger held up his hand to stop her, then furrowed his brow and replied.

"Better, miss, that you are simply a young hiker out for a bit of air, as you originally had intended, before the park's plans, and before that old woman, the odd encounter below, almost altered yours," the kindly old ranger responded.

"Sir, are you certain you don't need to…?" the young hiker tried to continue, but the old ranger held up both hands for emphasis.

"Miss, the mountains were here long before me, and you, and will be here long after we are no longer able to walk the majestic paths, marvel at the amazing views, relish the company of our family and friends, and momentarily dwell in the silences of our own reflections. Our names are fleeting labels that we carry for a while, then discard as we move up that eventual last trail. Let's walk, then I have to leave you."

Her face reflective after the ranger's unexpected, sage words, the youth simply nodded, and, walking along in silence, followed the old ranger up the trail.

As the two unlikely hiking partners neared the spot where the feeder trail split off, the old ranger commented on the young lady's intended path.

"Miss, I think you know that trail is only a few dozen meters, and ends near the cliff's edge, with signs prohibiting any climbing on the cliff itself."

"Sir, I know what you are thinking, but I never try to climb down the cliff. There is a spot…," the young hiker began, but hesitated to finish her answer, loathe to share knowledge of her friend's secret viewing spot with anyone, even a ranger who probably knew every nook and cranny on the mountain.

"…the Lover's Lament," the old ranger finished for the young hiker.

"Sir?"

"At least, that is what we called it in the old days," the old ranger continued, his eyes staring off into the distance. "A place of melancholy and sadness. It's good that you avoided the old woman, if you were coming to such a place."

"Sir? No. It must be a different spot," the young hiker declared, wondering what the ranger meant by his continued cautions on the old woman. "My…my friend's and my enclave is enchanting, happy, and a warm breath of solitude in a crazy busy world, sir."

"Miss, is the spot sort of hidden, surrounded by…? Wait, I'll walk over with you."

Quietly, then, the two unlikely companions turned off the main trail and stepped onto the weather-rounded boulders and huge stones that revealed little to the untrained eye in the way of a spur trail. The two continued to remain silent until they had arrived at the end of the path, both facing the nearby edge of the cliff, looking down over the waking city in the distance.

"Ah!" exclaimed the young hiker, throwing her arms up in triumph at the edge of the cliff. "There you are!"

Pushing back her hood, the spontaneous sound of triumph at reaching her viewing spot burst forth from the young woman with clear hints of the high quality tone of a well-trained, yet natural voice. A large puff of misty breath slowly rose above her black, cropped, slightly wavy hair as a brief smile rippled across the pale skin of her young face. Her eyes, instead of tearing, as she had feared, beamed at her triumph.

Suddenly, the mixed odors of the fallen leaves with the rocky soil and sparse ground cover, draped with the wispy fog's dew, took the young hiker back to the first time she had approached the rocky sanctuary. That delicious aroma, mixed with the fragrance of the trees and the perfume of the morning winds, caused the young lady to take a deep breath and seemingly float forward.

Leaving the ranger, the young hiker stepped off the path, glided around two ancient tree stump skeletons jutting into the air, and past a jumble of large, grey, almost guardian boulders. There she found her favorite viewing spot, a reclining cache of larger boulders and smooth stones in steel grey and dirty brown, streaked with dashes of white, waiting quietly for her arrival, where she repeated her earlier exclamation.

"There you are…!"

The happy youth's words bounced around the area of the cozy stone sanctuary, just large enough for two, if those two were small in stature like the young hiker.

Stepping back to the weathered stumps, the joyful young hiker could just see over them enough to spy the old ranger's face looking her way. To her delight, the old ranger seemed truly surprised. He walked over to the narrow space between the two tree stumps and, with difficulty, squeezed part of the way through, and then leaned in to take a look at her private sanctuary.

A low whistle, rare in the suspicious world of old Korea, came out of the surprised ranger. He did a quick bow with his head to his young companion.

"Miss, my highest compliments on your secret rock garden. Your sanctum sanctorum. Your refuge, far from the madding crowd. And, I commend you on your managing to keep it so secret. This is a safe place, I can tell. No need to worry about your…your friend below. Please take this pass and keep it safe, in case you need to show it."

Leaning deeper into the small enclave, the ranger handed the pass to the young hiker and nodded his approval as he continued.

"May I ask how you came to know this was here?"

Beaming at the old ranger's sincere surprise and poetic praise, the young lady, after stowing the pass in her coat pocket, wondered if she should make up a story, or tell the helpful official the truth.

"Maybe this is a place you've shared with a young...?" the old ranger offered with some amusement.

"What? Sorry, sir. No, not that sort of friend," the young hiker quickly replied, spots of red jumping into her cheeks. "My friend...."

Suddenly, no doubt due to the stresses of the previous few days, coupled with reliving memories of spending time with her best friend up in the mountains, the young woman allowed all her pent up feelings to flood to the surface and began to blurt out her story before she realized what she was saying.

"Oh, sir, a few years before now, before all the...all the public appearances, my best friend brought me up here and showed me the wonder of this hideaway," the young hiker called over the entrance. "This is...was my friend's favorite place. She had grown up not far from here, and she, she and her father had hiked this mountain every weekend. She liked other mountains, of course, but this one was special, as it was where she and her father could share their love of outdoors and get away, outdoors, away from...the pressures."

Just as quickly as she had burst forth with her jumbled, joyous words, the young hiker abruptly fell silent, while memories of her closest friend rushed back, filling her head with bittersweet images, and crushing her chest with a pain she felt only she could know, cutting short her hurried explanation and confirming to the kindly old ranger that something quite serious was indeed weighing heavily on the young hiker.

Yet, to his credit, the old ranger, well-versed in the ways of the world and, possibly, at his advanced age, all too familiar with personal tragedies, only stood silently, not questioning, not commenting, not judging, but simply standing, allowing the distressed young lady to speak freely, without fear.

"She loved nature," the young hiker continued, her voice settling into a quiet calmness, reassured by the old ranger's attentive and non-judging ear. "And, really loved this spot. Her spot. We never really got back together here after our debut. But, we had always promised each other that, when the fans were gone, the managers reassigned, the fair-weather friends moved on to the next rising prospects...that we would...that we'd never forget our simpler times. Our happiest times. From this aloof, protective shelter, we looked down over the town that we would conquer. Conquer...yet, we were woefully ignorant of how the city, the business, would, by and by, conquer us. How we could...how we would succumb. She was the smart one. She was the one who warned me. Protected me. I...I think I came to resent her. Her ability to see through the glitz and the carefully orchestrated façades. The last time we…I yelled at her, sir, the last time we spoke. Yelled at the one person who…loved me…loved me for me!"

The young hiker, torn by her veiled tragedy, leaned hungrily against the reassuring, solid rock of the sanctuary as she allowed her inner dialogue to find a voice.

"Why, sir? Why did I yell? Why didn't I listen? Why…? I can't fault her. She was right. She was always protecting me. Even…even to the end, she continued to protect me. Me, the one…the ungrateful one…the one who yelled."

Her lyrical, yet strained voice trailing off, the youth fell silent, lost in her own, obviously sad, tragic thoughts.

After the young hiker had been quiet for a long moment, the old ranger, no doubt sensing he needed to move away to give the troubled girl some privacy, yet, obviously concerned for the youth, spoke softly and offered to remain close by for a moment, just on the other side of the hidden entrance to her sanctuary.

"Miss, I think I need to sit for a bit, if you do not mind, and rest here on this well-worn stone and old tree, just beyond your castle's sturdy gate. I'll not intrude on your personal reflection, but, if you wish and would like an old, unassuming ear, I'd be happy to listen if you need to talk."

With that, the old ranger nodded to the silent young lady and disappeared behind the tree stumps and boulders, only the sounds of his feet rustling the leaves and twigs on the ground betraying his continued presence.

For several more minutes, the young hiker stood silently, leaning on the ancient rock for support. She then seemed to awaken from her quiet reflection and turned to look for the old ranger, while wondering why she had been so open with the stranger, an old man who probably thought very little of the Korean popular music scene and doubtless had little knowledge, nor cared for, the daily drama in the lives of its leading ladies and men.

Finally, spying the old man's back, surprisingly comforting, just beyond the tree stumps, the young hiker stepped back into the enclave and, carefully fitting herself into the natural embrace formed by three stones leaning against one another, she stood looking out over her city, while her thoughts returned to her friend.

"Sir, may I tell you a story? I need to tell someone. I think it would be good to tell you. Yes…?"

The young lady's voice was a mix of high expectation and real fear. She suddenly realized that she desperately needed a sympathetic, but discreet ear, and felt, in her very core, that the old ranger, as at home among the stones of her best friend's favorite mountain as her friend had been, was that caring ear. Yet, her years of studio life tempered every new personal approach with caution, so her voice betrayed her hesitancy to share, to show any vulnerability, to be honest, with herself, and with a near total stranger. Into her thoughts, she felt, more than heard, the old man's melodic voice drifting over the stones through the clearing fog.

"Miss," the ranger said quietly, his voice almost a whisper, "I'm going to sit here for a few moments and admire the city emerging from the morning mist. Probably monitor if anyone comes up the path, skirting the barriers from below, especially if aided by that old woman. I can also see a stretch of trail above us, so can monitor if anyone attempts to come from that direction. I do need to get to the next station, so may have to slip away without notice, so will apologize in advance if I am gone when you depart."

"Sir, grandfather, thank you," the young hiker replied, the sweet sincerity in her young voice revealing her heartfelt thanks more than her words. "I understand, sir."

Turning to the center of the small space, the sad young woman wistfully brushed a few barely damp leaves from the stones. Since her secret perch partially faced the rising sun, the rocks were neither too damp nor too cold, allowing the young hiker to settle and snuggle into the weathered space like a child cuddling up to the strong arms of a caring mother, or a loving aunt.

For several minutes, the young hiker simply looked out at the morning mist far below, peacefully watched the orange glow of the new sun bouncing off the tall buildings in the distance, and quietly marveled at the few brave morning birds winging about the dips and rises of the hills and mountains around the mega-city. The view down into Seoul as the fog lifted was unusually clear and, with so many trees denuded of leaves at that time of year, more of the city was visible in the distance. Mount Namsan and its iconic tower were just visible over a distant rise, and much of the center of the city was also visible, although layered in thin, early morning wisps of fog.

Unlike the first time the youth had seen the spot several years before.

Closing her eyes, the young hiker slowly forgot about the old ranger, the nosy lady hikers, the odd old woman, the tabloids, the social media pressures, her studio, and her duties to everyone. Exhaling deeply, she allowed herself to finally think back to those early days.

Quietly at first, the young woman, urging herself to be open, to be vulnerable, began to talk again, more to herself, not really thinking if she was speaking loudly enough for the old man to hear or not, but recognizing that simply talking seemed to relieve a good deal of the pressure she had felt in her chest over the previous few days.

Gradually, the young hiker, music star, and actress related her tale to the mountain, the aged stones, the dancing winds, and the happy forests, and, if he was actually listening and not dozing in the morning sun, to the kind old ranger who had looked deep into her grief and had blessed her with a brief span of solitude and inner comfort, allowing her to return to the days before.

The days before the fame.

The days before the money.

The days before the endless parade.

The days before everyone wanted his or her piece of the pie.

Back to the days of hunger, but full of expectation.

Back to the days of uncertainty, but of hope.

Back to the days of innocence, but with open eyes.

Back to the days of true friends being true friends.

Six long years before, the young woman and her truest best friend, also from the same studio, had both triumphantly stood on that very outcropping and had shouted their shared happiness at success to the world, startling passing hikers who could hear the shouts, but could not see the ethereal voices hidden by the trees and boulders.

That cherished moment had been amongst the flowering trees and renewed hope of the Korean spring, the weekend before their debut, before they were aware of how far that debut would catapult them to stardom.

On that happy day, the two friends had promised themselves that, if the fame and attention ever became too much to handle, they would meet secretly on the mountain and breathe free and untainted air for a few hours, far away from the lights, the cameras, and all the people depending on them.

After that trip to the mountain, their temporary group's debut had been a smashing success. A year later, both of the young friends had eventually debuted as solo artists.

As the months and years had passed after their solo debuts, the two had experienced wildly successful, but separate careers, with some rare overlap when the studio had needed a ratings boost. Yet, each had tried to keep in touch with the other. Each had secretly remained the other's best true friend, even when the press, the studio, or the fan clubs had pressured them to create drama.

Yet, in all those years, the two had never had the chance to get away, together, a second time to the mountain's warm embrace and healing solitude. While each had managed to secretly visit the mountain separately a few times a year, they had been unable to do so together. There had been several false starts, but one or the other always had something come up, or some fan group had discovered the two of them sneaking off together. No matter how hard they had tried, the young hiker reflected, life had always conspired to postpone their rendezvous with the mountain.

Until now.

The youth sighed, and, smiling, immediately thought of her long passed grandmother and how her grandmother had lovingly admonished her and her little brother if they had sighed, claiming it was bad luck. What I wouldn't give for a few minutes in my grandmother's arms, the young hiker thought, as she absently watched a black and white bird skim the tops of the trees below. Possibly a magpie, but too far to be certain.

Still smiling, the young hiker reached into her jacket's side pocket and retrieved her personal phone, opened her photos, and brought up the old photo of her friend and her, taken by an American stranger, an older man, who had been hiking with his wife's Korean family that spring day years before. She and her friend had walked and chatted with the small group for a few minutes, making small talk as she had enjoyed doing before the aloofness and suspicion of strangers that had inevitably come with fame. She chuckled at the memory of her boldly asking the American to take a picture of herself and her friend under one of the flowering cheery trees that lined the path below.

The American had been so kind and patient and, upon parting, had wished them good luck in their lives in a mix of English and his broken Hangul. His words had been curiously prophetic.

'Best of luck and talent on your schooling, lives, and careers,' the American had said, his words still resonating with the young hiker. 'And, never forget your friendship and your obvious love of this mountain and the solace it can bring. Especially as the pressures of career and life weigh more heavily as the months and years pass. 'Break a leg,' as they say on Broadway in New York.'

Smiling at the memory of the long ago encounter and the picture of her friend, who had been the more clowning of the two that day, the young hiker then fished around in her pocket for her ear buds, but realized they were in an inside pocket. She then simply thumbed through her music until she found the song, one of her friend's early, signature songs.

"Sir, if you are still there, I'm going to play a little music. Softly, so I doubt you will hear it well. I know the rules say no loud music. Just a short song, sir."

The ranger was silent, as she suspected he would be, so the youth touched play, and leaned back as the song began.

The sounds of the old folksong, recorded by her friend, with the young hiker singing backup, in the weeks before their debut, drifted up from the silent rocks and floated around the trail and the near-barren trees. She quietly hummed along with the tune, but so very quietly so as to not drown out her friend's soulful voice.

As the song's words and music wrapped themselves around the young woman, the rocks seemed to press in close to hear better, while the trees appeared to summon additional wind to help them bend closer to the earth to catch the nuances of the song. Even several small, shivering birds turned in flight and landed on the drooping tree branches just beyond the small sanctuary, their feathered heads cocked to listen to the melody.

The song was an old standard. One that often elicited groans from more youthful fans, but, once they had listened longer, they, too, were soon lost in the sadness and timelessness of the old standard. Elders, of course, always cried as it ended.

As she became lost in the song, the young hiker, her sadness nearly unbearable, slowly stood, and, as if in a trance, stared out over the city that had been both kind and cruel to her and her friend.

Stepping out of the secure embrace of her rock walls, the grieving young woman was soon swaying to the music far too close to the cliff's edge, yet was so caught up in the song, her memories of her friend, and the grand view from their special viewing spot, that she did not realize just how close to the edge she had wandered.

The brisk air carried the song far up and down the mountain, while the young hiker continued to sway close to the edge, struggling with a part of her mind that was reeling from creeping guilt that her friend was gone, while she was left behind. Another part was screaming in anger at the leeches who had driven her friend to…to irreversible decisions. Still another, deeper area of her confused mind longed for a rest…a sleep…a few minutes of bliss far from the madding crowd, as the old ranger had said.

Suddenly, from some unknown source, a darker mist crawled up the cliff face from below, intruding, unseen, into the distraught young woman's secluded sanctuary. The cold mist lapped at the young hiker's boots and then, slowly, like a snake coiling around a sapling, wound itself around her legs, then her torso, where the mist slowed to an eventual stop, seeming to struggle to continue.

Unaware of the mist, the young hiker continued to sway to the final verses of the old song, humming louder in her confusion of joy and grief, and even silently mouthing some of the chorus.

Yet, even as she felt the strong presence of her friend, the grieving young woman tried to shake off a strange, absent feeling that someone was calling to her.

Was it her friend?

No, too soon, the young hiker cried in her mind. Too soon!

Yet, someone was there, just outside of her awareness, calling, beckoning, inviting the young hiker to cross…to cross the barricades once again. To look beyond the moment, and think of what such a step might mean.

Freedom?

Just one step, the voice murmured in the young hiker's ears.

What?

You did it on the trail just below, young miss, you can do it again, the voice seemed to whisper to the young hiker, mixing its honey-draped voice with the closing words of her friend's song.

No, I want to finish the song, the youth's mind yelled at the strange voice.

Suddenly, the young hiker felt the crazed eyes of the old woman from the barricades digging into her, waving that twisted walking stick, beckoning to the youth to, again, cross the barrier.

Beckoning.

Promising a long rest.

Only to take a first step.

A first and…final…step.

As the last chorus of the song played, another voice, warmer, familiar, intruded just as the young hiker moved to the very brink of the cliff's edge to take in the dizzying view of the scattered rocks and trees far below, and the distant vista of Seoul.

The old ranger! Wasn't he napping, the young hiker wondered? She tried to hear his words over her friend's song, and over the increasingly brash murmurings of the crazed old woman.

"Mapo Bridge!"

The old ranger's blunt words from earlier abruptly drowned out the old woman's cries.

"Look inside yourself!"

The old ranger seemed to call even louder, pressing the old woman's now faint babblings into the far recesses of the young hiker's slowly awakening mind.

Seoul!

Are you laughing at me, city of dreams and nightmares, cried the young woman to herself. Are you? Daring me? Are you gloating at your triumph, wanting me to succumb to your infidelities and Janus perspectives?

No!

Abruptly, her mind finally clearing, the young woman threw herself backwards, away from the cliff's dangerous edge and, turning, exhausted, let her body fall softly back into the embrace of her rocky sanctuary.

The dark mist that had crawled up the cliff face slipped off the young hiker's body and swiftly cascaded back down, revealing only a small feathering along her sanctuary's edge as it disappeared.

As the song ended and her friend's haunting voice faded into the mountains, the saddened young woman held the phone close to her now tearful face, and gave her friend a quick kiss. She then gently tried to wipe her tears off the phone as she slid it back into her jacket pocket.

The tears continued for a while, just long enough for a small pool of the glistening drops to collect in the corners of the young woman's reddened eyes, and then, like emotional dams bursting their seams, the collected tears flooded down her face and fell, lightly, almost reverently, to the dark stone beside her, leaving a brief, gleaming stain of the young woman's crushing pain on the ancient rock.

Bong…Bong…Bong!

Somewhere, its origin masked by the peaks and valleys around her, a lone temple bell echoed around the cliffs and peaks, pausing at the young hiker's refuge, wrapping the distraught young woman in a momentary embrace, before continuing its reverberations down to the far valley below.

"Beautiful!"

The sudden comment, quite close, shocked the young hiker out of her private reverie. Looking quickly around, she wiped her eyes as she tried to find the source of the voice, but saw that she was still alone.

Cautiously standing, the young hiker looked over the boulders toward the path to see if the voice had come from the old ranger whom she decided had heard her friend's song after all. To her surprise, the old ranger was no longer sitting near the old tree, but standing some distance away, facing away from her enclave toward the branch trail.

Standing quite rigid, the old ranger was facing the odd old woman who had pushed the young hiker to cross the barrier. While she could not hear anything further, the youth did see that the two were talking. Or, more accurately, the old woman was talking and the ranger seemed to be simply listening.

Was that what I heard during the song, the young hiker wondered? Had the old woman been calling to me from the trail?

The old woman was quite animated and seemed to be angry with the old ranger. She was talking loudly, even though the young woman heard only low mumblings, and was waving the twisted walking stick around, almost like a weapon. However, the old woman did not advance, but kept about two meters away from the ranger.

The old ranger seemed quite calm and as immobile as the rock he stood upon while he suffered what must have been quite strong language from what the young hiker could see of the old woman's angry face.

Abruptly, the old ranger stepped forward, his right hand holding up something that the youth could not see, but she did see that, whatever the old ranger was holding in front of him, it had a profound effect on the old woman.

The old woman covered her eyes and, using the walking stick as a blind person uses a cane, walked backwards, feeling her way with the walking stick. Once she had reached the boulders that were about to hide her from the young hiker's view, the old ranger paused, reached out to the old woman and, roughly taking her walking stick in his free left hand, shoved the old woman until she fell back against the boulders, where she howled with more anger than pain, and then, abandoning her walking stick, scrambled like some feral animal out of sight beyond the boulders.

After the old woman had dashed off, the old ranger simply stood, both hands by his sides, looking off in the direction she had taken. His right hand held a paper or maybe his pad from earlier. His left hand held the old woman's walking stick.

Suddenly, the old ranger's legs seemed to waver and he looked as if he might pitch over, head first. He caught himself, tossed the stick aside, into some rocks, and then, staggering, as if he was unsure of his footing, found his way back to the flat stone he had been sitting on earlier, near the old fallen tree.

Just as she was about to call out to the old man, something in his manner caused the young woman to hesitate and then step back into her enclave to catch her breath.

What had happened between the two, the young hiker wondered? And, why did the old ranger suddenly seem older, frailer?

Peeking out between the two dead trees, the youth saw that the ranger had regained most of his color and had returned the paper or the pad to his pockets. He then turned and saw the young hiker's eyes staring at him.

"Young miss, your singing…your friend's singing is enchanting," the old ranger called, but his strained voice was not the soothing voice from earlier.

"Sir, thank you. She has…had…no, has one of the most amazing voices," the young woman replied, still worried about the old ranger's condition. "Sir, I don't mean to be disrespectful, but are you feeling okay? You and the old woman…?"

"You saw her?" the old ranger bluntly interrupted. "The old woman?"

"Sir? Yes, just there, where she slipped away, after…when you…," the young hiker replied, trying to find the proper words.

"You saw the old woman…," the ranger repeated, but as a statement and not a question. "Good. That's good, miss. That you know she is still interested. But, please, think nothing of her. She will, that is, she has, I think, retired for the day from this side of the mountain."

"Yes, sir. I think I should thank you, sir…?" the young hiker tentatively asked, not knowing how to interpret what she had seen, or what she had experienced at the cliff's edge.

"Thank me? For…? Oh, no, young miss," the old ranger replied, his face returning to its earlier warmness as a smile slowly formed. "You, your love for your friend. Your heart's pain. They are in conflict, young miss. Such conflict can attract, can elevate certain external awareness. The music, miss, brought that, the old woman you see, closer than she's ever dared, miss. Those notes of vulnerability, they are enticing to certain listeners, miss. I must apologize for the interruption, as I never expected she would venture so far. But, all is well. You can remain here without concern. I will rest here for a few moments, but will need to move to the higher trail soon."

With that last comment, the old ranger nodded to the young hiker and let his shoulders drop, exhausted. Then, as if on cue, two cats, both large, black and white females, hopped up from where they had been hiding behind an old log. After brushing up against both sides of the old man, the two new arrivals spread themselves out on either side of him, to lounge in the rising sunshine like two sphinxes guarding the trail. The old ranger then let his head and chin slowly drop to his chest and, from what the youth could see, began to nap.

Quietly turning back to the boulders, the young hiker, even more confused by the old ranger's rambling narrative, but wanting to let the poor man rest, decided to focus on the other voice, mainly to settle, in her own mind, that she had even heard it, and was not slipping into some sort of stress related delirium.

Looking up, the young hiker strained to see if some youngster had climbed to the rock above her and was spying on her, something she was quite familiar with down in the city. She did not think that the first comment of 'beautiful' had come from the ranger and she knew it was not the voice of the old woman, so someone else must be nearby, she had concluded.

No one was lurking above her, however.

Taking a deep breath, the young woman again stepped over to the dangerous edge of the boulders and, with care, slowly leaned out to look toward the ledge some ten or fifteen meters below, to see if some young couple had managed to sneak out there and had heard the song.

No one there.

Momentarily puzzled, the young hiker then shook off her thoughts of paparazzi or fan stalkers, and called out in a hushed tone, so as to not wake the napping ranger.

"Yes, quite beautiful. Are you a fan?"

The young music star then mentally kicked herself for using the timeworn, automatic question that she and countless other stars of music and entertainment tended to use when first encountering an admirer or even a complete, unimpressed stranger to their work.

At first, only the mountain wind answered the youth's call, as even the birds had gone silent, probably out of respect for the old ranger, the young hiker mused to herself.

Then, from somewhere just on the edge of the young woman's hearing, the voice called out again, its words seeming to rise up from within the protected enclave itself.

"A fan? Strange, we've been called many things, but never a fan. What is a fan?"

The deeply resonant voice was definitely close, the young hiker realized, looking around quickly for the source.

Older. An older voice, from the tone and the type of language. Probably a woman, but could also be a higher pitched old man's voice. Quite old, the young hiker decided, older even than the napping old ranger. The voice had the same politeness as the ranger, but was different, and was also similar in some ways to the old woman's, but less harsh. A quick glance back through the dead trees showed her that the old ranger was, if not fully asleep, definitely not talking to her with his head down and chin resting on his chest.

Momentarily annoyed, in a selfish way, the coddled pop star in the young hiker wondered why the old ranger had nodded off after his odd encounter and if his snoozing had allowed some unwelcomed hiker to take the rarely used trail across the boulders, just as the odd old woman had found them.

Unsure as to how to address the source of the older voice, since she couldn't tell if it belonged to a man or a woman, the young hiker hesitated to respond, since she would be rude if she guessed wrong and used the incorrect honorific. So, true to her Korean roots, she simply bowed her head and called out how sorry she was that she could not see the source of the voice.

"I'm so sorry. I...I can't seem to find you?"

The young hiker's faltering words caused the voice to chuckle, not maliciously, but more in an understanding way.

"Hmm," the voice continued, revealing an undertone of not unwelcome mirth. "Must apologize for confusing you and for intruding on your grief."

"My grief?"

The young hiker snapped her head up with her reply. Had someone been spying on her the entire time, she wondered? She involuntarily pulled her coat closer to her and wondered if she could jump over to the path and run for help. Run for the old ranger.

"The tears, young miss. The tears seared deeply, did they not?"

The young woman looked back to the spot where her tears had stained the rock and was surprised to see that they had already evaporated into the morning air, leaving an unusual mark of a small, white crescent moon on the darker rock. Assuming the voice was another ranger who was admonishing her for scarring the park's boulder and for straying from the designated path, she pulled the pass out of her pocket, and apologized.

"I'm sorry. I'm sure the mark will weather well, though. After a little time. Once it is fully dry. I have a pass."

The young hiker had raised her voice, thinking the unseen new ranger was standing off in the trees, waiting for her to step back to the path before he, for she had determined that the voice was probably male, wrote her a citation. This caused her to grip her pass even more tightly and shove it back into her pocket, lest a sudden wind blow it from her hands into the forest below.

"Time, yes, young miss. Time does heal all, we're told. Partly the salt, partly your intense grief, no doubt, caused the small memory mark. Or, guilt...? Yes, time heals all...but, don't believe everything you are told."

The voice, losing its earlier mirth and turning solemn at the mention of time, then turned slightly mischievous at the end of the sentence, intentionally leaving the young hiker hanging, wondering what might come next. Yet, the brief reference to guilt struck a discordant note with the young hiker.

Guilt? Is that what I should be feeling, the young woman wondered, becoming a bit annoyed with the unseen voice.

"Sir, I'm terribly sorry for straying from the path and creating an uncomfortable situation," the annoyed and somewhat alarmed young woman called, deciding fully that the voice was male. "I'm prepared to pay any reparations for any damage I have accidentally done. The other ranger was so kind. And, I really do have a pass."

The young hiker held her head high at that point, not wanting to appear docile in case the new ranger wasn't a ranger, but a fan stalker or, worse, tabloid press that had somehow followed her and was toying with her. She also knew that the unseen stranger could be recording everything, including video, so she had to be particularly careful with what she said or did.

"Deeply searing, miss, those tears, they are. Deep down into the very heart of the mountain. Deep down into the very soul of these old rocks, young miss."

Losing her feeling of annoyance at the sincerity of the voice, yet, not wanting to give a response until she had identified the speaker, the young hiker stepped out of the comforting pocket of the embracing boulders to look around, and, as she looked, stood ready to run back onto the path, either to awaken the old ranger, or to dash to the main trail.

If the voice was from another ranger, the youth had decided, she would simply call her personal assistant who would handle the matter and pay any fines that might be levied. If not a ranger, then she would simply challenge the person and, if she felt threatened, she'd press the fast dial special police number she had had in her phone since she had become a spokeswoman for policemen's issues.

Seeing no one, the young hiker mustered up a confident and strong voice, hoping she sounded more capable of handling an unwelcome approach than she actually felt. Just as she parted her lips to speak, the voice called to her again.

"Pray, please sit, young miss. Did not intend to interrupt your private moment. We were curious, yes, as to who woke our old friend. Yes, why was he here, so far from...so far from his usual post?" the voice continued, but now seeming to come from where the old ranger was napping. "But, will, of course, withdraw and leave you with your memories, pain and happiness, together, in this quiet place."

While still unseen, the young hiker felt, rather than saw, the disembodied voice withdrawing, shifting away, back to the mountain and back to the silence of the aged stones and the timeless trails. Clutching at her collar, the young hiker felt her pain and burden increase as the voice drifted away, causing her to throw caution aside and, for some unknown reason, beseech the warmhearted voice to stay a while longer.

Whether it was the voice's confusing, yet soothing tone, or its grandfatherly and, at the same time, grandmotherly common sense expressions, something told the young woman that the voice was something she wanted...no, needed to hear more of, even without knowing exactly who it was or why it spoke to her.

"Sir. Please, I'm truly, truly sorry for not being...for being a little confused. Grandfather, I'm sorry. Please...don't go," the young hiker called in earnest, using the honorific for elderly men. "The kind old ranger is just there. Resting. He had a...he sent the old woman away. You must have just missed her. I'm sure he must be exhausted, so will be available soon. I haven't thanked him properly for being so helpful today, so will wait to go until he has awakened. Stay, if only for a little while longer?"

In spite of her wanting to thank the old ranger, the crushing pain in the young music star's breast over her friend was the primary driver of her thoughts. In her mind, the fading, discorporate voice had seemed to draw out even deeper thoughts of her friend and her final few days. The young singer dearly needed, she realized, to have that old voice draw even more, otherwise, she'd be alone. Starkly alone, she felt.

Keeping her head bowed, thinking the voice's owner might prefer to approach without being stared at, the young hiker waited briefly at the entrance to her enclave, and then returned to the boulders' natural armchair. Pausing, she glanced back to the entrance and then gracefully settled back into the mountain's embrace.

And waited.

The young hiker was hoping that, once she was sitting and, unfortunately, in a more defenseless posture, the voice's owner would appear around the edge of the boulder. Partially fearful of her vulnerability, yet also excited at the prospect of greeting the old man of the voice, who evidently knew the old ranger, she repressed her momentary desire to flee to the safety of the city at the base of the mountain trail. And, yes, there was the old ranger, napping nearby, ready to help if she called.

No one else appeared.

"Sir? Grandfather, are you still there?"

The young hiker's voice was hopeful, surprising herself in its pleading tone of reaching out, especially to a yet another complete stranger. Maybe, she thought, talking with the napping old ranger earlier had helped open her to be more receptive and to not always be automatically suspicious of other's motives.

"Apologies, young miss. Thought you wanted quiet for your thoughts. Have not departed. Was lingering over the youngster."

"Thank you, sir. Thank you ever so much," the young hiker exclaimed, her breath finally calming and her heartbeat leveling off. "Youngster, sir? Oh, the ranger, sir? Yes, I suppose he could be young to someone older?"

Content that the old grandfather was still with her, the youth again let the silence of the morning define the atmosphere and then, after a moment, she reworded the question that had occurred to her when the voice had first spoken.

"Do you know the voice? The voice of the singer, my friend?" the young hiker asked, an unusual expectancy tingeing her question as she decided the voice belonged to some old-fashioned village elder.

"Know the voice? Know many voices. Know beauty when beauty sings. Know sadness when sadness mourns. Know happiness in the tears of pain you shed. How long since your friend passed?"

Initially lulled by the elder's remarks on her friend's voice, the young hiker was caught off guard at the directness of the elder's question.

'How long...passed?' the young hiker repeated in her mind and then went rigid with sudden alertness and alarm.

"How...? Sir, how did you...?" the young hiker began, but her voice faltered.

"Your own voice, your own sweet tears, both speak volumes, young miss," was the elder's quiet reply.

The young hiker, while still shocked at hearing the tough words, suddenly felt compelled to have the voice's owner understand her and, more importantly, her friend.

"Sunday morning. After...before midday."

"You were with her."

The voice did not ask, but stated the last comment.

"Yes. Oh, no. Well, no. The phone...."

"Yes, those phones. For your generation, the same as being in the room."

"Yes. Almost. I had a function. A...a commercial shoot. Near Incheon. The old Freedom Park. Too far. Too...far."

The young hiker choked up again and fell silent, tears forming a second glistening trickle down her already reddened cheeks.

"There, there, young miss. No need to hide the tears. Let them flow. Let them bathe your friend's spirit in their purity of heart. In their simple statement of how you cherish her."

The young music star was now fully sobbing, unable to hold back the flood of emotions she had walled off inside of herself, not only over the previous few days, but also over the years.

"She was ill."

Another statement by the voice.

The young hiker nodded in agreement to the rocks and trees around her, her head hung low, her chest heaving beneath her coat, her sobs muffled by her scarf, now wet with her tears.

"No one knew," the kindly voice continued. "Maybe…maybe only her mother knew…recently. Only you. Only her friend was burdened with this awful secret. Only you could comfort her. Only you could defend her after."

The young hiker suddenly jerked her head up high, fiery eyes ringed red from tears for her friend, and nearly shouted her angry response.

"Yes! Defend her! All the ugly press. The fickle fans. All the hangers-on. Only…her close studio people were…were civil!"

Rubbing the tears from her eyes and, finding a tissue in another pocket, the young hiker discreetly wiped her petite nose, and then continued passionately, carrying on a two-way conversation more with herself than with the hidden origin of the kindly voice.

"Why was she off her game, they wondered? Was it drugs? Was she, gasp, pregnant? Was she thinking of suicide? Was she gay and tired of hiding it in our messed up society?"

The young hiker clenched her right fist and shook it at the sky.

"Was she drinking too much, the fans demanded? Hah! No one even knows what drinking too much means in Seoul!"

The young hiker then smashed her right hand into her left, pounding something of a cadence to her angry words.

"Was her romance on the skids? Where was her boyfriend? Why was he gone? Why wasn't he at her side…?"

The young hiker then shook her left hand at the sky.

"She didn't love him! It was arraigned to sell that perfume line. She didn't want a lie…she didn't want to have a lie hanging on her neck at the end."

The angry young woman then let both her hands fall, but then pushed back her hair and glared at the rocks, the sky, and the forests as she continued.

"Did anyone try to find out the truth? The truth? What is the truth in our crazy world? Our illusion? Our circus?"

A low, grim laugh escaped the young hiker's heaving chest, then her eyes became distant.

"The truth. A few tried. One did…all the way. He was a young fan from New York. Shut down the hackers. He wouldn't take any money. He simply destroyed the hacked lab information. He doesn't know yet, but he will never have to pay for the rest of his med school. She saw to that. He will be surprised, but honesty is good, isn't it? So rare, she wanted to reward it. He could have sold the information. He has honor, that boy, in a world without honor."

Her face a confused mix of emotions, the young hiker looked around in vain for the voice's owner.

"Isn't it? Sir, I did the right thing? My being silent, like she asked? She demanded it of me. On our friendship, she made me swear. She...made...me...swear!"

Only the morning breezes, stirred to more activity by the rising sun, answered the tortured cries of the grieving young woman.

"Sir?"

A hollowness was descending onto the young hiker's heart as she waited for a response, wondering if her words had frightened off the elder.

"Yes, young miss, with you, still," the voice finally answered, restoring the young hiker's sense of warmth.

"Sir, am I...am I doing the right thing?" the youth asked, her frightened voice wavering, having spent much of her earlier strength.

The young hiker felt, rather than saw, the elder moving closer, even leaning over her in her saddened state, curled up in the stone cradle she had shared with her friend so many years before.

"Young miss, your friend was, and is, your friend. She knew the time was near. She knew that your world of glamour and fleeting fame would turn on her, and on you. Any weakness, no matter the cause, brings in the sharks to circle, licking absent lips at the coming feeding frenzy. She didn't want her family to suffer. No. Nor, did she want her one true friend to suffer."

Suddenly, a sliver of flickering light beckoned from the darker recesses of the young woman's grief-clouded mind and threw a new, half-formed thought into her breaking heart.

"Me, sir? Me? Not me. She didn't want them to know of her...of her problem, sir."

The elder did not reply immediately, but let the sliver of light grow wider within the young hiker before the voice finally responded, in hushed, embracing tones.

"True friends, miss, keep their friends' needs close to their hearts. True friends, and loving family, will sacrifice for family or true friends. True friends are true friends, young miss, whatever the adversity. She was your true friend."

"But, me? How would she...?"

The young hiker's eyes were suddenly wide and clear, the odd voice from the rocks driving her dawning awareness, pulling back the final curtain on her friend's last days.

"She...kept...the sharks off of...off of me!" the young music star gasped, clasping her hands to her face.

"True friends, young miss...."

The elder's words resounded off the walls of the enclave, reverberating through the very stone of the mountain.

Realization then struck the young hiker to her core, causing her to rock back into the boulders, gasping at the sudden revelation, something that had been there all along, but that had been obscured by the pain and the loss, and, yes, a level of self pity, the young star finally admitted to herself.

"Me! She had been protecting me! Even...even to the end!"

Silence.

The young hiker, as well as the strange voice, remained silent for what seemed like an eternity, but was only a minute or so.

During the silence, the young hiker, popular singer, actress, and budding philanthropist, reflected on the revelation the voice had gently suggested until full recognition had finally dawned.

Whether the voice had actually known, or whether the young music star had unconsciously added meaning to the elder's odd words, neither was important. What was important was that, after a few minutes in their old retreat, high above the city that had molded them and had taken one of them already, the young hiker, in a moment of clarity, finally understood her friend's insistence on secrecy, on swearing oaths to each other, and why her final request to the young hiker had been to take her friend's place at the Freedom Park photo shoot that day the weekend before.

Protecting her friend.

Protecting her.

Even in her own misery, in her own despair, the young hiker's friend had remained a true friend until the very end, and, beyond, as her friend had extracted an oath that the young star had sworn on her own sweet grandmother's grave that her friend's secret would never be revealed.

"Sir!" the torn young woman suddenly cried out to the disembodied voice. "How...how do you know these things? Am I...am I truly mad? Have I...? Are you...? Are you...?"

The young hiker gulped deeply the cold, moist morning air, and briefly felt dizzy as a jumble of confusing images from the previous few days flooded her memory.

Slowly, as the old voice answered, the young hiker's jumbled thoughts began to clear.

"Miss, we are only what we are. This mountain has seen much sorrow. This mountain has seen much joy. The joy of two young friends pledging their love and friendship forever in their secret garden of stones and wildflowers carries a powerful message into the very core of a place like this, young miss. We hear things. Not as well as we used to, young miss, but we still hear things. We want to be there for people in times of happiness and in times of sorrow. We want to protect in times of danger. Alas, we cannot always help...no, not always, just ask your friend there, who stood between you and that...the old woman from below. Someday, not today, we will tell you many tales of the wars, the last war, and so many before. These old stones and valleys gave refuge to many, and, sadly, remain the grave of many more. Lost. Alone. But, in the end, many had those friends or family as you do, at least in their hearts. Such caring, miss, carries beyond. The youngster...the old ranger, who traveled far, heard your pain and, even though such selfish thoughts are foreign to him, he was able to ease his own by helping you this day, miss. That was your gift to him. That is why he can rest now, for a while."

Lulled into a sort of dream state, the young hiker, the saddened music star, the grieving friend, slowly nodded at the voice's curious words.

"Young miss, don't mourn your friend for too many days. A proper mourning, of course. But, one day, not too far off, you will create some of your best art, your music, in her memory. Yes, even while the low minded still whisper in the shadows and the fat cats get fatter off her legacy, even in death, you will go your own way and write your own heart into your work, holding up her friendship for a desperate world to see. Writing with your heart to heal others as you slowly try to heal yourself. And, writing your own spirit into your work, so that others, others like your friend, will know hope and love. That is your legacy to your friend. Her love for you. Your love for her."

The young hiker, struggling to absorb all the words of the kind voice, spoken in the nearly lost, high, formal language of her grandparents, only nodded in quiet agreement.

A sudden cold wind, no doubt pushed from the east by the now fully risen sun and being chased off the mountain and down to the city below to chill the company men and women headed to work, while cleansing the stale air of the morning traffic jams, caused the young hiker to shiver suddenly and to pull her coat tighter and her scarf more securely.

The young hiker then called out, her voice a little weak from the emotionally charged encounter, to thank the new ranger, for she had concluded that the old ranger had encountered a colleague and had asked the colleague to take the old ranger's place as he had said he was needed at the other station.

"Sir. Grandfather, sir. Thank you for your kind words. I hope we can speak again, next time I'm up here," the young hiker called cautiously to the trees and stones around her.

Silence.

No reply.

Only the chilling wind responded to the young hiker, stirring a few leaves and small twigs on the short path from her quiet retreat to the rough path across the boulders. Rising, she looked again over the top of the stumps and the boulders to try to find the elder of the warm understanding, but only saw the same barren stones as before. Sighing, she took a quick look at the clock on her phone and, pushing it back into her pocket, looked longingly back at her comfortable, now reverent enclave, bowed ever so slightly at the fading shadows of her friend, and then stepped toward the path back to the main trail.

The young hiker then looked over to where the old ranger had fallen asleep, but, to her surprise, he was nowhere to be seen. Even the two old cats had also disappeared.

"Sir? Are you still here, sir?" the young hiker called out in alarm to the old ranger who had been her escort and temporary sanctuary guard. "Sir, I so wanted to thank you, again. Sir…?"

Her eyes no longer reddened from her tears, but wide open and gleaming in the light of finally understanding what her friend had done in trying to protect her, the young hiker then looked boldly around for the origin of the elder's voice, or any evidence an elder had been there, or had replaced the old ranger.

Nothing.

Even the twigs that had lain across a section of the trail protected from the winds had not shifted since she had arrived with the old ranger.

Pausing, the young hiker marveled at how the old ranger had departed so silently, then let her eyes wander down to the city below and wondered if the elder's words would come true. Would the young hiker and music star be able to honor her friend's memory in such a dramatic way? Would she be strong enough? Would she have the nerve?

Friends.

The elder's voice had spoken of friends and family.

The young music star suddenly realized, for the first time in years, that she actually had many real friends. Friends that were there for her and would support her, both within the frantic world of the studios and outside. She had family. Strong family, in spite of the tougher, earlier days. Why had it taken kindly, strange voices in the mountains to bring her to realize her good fortune, she wondered?

The young hiker suddenly smiled broadly and warmly, realizing that, unlike so many down in that city of lights and chaos, she knew, deep down, for the first time since childhood, that she had loving friends and family.

After a long, lingering glance back at her…at their sanctuary, the young woman pledged, on her friend's heart, that she would honor the words of the strange elder in the mountain, and celebrate her friend's short life. She would write those songs, soon.

The young hiker finally turned and stepped through the two old, dead trees onto the path that would take her away from the cliff and the enclave.

Emerging from the protected boulders, the young hiker startled two cats, one a black and white old tom, and the other an old, battle worn, ear-scarred, tiger stripe. She called to the two, but the old mountain beasts sensed, rightly, that the slim young woman who had magically appeared from beyond the cliff had no treats, so the two played deaf to the young lady's calls and silently slipped away, no doubt to find better sunning rocks. Later, once they realized no other humans would be trekking their trail that day, the young hiker mused, the two furry compatriots would venture over to the alternate trail to accost treat-laden youths with their selfie cameras and cooing friends.

Watching the mountain's silent citizens slink away, the young hiker smiled and stepped onto the main trail, making a mental note that she had to remember to bring treats next time. She then marveled that she could think of such things when, mere moments before, she was on the edge of despair.

Just before she turned right to head down the mountain, the young hiker looked up to the summit and was surprised to see a young man, dressed in sharp ranger gear, newer than that of the older ranger, coming down the trail from above. She continued on to the first bend and, then paused, thinking that she should commend the old ranger to someone in authority, so waited at the junction for the young ranger to gain on her.

"Hello?" the young ranger called with an air of distinct superiority, upon seeing a civilian in a restricted area. "Hello, did you not see the signs?"

"Signs? Oh, yes, sir," the young hiker, her earlier, emotional voice hidden, replied with matching authority, while realizing a younger ranger might recognize her, so pushed her scarf up to cover more of her face as she continued, wishing she had left her sunglasses on. "Yes, but I have a pass. The older ranger gave it to me. I'd like to write out a thank you...a comment card for him?"

The younger ranger was looking at his watch, obviously cross at having to deal with a scofflaw so early in the day, and was almost ignoring the young hiker and her comments.

"No, miss. No other rangers on this trail this morning. Only me," the young ranger said absently as he scanned the surrounding area for any additional lawbreakers. "You're alone? Yes? Okay. Let's go down to the welcome station. You can plead your case to the supervisor."

Without waiting to listen and ignoring her attempt to get his attention, the ranger waved at the youth to follow. Walking at a fast clip, he continued down the trail to the visitor plaza below.

"Wait...!" the young hiker called to the new ranger as she hurried after him, barely managing to keep abreast of his pace by nearly running behind him a few meters. "I have a pass!"

Her entreaties ignored, the young hiker resigned herself to following the self-absorbed ranger and, the farther down the mountain they hiked, the more she returned to her former, self-important persona and began thinking of ways to make the rude young ranger pay for his indifference to her. The fact that she had hidden her identity was immaterial in her growing anger at not being recognized as a special person who always expected and received special treatment.

Special treatment…?

Suddenly, the young hiker and music star came to a dead standstill in the trail, watching the young ranger grow smaller as he descended the trail far down in front of her.

Special treatment…?

Slowly, the young hiker turned back to look up the trail, realizing she was falling back into her old, suspicious and imperious persona only minutes after her emotional revelation on the mountain. The blatant hypocrisy of the moment caused her to stamp her feet and laugh a grim, fatalistic laugh at herself.

"Hah! Am I so self-important that I can't see the gift you have given me, my mountain strangers…my guardians of the forests and cliffs?" the young music star called at the top of her lungs to the trail, trees, and rocks around her. "Am I so blind?"

Shaking her head violently, the young hiker then turned back to the trail and broke into a full trot, missing, in her haste, the lurking figure of an old calico cat that was perched on a rock overlooking the barricades from earlier.

With her natural limberness and dance training in full gear as she ran, the young hiker and music star slipped effortlessly through the barricades that had seemed so insurmountable earlier, and eventually gained on the distracted young ranger, who had not looked back at all. Catching up to the young official and then matching his pace, she remained silent and followed his steps toward the ranger station at the base of the trail.

As she passed others heading up the trail, the young hiker made an uncharacteristic point to say hello, especially to the older ladies' groups, feeling a twinge of guilt from ignoring the purple clad lady from earlier. She quietly resolved to stop and speak to the woman if she saw her on the next visit. None of the visitors seem to recognize her, but she had already shed that concern by dropping her furred hood to the back and letting her warm scarf hang loosely about her neck. Her sunglasses were still in her pocket.

At the large glass doors of the ranger station, the only acknowledgement the young ranger made of the young hiker's existence was to pause and open the door for her to enter first, in an oddly western show of politeness. The young man continued to look at something on his phone and simply strode past her once inside, and absently pointed at a small desk to the rear, which was faced by two hard plastic visitor chairs, of a faded hunter green.

There were only a couple of other people inside the station. One was partially out of sight in an office where the younger ranger had stopped at an open glass door to speak. The other was a young woman, not in a ranger uniform, but in working clothes, possibly a secretary, from the look of the desk she sat at across the wide room.

The station's main room was quite long, with large maps of various types across one side, near the young secretary, and several glass display cases showcasing historic items from around the park. A long table near the front of the room, near the entrance (and exit) held various brochures and pocket maps for visitors.

Taking one of the offered chairs, the young hiker settled in for whatever the wait might be, wondering how long she would be able to remain anonymous. Part of her wanted to reflect on her experience on the mountain, but she decided to repress thoughts of the encounter until she was well away from the prying eyes of the officials and their staff. However, she did want to write a nice comment card for the old ranger, so looked around the wide room for anything that looked like a comment card, or a web link where she could submit something. For the briefest of moments, she considered having one of her staff write up a nice, clever note, but then shook off such thoughts, determined to write it herself.

To keep her mind off her experience at her enclave, and to look for a comment card, or a web link, the young hiker turned her gaze to scan the various displays around the station. As she looked, she noticed a large bulletin board covered in posters of the mountains, visitor snapshots, various announcements, and a number of news articles. Hoping the articles or announcements would have information on how to make comments, and also help take her mind off the morning's strange encounters on the mountain, she then stood and walked over to the board. Surveying the many items describing the park and the vast responsibilities of the rangers, she also looked at the photos for any familiar vistas that might help her forget her earlier indignation at the younger ranger's indifference.

Suddenly, the young hiker stopped at one of the older, more faded articles and leaned in to read the text after recognizing her old ranger in the accompanying photo. The paper was yellowed from age and the photo faded, but she was certain the photo was of the kindly, old ranger. Unfortunately, before she could finish trying to read the faded text of the article, something about a rescue years before, the young ranger returned and motioned for her to retake the visitor seat at the small desk. She complied, again wondering why the rude young man had failed to recognize one of the nation's brightest young stars of music and drama.

Finally, after what was no doubt the appropriate wait time imposed on hardened violators of park rules, a middle-aged, somewhat stocky, but not portly, supervisory ranger appeared from the office behind the glass door and stepped to the visitor desk's large armchair. The man then sat, all the while reading over a small slip of paper in his hand.

Mumbling to himself, the supervisor opened a large bound notebook at the edge of the desk and flipped through a few pages until he uttered a low cough and then looked up at the near-felon of the young hiker.

For the briefest of moments, a startled look of recognition darted across the supervisor's face when he first looked at the young hiker, but, as if to tell himself that he was seeing things, he immediately shook that off and leaned back in his chair.

"Broke through the barricades did you, young sister?" the supervisor asked, in a tired, high-pitched voice, which was also a bit grating in a slow, long-time bureaucrat way. "What do you have to say for yourself?"

Placing as much charm as she could in her voice, the young hiker handed over her pass to the supervisor as she spoke.

"Sir, I know the barricade was there, but I did not break through anything. I have a pass, as you can clearly see there," the young hiker replied with a hint of self-righteousness, yet with the proper respect for the senior ranger.

The supervisor wrinkled his brow at the brown slip of brittle paper that the youth had handed him. She herself, upon seeing the pass's condition, was shocked since, just that morning, it had been a cheerful, crisp, canary yellow.

For a few seconds, the supervisor stared at the pass, his eyes gradually widening and losing their earlier bureaucratic look. He motioned to the young ranger who then looked at the pass and closely examined it as well.

The young hiker was able to catch a few phrases during the subsequent whispering between the men.

"Date's correct...?"

"Handwriting matches...?"

"How the devil...?"

"Can't be...can it?"

For nearly a full minute, both of the rangers then simply turned their gazes on the youth before them and stared at her, making her extremely uncomfortable with the blunt suspicion on both of their faces.

"Where did you get...?" the younger ranger began, but was cut off by the young hiker's interruption as she attempted to explain about the older ranger and the pass, while omitting her encounter with the second, unseen ranger, and the strange old woman.

"Sirs, please. The old ranger was quite helpful, and he made it clear I was not violating any rules, hence the pass," the young hiker stated with firm conviction. "In fact, he's the one in the picture over there in the article on that rescue some time ago. I'm certain that is the ranger who was so nice to me. The one in that photo there."

During the young hiker's interruption, the supervisor had stood up to whisper something to the younger ranger. Now the two men, keeping some distance from the law-breaking youth, made a wide circle around her to get a better look at the article she was pointing toward.

The senior ranger looked at the article, became even more wide-eyed, and then looked at the brittle pass in his hand. The younger ranger looked even more perplexed and started to back toward the desk, not taking his eyes off of their youthful offender.

The supervisor then mimicked the younger ranger's return to the desk, and, as he took his chair, whispered something to the younger ranger which caused the younger man to give the young hiker an odd look, a cross between disbelief and minor fear. He then backed toward the exit doors, and, without saying anything, turned and ducked out of the station.

The senior ranger, still staring at the pass, ignored the retreating younger ranger and only looked up when the doors slammed behind the escaping younger man.

"Miss...? Miss Lee, is it? According to your...this...uh, pass...?" the senior ranger asked, his voice wavering between rasping and choking on the words.

"Sir, am I in trouble? The grandfather...the elder ranger from the trail was quite pleasant and assured me all I had to do was show that pass and everything would be fine. He was so very kind," the young hiker answered, her voice sincere and strong. "So, I wanted to write up a comment card for him."

Slowly, the senior ranger leaned over toward her and, extending his hand, returned the pass, which she gently took, afraid it would crumble from its sudden brittleness.

With the senior ranger's eyes staring into some far off place, he spoke in a clear, almost reverent voice, giving the young hiker quite a start, such was the contrast with the man's earlier, bureaucrat-laden voice.

"Miss, the old ranger had a warm, welcoming voice, deep, with rich phrases from the older, more formal language that one rarely hears today?" the senior ranger asked, his eyes staring into an imagined distance.

"Sir, why yes. That's his style exactly," the youth replied. "One rarely hears."

"And, his eyes, miss?" the senior ranger continued, interrupting. "His eyes were hazel-brown and twinkled when he smiled that disarming smile of his, causing you to want to tell him all your dreams? And your sorrows?"

"Sir? What are you saying, sir?" the young hiker asked, her voice reflecting a mounting, unknown fear over the odd wavering in the senior ranger's voice and the desertion of the younger ranger out the door.

"Miss, little sister, I hope you have a great day and a good life, miss," the senior ranger replied, his voice returning to normal, strong and in charge. "There is no citation, you may go at your pleasure."

The senior ranger then turned abruptly and headed back into his office. The young hiker saw him pause at a display board at the side of his office and, suddenly coming to full attention, the ranger then bowed low to his waist toward the board.

The young hiker, confused by the sudden and unexpected reprieve, and alarmed by the senior ranger's odd behavior, and not a little disoriented by the morning's odd events, rose, and walked over to the large office window and peered in, trying to see what the ranger was bowing to, as that might explain all his odd behavior. Just as she leaned closer to the window, the ranger bowed a second time and, with his upper body out of the way, she was able to see what was on the wall he was facing.

A photograph.

A black and white draped photograph.

Of a ranger.

An older ranger...?

Her older ranger?

In...a...black...and...white...draped...photograph?

A silent gasp welled up in the young hiker's throat, and she stumbled backwards, finding herself back in the visitors' area just opposite the article on the wall. Turning to the article, she leaned toward the yellowed paper, and, slowly reaching out to the left corner, which had folded over years ago from a missing tack, she gently pushed the corner up to reveal the date of the article.

Decades before.

The young hiker's hand jerked back in a flash, as if a snake had struck her fingers at the end of that old, old article. Confused, with not a little fear rising up in her chest, she turned to see the senior ranger standing at his door, his hat in his hand.

"How...?" the young hiker started to ask, looking back and forth at the article and then at the photograph through the office window.

"...can it be?" the senior ranger finished her unspoken question as he motioned with his hat, walked over to the exit, and opened the door.

The young hiker, confused, but silenced by the ranger's words and his solemn look, stopped short of asking anything else, nodded a silent bow to the old ranger's article, and walked out the open door, with the senior ranger following behind.

The two walked in silence to the main entrance of the park, passing a few hikers and even a couple of vendors who greeted the ranger. The two then stopped near the main plaza entrance, the sun's rays finally having burned most of the morning fog away from the plaza and the edges of the village just beyond.

Turning to the young hiker, the senior ranger, no doubt a supervisor of some years, then thanked the young woman and parted with a short, but powerful farewell. His eyes were on the mountain above them as he spoke, his voice low and his words soft, meant for only her ears to hear among the late morning hikers trickling into the popular park.

"Miss, you've been given a…a gift today. Rare and, frankly, hard for me to fully comprehend. Use the gift wisely. My uncle was a great ranger, an inspiration to us all. I spent many hours as a youth tagging along behind him in these mountains. Learning from him. Listening to his tales of the war. The hard times. And, the good times. He gave his life all those decades ago to save an old man, disoriented and lost among those boulders and storm-ravaged trees. That old man was my father, his younger brother, distraught at a business reversal, shamed by the unrelenting pressures of our unforgiving society. Yet, my uncle never lost faith in him and went up onto the mountain on that stormy morning to bring my father back to those who loved him. Two men went up the mountain, only one came down. My father swore until his death that my uncle had carried him halfway to the station, after my father had been hit by a falling tree. Witnesses testified they had seen a second man, but that the second man had departed by the time the other rangers had come to the aid of my father."

A single stream of reluctant tears was flowing down the senior ranger's left cheek, causing the young hiker to fight back her own tears at hearing the man's story.

"Miss, he was never seen again," the ranger continued. "There are a lot of deep crevasses in these mountains and the rangers and police all assumed that, after days and nights of fruitless searching, one of those deeper ones was…is his final resting place."

Wiping the budding tears from her own eyes, the young hiker, respectful daughter, and quiet music star, nodded and bowed to the senior ranger, bonded now without the need for words. He attempted a smile and returned her bow with his own before she turned toward the exit. She then reached for her phone and, pulling it out, also pulled out the fragile bit of paper.

Staring at the kind old ranger's note, which accompanied a sense of deep well being at all his efforts on her behalf that day, the young hiker stopped, and gently called to the senior ranger, who checked his stride and walked back to her.

Holding out the small, yellow-brown pass, which the senior ranger had dutifully returned to her, written across the years by the saintly hand of the senior ranger's uncle and hero, the young lady spoke softly, her voice more relaxed and more heartfelt than she could remember it being in years.

"Sir, you should keep this. He wrote it to help me, and help me he truly did, but he wrote it for you," the young hiker said with a deep sincerity, her heart almost in her throat. "His gentle words, and those of his unknown friend, were a solace to my own…my own troubles, sir. I will always hold them dear."

The senior ranger gently accepted the small slip of brittle paper, and carefully, gingerly, placed it in his own small pad, and then held the pad with its precious content to his chest.

The senior ranger then straightened to his full height, and, with a calm look and lowered eyes, bowed deeply, with measured formality, to the young hiker and now friend, forever bound by shared life advice from the same man.

The young hiker drew herself to her full, one hundred and (almost) fifty centimeters, and, shaking off a momentary tremble, returned the bow with an inner grace and authenticity that she had forgotten she had.

With that ageless gesture, oblivious to the hikers and hawkers nearby, the two new friends parted.

The senior ranger walked slowly up the main trail, no doubt to spend a few minutes reflecting on the unique encounter of the morning.

The young hiker, pop singer, poet, actress, and true friend walked out of the park and off the mountain, more mentally prepared to return to the hectic frenzy of her everyday life than she had ever been.

Return, yes, the young hiker thought, but with a renewed sense of value and mission, even though more time would be needed to fully come to terms with her friend's passing. Time, she told herself, she would use more wisely as the years unfolded.

Wandering back through the outskirts of the neighborhood, the young hiker looked for and found the small mom and pop bakery that she had dashed past that morning. She had rarely visited the place, given her strict dietary guidelines, but she stepped to the door to stand in line, and bought a double espresso and several orders of those little round, Chinese doughnuts that she had always denied herself, in spite of their aroma's siren call. She also looked around for the little girl and her brother from the morning, but did not see them. Next time, I'll buy them a bag of treats, the young music star said to herself.

After taking a sip of the espresso and munching a couple of the warm, embracing treats while standing in the small terrace of the bakery, the young hiker closed up the bag and continued on. She then paused at the corner of the long street leading away from the park entrance, and said a quiet thank you to the mountain, the rangers, both current and helpful old souls, and, yes, the unknown elder's voice.

The fog was nearly gone and, just as she ducked into the rabbit warren of streets that led to an ever-increasing number of taller buildings which obscured the views to the mountains, the young hiker thought she could just make out the ridge that held her secret refuge. Her quiet place of rendezvous with her true friend who had helped her, even in…even though absent, regain what had been a fleeting appreciation of life.

Holding up the small, steaming cup and the bags of warm treats in homage to her friend's own sweet tooth, the young music star hummed a new melody that had suddenly slipped into her mind.

Approaching the newsstand of the kind old woman whom she had ignored earlier, even the glaring, accusatory headlines didn't deter the young singer from stopping, saying hello, apologizing for the morning, and offering the sweet lady some of her doughnuts. The old woman chuckled at the young girl's out of character gesture and, after failing to wave off the warm gift, accepted several of the doughnuts, and then handed the young hiker a copy of a magazine the girl usually purchased, refusing any money.

As the young singer thanked the old newsie, as such sellers of traditional media were called, she took a mental note of the address and, taking out her phone at the end of the block, took a discreet picture of the kind old woman, bundled up in worn, but mended layers against the morning chill. Later, the young singer would give the photo to her lawyers to research and buy the empty corner shop a few doors down, for a silent partnership with the kind older lady.

Passing the other newsstand, the young music star ignored the sudden silence of the obnoxious, chattering hawker at seeing the subject of many of the tabloid headlines boldly strolling by, without sunglasses and without her hood up to protect her face from prying eyes. She did glance back, however, at the end of the block and was amused when she saw the hawker shake his head and, obviously disbelieving his own eyes, turn back to his calling out the morning news.

After finally arriving at the prearranged pickup spot, by a closed ramyeon shop, the young singer spotted her car slowly moving down the street and so waited for the driver to bring the large studio limo to her.

As the driver hopped out to open her door, the young singer turned and paused, her eyes looking upward.

Before she stepped back into the limo and into her micro-managed life, the young lady looked up to the summit of the mountain behind her, barely visible between two grey office towers. She then traced the lines of the mountain downwards until she felt she was looking at the area of her once lost, but now regained, late friend's secret retreat, and smiled an honest, no one was looking, full smile, ignoring the smile wrinkles and all.

"Thank you, grandfathers, all of you, for your kindnesses," the young hiker, soon to be back in her role as a reigning K-pop star, said quietly, hoping the morning breeze would carry her words up into the embrace of the mountain and its aged guardians.

Stepping into the car, the young singer thanked her driver, surprised him with a bag of pastries, and, forcing herself to control her emotions, spoke to him in what she hoped sounded like her routine, crisp, diva voice.

"Make a note. Same day, same time, next month. Every month. Tell the assistant to blank it on my calendar. No changes unless it's a concert or filming day, or I'm out of the country."

"Ma'am? Every month? I don't think your producers will want…," the driver cautioned, but then grinned when he saw his employer's serene, but determined face.

The young singer's return look was enough to convince the driver, who also served as one of the three personal assistants to the music star, to not ask twice. He then closed the heavy door very gently after his precious, perishable cargo.

As he ducked back into his seat, the driver's eye caught the sun's mid-morning rays reflecting off a jumble of boulders about halfway up the side of the mountain, causing him to comment to his charge as he placed the bag of pastries on the console, engaged the gears, and sped off into the nightmare that is the weekday traffic of modern Seoul.

"Ma'am, I think I need to get out more and hike with my wife and kids. This park must have many wonders. If I may say, you look healthier than you have in months, ma'am," the driver offered, obvious concern in his voice, mixed with surprise at his charge's brighter outlook, much more so than when he had let her out in the morning, given all the press swirling around her and her close friend.

Smiling back at her long time assistant and trusted driver, the sad, grieving, nearly lost young girl who had gone up the trail in the morning and had then come down from the mountain a much wiser young woman, nodded to her confidant and, winking at his searching eyes in the rearview mirror, playfully replied, in a voice both musical and angelic, but calmer, and a bit older.

"Hey, find your own mountain," the young hiker, singer, and, for a time, K-pop princess, playfully called to her trusted driver. "This one is mine…ours. Ours, that is. This one is ours. My best friend's and mine!"

The driver nodded and then turned his full focus to the road, while the young star smiled another warm smile and amended her initial reply.

"Yet, I'm sure the mountain is big enough for all of us to share," the young singer added, comforted that her mountain refuge, and the refuge of so many others, would always be there, watching over her, her family, her friends, her staff, the rangers, the news lady, the baker, those little children, the purple ladies, the endless hikers, and, yes, even her fans.

INTERLUDE II

For several long, nervous minutes after he had finished relating the surreal tale of the K-pop singer and the mountain, the writer sat in silence, hoping the creature would, at least, tolerate the tale and, hopefully, ask for another. Watching the creature, the writer was at a loss as to how to ascertain any hints from the beast's jumble of rags, twitching limbs, and grotesque mash-up of a face.

Finally, the creature stirred in its massive stone chair and leaned toward the writer.

"You, this foolish girl, called her princess, your story did?" the creature asked, its voice low and menacing. "You beasts banished your special, tastiest blood. Into hiding, most have gone. How is this princess known?"

The creature's eyes were hidden by a greasy flap of filthy cowl, with only the lower part of the beast's pale, yellowish jaw visible to the writer.

"What? She's not. Oh, right, a princess," the writer replied, recalling he had casually used the reference to a 'K-pop princess' near the story's end. "Not the old ways of a princess, vile sir, but a new kind. A kind born, not of blood, but of the people. At least, from the view of the studios that profit off of these new princesses. It's a term used today to apply to a range of 'princesses,' here and, basically, everywhere. From Chaebol princesses to Disney princesses. I call my niece 'little princess,' at least, I did when she was younger."

"Trickier, this is, little man," the creature hissed, pulling its cowl even further down, obscuring its entire face, but continuing in the odd, singsong voice. "Protection, the special blood has. Special goblins. And powerful fairies who rob the night of our terror. Drag my cousins, these did."

Intrigued by the creature's odd behavior, the writer dug deep in his memory for anything about the old royal family in Korea, but didn't think his meager knowledge would be able to keep the creature talking. So, the writer chose ignorance.

"The royals had…have special protectors?" the writer asked, putting emphasis on 'protectors.' "What were…are they called?"

"Trickery!" the creature suddenly yelled, throwing back its cowl and rising to its full, monstrous height. "Nay, you'll not get me to utter their vile name. They know, they do, when one of my brethren dare to speak of them. No! You're for the pot, you are, vile human. Trickery!"

The creature then lunged at the cook pot, grabbed for the tinderbox, but, seeming to be confused, just stared at the fire-starter with a look of something lost. Finally, the creature turned, shaking its head from side to side.

"Not? Not of the old blood? The blood that feeds the countless wars of the humans? Not a true special one, your princess?" the creature asked, its mind finally grasping what the writer had tried to explain.

"No, certainly not. I mean, maybe one of the descendants has gone into music or, I mean, no. She's a product of a long and complex system," the writer answered, his words coming fast as he watched the creature continue to toy with the tinderbox. "Well, the one in the tale is still a real person, under all the glamor and glitz, hence the story, but a product for the masses of fans. People who like her music or her dramas, or whatever she does. So, in that sense, she still serves as an inspirational dream for millions, as did princesses of old."

The creature stopped turning the tinderbox over in its hands, but continued to hold onto it as the beast returned to its chair by the massive stone table. The creature then sat, placed the fire-starter next to the gruesome beer stein, and spoke slowly, looking around as if it expected one of the special goblins to jump out of the darkened trees.

"Few remain, the protectors who lurk in the deepest of shadows, human. You take care not to speak their name. Not to tell their tale. Not to tell them...," the creature whispered as it leaned toward the writer. "My mountain, not to tell?"

"No, certainly not, for I know not of what you speak, old spirit," the writer replied, honestly, as he had no idea what goblins the creature feared, and he certainly had no intention of seeking out such creatures, when and if he began to believe in them.

However, the writer was painfully aware that his captor, a seemingly all powerful, vile beast, while maybe not afraid of the royal protector spirits, definitely did not want to encounter such special goblins.

"What did you think of the story, great beast?" the writer then asked, to both get the creature's diseased mind off the protector goblins and back on the writer's tale and, with luck, the next tale.

"Lonely are those in the midst of crowds, yes? The human prin—, girl, like most of your kind, was not protected by a special protector? Hah! Had one of my cousins, who lurk about the high cliffs up there, met your little morsel, hers would have been a shortened day," the creature chortled, its eyes gleaming at the prospect, but then hardened as the beast challenged the writer.

"Clever, the story was. Sad that the morsel escaped the witch, and the old ones, who also need morsels from time to time. And, no, we fear not your human witches. We let them think we do, but my cousins work around them, as they harvest many souls, so my cousins linger about, dance for the witches when asked, and drag a few souls when they throw them our way, we do."

"Just your cousins?" the writer asked.

"Cousins? Only the lower cousins. I can't resist the snap of the soul of the witches, fat and juicy with the misery of so many," the creature replied, with what sounded like a low chuckle. "One day, human, visit one of those old way witches and, don't look at her, but let your eyes drift to her sides, count backwards for a bit to clear your head and you will see my cousins lurking there. Shadows in your eyes, but waiting for the morsels who throw their gold at the witch. One day, it's the witch who must be wary."

The lustful leer on the beast's pallid face caused the writer to momentarily hide his own face, as it had blanched at seeing the creature's lurid excitement over tricking witches.

"Wait! How is this a story of goblins and fairies? I smell only the old stones and pitiful witches," the creature called as it turned to look back to the cook pot, letting its hand linger over the tinderbox to send a clear signal to the writer, but continuing to speak. "Unless? Unless the tearful human girl was driven to betray her friend by one of my cousins? Maybe the night crawlers who haven't, who never become, not sure of your word, human, but they slither and never learn to fly. Yes, maybe her foolish friend had a long term companion of one of my cousins?"

"Possibly," the writer agreed, wanting to keep up the creature's challenge from earlier, hoping it would lead to requests for additional tales. "There could have been unseen forces at work against the singer's friend."

The creature then waved the writer to silence.

"Yet, I do seem to have memory of songs like the one she…of her friend sang. Long ago. Before," the creature, its mood calming down from its earlier agitation, suddenly volunteered, its speech changing again. "My mother used to carry me, in one of those old podaegi carriers, and sneak into a big house where a crowd sang, but she was there to hear a certain lady sing, with many tasty humans watching and crying. The human female sang of tragedy and betrayal. Of secret loves. Of being cast aside. Of great movements. My mother and cousins waited in the alleys near the big house for those who were so moved by the singing lady that they were weak and easily taken. She sang in many funny tongues, the lady did. Kim? My mother spoke often. The only human she would not permit her cousins to drag. Bok-hee? She moved my mother, who was weaker than my sire's troll and ogre side, to such tears that my mother gathered only a few morsels those nights. My early hunger doesn't let me forget the singing lady."

The writer, scanning the next pages in the book, looked up at the creature and realized the beast must have been talking of an old concert hall. Probably an old opera star, given the multiple languages.

Notably, the writer realized, it was the only time the beast had not only named someone, he had used the more polite term 'lady' for the old star. No doubt a throwback to his mother's guidance, the writer decided.

"These new show girls and singing boys, so many, my cousins used to avoid, as their empty souls could poison even the strongest of the street goblins," the creature hissed, its mind seeming to drift to another time.

"Ghouls, they would feast, the selfish oafs, made stronger by the misery of those child-women and man-boys."

"But, what of the managers? The studios who put them to work? Do they not deserve to fall to your cousins' ghastly appetites?" the writer asked, not out of some sense of justice for the music machine kids, but more of a way to keep the creature talking.

"Manager? Oh, the boss men, you speak of, human," the creature openly chuckled. "Protected by a loose guild of ghouls and goblins, they are. Not as the prin—, not as the ones we will not speak, but kept corralled for later. A young cousin dragged, long ago. Taken to the woods he was, by the goblins and fed to the nether ghouls. Can't have the suppliers angry."

"Suppliers of…?" the writer asked, making another mental note to ask later what a 'nether ghoul' was.

"The frenzy of the adorers of these show girls and singing boys breeds much, much juicy morsels in the dark corners of the city. And, even in the bright rooms of your high stone, hive-like huts, human," the creature answered. "My cousins will wait until the sounds have softened to drag or nibble, as the new sounds hurt their heads, sorely, it does.'

"A guild? Between opposing factions of your world?" the writer asked, somewhat surprised at the creature's musings, but noting that it and its cousins avoided modern music. "And the managers are in league with this guild? Absurd! Barbaric!"

"Fool. Since time began the strong send the weak out to sing or dance for coin. Why question the way of nature, boy?" the creature rebutted.

"Barbaric!" the writer mumbled, shaking his head.

"Humans, you are fools. We just play you, drag your souls, milk your fears. Judge you, we do not. You throw your hard won coin for the song and dance. You give the bosses what they demand. Ah, then the fickleness of the mob, desires shift, throw away the also ran, bring in the new, shiny bit for the mob. So it goes, for endless cycles, fool," the creature hissed, appearing to enjoy the discomfort the writer was exhibiting.

"Yes, but…," the writer began, but was waved down by the creature.

"Enough, human!" the creature barked, its voice becoming more menacing. "Enough of your spewing tongue. Mayhap I should call on one of the little ones, maybe one of the imugi, one of the ones damned to dwell in the in-between, to…to tenderize my supper guest before the cook pot?"

"Imugi?" the writer asked, letting his eyes dart to the shadows beyond the firebox. "Your little ones are…have serpents as companions?"

"Enough, human, enough," the creature spat back. "Do you wish to swim in your own oils and juices now, or tell me another tale of human weakness and goblin might?"

"Of course, another tale, oh vile oppressor," the writer quickly replied. "On to the next."

"Yet, little human, no goblin filled his belly in your story. Only an old soul who fell into the mountain's abyss," the creature grumbled, relapsing to the creature's promise of revealing where its cousins might have been hiding in the tale. "Songs. No goblins. Maybe a fairy. Or, ghoul? The old cat. She might have been a cousin. Maybe a human witch? You should have let her boil the pesky human girl. Exciting, boiling the foolish young. Are you sure your humans read these scribblings of yours?"

"The voice, good goblin-troll, sir. The mountain itself felt the girl's agony," the writer replied, tapping the stone bench and ignoring the insult. "Are these very singing stones not alive, giving, in their way, even you some protection? Do they not allow you to dwell here at their whim…?"

The writer was grasping at any imaginary straw he could think of to keep the creature interested and its mind off the cook pot, mixing and conflating all manner of Korean and even western superstitions, hoping to hit on anything that would hold the beast's interest.

"Gone, they are," the creature answered, a hint of almost human-like remorse in its gurgling voice. "Only the dumb singing remains. An echo of the old ones who came before. My sire spoke of them, before he departed. Many have vanished, they have, from his mountains as well. Many have faded into the blackened roads and massive hive huts you humans build, that their once grand and terrifying voices have been silenced here for so many, many cycles. North? Maybe a few remaining up there? Maybe far away at Heaven's Gate? Maybe some of the islands…? Some of your kind can see us…see even the old ones. Those are special. My mother's clan avoided those who might be able to see us, even a shadow. Too afraid that they would wrap you in a talisman and burn you in the fire. Yes, mayhap the human girl heard one of the lingering voices? Or, maybe they were just in her foolish head?"

"What of the stain? In the rock? From her tears?" the writer demanded, noting the creature's slip about the power of talismans, even though the creature had ridiculed human witches just moments before.

"There are many stains, boy," the creature grunted, pointing to the ghastly, marred edges of the stone table and the top of the firebox. "Blood and tears make for permanent markings. Like little runes that anyone can decipher, of the demise of chatty…very chatty humans."

"Do your kind not move to the sadness of the old songs? Or the heart rending songs in the old style?" the writer called, trying anything to keep the creature thinking, instead of eating. "Even I, with pretty poor Korean, teared up when I heard that young singer's version of Lee Yong's 'Forgotten Season' on an old drama. Why, even the beasts of the forest weep at certain old songs. Does not the very stone of your mountain lair sob at the death songs of your victims?"

Suddenly, the creature revealed, when it visibly winced at the words 'death songs,' that the writer had hit on a key element.

"Death!" the writer then cried, watching the creature's reactions. "Death lurks everywhere, especially in the old places. Ready for us all, death is, even for ones so young. Yes, even when disguised with the new that you disparage so."

At the writer's blunt words, the creature leapt up out of its chair and, extending its rail thin arms like two swords, began swinging them around the small enclosure, causing the writer to lean back as far as he could on the bench to avoid being skewered by a bony hand.

"Where?" demanded the suddenly nervous creature, its voice strained as it shouted. "Where, damned human? Do you see? I've heard many a human cry out her name just before the cooking pot. Where, you devil's cur?"

"The story...," the writer finally answered, thinking he might have pushed the creature too far. "The story...and, the next story."

Stopping its flailing arms, the creature, its foul breath coming quickly, but slowly easing, leaned into the writer, and, placing a thin, gangrenous finger on the man's chest, nudged him so hard that the writer fell backward.

"No tricks, human. If you see d—...see her before the pot, it means she could be here for either of us, or both," the creature hissed, almost in a whisper, its eyes darting all around the enclosure. "Don't temp me...to...to summon her, to satisfy her before she can stalk me."

"No...no tricks," the writer whispered, sitting up and trying to talk while holding his breath against the stench of the creature. "The next story...?"

The creature tapped its captive's chest a few more times and then slipped back into its chair. The creature's eyes were wild, and darted from one dark recess in the enclave to another as it finally answered the writer's plea for another tale.

"Proceed, boy, but do not use any veiled incantations to summon her behind my back," the creature warned, its slithering tongue catching on a rotted tooth, slurring the beast's words. "I've fought her before and...well, came to a draw."

Shuddering inwardly at the creature's sudden revelation of its own deep fear of the angel of death, the writer's mind raced as he thought of the next tale, wondering where he might need to alter the story in order to appease his captor.

"Let's turn to an area across town, not too far, where the students like to gather, housewives will shop, old men will gawk, and shopkeepers still have a touch of Old Seoul courtesy," the writer began. "Hongdae...."

"Ah," the creature abruptly sighed, visibly relaxing from its earlier frenzy. "Before I was cast out, my mother's brothers used to take me to haunt those narrow, abyssal alleys. Tricking students when I was young. So many artists and musicians. It's the creative types who see us sometimes before we can grab them, so we had to be exceptionally clever to drag one of those down into the drain holes or into the dark alleys behind the darker shops. Yes, I well remember those twists and turns, boy. Maybe I will recognize your…the story places. Banned from there, these many, many cycles. Broke a truce, between shop goblins and school goblins. There is a patch of land, a plaza like the one above us. The two clans of goblins had a, what do you say, neutral place? Ensured that two goblins from the different clans didn't latch onto a juicy student at the same time and render the pitiful human worthless before either could drain its shallow soul. Yes, good times, those were, angering the elders and terrifying those prancing, creative morsels. Listen I will, closely, for my cousins will be all around your story's pitiful humans. Yes. Proceed."

"You broke a truce…?" the writer asked, knowing each additional sentence or long rant by his captor kept the writer out of the cook pot longer.

"A truce? Oh, the neutral ground. Yes, I dragged the wrong student at the wrong time, I did," the creature replied, a deep chuckle rumbling in its chest. "Dusk, it was, when we can slip in between the coming shadows and the fleeing light. A human girl student. Not old. Was…yes, I remember, was taking a shortcut down an alley just on the edge of the neutral area. Well, some of the shop goblins shoved her, but did not drag her, causing her such a fright that she abandoned the alley and took off across the plaza. Well, I was still young and thought the shop goblins had tried to drag her and missed, so I, wanting to show my mother's family that I was as good as any pure blood, chased after her, staying to her shadow and the shadows of the tall huts. Just before she crossed that big, massive gate, I dragged her. Surprised me, she did. She had an un-human toughness to her, and wouldn't let go of her soul or her flesh so easily, so I took a nip of her left ear. Just a nip, as the ghouls do, to set their mark so other ghouls leave a marked human alone. Well, that didn't work either and only enraged the girl, who began spewing all manner of vile spells and witch words that hurt my head. Terrible words of goblin demise and dokkaebi suicide, she used. Horrible. So horrible that, when she stepped over the threshold of the gate and into the school goblin domains, four gate dokkaebi on the school side fell hard to their early dust at the girl's anger and her powerful spells. I was alone in the plaza. The humans, of course, just walked by me, the carriages just whizzed by, but my mother's kin, the shop goblins, and the school goblins, all saw how my antics had killed a few of their school goblin brethren. Yet, they were also a little afraid. Afraid because the girl's terrible words had no effect on me, other than a headache. That's when the whispers started. I was different. The old spells bounced off me. Four good goblins dead and the vile mix of troll-ogre and dokkaebi survived without even a new wart. Yes, that was the beginning, you might say, of my end."

"Tragic," the writer commented after the creature had fallen silent. "Shall I begin?"

"The biggest irony?" the creature interrupted.

"What?" the writer asked.

"The human girl fool wasn't even a student there. She was a human scribbling major from old Yonhi. What is the new name? And, foreign scribbling at that," the creature chuckled. "One day, I will find her again."

"Really? You can tell all that from a nip of the ear?" the writer asked, trying to drag out the creature's story.

"What? Ear? Oh, only partly, fool. She dropped a book, in a black cover. One of my cousins could read the book scribbles within," the creature replied. "Some study of one of those Yeongguk, Englander, women writers, it was. I could not read it then, but it was in the same scribbles as your notebook there. One day, I will find that death spewing girl with the nipped ear."

"Ah, it was in English," the writer answered, looking at the next tale he hoped to read to the creature. "How? Why do you say she was Yonhi, Yonsei?"

"Enough!" the creature grumbled at the writer. "My belly might begin to think it's as empty as the little ones', lurking just beyond the shadows to sample your morsels, boy. Better to take me back, swiftly, to old Hongdae, human. Read or boil!"

Nodding quickly at the creature's outburst, the writer was actually a little happy that he had pushed the creature a bit too far, because the episode had allowed the writer to better tell from the creature's body language when the time for banter was over. So, settling into the bench and, after taking a couple of deep breaths, while wondering why the stench didn't bother him as much as earlier, the captive dinner guest, or entrée, pushed his voice lower to set the mood. Also, he was sorely wishing he wasn't about to relate a tale that took place in the midst of a hundred restaurants, so hoped the twists of the Hongdae tale would push that fact to the background.

3

AN ANGEL OF HONGDAE

Due west of Mount Namsan, about thirty minutes by car or a little longer by bus or subway, at the foot of an arguably much smaller hill, fanning out westward from one of the top art and engineering schools in the country, an edgy neighborhood was waging a decades-long fight with gentrification to retain its artistic and alternative roots in a city where conformity was king and new buildings routinely swallowed tradition. Embedded in the Korean capital city that never sleeps, the area of Hongdae, Zandari before the nearby University of Hongik lent its name, boasts youth's entire rainbow of guilty pleasures in its narrow streets and winding alleys. The area plays continuous host to thousands of artists, musicians, shoppers, students, coffee drinkers, diners, barflies, and groups of friends looking for memorable evenings flavored with a touch of old Seoul.

Inevitably, as history tells us, the ultra hip areas of the world eventually fall prey to real estate speculators and chain boutiques. Anyone who can recall Notting Hill and Portobello Road before the influx of condos, Greenwich Village before the steamroller of progress, Kennedy Town before the espresso bars, or countless other rare enclaves of human creativity, will agree that Hongdae was fast marching down that road to creative perdition. However, for the moment, quaint mom and pop shops, struggling musicians, starving artists, serious alternative lifers, and chaebol heirs alike, along with the quirky restaurants, trendy nightclubs, dive bars, and kitschy, but adorable character cafés, survive and thrive in the cluster of back alleys and side streets with no imminent development prospects.

It was down one of those more twisted back alleys, a week or so before the Lunar New Year, where I was meeting up with a few friends while in Seoul on business. Our agreed to destination, a barbeque joint, on a corner across from one of the best, old-style fried chicken places in Seoul, was known to all of us, as we tended to gravitate back to the familiar smells, tastes, and sounds of the decades-old mom and pop restaurant when meeting in the shadow of Hongik University, just a few blocks to the east by the main avenue.

Exiting the taxi at the outskirts of the village, an apt term for the quainter neighborhoods in large cities, a strong whiff of old Seoul slammed into me in the cold air. Looking around with wrinkled nose and deep nostalgia, I wondered how long such an obnoxious, yet heartwarming aroma would survive development. With the old smell of a Seoul fast disappearing as the town sped into the future, I was encouraged when I also saw that the darker doorways and less than welcoming back alleys of the old days were still evident, causing me to be a little more careful with my out-of-town appearance.

Fortunately, blending into an international hub for the modern traveler usually meant black jeans or slacks, a dark shirt, high-end shoes or boots, a dark sports jacket or suit coat, and a black or dark grey coat, with a branded scarf. I was wrapped in all those, so I felt I'd be able to pass by most without a second look.

Pulling my coat tighter and tucking in my grey scarf, I pointed myself in the general direction of the winding side street that held the barbeque joint. While it had been a couple of years since I had wandered Hongdae, a glance at my phone's map app to jog my memory let me relax and enjoy the few minutes' stroll.

Walking for a few blocks, even in the cold, allowed me to recall familiar sights, breathe in the amazing aromas from all manner of foods, especially the bakeries, and reacquaint myself with a few of the old shops. I passed countless patrons simply wandering narrow streets while window shopping, saw a few groups of local hipsters heading down blind alleys following the next great band, and spied cluttered signs proclaiming high end shops next to struggling mom and pop, hole-in-the-wall eateries. The even darker, narrower alleys hinted at the promise of somewhat more illicit meetings and alternative adventures to break up the monotonous life of the company men. Dark rooms over seedy shops in those back alleys held secrets close and kept the authorities at bay with age-old methods.

Lively music spilled into the streets, to be met by the sounds of random startup bands hoping to be the next discovery. Groups of friends wandered the selection of fare in search of that day's prized food, the search changing often in the modern, networked world of collective, instant gratification. Students, locals and those from other neighborhoods, scurried about, worried about the coming semester, but always looking for a brief, often alcohol-aided escape. Dutiful first and second sons and daughters chased art, engineering, economics, law, and medical degrees from the school,

Honggik, just beyond the shops and restaurants. From the two just to the north, Ewha, the traditional women's school, and Yonsei, with women and men, a similar hormone driven mix added an almost tangible electricity to the youthful haunting of the streets and alleys of old Hongdae.

While there were no current Banksy equivalents that I knew of, a great deal of the local tagged art, the thinking man's graffiti, was quite good, and depicted all manner of modern life, both real and bizarrely imagined. I was also happy to see a few brave, solo musicians busking in the chilly night air, and left a few bills in their guitar cases and one violin case.

Yet, even with the map app, I managed to wander down a couple of blind alleys, one full of leather-clad youths draped about very pricey motorcycles, acting as if they were waiting for friends. They barely looked in my direction, but a couple did smirk a bit when I had to backtrack out of the dead end. Another alley's denizens were less welcoming and I quickly turned back to the main street after several tough looking youths looked crossways at me, an obvious outsider, as they crowded two painted girls out of a small car and into one of those darker entrances. Catching a fleeting glimpse of the vacant, dead look on one of the painted girls' faces, I was shocked, but only fleetingly, before I turned away, writing it off to how the real world operated.

Finally, after weaving through a large crowd of students waiting outside a lively bar with loud, but fairly interesting, live music spilling out of its open doors, I spotted my destination, comfortably nestled along one of the tree-lined, one-way lanes suited more for pedestrians than cars.

Through the restaurant's open sided corner, which, even in winter, allowed passerby to sample the aromas and see the sizzling pork and beef on the tabletop grills, luring new patrons inside, I saw that the place was not yet full, a good sign for a better table. Not too far from the former Hello Kitty Café location and only a couple of blocks from the school, the restaurant was a popular local institution, so arriving early always helped with scoring a better table, or a shorter wait.

Stepping through the blast of warm air from the vent overhead of the wide opening, keeping the frigid air outside and the inside air tepid, I paused to take in the scene, the sounds, and the smells all around me. The air just inside still had a bit of a chill due to the open sides, but, I smiled to myself as I looked around for my friends, I knew the grills warmed up the place and the steaming bowls of soup gave it just the right humidity.

"Hello!"

Turning at the boisterous call, in English, so had assumed it was directed at me, I was delighted to see one of my colleagues, the manager of our firm's local office and a long time friend, waving from one of the longer tables near the middle of the floor, packed in close to the others around it. From the look of the nearly empty table, it appeared I wasn't the last to arrive.

I waved back at my friend, and, with the help of the younger of the two old ajumma women who were fixtures in the restaurant, wove through the bustling tables of mostly students to join him. Sounds of excited chatter rose up around me, mostly Korean, with some Mandarin, a scattering of English, and even Russian, confirming the wide appeal of the old place.

All the while, the younger ajumma, her cherubic face flush with the heat of the kitchen, chattered about the food, what I might like, what was freshest that night, and pointed at various grills sizzling with pork belly, a favorite with the student crowd. I could only catch the major words, as my Korean was woefully inadequate, in spite of having married into a stateside Korean family nearly ten years before.

About halfway to our table, I profusely thanked the old lady, bowed to her, which made her giggle afresh as she then headed back to the kitchen, beaming at the satisfied faces around her. I watched her for a few seconds and then stepped around a lively group of young people already heavily into the beer and pork.

Suddenly, as if out of nowhere, a waiter, carrying a heavy iron bowl of bubbling hot soup, seemed to be unwittingly backing into an older couple who must have just entered the restaurant from the more civilized front door just to the left. The waiter, a brutish looking, middle-aged man of short stature, sweating through a grizzled, pock-marked face, and sporting a soiled uniform, didn't notice the older couple and was about to bump into the old woman, and no doubt spill the hot soup all over her.

Quickly stepping away from the chair being offered by my friend, to his questioning look, I forced myself in between the old woman and the brutish waiter just as the waiter turned with the heavy bowl.

Fortunately, I was ready for the oaf's fumbling delivery, so was able to steady his hands just as the bowl touched my mid-section.

I could feel the heat of the iron bowl through my clothes, even with a coat on, and a few drops of the scalding liquid landed on my left hand, which I quickly shook off once the waiter was stable and had moved on, gruffly bowing and mumbling a half apology as he retreated. I then stepped aside to allow the old couple to pass by, bowing slightly to show respect.

The old woman smiled briefly at me as she passed and acknowledged the bow with the benevolent imperiousness of an older Korea matron of a good family. The old man, his eyes deep pools of dark, long life mysteries, bowed slightly as well, but paused as he passed, and then clasped my hand, inspecting it closely to ensure there was no scalding. Satisfied, the old man smiled and spoke, his voice deep with the wisdom of his culture, adding a certain elevation to the bustling restaurant's atmosphere. Yet, he also spoke in perfect English, with formality and grace.

"You are quick, young man, and thought only of my dear wife's safety, not your own. We are in your debt, twice. For, fortune has smiled on you and you were also not burned, which would have been unforgivable as a guest in my homeland. You are a good man. Remain so."

I could only bow and then smile my thanks to the odd comments from the old man as he then moved on.

My friend's eyes were dancing with mirth, but he was too well bred to say anything while the elderly couple was still within earshot.

As they passed the mostly youthful tables on their way deeper into the restaurant, the old couple smiled at the many bowing heads from the polite youth.

One younger boy, intent on gorging himself on kalbi, beef ribs, did not see the older couple, so the boy's older sister or cousin, kicked him under the table and admonished him for not acknowledging the older couple. The boy's face at first showed annoyance, then, once he had seen the older couple, he gulped down the meat, which had been bulging out of his cheeks, jumped up, turned and bowed low, loudly asking for forgiveness for being such an unworthy child.

The old man of the couple paused, turned back to the boy, and smiled at the top of the boy's bowed head. As the old man spoke, the sounds of conversation and cooking quickly subsided in a wave around the old man and his companion. All in the restaurant had turned to look and listen to the eerie peacefulness of the old man's voice, now speaking the highest-level Korean to the small boy, quite an honor for the boy.

"Son, no need to be so formal. Yet, I thank you for your kindness and your sister's adherence to the old ways. Please finish your dinner. Eat well. Grow well. Live well, young man."

The old man then placed his aged right hand on the boy's shoulder, causing the boy to initially stiffen, but then relax as the old man nudged the boy to raise his gaze. Smiling, the old man patted the young boy on the shoulder, and then, as if plucking the item from thin air, he handed the child a small, multicolored silk packet with gold lettering.

The young boy, his eyes wide with wonder, knew immediately that the small pouch was a Lunar New Year gift.

"Grandfather, sir, thank you, but I can not accept. I am not worthy. I did not greet you with respect as you and Grandmother passed...!"

The old man waved the boy to silence and spoke one last time as he turned away and took his wife's arm, to continue to one of the private rooms at the back of the restaurant.

"Son, you are more than worthy. To have honored an old man in his twilight with your sweet words. Live long. Have many children. Love your sister, your parents, your friends, and your wife. May you never know the sadness of living too far beyond your own offspring."

At that point, the entire restaurant was silent, out of both respect and sympathy for the older couple. A few of the female college students closest to the old couple were actually tearing up at the old man's words of loss.

As I watched the old couple disappear into the farthest of the private rooms, the sounds of cooking mixed with conversation and laughter returned in an opposite wave.

"Funny, never knew they had private rooms."

Turning back to the voice, I smiled at my robust and always ready to eat friend and colleague of many years, Tae-hyun.

"You're right. I didn't know, either," I replied as we greeted with a robust, but discreet man-hug.

After we had exchanged hellos, Tae-hyun introduced his current girlfriend, Ji-su, a stylish marketing grad student from Ewha. Whether she was the first of the coming New Year or the last of the current year, I never did figure out. One never knew with my happy friend.

A few minutes later, our other mutual friends arrived. Both only a year older than the rest of us, they nevertheless loved to play up the age difference and the need for formal language and demonstrated signs of respect, especially as the evening grew longer and the beer more abundant.

Ji-hye was a lawyer out of Seoul National University, recently a deputy minister of some sort, even though she was quite a bit younger than her peers, and stunningly beautiful. Her long-time beau, Ji-hoon, sporting a likable round face with a hint of baby fat, was from one of the usual good houses, school not mentioned. Our other friend, who preferred to be called by her English name, Jenny, also Ewha, and her colleague, Ji-song, who had gone to UCLA in Los Angeles, were both in the music industry, as very successful studio producers. Jenny had that imperious Korean air of a much older dowager, but with the looks of a coed, and her beau had the classic good looks of a drama star, easily mistaken for much-admired actor Kim Soo-hyun. Rounding out the group, and a stranger to me, was the last arriving Yu-na, an attractive Yonsei grad student in foreign affairs, and a friend of Tae-hyun's date, Ji-su.

Once the seating was all arranged, we shed our coats and, in unison, rubbed our hands in anticipation of gorging on meats, veggies, and various pan chon, the multitude of side dishes in any Korean restaurant worthy of the name. Ji-su had placed the single woman next to me, the old married guy, more to protect her from the inevitable advances of the other single men than to try to lead me, her beau's old drinking buddy, astray.

After the first round of meats had been ordered, pork belly and some sort of beef strips, and the first round of drinks had been downed, the conversation turned to the change I had noticed walking through Hongdae to the restaurant.

"Is this the new Itaewon?" I asked to the table in general, referring to the former American soldier hangout turned high-end-shopping area.

"Where are all the starving artists going to find galleries and the hungry bands find gigs when all the rents go up?"

As a group, everyone, except the Yonsei student, replied in waves of protests that the developers were still years away from converting the Hongdae area into an overpriced coffee bar and condo haven.

Jenny was the most vocal, letting her thoughts, and persuasive voice, drown out her friends.

"Look around you at this place, for example," Jenny cooed, pointing at the tables in the restaurant, full of students, some older groups, and a few obvious band members. "Look out there, at the street. Across the street. Crane your neck and look down that darker alley over there. No doubt one can still find his, or her, heart's desire in those lonely, unregistered rooms."

Winking at her beau, Jenny laughed, and the table returned her laughter in kind.

"Yes, the old ways are still here," Yu-na finally added, mostly in English for my benefit, with almost a sad, far off look of one thinking back to happier times. "But, much of what made this place is fading. The magic of the old people. The music of the children. The smells of old Seoul. Those…those are drifting away, like the shriveled, dead leaves of fall finally flowing out on the Han River to the far, unforgiving sea, this bitter winter evening."

Initially, no one replied to the young woman's overly heart wrenching comment. Then, Ji-su, her friend, giggled, and scolded Yu-na for being too serious.

"What? Really? Which Bronte sister are you now?" Ji-su called from the other end of the table. "Better drop out and seek a spot at Hongik with the artists. How can you be a progressive foreign ministry officer if you see poetry in the back alleys of the world?"

Yu-na's cheeks and neck immediately colored pink, and she lowered her head in mock acquiescence to her friend, and then laughed at herself to ease the momentary tension. That allowed the conversation to return to ordering the next dish and determining which beer, local or foreign, worked with whatever was being ordered.

Looking at the silenced grad student out of the corner of my eye, I could see she was still thinking about the old days, which I thought was a little strange for someone of the younger generation, yet also comfortably reassuring.

"No need to worry," I said quietly, looking at the food, but talking to Yu-na. "Your observations are sound and, I hope you don't think me patronizing, for your youth, quite insightful. Don't lose that perception as it will serve you well in foreign lands, and at home."

Yu-na smiled and said a quick thank you under her breath, and then rejoined the food revelry with the rest.

After the third round of beers, while I was still nursing my second glass, the loud conversation moved between world events, sports, food, recent celebrity pair ups and separations, alcohol, more sports, fashion (briefly), bosses (good and bad), more food, and which school had the smartest students.

The last topic was promoted by Tae-hyun, mainly to see what would happen at the table full of cute coeds just beside ours. The louder he proclaimed his alma mater, Chung-Ang, as the best, the more the coeds and other tables looked at him with mild annoyance. Korean protocol dictated that the younger diners could not openly challenge someone so obviously older and, therefore, superior to them. Yet, my friend's somewhat tipsy, continued poking finally raised the ire of one of the youngest looking coeds, a slim, probably under fifty kilos, waif of a girl in a cream colored, woolen outfit.

The young woman stood, bowed low to our table, and, with the utmost care in choosing her words, proceeded to enumerate countless statistics on the various schools in Seoul and beyond, citing sources and dates, placing Chung-Ang in its appropriate ranking (some which were the highest, some which were less so). Finishing with a flourish about her own school, Hongik, she bowed to the shocked silence around her table, collapsed back into her chair, and appeared to immediately pass out, her small form no match for the stress of her soliloquy oiled by too much fermented courage.

Tae-hyun, amusedly, also shocked into silence during the girl's speech, stood up at the girl's final bow and, lifting his glass to her and her colleagues, cried out in hearty endorsement.

"Geonbae! Geonbae! Drink up for your brave, fallen colleague," my tipsy friend called to the youth around him. "Carry her carefully on her shield back to her far castle, so she can sally forth another day to do battle with my addled wits. Geonbae! And, someone get her name. We need to hire her!"

Dropping back into his own chair, Tae-hyun smiled at his muddled chivalry and proceeded to call for the fourth, or was it fifth, round as he also tried to sing that recent novelty satire song about Korean girls, set to the tune of 'California Girls,' so far off key that he sounded like cats fighting.

Fortunately, Tae-hyun was too lubricated to get more that a few of the parody words out.

"…and, those Jeju girls really…really…something, something…my, my, my boat! And Busan girls, uh, Busan…?"

His efforts at singing exhausted, Tae-hyun continued with the beer order, choosing domestic out of national pride after mumbling an additional line about 'Incheon girls really…,' or some such nonsense.

After the brief interlude on the merits of one leading school over the other, the conversation moved on to subjects of romance, which led to marriage talk, which then led to arguments on retirement investments.

Tiring of the predictable directions of the table talk, I began to pay more attention to the restaurant around me, wondering, absently, if I could spot the local students, versus those from just north or from across the Han River. I enlisted Yu-na's assistance and soon learned she had a keen eye for detail, pointing out the specific brands typically worn by each school, the subtle differences in appearances, and the shoes and high heels, which seemed to give her the best insight into the many groups and cliques that made up Seoul's youth.

After a number of minutes at the mindless game, we determined, with the added help of Ji-song and Jenny who had joined in, that the room held a fair representation from all the best schools and a few of the good schools, to include a few of the more famous high schools, with the glaring absence of beer as the main indicator of age. Yu-na was happy to have discovered her own high school in the mix, Daewon, one of the top foreign language high schools in Seoul.

"Yet, with such a diverse crowd in this main room, I still wonder who gets the private room treatment," Yu-na offered to the group, straining her neck to see into the far recesses at the back of the restaurant.

"Older, local couples, I would imagine," I replied, adding that the couple who had spoken to me seemed very well off and highly educated.

"Interesting, isn't it," Yu-na commented, "that the waitress only brings out empty trays, but doesn't seem to take any full trays in."

"What?" Jenny asked, half turning her head in mock concern. "Are they starving those dear old people?"

"Maybe you just missed the food trays earlier, Yu-na," Ji-song suggested.

"Yes, that's probably it," Yu-na acknowledged, turning away from looking into the back of the establishment.

Over the course of the next hour, amused by the young grad student's observation and, always interested in a mystery, I also began to watch the waitresses at the back of the restaurant. From what I could tell, other than drinks (not beer), no actual food was taken into the back rooms. Four rooms lined the back, from what I could see. Yet, as Yu-na had pointed out, every now and then, the waitress would emerge from the curtained doorway to one of the rooms carrying an empty tray. And, it was always the same waitress, an older woman with a stern look and a quick, shifting eye.

With my friends pretty well plastered at that point, I let the little mystery of the rooms occupy my thoughts. I noticed Yu-na watching my interest and, with a little sheepishness, I confessed my puzzlement.

"Seems you were right," I commented so that only Yu-na heard. "And, given the way this building sits on the corner, backed up against that slight hill at the rear, I don't think those rooms have an extra door that we can't see."

Yu-na, who had also stopped drinking some time earlier, begging off from her friends that she had an early appointment the next day, perked up at my interest in the puzzle of the back rooms and motioned for me to continue.

"Maybe, if I time it just right...?" I mused, giving the young grad student a quick smile.

Standing, using the motion of washing my hands to signal my intent to my friends, I headed back to the men's room, knowing that it was already occupied, which I hoped would give me enough time to peek in the fourth room when the waitress pushed back the curtain, either coming out or going in.

Waiting at the back of the restaurant, dodging the same clumsy waiter from the soup bowl incident earlier and some of his younger colleagues, I had a few minutes to look over the entire dining area from both being in the back and from being taller than most patrons.

What I saw confirmed my earlier assessment. Mostly students, with a few business groups, like ours, mixed in. Later in the evening, no doubt it would be more business groups after an evening of drinking and fewer students, who had to filter back to dorms, apartments, or homes to study and prepare for the coming semester. Or not. The students, since most were probably on break between semesters, might actually outlast the older patrons and close the place down in the wee hours of the morning.

Finally, after a couple of long minutes, with the door to the men's room still reading 'occupied,' the primary waitress for the back rooms squeezed by me and stepped to the curtain covering the fourth private room. There, drawn by the movement of the waitress, I noticed that there were three sets of shoes at the entrance, left there in deference to the old style of dining. I surmised the third set was from someone the old couple was meeting and who had already been in the restaurant when the sweet old couple had arrived.

When the old waitress lifted the curtain, I felt a little guilty staring at her and the doorway, so briefly averted my eyes out of politeness.

Just at the moment I shifted my gaze to the kitchen area, out of the corner of my eye I saw the waitress pause and turn to look in my direction. For the briefest of moments, I felt a sharp chill at the back of my neck, similar to the feeling of an unexpected blast of cold air from an abruptly opened window. Yet, there were no such windows near me, only the piercing stare of the old waitress.

As the waitress dropped her gaze and turned back to enter the room, I was able to shift my view to see a few fleeting scenes in the private room.

Ornate, yet subdued, was my first thought after flashes of vivid color, streams of stark white embellishments, and elaborate décor reaching far beyond the room's doorway caught my eye before the curtain fell.

Suddenly, the men's room door opened and stepping aside, I allowed the occupant to pass me, and then I stepped in, where I completed my business quickly, washed my hands, and returned to our table, glancing back to the private rooms only once.

Reaching my chair, I saw that no one, other than Yu-na, even noticed my return. So, sitting, I let the images from the fourth room sink in before mentioning anything to my young co-conspirator.

"Well, detective, anything?" Yu-na finally asked, unable to keep her curiosity in check.

"Yes. But, oddly arranged, the few images I saw while the curtain was pulled back. Quite odd, actually," I replied, my mind still struggling with the array of incongruent imagery from the briefest of glimpses.

"Odd, how?" Yu-na asked, leaning her youthful, uncomfortably attractive body in close to hear more clearly.

"Well, first, it's huge. The room. I'd say half as large as this front dining area, and deep. Lots of colorful appointments, almost like a museum or an old-fashioned home. But, with white embellishments, like a Catholic mass from my youth. Incense, somewhere out of view, but it was definitely there."

"What fragrance?" Yu-na asked, her eyes wide.

Looking back to the rear, I tried to mentally bring up the smells I had just encountered, but nothing seemed out of the ordinary.

"Fragrance? Hard to say with all the kitchen smells back there," was the only answer I could offer, then continued. "I did see the old woman, but just briefly, from the back. She wasn't wearing her coat, but I recognized her profile. I did not see the husband. She was sitting, traditional style, at a low table, full of pan chon and meats. Symmetrical."

"Symmetrical?" Yu-na asked, her voice quiet and with an added hint of what sounded like concern.

"Yes. It almost seemed like it was set up for a photo shoot. Not to actually be eaten," I replied, recalling the carefully spaced and placed items on the low, highly polished, lacquered table. "Reminded me a little of my niece's Dol some years ago."

Seeing Yu-na's brow furrow even more, I shrugged, and continued.

"Well, it appears I'm not the best detective. Maybe you should have a try?" I suggested.

Yu-na immediately recoiled and shook her head in disagreement, attracting the attention of her friend at the other end of the table.

"Hey, Yu-na," Ji-su called, her words slurred a bit. "What's going on over there with you two?"

Coloring up beet red, Yu-na said something quickly to her friend about having too much to drink already and just didn't want anymore, causing her friend to wink and laugh, and then turn her attention back to Tae-hyun.

"I can't do that," Yu-na whispered under her breath to me, calming down, but leaning back into the conspiracy. "Could I...?"

I waited, wondering if that elusive adventurous element, often repressed in young Koreans, might find a brief home in Yu-na's personality. As I watched, I was happy to see the seed of new possibilities begin to appear on her face and, as if she were having an internal revelation, the young grad student's brow went from puzzlement, awareness, and then resolve in the expanse of a few seconds.

"Yes!" Yu-na stated, resolutely. "Why not? I can take a quick look."

Rising, Yu-na dashed off to the back of the restaurant, without any of the washroom antics I had put on, and parked herself at the kitchen entrance as if she wanted to say something to our waitress. However, Yu-na was well aware, as was I, that our table's waitress had stepped out to fetch some fried chicken from the sister place across the alleyway in order to satisfy Tae-hyun's sudden craving. This absence allowed Yu-na several minutes of hanging around the kitchen entrance within full view of the back rooms.

As I watched, I noticed the old waitress, who was working the back rooms, pause and say something to Yu-na, who smiled and waved her off, pointing into the kitchen. I saw the old waitress slowly nod and continue on to the fourth room and, without looking back at Yu-na or anyone else, pulled back the curtain, and, for a full half minute, held the curtain open while she seemed to be talking to someone inside the room.

I strained a little to my right, but was unable to see into the room, given the distance and all the patrons between the rear of the restaurant and me.

Turning back to watch Yu-na, I noticed she had stopped her ruse of looking back and forth from the kitchen to the main dining area and was staring, immobile, at the fourth room through the open curtain.

Even when I saw the old waitress drop the curtain, Yu-na continued to stare at the room's closed doorway.

Finally, a bump from the clumsy waiter seemed to awaken Yu-na, who, initially walking backward, stepped away from her position and seemed to be heading for the front exit. As she progressed, I noticed her frozen look thawed a bit and she began to look around, almost as if she was disoriented and didn't remember she was in the restaurant.

No doubt too much beer I thought, as I considered calling out to the young student.

Suddenly, as if out of nowhere, the clumsy waiter and the old waitress from the private rooms were both standing in front of Yu-na. The two seemed to be encouraging the grad student to accompany them to the back of the restaurant. As she turned and took a hesitant step with them, something about the two bothered me. While my concerns were undefined, something in the back of my mind told me to step in.

Leaving our table, I intercepted the odd little party of three just as Yu-na had seemed to awaken and politely protest the two's insistence on her following them.

"Hey, my young friend," I called to Yu-na, for some unexplained reason not wanting to use her name in front of the two staff members. "Were you able to find our waitress? Your friends are worried you might have forgotten their order. More pork belly. Remember?"

As I had been talking, I inserted myself between the two staff members and Yu-na and, with care, touched her shoulder to remind her of her ruse.

Looking into the young woman's eyes, I saw both fear and confusion, then a moment of recognition when she realized what I was saying.

"Yes…more…pork belly," Yu-na mimicked, finally looking as if her head had cleared of whatever had been troubling her. "Oh, there she is now."

Fortune smiled on us as our table's waitress, having just returned and delivered our friend's chicken, saw us with the other two staff, and hurried over to see to our needs, bowing both to us and, apologetically, to the old waitress from the private rooms.

We repeated our new order, which seemed to satisfy the old waitress as she bowed, but only just, and led the clumsy waiter away. I then led Yu-na back to our table and let our friends know, a little too loudly, that the fresh pork belly was on its way.

For a few minutes, both Yu-na and I sat silently, listening to the conversations of our friends and nodding in agreement now and then.

Even after the arrival of the pork belly, delivered by the old waitress of the private rooms, who smiled like a Cheshire cat at me, and then attempted to get Yu-na to look her in the eye. But, Yu-na, feigning something important on her phone, refused to allow her eyes to connect with those of the old woman.

After fussing about with the grilling meat a little too long, as even my tipsy friends were beginning to make comments about how they could grill the pork, which was part of the fun of such places, the old waitress from the private rooms finally laughed nervously and backed away, while, even in her retreat, trying to catch Yu-na's eye.

Once the old woman had finally disappeared into the back, I heard Yu-na let out a long, exhaustive breath. Then, the young woman, keeping her eyes averted downwards, leaned over toward me as she poked at a couple of pieces of pork with her chopsticks.

"Is she still there?" Yu-na, asked, her voice a shadow of its earlier, more robust tone.

"Tell, me. Is she there?" Yu-na repeated, sounding alarmingly desperate.

"No. She's gone into the back," I replied, my own voice showing a level of alarm at Yu-na's odd behavior. "Hey, what did those two say to you? Should I have a word with the manager...?"

"No, no, no! Please, don't," Yu-na cried, her nervous voice a low whisper. "Don't."

After Yu-na's plea, we simply sat, me out of respect for the young woman's wishes and Yu-na, I think, out of something akin to fear.

"Yu-na, we need to powder our noses," Ji-su said, holding Jenny's arm, who was, in turn, leading Ji-hye. "Let's go."

Yu-na, not wanting to raise any eyebrows, but obviously torn between joining her friend and avoiding the old waitress at the back of the place, was in the midst of begging off from Ji-su's summons, when the old waitress passed our table and headed out the side door, bundled up to her neck against the cold. Realizing the old woman must be on a longer errand, Yu-na jumped up and preceded the three others to the ladies' room.

While the women were away, Tae-hyun and Ji-hoon moved over to sit closer to me and Ji-song, and, after my failing to take the bait on their beer-fueled male innuendo about my possible interests with respect to the young grad student, the three turned to talking about business.

All three men were models of success in modern Korea. Ji-hoon by the traditional route of wealthy parents, born into one of the top houses in the country, and via the best schools money could buy. Tae-hyun, while not at the same level as Ji-hoon, had been afforded a good life and the best schools, while choosing the right jobs, the best personal and professional networks, and the right mentors. Ji-song, educated first in Korea and then in Los Angeles, carried that air of the music industry invincibility, as long as the latest acts were successful. All three of the men were solid examples of Korea's economic progress and were, by staying in Korea and not permanently emigrating to Europe or America, harbingers of the country's future, as were the highly successful ladies in their lives.

Finally, after a number of minutes, the young women returned, shooing Tae-hyun and Ji-hoon back to their respective seats.

Yu-na, looking somewhat refreshed, but still distant, took her seat casually, and, as if nothing had happened earlier, began to chatter away with Ji-su, Jenny, and Ji-hye on all manner of subjects unrelated to the odd private room in the back.

As the evening wound down, try as I might, I could not get the young woman to reveal anything from her observation of the private room. Nor of her encounter with the two staff. Frustrated, and, fueled by both boredom and a little more beer, I decided to wander back to the rooms and see what I could see.

Yet, before I could rise, a young child, looking a lot like the one the old man had spoken to earlier, but somehow less wholesome and with more hunger in his eyes, suddenly stepped into my view, a couple of tables over.

The strange child just stood and stared at our table, first at one end and then the other, where Yun-na and I sat, as if he was searching for someone.

"Hey," Tae-hyun called, noticing the odd child. "Hey, did anyone lose a kid...? Doesn't look too bright, so might not know who his parents are."

Chuckling to himself, Tae-hyun looked around the table for endorsement of his slightly inebriated comments when he suddenly started to gurgle and gasp, as if choking on his beer. For a few seconds, his eyes bugged out and his face became red, then nearly blue, all so quickly, no one was able to react before he collapsed back into his chair, visibly gasping.

Just as quickly, normal color returned to Tae-hyun's ample cheeks.

"What the hell...?" Ji-su said as she leaned over her beau and wiped his sweating forehead with a napkin. "You okay, honey? Too much beer? Better stop, okay?"

Tae-hyun nodded, not trusting himself to speak, no doubt fearing he'd begin choking again. The rest of us relaxed, a bit rattled, but content our friend was okay.

I then returned my thoughts to the back room and, dismissing the odd kid who had moved farther away during Tae-hyun's incident, but continued to stare in our general direction, I pointed with my head to the rear of the restaurant to let Yu-na know I was heading back into the breech. However, just as I pushed my chair out to stand, a light, yet steely grip landed on my right arm, nearly crushing my wrist.

Startled, I looked into Yu-na's eyes and, shocked, more at the intensity of her gaze beseeching me to abandon my quest than her iron grip, I slowly nodded, and slid my chair and myself back to the table.

Yu-na's eyes softened, but her tight grip remained until I had acknowledged her unspoken demand. Of note, her eyes would drift toward the room in the back, but then jerk back to me, as if she didn't want to look upon the room, or, coincidentally, on the odd kid who had moved all the way back to the restrooms near the private rooms, where he suddenly stepped away, out of sight.

"Yes, a bit silly of me," I said casually, feeling Yu-na's grip loosen at my words. "I suppose some secrets are best left to others."

With that last quip, I felt Yu-na fully release my wrist and, turning away, she slumped sideways in her chair, as if exhausted. Her friend, Ji-su, noticed, and began to hint at departure all around.

After a brief argument over the check, which was won by Tae-hyun, being that it was his turn in the complicated math of Korean social responsibility, we all finished up our various drinks, and began the long goodbyes associated with such parties. We all also ganged up on Tae-hyun and playfully berated him for giving us a scare with his choking incident. He played along, but had the oddest look in his reddened eyes.

I soon learned that the three couples had planned all along to go to the latest dance spot just a few blocks over, where one of the hotter indie bands was to start playing soon. I begged off since I had to work very early the next day. Yu-na also excused herself, using her earlier pretext of a morning appointment.

Once we sorted out the coats and scarves from the backs of our seats, we made our way through the crush of tables and chairs, which delayed our progress enough for me to wave farewell to the more pleasant of the waitresses, the younger ajumma who always waited on us. We finally reached the hanging sheets of heavy plastic that passed for walls as the night had progressed, and we then all crowded outside into the still bustling street.

The third, or fourth, round of goodbyes were then given and the couples prepared to fade into the crowd heading east, but not before Ji-su had demanded I escort Yu-na to the subway, in case she was enticed to stop in at one of the many bars and not return home. I agreed, of course, and, yes, I also offered to give her a lift in my taxi, but, as was proper for a woman her age, she refused as being too far out of my way.

Just before the couples departed, Tae-hyun grabbed my arm and, whispering, suddenly spoke of his brief incident.

"Man, I thought I was really a goner. For real. Saw things as I was trying to breathe. Weird things," Tae-hyun said, trying to keep his voice low so no one else could hear. "Be careful what you eat, next time. Crazy. I could swear I heard my grandmother calling me just before I started breathing again."

"Did something get stuck in your throat?" I asked, noticing that Yu-na seemed to be listening.

"Throat? Yeah, I guess. I…I don't know," Tae-hyun replied, then leaned in closer to my face and added. "She passed when I was six, bro. Six. Didn't think I even remembered her. Clear as day. She was calling…calling to me."

"Maybe you should head home and get some sleep," I suggested as Ji-su and the rest pulled Tae-hyun away.

My friend just laughed, recovering from his momentary reflection, and, as he and his friends faded into the crowd, called back to me that the night was still young and the music new.

"He was lucky," Yu-na said as the couples finally disappeared in the Hongdae throngs, reminding me that the young grad student was still with me.

"Yes. But, he's a tough one," I said, not wanting to break my friend's confidence.

While standing in the cold streets of Hongdae with such an intriguing young woman, I had briefly thought of suggesting a late night espresso before walking to the subway, but that might be wrongly construed, especially by one so much younger. One of the oddities of adult Korean life was that women, single or in relationships, seemed to rarely have male friends after college. However, a moment later, I found I was not the only one thinking of warm drinks.

"That café, just there, serves amazing cakes and coffee," Yu-na suggested out of the blue. "That is, if you'd like to warm up before heading out?"

Surprised, but delighted, I assented, and we ducked into a small corner bakery just on the other side of the street from the restaurant. The café was one of those ubiquitous, but consistently tasty, Parisian-style chains one sees around Seoul and, recently, in major cities across Europe and America. The Eiffel Tower motif was a welcome sight on a cold night.

After ordering a couple of cakes, and tea for her and espresso for me, we found a small table at the side, away from the chill of the door, and, coincidentally, facing the BBQ joint. We sat quietly for a few minutes, both lost in our own thoughts and neither wanting to be the one to first bring up the odd private room at the restaurant, no doubt the reason the young grad student had suggested the café.

Ordinarily, modern Seoul women did not 'hang out' with men who were near strangers, nor did they have long term, platonic relationships with men they did know, especially older men, whether married or single. It was one of the quirks of culture that I had come to accept, after years of trying to understand it. Other than the required interactions at work or with family, one rarely saw opposite sexes enjoying each other's company unless they were in a serious, romantic relationship. Sad, really, all around.

Yu-na spent most of those first minutes trying not to look me in the eye, so I made a point to gaze out at the crowds and to try to look disinterested in what she had seen during her peek into that back room, but had been unwilling to share.

After about half a cup of espresso and the same for her tea, we both suddenly looked at the other and tried to speak at the same time. With a nod to American chivalry, which was hard to break, even though it greatly annoyed such obviously independent Korean women as Yu-na, I silenced myself, and nodded to my companion.

"Thank you," Yu-na began, "for back there and for being patient with me. It's just…it's just that I didn't think that happened anymore…I mean, that those rituals were only legend. I don't truly understand…and, that…that creature…that…child."

I let Yu-na, who visibly shuddered at mentioning the odd kid that had appeared just as Tae-hyun had had his incident, fall completely silent before I interjected my thoughts, which I did slowly and carefully.

"Yu-na," I said quietly, "something back there obviously tripped some sort of puzzle for you. I'm sorry if I pushed you into breaking some taboo by peeking into the room. Wait, if that's the case, some sort of cultural taboo was violated, I will walk back and apologize to the couple."

"Oh, no, you don't have to do that!" Yu-na responded with alarm. "The old couple are sweet and dear people, they do not have any bad feelings, I think. Only the mudang, the shaman, and her familiar."

"The what?" I asked, my ears perking up, wondering if I had heard correctly.

"What? I can't believe I'm saying this," Yu-na moaned, her face a contortion of emotions. "I have a double major in English and Economics. I do come from a family of Buddhists, but don't practice. I've traveled to a dozen other countries. I even spent a semester abroad in the states two years ago. I'm studying the intricacies and social science of complex foreign affairs. Why in the world would I suddenly be afraid of some old folk tale?"

I just sat silently as the young, modern woman talked her way through her emotional, culturally specific dilemma.

"I mean, who would have thought such things would be right here?" Yu-na asked, more to herself, than to me. "Right in the middle of the city, and not in some cut off village, or a lonely, wind-swept mountaintop in the south, or along the more isolated sections of the coast? I mean, we've all seen the festivals and holiday celebrations, but those are more like nods to our older culture. More camera opportunities, than some deep revelation."

Looking around at the patrons in the small café, Yu-na then leaned over toward me and whispered her next words.

"Who knows how many of these seemingly normal people might also know what's going on over there? How can the locals not know? Do they just turn a blind eye? Or, is it so routine no one thinks twice about it?"

Finally, after seeing the conflict in Yu-na's eyes, I felt I should speak.

"What has upset you, if you are okay telling me, the ultimate outsider?" I offered, speaking quietly as well.

"Outsider? Yes, maybe that is why you were able to see as much...? You...you were correct about the symmetry of the food, the offerings, and the ornate trappings," Yu-na whispered, almost too quietly. "It's not a dinner, at least, not for the living."

Silence.

I mulled over her last comment as Yu-na fidgeted.

'Not for the living.'

I waited, letting her speak at her own pace.

"A ritual," Yu-na continued. "One that mountain children hear about at bedtime. School kids hear about these if they go to the summer camps in the country. One that old grandparents, beyond senility, call for in their dementia. A...what is the correct English? Altar? Where you leave offerings? Like in a shrine or a church, but more...more ancient. Ancestral rites for those who passed long ago."

"So, the old couple was praying? In the back of the restaurant?" I asked, my own voice soft, so that it only carried to Yu-na's ear. "Is that so unusual?"

"Praying? Oh. Probably. But, there was more...," Yu-na replied, her eyes growing wider. "I think...I think a funeral. Or...I don't know. Something like a funeral being prepared."

"Well, it's not unusual to have a meal after or during the mourning period, Yu-na," I added from my limited knowledge of Korean funeral rites. "Food is pretty common across all cultures at funerals. In the U.S. south, where I grew up, food is a huge part of the after funeral ritual."

"Food, yes. But, those older rituals are ancient history in Korea," Yu-na said, her voice becoming more agitated. "Not today. This century. No one seriously believes in those...those older ways."

"Maybe it's just an innocent reenactment, or a bunch of older history nerds?" I offered, trying to soften the young woman's rising concern.

"Maybe...do you think...? But, what of that...that child-thing? No, not in this day and age," Yu-na mumbled, half in English and half in Korean.

For another minute, I just looked at the confused young woman as she struggled with her heritage and her culture, myself quite unsure as to what the room, those trappings, and even the obviously disturbing appearance of the odd little child truly meant. Then, seeing that she was on the cusp of some sort of revelation about her understanding, but still hesitant to speak, I decided to relate a few of the odd encounters I had had over the years, hoping to help her see more clearly, and to calm any fears that she might have about confiding in me, a near stranger.

"You know, I was in Ireland years ago, taking a coach tour, not something I usually do, but was glad we did as the driver was quite knowledgeable," I began, thinking back on that odd June day. "Somewhere, about an hour west of Dublin, on a long, straight motorway, newly built, the driver called our attention to an odd bend in the road. A true bend. For no apparent reason, this highly engineered, modern super highway took an odd detour around a craggy old thorn bush in the middle of nowhere. There were no geologic reasons for the bend, no dips in the landscape, no structures to avoid, just this old thorn bush that happened to be dead center of the new road's path. As we weaved around this anomaly on a long, curving crook in the motorway, the driver chuckled and pointed out that no one had taken responsibility for the odd bend in the road and none of the engineers or construction crew had admitted that the bend was there to protect the old thorn bush. Turned out, no one who was born and bred Irish would dare dig it up or bulldoze the thorn bush, out of fear and respect of the old ones, the old spirits. Modern, highly educated men and women. But, still giving a bow to an age-old superstition, that spirits lived in the thorn bush and to cut it down was to bring disaster upon anyone foolhardy enough to do so."

Yu-na simply frowned at me, her face a mix of confused emotions.

"Another time," I continued, trying to soften her concerns about old traditions and mysteries, "years before that, I had the pleasure of living on the island of Crete, in Greece. It was full of superstitions, most of which were remnants of the previous civilizations. Yet, there were times when, jogging on the beach in the evening and looking up at the night sky, you would swear you were looking through great windows into Mount Olympus and the warring gods, and not a thermal inversion as the weather guys would say. It was as real to my eyes as the street scene we are looking at out this window."

"Yes, I know, but...wait, look there!" Yu-na cried, causing a few heads to turn to look in our direction, all of which then turned away.

Across the narrow street, emerging from the shadows of a side alley just to the south of the barbeque restaurant, the old waitress for the private rooms was hustling a young woman, more of a girl, in front of her. The waif of a girl, thin, emaciated, and obviously in dire economic straits, was wearing the scarf of the old waitress, the one that had protected the old woman's neck earlier on her exit.

The young girl looked frightened, but also hungry. Deathly hungry. No doubt the hunger, with a probable promise of a warm meal from the old waitress, was driving the weak girl's faltering steps. As the old woman arrived at the side door, which was opened by the odd little child from earlier, I saw the girl hesitate, and actually start to unravel the old waitress' scarf, but her thin hands were checked by the old waitress, who said something into the girl's ear, causing the young girl to drop her hands listlessly by her side, while her head and shoulders also hung low as she stepped into the doorway, obviously defeated.

As the whisper thin girl was pushed into the restaurant by the old woman, and, as the strange child reached out for her hand, the young girl's eyes turned outward, as if searching frantically for anyone, any soul who might look upon the starving waif with even a modicum of compassion. She turned her head first up the street and then down. Several groups passed, but none seemed to even see the near child only steps away. The young scarecrow's final, pitiful gaze found our little café, and her eyes seemed to burn into mine, and, to my belated realization, Yu-na's, as the restaurant's side doorway slowly swallowed the girl.

Without uttering a word, Yu-na was out of her chair and at the restaurant doorway before I could even stand. I watched with some trepidation as Yu-na then disappeared into the restaurant just a few steps behind the odd group, none of whom had seen Yu-na, as the old waitress and the boy were focused on the waif.

For the briefest of moments, I wondered to myself if it might be better to simply walk away and not get involved in whatever cultural conflict was imminent. After all, I had just met Yu-na and, arguably, had more in common with the two ajummas in the familiar restaurant, than with the newly met young grad student.

Yet, my southern United States upbringing and my simple sense of fair play would not let me abandon the young student, even if she didn't want, or need my help.

Sighing lightly, I left a small bill for a tip and stepped into the bustling street. Looking longingly at the next street, just over where a closer taxi stand stood, I shrugged, and made my way through the crowds, and then through the side door to the restaurant. As I entered, I looked around, but did not see Yu-na, nor the old woman and her young charge, nor the odd boy.

I then turned to head to the back rooms when the younger of the two ajummas found me and tried to drag me to an open table just beyond the door. I thanked her and begged off, but the ajumma was persistent. I finally had to be firm and, standing my ground, told the kind, old proprietor that I had to see the fourth room.

Silenced, the younger ajumma only bowed low and, walking backwards, bowed and apologized and bowed some more. Never connecting with my gaze after I had mentioned the fourth room.

As I passed the kitchen door, the clumsy waiter appeared and blocked my way to the back rooms. Feigning being unable to understand my broken Korean or demanding gestures, the waiter managed to delay my progress for a full minute.

Finally, with the curtained doorway of the fourth room only a meter or so away, I simply pushed by the waiter, who finally acquiesced and did not try to stop me.

At the curtain, where a tiny pair of dirty street clogs had joined the original three sets of shoes, I reached out without hesitation and, grabbing the fabric, silk from the feel of it, pulled it aside and stepped into the room.

Into the past.

Some distant, unknown, and, to me, unrecognizable past.

To my left, the ornate structure that I had seen earlier and that Yu-na had mentioned was an altar, was full of incense and offerings of food, random household items, books and pens, and what looked like cash. Lots of cash.

To my right and just before me, the long, ornate table was missing the food from earlier, but held all manner of other items, very few of which I recognized, so I didn't waste any brain power there.

To the far right and near the back of the cavernous room, I saw Yu-na in heated discussion with the old waitress. Yu-na, who had evidently pulled the young waif away from the old waitress and appeared to be defending the girl, was being backed into the deeper recess of the room by the old woman and the strange child, who seemed taller and thinner in the dim light of the private room.

The old couple was nowhere to be seen, but a large table or block of some sort was positioned in the deep recess, just behind Yu-na and the old waitress.

At that moment, Yu-na suddenly saw me, grimaced at the old woman, and, grabbing a bundle of what looked like reeds from the table, shoved the strange child back and pushed the skinny girl in my direction, yelling as she did so.

"Get her outside! Outside! Now!" Yu-na called, with a commanding, no nonsense voice. "Don't touch the boy!"

Recognizing that Yu-na seemed to be fully in control of the older waitress and the now truly weird, even taller child, and didn't need my help, I followed her command and, grabbing the skinny girl by her far too thin, bony waist, I stepped outside of the room.

Holding the curtain open and spying the younger of the two ajumma's just entering the kitchen, I called to the familiar face to take the girl.

The ajumma was obviously confused to see me standing there and was certainly bewildered by the waif of a girl I was thrusting in her direction. The ajumma stood frozen until I barked the order again and fished out the equivalent of twenty dollars to sweeten the request.

Whether it was the commanding voice or the hefty bribe, the younger ajumma stepped over, took the girl, objected to, but took the money, and then dragged the girl into the kitchen and disappeared.

I then turned back to the scene in the room, which now included an even older woman sitting in front of the ornate altar, holding incense in her left hand and, swaying side-to-side, chanting something unintelligible. Around this new apparition, a thick black cloud of nearly mesmerizing smoke seemed to sway with her motions.

The chanting then permeated my every pore, even though it was gibberish to my ears. I seemed to suddenly have very heavy feet as I stepped into the room and slowly made my way over to where the old waitress was literally pulling Yu-na into the deeper recess at the back of the room.

The old waitress' face showed a horrid, twisted grimace, with malice and hate filling her now bloodshot, reddened eyes. The odd child was nowhere to be seen.

Once I had reached Yu-na, I grabbed the old woman's arms and separated her from her young prey, shouting at her in my best Korean to stand back.

The old waitress seemed to see me for the first time and, instead of fighting to continue to drag Yu-na into the recess, the old woman relented, bowed low to me, and, turning, dove headfirst into the dark recess.

Dove?

My head was beginning to ache from the other woman's incessant chanting and strong, sickly sweet incense, so I thought I had been mistaken.

A splash.

Water?

Behind the room?

I felt Yu-na pulling at my arm and calling, as if from a far off distance, to get out of the room.

As Yu-na struggled to drag me back toward the doorway, the kindly old man from earlier appeared out of the blackness at the back of the cave, for, suddenly, quite clearly, I realized I had been looking into a deep cave hidden behind the room, behind the restaurant.

Abruptly, the woman at the altar began hissing, sounding the world like a snake or an angry cat. The smoke around her seemed to sway even more. It then slipped off the altar and slid over my shoes. As I looked down at the smoke, I seemed to see it shimmering with a rainbow of colors, just as scales on a fish might look, or the scales on a…on an eel?

Shaking my head vigorously, I tried to also shake off the feeling that the smoke had somehow wrapped itself around my right leg and was slowly forcing me toward the back of the cave, toward the looming dark maw of a black mouth.

No!

I shouted to myself, and, finding Yu-na's face, which seemed to waver in the shimmering water that was all around me, I shouted again.

No!

As I yelled to myself again, and struggled to remove the crawling smoke from my leg, I heard the old man shout a blunt command to the woman at the altar and the chanting mercifully came to an abrupt halt as the woman, who, for the life of me, looked liked a female version of the strange child from earlier, grumbled something unintelligible and folded herself into a sitting position on a wide cushion just beside the altar.

The smoke on my leg slipped away and returned to linger over the altar, just beside the odd woman.

My head slowly clearing, I finally understood what Yu-na was trying to do and, turning, grabbed her arm to escort her out of the room, only vaguely realizing she was escorting me.

At the door, I turned, and, for some unknown reason, asked a question of the old man, who seemed to waver as well, indicating that my head was not altogether clear.

"Sir, you are of the old ways, so I will not insult you by asking for your assurance that no harm will come to this young lady?" were my words, but in a voice that sounded out of body.

The old man, or rather the old man's head, as that was all I could see of him against the black recesses of the cavern behind him, spoke in his fatherly, kind voice from earlier in the restaurant, and what seemed ages ago.

"Kind young man, you are certainly excused, and I bear no insult from your learned words. And, yes, your friend, and the little sister in the kitchen, are free of any encumbrances, even though your friend is of an old, very old bloodline, and should know her place. And, the little one, like so many countless others whom we graciously save from themselves, will soon be back in the streets, well fed, for a day, maybe two, but soon to suffer unknown fates. You come from a worthy line, and we will not break our vows to you. Go with your gods. We go with ours."

With that, the old man faded into the impenetrable darkness of the back of the cave.

Stepping through the curtain, I had one last glimpse of the altar, which showed that the woman who had been there just a moment before was nowhere to be seen, and that the dark smoke had turned white and grey and was flowing toward the far cavern. Shaking my head, I then turned away fully.

Making our way a few meters into the restaurant from the fourth room, I helped Yu-na into an empty chair at an empty table. I stood over her, facing the private rooms, irrationally waiting for some banshee from a Korean hell to appear and try to claim me, or the grad student, in spite of the old man's assurances.

As I stood there, both the older and younger ajummas appeared with cold water and hot tea and placed them both on the table. Behind them, the young waif followed meekly, her frozen gaze shockingly reminding me of the dead eyes of the sad little painted girl I had turned away from earlier.

After bowing to the two ajummas, ignoring me, and giving Yu-na a longing look, the frightened night fawn of old Seoul darted out the restaurant through the hanging plastic and not the side door of her painful entrance. In seconds, the girl had disappeared into the Hongdae night crowds, the shuffle of her worn out clogs fading quickly into the night.

The two courageous old ajumma sisters then did an odd thing.

Holding hands, they bowed to us, and then walked to the entrance of the bizarre private room we had just exited, stopped barely a stride in front of it, and then bowed low three times, all the while holding hands. As they did so, the curtain bellowed out, as if someone, or some thing, was trying to exit the room, but was held back by the sheer will of the two ajummas.

After the third bow, the old ladies remained bowed, frozen in that position, while the room's curtain gave one last bulging attempt, but then fell straight, undisturbed, eerily unmoving.

"We...we need to go," Yu-na suddenly spoke, but softly, her hand gripping my arm for support as she pulled herself out of her chair. "They will remain like that until we are at least a block away."

Still a bit numb from the bizarre room, I decided to err on the side of Yu-na's judgment and nodded. Stepping around the table, I put myself between Yu-na and the private room guarded by the ajummas as we exited.

Arriving at the door, I took a look around at the chattering patrons, the mostly young and the few middle-aged, and wondered if anyone suspected what had just happened. No one had looked our way. No one had called out. The bowing of the old ladies seemed to be ignored by all. Even the clumsy waiter was back, weaving between the tables, oblivious to us and to the bowing ladies at the back of the restaurant.

Holding the hanging plastic open for Yu-na, I looked out into the street at the Hongdae throngs, full of young students arming themselves for the modern age, with the best education and the best experiences, just as Yu-na and our mutual friends had said earlier in the evening. None seemed to carry superstition and fear as companions. Their burdens all seemed just a lust for life and the next new thing.

Standing in the street, with the young crowd moving around us, the blast of cold air helped clear the final strands of the chanting and incense out of my head. Yu-na also seemed to perk up, and appeared to shake off the effects of her near abduction.

"Police?" I asked, knowing the answer.

"They would just laugh. The room would be cleared, the entrance to the cave hidden too well. No one, including the girl, if she could be found, would side with us. We'd only increase our own…our own danger," Yu-na replied, a small part of her modernistic dreams dying a little in that cold alley of old Seoul. "Let's go, please."

Just as we turned to walk to the subway stop, we both froze when the old waitress from the private rooms suddenly appeared from the side door and glanced our way. She then hid her face from our gazes with her scarf and scurried off to be absorbed by the encroaching darkness of the alley, no doubt in search of another youth for her rituals. As the door slowly closed, the odd little boy, or child-thing, as Yu-na had called him, poked his chubby head out the door and, staring at us, grinned like a drunken sailor, shocking me and causing Yu-na to actually stumble. He then withdrew, a dark haze engulfing him as he slithered back into his lair, waiting patiently, as he had done for millennia, for the next offering.

Shuddering, my mind wrestled with crazy images and confusing thoughts. I helped Yu-na regain her footing and, turning my back, but not my mind, to the restaurant, I helped the young student down the street, hoping we were headed in the right direction, but knowing we were putting physical distance between ourselves and the ancient, hidden rites of that dark, Hongdae alley.

About a block or so away, I finally allowed myself a glance backwards, irrationally wondering if someone, or some vile, hidden, otherworldly companion of the cavern's inmates might be in the crowds passing us. Shaking the crazy thoughts out of my head, I finally let go of Yu-na's arm. Without words, we both acknowledged that we had been lucky, even though I was unsure as to exactly how, or why.

A well traveled, but astounded outsider, an American, and an intelligent, well educated, modern Korean woman, in conflict about elements of her heritage, had both accidently stepped, for the briefest of moments, into a hidden, ancient tradition, born of primeval superstitions from more distant and more violent times. Traditions shockingly kept alive in the dark, secret places of the sleepless city, by those stealthy enough and powerful enough to keep the old rituals alive by hiding them in plain sight.

As we stepped out of the tree-lined, curved alley onto the main thoroughfare, throngs of youth swirled around us. For a few of those young people, when they found themselves down and out, with no more prospects, and abandoned by all, salvation, of a sort, would be offered, and those cast off waifs of the gleaming city would continue to feed the rituals of life and death in the back rooms, shadowy alleys, and all but forgotten, dark caverns of old Hongdae.

INTERLUDE III

As the writer's concluding words echoed into the darker recesses of the enclave, the creature snorted and then picked up a large stick from the ground and proceeded to chew on it, almost like a toothpick, except the beast's use of such a hygiene device gave the writer a fear that the creature would dislodge one of its many diseased teeth.

"Better, human, scribbling. A proper set of goblins and ghouls inhabit the edges of your story's pages. Yes, my cousins still love those darker corners of old Hongdae," the creature hissed, its voice particularly syrupy. "Had my first foreigner, a Russian fellow there, I did. Pudgy chap, so full of soju I nearly collapsed in a stupor. I was young."

Tossing its stick toward the stove, the creature let out what might have been interpreted as a nostalgic sigh, in other circumstances.

"A tale of old superstitions is more to your liking?" the writer asked, wondering how he might be able to alter other tales on the fly to hold the creature's interest.

"The old ones remember. I've heard such stories. After the mourners would depart, easy to slip into the burial rooms and pick out the juiciest of the wretches left there as the sunjang offerings, sacrifices," the creature added, its eyes bulging with the thought. "Yes, life was easier for my cousins then, when you humans didn't care much for the lives of others. Not that you value such throwaway lives now. Your story was clear on that. A few of my cast off little ones would have views on that, were they to have views any longer."

The creature snorted again, and then shook its hand and arm at the writer.

"Now, you sad humans hurry up your burials. You throw some old food and a few coins at the departed, after stuffing the morsel with poison so my cousins can't have it," the beast lamented, swaying its head from side to side. "Or you burn them beyond taste, turning them to simply ashes, trapping the fools' lesser morsels."

"Poison?" the writer asked without thinking.

"Talismans. Mudang and baksu scribbles. Saju trinkets for fortune telling. Poison, all," the creature answered, snapping its teeth, which sounded more like several fleshy, rotten fish hitting a dirty counter.

The creature then seemed to drift away, its mind, or whatever occupied its diseased skull, lost in something akin to deep thought.

The beast's reflection did not last long, however.

"You've earned another reprieve, you have, boy. Your right arm, maybe?" the pile of rags then called out as it stood and walked a circuit around the bench, its eyes trained, not on the writer, but on a group of youths who were passing close by at that moment.

Suddenly, the creature stopped by the edge of the trees, and, waving its left arm, seemed to move the branches a bit so as to see the youths more clearly as they climbed the path to Namsan Tower. The creature then reached out and, with its hand and arm appearing to turn into grey mist, stroked the long, copper-black hair of a young college student.

"Was the shaman's hair as shiny as this girl's, boy? Did it have the fragrance of fish? Like this child of the sea? Or, the scent of a thousand boar, as consumed by the fat one just there?" the creature asked, its voice frantic. "Which was it boy?"

"The hair? Oh, neither, good troll-spirit. The shaman's hair was more the image of eels, trapped in a drained pond, like ones we used to see at the edge of the rice fields," the writer hastily replied, trying to pick something that did not remind the creature of any of the students within its reach.

"Eels…? Oh, those slimy little brothers to the land snakes. Yes, I know them. Delightful in their…," the creature answered, then stopped itself and withdrew the mist of an arm and allowed the students to go on their way, unmolested.

The writer watched with disappointment, as the trees seemed to move back and block the momentary escape route. Turning his eyes back to the notebook, his brow suddenly furrowed at the title of the next story and wondered if he should skip it, given its focus on….

"Ghouls, boy! Tell me stories of the ghouls," the creature suddenly demanded, continuing in its pacing around the bench, its tongue clicking. "Most are gone, from Hongdae, I think, or your story would have ended more favorably for my kind and not for your gold draining shaman. Gangnam used to be a favorite haunt of those hideous cousins. So many souls were snatched from the self-important. But, alas, when the humans became even more ghoulish in their business and home life than my cousins, well, it was only a matter of time before they were unable to tell which was which. One of my uncles used to tell me he knew of two of the last old school Gangnam ghouls, who haunted that street, somewhere in Sinsa-dong, full of ginkgo trees and coffee shops, since ghouls love ginkgo trees in the fall, as the stench from the fallen berries of the females hides the stench of the ghouls lurking about in the alleys."

"The last two?" the writer asked at the creature's pause.

"What?" the creature asked, seemingly confused. "Oh. Yes, the last two were so confused by the bile and self-serving greed of the humans…they were so confused one night that each latched on to the soul of the other and, before they realized it, sucked the soul right out of each other, fading into that nothingness from which no one returns."

"Oh, that's a pity," the writer offered. "Souls, though? I was not aware such, uh, entities had souls."

"Souls. Life force. Whatever drives the inside. It has many names, boy. Tell me a story about the soul eaters, you have?" the creature then asked, stopping at the end of the bench and sliding onto it, draping an arm on the writer's shoulder as the beast sniffed the air around the writer. "Do your flimsy pages have a story on my lesser cousins? Or, do I need to light the firebox?"

The creature's grin was so intense, the writer could see one of its gruesome teeth being shoved sideways, nearly out of the beast's mouth, like the under bite of a Shih-tzu puppy, but, without the cuteness.

Shaking off a sudden shiver, the writer nodded, and, running his finger down the story listing, he struggled to contrive a ghoul out of one of the remaining tales. He had some draft notes for a tale that might work, but was not satisfied he could alter it enough to appease his captor.

Finally, hitting on an idea that would only require a few embellishments of an existing tale, the writer looked back at the creature with what he hoped was as grim a look as the beast's, and nodded.

"A tale of mystery and ghouls, wretched troll-goblin, I have for you," the writer answered. "Pray sit back, and imagine yourself on a brief day trip out of the noisy, bustling city, and, as in the days before the grand airport with its modern flying machines, you've traveled to old Incheon for a beach picnic amongst the former gun emplacements and war batteries. Yes, just sit back and close your eyes, if you will, or not, and imagine how you and others long for the bustling fish stalls, shouting market hawkers, expansive parks, and silent battlements of a long lost Incheon, from before the shiny new glass and steel of yet another manufactured city. Yes, sit and listen to a brief tale of Incheon, between the old and the new."

4

THE FISHMONGER OF INCHEON

About an hour and a half by train or car from Mount Namsan, in the old Chelumpo section of the western coast, the shining beacon of the new city of Incheon had been growing for several decades, leaving its almost rural, coastal village identity far behind in favor of the Seoul city fathers' vision of a mega-city to rival downtown Seoul. While only a scattering of the older haunts had survived the march of progress, those in the know can search them out and enjoy a fleeting experience of old Incheon, before the glass and steel, and the added 'e' in the name on English maps. Those encounters are brief, however, and, unless you know someone who knows someone, finding the few shops, fish markets, small restaurants, and quiet bars from the old days is nearly impossible. Fortunately, there is one fish shop still near where outsiders might pass that harkens back to the old days. Close to the older lanes, not far from the water, with no fancy, lighted sign, the old shop, with a small restaurant, happily admits any customer who can find its shaded doorway amongst the neon flash and tourist traps of the modern Incheon waterfront. Not far from the former garrison island of Wolmido, but not too far south, the more modern waterfront shops leading to the fishmonger's place are usually all shuttered early in the morning. However, a savvy visitor could find the place by following the night fishermen as they emerge from the early morning's grey mist to deliver their catches, usually routine, but, sometimes, very expensive, exclusive bounty, and, other times, the trash fish of the sea. Whatever Pungeo-shin, the fishing god, provides. One of those traditional fishermen was calling at the shaded door of the small fish shop, a shop many a stranger to the area would pass by in search of brighter fare. Just there, down the lane, beyond that old column, near the quickly fading memory that was old Inchon.

"Hey, oy!" called the grizzled, leather-faced fisherman to the darkened interior of the small shop, in a voice worn salty and throaty from decades in the open sea air. "Only have a minute. Get your catch, you lazy pig farmer."

The old fisherman laughed at his little joke, knowing his long time friend, somewhere inside the darkened interior, would also get a chuckle, while relishing that the resident mother-in-law would be highly offended at the humorous slight.

"Find your own way, you bloated son an octopus, you!" a muffled voice called from the darkened shop. "Can't turn on the lights until the hour. Mother-in-law rules."

"Ha, ha!" laughed the fisherman, who had been joined by a younger apprentice, who grumbled as he tugged at his boss to get moving to the large, modern fish market a few blocks away.

The old fisherman laughed off the apprentice and, waving at the awkward, anachronistic, wheeled cart, indicated one of the choice bins holding the top catch. The apprentice then grudgingly grabbed the large bin full of still wriggling fish and, under the boss's watchful eye, dragged the bin through the darkened door.

"Light! Light, you old miser," called the fisherman as he squinted in the doorway, listening to the apprentice drag the bin through near darkness to the shop's main display cases, which emitted just enough low-level light to see to walk by.

Suddenly, the entire shop sprang into full view with the illumination of the shop's main overhead lights. Old, somewhat battle-scarred by years of hard work, the shop was, however, quite clean, with pristine, if dented, shelving, clean cases, spotless cabinets, and a few wobbly, but clean old tables and metal navy chairs left over from occupation days.

The walls of the small shop held a few faded, cheaply framed photos from a bygone era, several nautically themed watercolors done by some long forgotten student, and a couple of weathered fish nets draped for effect, which seemed unnecessary in a place that reeked of fish. The few tables were bare, except for miss-matched ashtrays and random bottles of simple sauces. The counter, near the cash box, held a vase of fresh flowers, white and yellow daisies, which brightened up the small room with a touch of light.

Sitting atop an old sea chest wedged into the far corner, the resident cat, a large, lithe animal of Siamese and possibly tabby street cat heritage, watched over the shop with imperious demeanor. The old fisherman nodded to the sleepy guardian, as he had done a thousand times, then called out to his friend.

"Ah, must be the witching hour," chuckled the old fisherman as the apprentice shoved the sloshing bin into the center case, slammed the case shut, and turned to leave.

"Wait, wait," the fisherman demanded, placing his weathered right hand on the younger man's shoulder. "We must say good morning to our friend."

From somewhere overhead, heavy footsteps were heard moving from the front, street side of the shop's building to the back, then on creaking stairs as someone descended from the first level of three floors of living quarters over the shop, to the sales floor and small restaurant below.

"Greetings, you old shrimp bait," the voice from earlier called from a deep corridor at the rear of the shop.

Suddenly, the voice's owner appeared at the doorway, bringing with him an air of strength and optimism, surprising for so early in the morning. He was not too fat and not too thin. Taller than most of his peers, with a full head of still naturally black-brown hair, piercing brown eyes, leather skin showing years of baking in the sun on the sea, and clothes that fit the job. His fishmonger smock, old LL Bean boots, authentic, not Itaewon knock offs, and his heavy canvass jeans all screamed of fish and fish guts. Decades worth.

After an obligatory scratch of the shop mascot's ears, and a quick glance to inspect the load just deposited in the center case, the lord of the small shop grumbled his thanks.

"Well, I doubt any of these puny minnows will sell. Maybe the beggar woman of Wolmi will trade some colorful bits of sea glass for them," the fishmonger grumbled at his friend, raising his eyes at just the right moment to give a telling wink.

"Why, you old buzzard. These are the finest gulbi you will see this season," declared the old fisherman. "Hmph! Maybe I'll just pass you by tomorrow morning?"

"Aye, see that you do, old man. You need new glasses if you think these puny excuses for fish are worth more than the foam on our last beer," countered the fishmonger, who then walked over and gave the fisherman a resounding clap on the shoulder.

Both men then chuckled at their morning routine, while the young apprentice simply rolled his eyes at his boss and the eccentric fishmonger. The two older men then sat at the sturdiest of the tables and spoke of small things. The fisherman related the various ups and downs of the morning run and the fishmonger related the juiciest gossip for the fisherman. After only a couple of minutes, the two men then stood, shook hands instead of bowing, and parted ways.

The apprentice noticed the envelope as the fisherman shoved the payment into his jacket. One day, the apprentice thought, he'll actually see that fishmonger hand that envelope over. Odd how that is never seen, thought the younger man, as he backed out of the shop, giving the older shopkeeper a quick, but respectable bow.

"Can we just go?" the apprentice asked when his boss paused at the doorway. "I don't know why we have to drag this smelly old cart, when Chin-hae gets to drive the bulk of the catch over to the market. And, this alley always gives me the jitters. I'd swear someone is always lurking about here, watching us. Maybe ready to jump us."

"Get on, with you," called the fisherman, taking a swipe at the youth's head. "I'll be along. Get on and don't forget to tell Chin-hae to sign in with the foreman!"

With that, the apprentice shrugged off his skittishness and, lifting the cart's long poles, began wheeling the mid-century relic the remaining two blocks to the monstrous fish market. Looking back at the shop, the apprentice watched as his boss stepped out of the shop backwards, bowed twice to the empty door and, licking the back of a piece of paper in the man's right hand, stuck a yellow and red paper on the doorjamb, but just under the curtain that hung there. The boss then turned and hurried after the apprentice, who jerked his head back around so that the boss would not yell at him for having snooped.

The fisherman caught up with his apprentice after just a block and, for good measure, whacked the youth on the back of his head.

"Hey, up? What's that for?" the apprentice complained. "I'm wheeling here. I'm wheeling. Just as you said."

"That's for snooping on me, after," the youth's kindhearted, but stern boss replied. "And, if you weren't, it's to remind you to not snoop on me."

With that, the two men fell silent as they covered the remaining block to the grand, expansive, modern fish market, and disappeared for the morning, with hundreds of their brethren, into that cavernous mecca of seafood and seafarers.

Back at the shop, the fishmonger appeared at the door, just on the threshold, looking after his long time friend and the young apprentice. The old man then looked back down the long street that, in its glory days, had been little more than a worn, wood and concrete pier before the city had reclaimed the land, laid out a paved street, removed the old gun emplacements, and installed a family park where boats used to lay in repair.

Sighing at the fading old days, as he had done every morning for decades, the shop owner then turned, his shoulder brushing the spot where his friend had pasted the bit of paper against the doorjamb. Staring at the feeble writing and the tell-tale symbols used by old Jihee, the fortuneteller of Water Lane, the shop owner almost ripped the paper down. But, thinking of his friend's concern and smiling at his friend's continued battle with the fishmonger's imagined foes, the old man patted the paper instead and mumbled a quiet thanks to his friend as he stepped back into the shop.

After the fishmonger had returned to the peaceful interior of the shop, the only indication to passerby that the shop was open was a small sign, white with black lettering, written in Hangul, English, Russian, Chinese, Japanese, and French, declaring the nearly hidden establishment 'Open.'

About a quarter of an hour after the fisherman's visit, the old grocer, whom the fishmonger had known for nearly forty years, also appeared at the door and, in a similar ritual as the fisherman, bantered with the fishmonger, handed over choice vegetables, took his payment, cash, of course, and quickly departed. However, before he left, the grocer also performed a small ritual at the door and, just like the fisherman, pasted, using clear tape instead of spit, another talisman to the other side of the door.

Over the next hour, two other shopkeepers, one who sold the fishmonger the oil for his cooking, and the cleaner who kept the few uniforms fairly free of fish guts and blood, also stopped by, and, yes, they also carried out small, separate rituals, and pasted small bits of paper at the sides of the main door as they departed.

Each time, the fishmonger would appear after the other shopkeepers had departed, look at their superstition-laden postings on his doorjambs, shake his head, consider ripping them down, but then duck back into the shop, leaving the bits of paper where they hung.

As the foggy morning progressed into a mid-day partial haze, quite a few locals, mostly older housewives, came, lingered for a few moments while making their small purchases, many on credit as times were always hard for Seoul's exploding population of older couples and single older ladies, and then went on their way. Once in a while, one of the older couples would sit at one of the tables and the fishmonger would cook their purchase for them. Often the older couples would eat a small bit of the cooked fish and then wrap up the rest to take home for dinner with some rice, a few pickled veggies, and, of course, homemade kimchi.

Only rarely did any of the customers linger more than the time needed to purchase and have the fish cooked, or to take a quick cup of tea or a small bite. Most observers would attribute that to the shop owner's gruff manner and near total lack of customer service skills. The locals obviously loved the shop and tolerated the owner, so the place, in spite of its odd location away from most of the other shops and restaurants, was always moderately busy.

Yet, somehow, on that particular day, a day of no outward significance, a day like so many others in the work-a-day world of Seoul's laboring classes, none of the fishmonger's friends or longtime acquaintances had any desire to linger too long at the old man's shop. Most who knew him and were not incidental shoppers, actually appeared to rush their small orders and depart, shielding their gazes from the old man's talisman laden door frame.

Of the few customers who did tend to linger, the single ladies, mostly older women of the same age as the fishmonger, who had either lost their husbands through death or, as is all to common in Seoul, divorce, or had never married, would linger and try to offer their help, hoping, in some small way, to kindle a late in life romance with the man, or, as often as not, simply wanting to have a conversation with someone other than one of their old lady peers. The shop owner, just at the end of the traditional three-year mourning window, simply smiled at the ladies' mostly good intentions, but avoided anything else. However, on that particular day, the single ladies were more standoffish and even the old man's most ardent pursuers curtailed their lingering.

Throughout the day, some of the customers were treated to a rare sighting of the shop owner's aged mother-in-law taking the small dog, a terrier of dubious, but expensive parentage, out for a morning walk, or, rather, to supervise one of the local urchins to whom she paid a small sum to walk the little creature, collect its droppings, and generally nod at the old woman's comments and observations. Later visitors would catch the imperious old lady when she would be heading out with other older women to lunch, shop downtown, or attend some church function. Prior to such grand departures, she would spend three or four minutes gently verbally abusing the fishmonger, to ensure anyone within earshot knew that the mother-in-law, in spite of her daughter's passing, was still calling the shots in that household, and was keeping the fishmonger on a short tether. In addition, her domineering actions ensured the ladies who might have romantic intentions toward her son-in-law were always ready to flatter the mother-in-law and express sympathy at her recurring lamentations of advanced age.

The old man's mother-in-law was particularly fond of taking the poor man to task over his generous extension of credit to the growing number of the less fortunate in the neighborhood, almost, but not quite, embarrassing the fishmonger by publicly alluding to her having to pay some recent domestic bill or small extravagance out of her late husband's ample pension and holdings. While she was careful to never directly insult the shopkeeper, she certainly pushed the social envelope a bit.

For his part, the fishmonger, usually gruff and blunt with customers, was painfully polite and went out of his way to ensure the comfort of the mother-in-law, often to his own discomfort. Yet, he suffered in stoic silence and even his closest friends had never heard the man say one ill word against the badgering old battle axe, as some of his friends had labeled her, or even hint at any displeasure of her perceived ill treatment of him. Many of his friends had lobbied for the shopkeeper to ship the bothersome woman, as they saw her, off to one of her absent sons' homes, one far to the south, in Busan, the other even farther, in America, arguing that the sons had well paying jobs, nice homes, and doting wives the mother-in-law could dominate instead of the fishmonger.

However, the fishmonger would have none of it, to the continual puzzlement and frustration of his friends.

The man's secret to surviving his mother-in-law's never-ending harangues?

Love. Yes, true love.

The old fishmonger, in spite of his outward appearance, had dearly loved his deceased wife. Even with her gone to the heaven she had deserved after years of backbreaking labor on the boats and then in the shop, the old man still loved that woman dearly. His wife had loved her mother and, on her dying bed, had worried about what would become of the old woman once the daughter had passed on and the husband's obligation had ceased. The old fishmonger had assured his dying wife that the mother-in-law would always be part of his house and that he would never turn her out.

The mother-in-law, of course, knew of her daughter's wishes and her son-in-law's vow, so was free to lord over the man every waking minute, even when she napped most of the mid-day, slumbering in the expensive massage chair, Japanese made, of course, that he had gifted her several summers before.

Sometime after the lunch hour, one of the mother-in-law's lady friends, a few years younger, from the same high school, so was often fawning over the older woman, arrived at the shop, spoke briefly to the owner, and then stood by the entrance and waited. After a few minutes, the slow creaking of the rear stairs under the dowager's weight, which was not of an unusual amount, but was taxing on the ancient stairs, signaled that the empress of the house was ready for her excursion.

The obligatory nagging of the fishmonger was oddly good-natured for a change, after the old woman had paused and had briefly closed her eyes when she had seen the simple display of daisies, her daughter's favorite flowers. The mother-in-law then shuffled her way to the door, pulling her shawl around her shoulders at a sudden chill that settled on her and her fawning friend as they passed through the doorway.

"Mother, please be home before dark," the fishmonger called from the cashbox stand. "There may be a storm coming."

"Daft man! There's nary a cloud in the sky, and the weather reports speak of no rain until Sunday," the old woman called back through the doorway, her gaze momentarily resting on one of the talismans, then darting back to her friend. "Storm indeed. Hmph!"

With a knowing look to her visibly subservient, younger friend, the old matriarch of a house of two shuffled along the street, holding the arm of her friend as she was led to the small grey car parked just at the corner. Stepping into the car, helped by her friend and another little lady who had been waiting by the open car door, the old woman paused and looked back at the shop, rubbing her eyes when she thought she saw a drifting shadow of a woman just beyond the doorway.

Could it be…?

No, the old woman told herself. Just a little bit of indigestion from the morning's rice porridge and salmon, she thought, as she settled into the back seat of the car.

As the small car slowly left the curb and entered the mid-day Incheon traffic, the old woman did turn her head back to stare at the shop until it had faded into the jumble of storefronts and warehouses that populated much of that part of working Incheon.

Back at the shop, several youths had arrived at the doorway, with one, obviously not a local from his blond hair and nearly six-foot tall frame, arguing with the others to try the fishmonger's shop. The others were arguing for the vast diversity, and more girls, at the large public market just a couple of blocks away. But, the blond youth, waving what appeared to be an old photo, was steadfast, and ducked into the shop. His three friends all finally threw up their hands in surrender, and followed him in.

Once inside the quaint, rough looking shop, the three friends renewed their efforts to extract the blond youth.

"Seriously, Jim, who knows how old the stuff is they serve here…?" Yong said under his breath to the tall blond youth.

"Or, if it's even fish," Kwan added, turning his nose up at the imagined stench of the place.

"Look at those tables? Do you think they could ever be germ free?" Cho suggested, grimacing in mock revulsion.

"Help you?" the fishmonger called loudly and bluntly from behind the counter, the large butcher knife and spots of fresh fish blood on his smock convincing Jim's friends to quickly fall silent.

"Yes," Jim answered, waving his friends to one of the many free tables. "Yes, we'd like some of…well, what do you recommend for a small, late lunch?"

The fishmonger, while old and gruff, had an immense database of faces and names in his head, and the youth seemed to match one from many, many years before. The shopkeeper did not answer the youth right away, but stepped from behind the counter, large knife still in hand, and leaned close to the blond youth, staring at the young man's face.

"Your father?" the fishmonger suddenly asked. "He was at the American base in Suwon? No, not Suwon. Osan? Yes, he was at the base in Osan?"

Shocked at the apparent immediate recognition, the youth stepped back and gasped in surprise.

"Yes! How…? Seriously, after all these years?" Jim replied. "My dad is not going to believe this!"

Jim then pulled the picture he had been waving at his friends out of his pocket and offered it to the fishmonger, who looked down at it and smiled. The fishmonger then nodded, dropped the knife behind the counter on the wide cutting board and, wiping his hands on his apron, turned to the cashbox and, banging it on the side, opened the drawer, picked it up, and rummaged through a stack of old papers hidden underneath.

After a moment's searching, the old man let out a grunt of victory and extracted another photo, an old Polaroid print, somewhat faded.

Holding out the old photo, the fishmonger placed it beside Jim's picture. It was a match.

The two photos, obviously taken at the same time, were of two young men, one Korean and one American, with the shop and street scene behind the two from another era.

"Your father...?" the fishmonger asked, hesitantly, as so many he had known had already passed away.

"Quite well, thank you, sir," Jim answered. "He's getting on in years, of course, but he sends his best wishes and I would have been carrying a letter if he had had enough warning of my last minute trip."

"Good, that's good, young...?" the fishmonger asked.

"Jim, sir."

"Jim...that's it. Jim. Yes, I remember," the old man replied, looking back to the photo. "I keep it in the drawer, now. It started to fade, years ago. Never thought I'd see you again, Jim...I mean, see his son."

The old man seemed to be drifting back to the old days, the days of his own youth, so the tall American remained silent.

"It was over that time after the president had been...well, in those days it was not unusual for the presidency to change hands through means other than elections," the fishmonger said. "Your father used to visit the base up there. Once or twice a month, for the year or so he was in Korea. He would stop here maybe once a month. Sometimes twice. With his friend. Darker hair. Wore glasses. Do you...?"

"I'm sorry, no, I don't know who that might be, but I can ask," Jim replied, taking out his phone. "Was he Air Force, too?"

"Yes, I think so," the fishmonger replied.

However, before Jim could send a text or ask the shop owner for a photo, and before the fishmonger had fully recovered from the shock and surprise of a fresh face from the past appearing out of the blue, especially on that particular day, a loud bang came from the front of the store, as if something had crashed into the door or the small terrace wall skirting the edge of the pavement.

Bang! Clang!

Again, a confusing noise came through the door, causing the old man to turn away from the youth, apologize, and step outside.

As the fishmonger stepped into the muted brightness of the overcast daylight, quite a spectacle was unfolding in front of his shop.

Two of his shopkeeper neighbors, one who sold trinkets and snacks to the tourists in a small, New York style bodega a block or so up the road, and the other a more proper, in his own mind, businessman who owned a string of three bakeries, were fighting over what appeared to be a large temple drum or wide bowl gong, the fishmonger could not see it clearly. The snack shop man seemed to be getting the advantage over the baker when the fishmonger waded into the two combatants and, with immensely strong arms, dragged the two men apart from each other, shook them forcibly a couple of times, and then released them.

"You two old...! Do you realize what it looks like to have two old geezers fighting like children in front of my shop?" the fishmonger grumbled at the two disheveled men, while trying to hold back a sudden urge to laugh at their antics. "Have you no shame? At your age?"

"Was my idea!" declared the pouting owner of the small baking empire.

"Your idea? My drum, you portly pile of spoiled dough...," the snack shop owner retorted, grabbing the large, kettle shaped object from the ground.

"It was my money that paid the mudang...," the baker began, but then clammed up when he realized what he had said.

Both men then immediately forgot their differences and turned to their friend, the fishmonger, and began to talk over each other as they tried to explain their way out of an apparent corner.

"It's not what you think...!"

"We've only just been walking by and happened to...."

"Think of the children...."

"The children...?"

"What the old woman will do if she finds out...."

"Which old woman...?"

After a bit, the two colleagues began arguing about how they should explain away the little altercation and the odd presence of a temple drum. In fact, they became so heated in their disagreement on how to explain their earlier disagreement that the two men appeared to be ready to grapple on the pavement again.

"Inside, the both of you!" roared the fishmonger, in his old sailing voice, which shook the two men, and any passerby, to their very core.

Looking sheepish, the two men nodded and, with a quickness of step unexpected in men of such well-fed nature, the two ducked inside the doorway, both pausing briefly to inspect the talismans posted there.

Once inside, the two men found that their favorite table, one they and other friends had considered their special table, was occupied by three insolent looking youths and a suspicious looking American.

Cho, quick to catch the meaning in the eye of the snack shop owner, nudged his friends and they all moved to another table, a respectable distance from the older men, or about one and a half meters in the small dining area.

Once the fishmonger had joined the two older men, he looked over at Jim and, smiling, gave Jim a look that let the youth know the fishmonger would pick up their conversation shortly, as soon as he had straightened out the two old shopkeepers. The fishmonger then pointed at the drinks cooler and waved the four youths over to pick out something to tide them over while he sorted out the two old men.

For a couple of long minutes, the fishmonger simply sat across from his two friends with his arms crossed, his hard gaze digging equally into the very souls of the two men.

Finally, the baker, who had already proven he was a softer touch, blurted out their defense.

"You know what day it is. We…we had to!" the baker stated, his voice a little high pitched and in obvious discomfort sitting in the shop. "Can we talk outside…?"

"You?" the fishmonger then asked of the snack shop owner.

"Young cousin is right, you know. Today is the day. Were we to simply stand by?" the snack owner answered, his voice more challenging. "Besides, she's my wife's cousin."

"How much did she take you for?" the fishmonger gently demanded.

"Pennies. Mere pennies…," the baker responded, shifting his chair until he was directly under one of the overhead lights. "Really, can't we talk outside?"

"How much?"

"Less than the going rate. Thirty percent discount," the snack shop owner replied. "A bargain."

"And the drum?"

Both men looked around the room and tried to escape the fishmonger's gaze.

"The drum…?" the fishmonger repeated, slowly.

"Borrowed…," the baker replied, his voice low.

"Borrowed? From…? No? Not…not that?" the fishmonger replied, letting a long sigh escape.

"They'll not miss it until tonight. Really," the snack owner replied, waving off the fishmonger's accusing gaze. "We're taking it back before then."

"And do what? Sit outside my door until…?" the fishmonger began, but, looking over at the four youths, cut off his question.

The fishmonger then waved his two friends into silence and stood. He walked over to the display cases and tapped on the glass above the gulbi.

"These just came in this morning, Jim. I will fry these up for you and your friends," the fishmonger called. "Only a minute. You might want to eat on the terrace seating, those three small tables just to the right of the door as you exit. Fresh air, you know."

Cho, still the fastest thinker in his group, nodded and bowed as he stood and waved his friends out to the small terrace. Jim smiled and gave the fishmonger a wave as well, signaling they could take up the semi-reunion once the older man had finished the mysterious arbitration with his two shopkeeper friends.

Once outside, Jim took the opportunity to explain to his friends that his father had frequented the old fish shop years before, when his father had been in the U.S. Air Force, assigned to a large air base south of Seoul. The shop owner and Jim's father had developed a brief friendship, which had faded over the years in the time before instant communication. Fast forward decades later and Jim was studying in Hong Kong and had made a last minute trip to Seoul with some classmates. After talking with his father, Jim had insisted on taking the train out to Incheon that morning. Once Jim had explained the side trip, which he had hesitated doing so earlier as to not jinx trying to find the old shop, his friends relaxed and focused on the few passing girls heading to the more popular, modern market a couple of blocks away.

Back inside the shop, the fishmonger quickly prepared several choice fish for the son of his long ago friend and the other youths, while his two shopkeeper friends grumbled at the wait.

At one point, the baker, still skittish about remaining inside the store, made a futile dash for the door, with the fishmonger deftly stepping in the baker's path, and staring him down to return to the table with the snack bar owner to wait.

After only a few short minutes, the fishmonger had completed the frying, plated the hot fish, and, grabbing several bags of crisps and a few small pan chon bowls, put it all on a large tray and stepped outside to serve the youths. On his way out the door, he flicked on the switch to the old radio system that barely squeaked out tunes on decades-old speakers, both inside and on the terrace. He could just make out some boy band singing about something unintelligible, at least to the old fishmonger.

"It's hot, so wait a moment before digging in, young Jim," the fishmonger said, giving Jim's friends a quick look that told them to ensure the foreign guy didn't burn his tongue or the fishmonger would blame them.

Returning to his two friends, the fishmonger sat, took a deep breath, and leaned back in his chair.

"The drum…?" the fishmonger repeated.

"No worries, old cousin," the baker replied. "We've got that covered. Long before midnight, it will be returned."

"So, who is going to watch your shops while the two of you rant about in front of my store?" the fishmonger asked, sarcasm dripping from his words.

"We have assistants who are more than happy to watch the shops," the baker answered, tugging at his over-starched collar and nervously eyeing the door. "So, shouldn't we be sitting outside, with the drum and the incense?"

"Modern age superstitions. You two should be ashamed of yourselves," the fishmonger replied. "Although…maybe your antics will attract some curious tourists who will pay too much for an early dinner and floor show."

"Really? You laugh at us? What happens when your soul is dragged from the store, its silent screams unheard by your dead eyes? What then? What then?" the baker suddenly yelled, shocking both the fishmonger and the snack bar owner with the baker's gruesomely poetic speech. "Will you so easily let your entire life's work pass, without a fight, to that dowager who treats you…?"

"No ill words to my wife's mother, young cousin," the fishmonger said in flat, cold tones.

"What of your boy? In Jeju? Don't you want to see his sons some day? Well, when he has them?" the snack bar owner asked, joining the baker's line of questioning. "At least let us, your friends these many decades, try the mudang's ideas."

For a long minute, the fishmonger simply sat and stared at his friends in silence. Behind him, he could hear the low talk of the four youths and the growing bustle of the pavement beyond.

The baker shifted nervously, trying to avert his eyes from looking at any dark corners around the shop. He also avoided looking at the old shop cat, seeing only devilry in its eyes. With cold sweat beading off of his brow, the baker looked as if he'd either fall over dead any moment, or bolt out of the store screaming.

The snack bar owner, a little less imaginative than his friend and much more practical, fidgeted by tapping on the table top with his fingers, roughly mimicking a catchy, older J.Y. Park tune coming over the radio. Finally, he ceased his tapping and, letting out a long sigh, stood, and leaned over the fishmonger.

"Old cousin, I'm taking our doughy friend here outside before his veins burst," the snack bar owner said in a somber, level voice. "We will sit just beyond your store, on the wall, and quietly play the tune the mudang taught us. We will stay until dusk or after…after your guest has either turned away, or entered and taken what he will come for. Whatever happens, old cousin, we will not turn away, nor can you scare us off with your sullen stares and your loud brashness. We are old. Many of our friends have passed. As have yours. We three have been friends for many years. Many of your other friends have left various talismans to help with the visitor, which I see you did not rip away. We can do no less."

The fishmonger, at a loss for words to counter his old friend's sincerity and eloquence, simply nodded gruffly and also stood.

The fishmonger then bowed and, turning back to his counter, waved his two friends out, shielding his misting eyes as the baker dashed past him and the snack bar owner slowly moved to the outside.

Once outside, the two men saw that the youths had taken the most spiritually advantageous position in the small terrace seating, at least, according to the mudang who had advised them. Grumbling, the two men took seats just opposite and, staring at the youths eating the fried fish, bided their time until the four young men would be finished.

A few moments later, the fishmonger emerged to check on the youths and waved off Cho's suggestion that they move again so the two older men could take the seats that were obviously of some value to them.

After the fishmonger was satisfied that the youths were eating well and had said a few words to Jim about his father, the old fish store owner, suddenly showing his age, slowly returned to the shop, pausing briefly to look at the explosion of talismans arrayed around his doorway. He then ducked into the darker interior.

"Hey, Cho, you're the classic scholar," Yong suddenly said. "What's with all those papers by this shop's door?"

Cho almost choked on a piece of fish at his friend's sudden question. He gave Yong a quick look meant to silence his friend, but it only made him more curious.

"Seriously, we have a chance to show Jim here some of our lesser known cultural realities," Yong continued. "What do the papers mean? I know from my grandmother that they are some sort of defense against the dark arts, to cite Rowling."

Cho looked hesitantly at the two older men, one clutching a temple drum, which was normally never out of the temple, and one looking as nervous as a wet cat as he looked back and forth, up and down the street, with such jerking motions that Cho thought the man would crack his own neck. Finally, Cho spoke, trying to keep his voice low.

"Something wicked this way comes," Cho said. "And, I don't mean Ray Bradbury or Shakespeare."

"Something wicked?" Jim asked, his interest in the shop owner genuine, wanting to take back memories to his father, in addition to a few pics he had snapped. "What do you mean?"

Cho, his voice catching, was cut short by another voice, one older and considerably worldlier.

"Payment, young man. Payment for a long overdue debt," the snack bar owner said, while trying to calm the baker. "Whatever you want to call it, in the end, it's simply payment due."

"What sort of debt?" Jim asked, looking back to the front of the shop at the array of strips of paper flapping in the afternoon breeze.

"Cousin!" the baker admonished the snack bar owner's openness with the stranger.

"The boy is the son of old cousin's long ago friend. He can hear," the snack bar owner said. "The others, well, they will never tell."

A sudden stillness settled over the youths and the two old men as the snack bar owner related the events that had led to the two friends arriving that afternoon with a kidnapped temple drum, some overpriced incense, and a long poem or incantation sold to them by one of the pricier mudangs working the western sections of Seoul. Jim and his friends listened in awed silence to the snack shop owner, unsure if they believed what they were hearing, but all four were wise enough, even in youth, to hold back any comments or to cast any dispersions on the two old men, who both seemed to fervently believe what the snack bar owner was saying.

"Some years ago, just after our friend's hwangap, his sixtieth year, his dear wife fell ill. He was distraught. Spared no expense. Don't let this worn old shop fool you. Our friend has long invested well. The doctors, many of the best, passed on her, saying she was beyond treatment. Most suggested a mix of drugs to keep…to keep her sedated to avoid the pain. His son even brought her to Los Angeles for tests, but the results were the same."

"She was an angel, his wife. She complained not once. Her only concerns were for our friend, her child, and her aging mother. She suffered in silence. Took some of the drugs, but hated them as they put her in a stupor, almost like a zombie, she said. So, she slowly began to refuse them. The pain was still there, you could see it in her eyes. For him, every time the pain came, he felt it in his own gut. Watching her agony was slowly killing him, as well."

"The mother-in-law, she was hard on him. Kept urging our friend to use the old ways. To go to the fortunetellers. To use the stars. Well, she was hard, that old dowager. But, oddly, she was probably right, in the end. She had her friends pray for her daughter in church. Donated large sums to her church. Paid scholarships for some of the youths."

"On the other hand, she also contributed to the local temple. She even consulted with the fortunetellers herself. Or, more frequently, through intermediaries as it was unseemly for someone of her high birth to be seen with such elements."

"Nothing worked, of course. Nothing removed or even dampened the pain. She continued to suffer. Our friend continued to decline. He was nearly all skin and bones that night…."

The snack shop owner paused as his voice faltered.

"That night…," the baker chimed in, but then fell silent again as the snack bar owner regained his composure and continued.

"Our friend was at his wits' end," the snack bar owner said, his eyes staring into the distance. "He had one foot nearly in the grave, to quickly follow his wife. I was coming by for a visit, when I heard the cry. Unearthly. Like a newborn crying for his childbirth dead mother's milk that he will never taste. Like the screech of a death owl of old. A horrible sound. A sound of a desperate man's final breath."

The snack bar owner turned slowly to face the doorway, and continued.

"That's when I saw…that's when the visitor arrived. No fanfare. No footsteps. No warning. Just arrived. Smelling, sensing, feeling the abject desperation of our friend."

"The visitor would not step across the threshold. No, such a creature has to be invited in. The…the shadow simply stood there, in that doorway, its tattered robes, witness to so many like our friend, barely stirring in the strong, westerly wind that evening. A little later than now. Just stood there, listening to the deathly cry, the soul wrenching call of our defeated friend."

"I was frozen to my spot on the pavement. I could neither advance, nor retreat. It was, I don't know, macabre fascination? Fear? Blindness? I simply stood, waiting for the inevitable."

"Suddenly, our friend stumbled out of the doorway and swept the shadowy figure to one side, passing his right arm through the creature's rags, and collapsed at the wall, just there. Yet, he remained upright, but quite feeble and stared straight into the black depth's of the creature's shaded face and spoke. Yes, he spoke to the beast."

"'Ease her pain!' our dear friend cried to the apparition. 'And I will take her pain. Take her softly, with no violence in the end, and you can render me from Paektu to Jeju for a thousand years,' he said. With that, our friend then…then slashed his hand on the wall, just there, at that black spot, and dripped the blood from his hand onto the outstretched…I couldn't see clearly…maybe the beast's hand? Our friend then nodded slowly and, standing, bowed to the shadow, only once, and said something that sounded like three years."

Snap!

Snapping his fingers, the snack bar owner shocked the youths and even the baker into jumping.

"Then, gone. Snap! Just like that. I was able to move again and rushed over to my friend. He looked at me as if seeing me for the first time. When the fog had lifted from his eyes, he finally spoke."

"'She will be okay, cousin,' he said, and then turned back into the store."

The snack bar owner then found a chair and sat down, his eyes never leaving the doorway. The baker rose, walked over to his friend, and held the man's shoulder as the baker then spoke.

"She did not recover, of course, from the disease, but her pain did vanish," the baker said in hushed tones. "Her mother attributed it to all the prayers. She lingered for a few more weeks, and was even able to take walks along the old boardwalk from time to time. Our friend, he put on some weight again, as his wife could actually eat, so he ate to encourage her. For a few weeks, they were as youths again. Romantic, happy youths. She passed quietly, one cool evening, not unlike today. In his arms, with her mother and some close friends looking on. Her son was not able to arrive in time, but was here the next morning."

The baker then fell silent, his face a mix of sorrow, with a hint of fear.

"Now, the debt must be paid. The deal closed. Unless...," the baker added, but his voice faltered.

"Unless we can stop it," the snack bar owner continued, his hands closing into fists. "Unless...."

Jim and the youths simply sat quietly, until Kwan was about to make a comment and Cho literally placed his right hand over Kwan's mouth to silence his friend.

"Grandfather, we are honored and humbled that you would share this with us," Cho said, with sincere reverence. "While this is beyond our meager minds, we offer ourselves to help in any way."

"What...?" Kwan managed to mumble, suddenly wondering why his friend just volunteered them to take part in some ancient, scary ritual that probably involved some sort of pain.

"Thank you, young man, but we are ready to confront our own demons and those of our friend," the snack bar owner replied. "Best you all be on your way before dusk falls, however, as we are unsure how the evening will unfold."

"Yes!" Yong exclaimed and stood, placing some cash on the tray to pay for the meal, with Kwan jumping up as well. "Let's go."

"Wait," Jim interjected, then leaned in toward the two old men. "Does my father's friend in there know what the two of you are up to?"

"Yes, and he does not approve, the stubborn old goat," the baker replied. "He is a fatalist. Claims his fate is sealed and, when the debt is due, he will honor it."

"There is something noble in that," the snack bar owner added. "Yet, we can't sit idly by and watch our friend have the life force dragged out of him, before his time."

"With all due respect, sirs," Jim then asked, "whatever event might happen tonight, or however terrifying this visitor might be, do you think your actions can have any effect, especially if the store owner believes as he does?"

"We can only do what friends can do, young stranger," the snack bar owner replied, in a strong, but kindly voice.

The two older men then waved the youths into silence and moved back to their spot closer to the doorway. There the two men sat and spoke in whispers, occasionally tapping the drum as if testing the sound. At the same time, Jim convinced his friends to wait, which they did, in spite of their concerns.

From time to time, the old fishmonger would emerge, have a few quiet words with his friends, throw up his hands, and duck back inside the store, but not before checking on the four youths and exchanging a few words with the young American.

Over the next hour or so, there was a steady trickle of customers. Mostly regulars, who all bowed respectfully to the baker and the snack bar owner before entering the store, and upon departure. A few tourists were attracted by the old men's traditional hats, which had emerged from a large bag the baker had stashed behind the wall, and the soft sounds of the drum, which the snack bar owner had begun to tap continuously as the late afternoon sun had begun to hover lower in the sky above the Yellow Sea.

After badgering their American friend about the time wasted at the shop, the youths eventually managed to convince Jim to take a couple of pictures with the old shop keeper friend of his father, and then head to the large market and other nightspots nearby.

"Right. Only, let me speak to him one last time," Jim asked as his friends were piling cash on the table to pay for the meal.

Just as Jim stood, the fishmonger appeared and, seeing the money, waved the youths off, telling them that the meal was his treat, for the young American bringing back so many good memories from long ago.

"Are you certain we can't pay? No? Okay, but can we…?" Jim asked, holding up his phone to indicate a picture.

The fishmonger grunted approval for the picture and Cho, taking Jim's phone, took several pictures of the old man with the young American. Afterwards, Jim exchanged phone numbers with the old man and, gripping his arm, wished him well.

"Sir, if my father were here, I'm sure he'd spend the rest of the evening with you, remembering old times. I don't have those memories, but am willing to remain until you have more free time to talk?" Jim asked, trying to not look at the baker and the snack bar owner.

The fishmonger, smiling sideways at his two older friends, chuckled and replied.

"Don't listen to what these two old windbags are telling you, young Jim," the old shopkeeper said. "They live in a fantasy world of the fading old days, mixed up with what they hear among the gossips. Go with your friends and enjoy your few days in Seoul. You are young. We were all young men once, even those two. Youth gave me your father as a friend. And, youth, yes, youth gave me my dear wife. Funny thing. Your father was here when I first met her. He always joked that it was his insistence that I walk over to the bakery just there and talk to her. Forced me to buy her flowers, daisies. I, of course, believe it was my own initiative. Whatever the truth, she didn't run away, and we had many, many happy years together."

"Had, sir?" Jim asked, his voice low, respectful, wanting to her of the wife from his father's friend, in addition to what he had already heard.

"Yes. Please let your father know she passed peacefully several years ago," the fishmonger said, his voice resigned, but cheerful. "I don't dwell on her passing, only on joining her one day. Your father will understand. He met her a few times. And, yes, that we have a son. Not much older than you probably are. He lives down south. I just spoke to him...last night."

"I'm so sorry to hear about your wife, sir," Jim replied, making mental notes to ensure he related the story to his father correctly. "I'll let him know. But, sir, I'm happy to spend the rest of the evening chatting. I can meet my friends later?"

"Thank you, young Jim. But, you need to remain in the modern era. I know what you are really saying and, like your father, I respect you for that. But, better that you head out with your friends," the old man replied, with resolve, and, after shaking the young American's hand and nodding to Jim's three bowing friends, he waved them onward toward the market down the road.

"Did the American really do that?" the baker asked after the youths had departed, surprised at the bit of old intelligence he did not know.

"Yes. Well, maybe. It is so long ago, now," the old fishmonger replied, rubbing the back of his neck. "That bakery is long gone, replaced by that noisy arcade. But, maybe."

With that, the fishmonger returned to his daily routine, while his two friends continued to haunt the terrace as dusk approached, and practiced their lines and songs for the evening's supposed event. People came and went as usual. Even a few of the old, romantically inclined ladies stopped in for brief chats as the day drew to a close. The urchin appeared and took the little terrier on its afternoon walk and, upon returning, had to pick up the complaining little animal as it refused to cross the threshold, to the knowing looks of the two old men mumbling incantations. The child then deposited the little pooch at the back stairwell, where it rushed up the flight of stairs to collapse in its bed until summoned to a late supper.

Of particular note, the old part-Siamese cat, a fixture in and around the fish shop, who relished testing the little terrier's resolve by taunting the dog at every opportunity, had remained strangely absent after his initial, early morning appearance. The fishmonger wrote it off to a cat being a cat.

Shortly before the last, orange and red rays of the dying sun painted their final colors on the storefronts of Incheon, the fishmonger's mother-in-law, with her two friends in tow, approached from the parking lot just down from the corner. From their chatter, it appeared the two friends were going to join the mother-in-law for dinner, possibly in the fishmonger's shop, or, more likely, in the quaint little sushi parlor several doors down, owned by another old friend.

As the three old women approached, one of the friends, the one who had collected the mother-in-law earlier, was the first to see the two old men engaged in their odd activity. The little lady immediately tried to steer the older woman away from the shop, even trying to redirect their path across the broad avenue to the seaside pavement. However, the old dowager would have none of it and, once she had seen the two local businessmen decked out in partial traditional dress, her face hardened and she made a beeline for the two older men.

The two men, lost in their whispers and their attention to the mudang's poem and chants, were startled by the abrupt arrival of a formidable shadow cast by the fishmonger's mother-in-law. The baker, nerves already frayed from the extended wait, immediately covered his eyes and wailed at the fearful apparition he thought he saw.

"Oh cruel stench of justice, I humble myself before your terrifying grotesqueness! We beseech your hideous other worldliness to hear our cries for mercy on our friend!" the baker wailed, his eyes covered by his hat as he swayed in rhythm with the tapping on the drum.

The snack bar owner, a little less startled than the baker, stopped his drumming, reached over, and slapped his right hand against the back of the baker's neck to knock the old man out of his babbling reaction to the unknown shadow. Once the baker had dared to lift his eyes, he saw the angry face of the fishmonger's mother-in-law and let out a small squeak of fear. His immediate thought of flight was checked by the snack bar owner and the sudden appearance of the fishmonger himself.

"You old fools!" the mother-in-law scolded the two friends of her son-in-law. "What are you up to now? Trying to get a few won coins thrown at you by the foreigners? What? Are you trying to bring shame to my door? Speak! Bark, you dogs!"

"Mother, really, they mean only to do good," the fishmonger interjected, emerging from the doorway and standing between his wife's mother and his two friends. "They were...they are testing a new poem for the winter solstice, yes, that's it. Testing a new poem."

The snack bar owner nodded in quick agreement with his friend, while the baker just kept bowing and mumbling his apologies to the formidable woman.

For the blink of an eye, the old mother-in-law looked as if she would counter her son-in-law's feeble explanation, but something in the fishmonger's expression stopped her. She leaned in closer to her wife's husband, and, taking her hand, touched his face, drawing her hand back quickly. She then turned to the entrance, seemed to think about something, and then beckoned to her two friends, both of whom were whispering about the talismans they had just seen arrayed around the doorway.

"Sushi! I think I want sushi now. And, maybe tuna jaw," the mother-in-law declared and, letting her gaze linger on her son-in-law and his two friends, she then led her two ladies-in-waiting to the sushi parlor just a few doors down from the store, and disappeared inside.

"She's gone. You can stop demeaning yourself now," the snack bar owner said quietly to the baker.

The baker looked up, uncertain whether to believe his friend and, only after the baker had looked around, and up and down the street, did he sit back up and take a long breath, letting out an even longer sigh of relief.

"Well, gents, it's dusk and the two of you are still here making fools…carrying on like old women," the fishmonger said, watching the final rays of sunlight light up the sea's distant horizon.

For a few moments, none of the men spoke. Only the sounds of the night drifted into the small doorway and terrace, with the dinner crowds beginning to populate the pavement on both sides of the avenue.

The fish shop's guardian alley cat took that moment to decide to appear. He walked over to the fishmonger, rubbed his back on his human's legs and then, instead of heading into the shop to inspect any leavings the owner might have saved for him, the large cat walked over to the two friends, eyed them with a suspicious look, hopped up to a perch on the wall between them, and immediately seemed to fall into a nap. The fishmonger, smiling at the cat's new found affinity for his two worried friends, clucked at the little beast, and then, with his eyes, told his two friends that even the house guardian was bored with their antics.

Suddenly, the baker grabbed the parchment-like paper from the snack bar owner and began reciting the first of several chants the mudang had sold the two men. His grasp of classical, old style Korean was rough, but his sincerity made up for his mispronunciations. The fishmonger and the snack bar owner stared at their distressed friend and moved to take the papers away from him, lest the poor baker faint from overexertion.

Just as the fishmonger's hands touched the papers, the snack bar owner then suddenly began to beat the drum in earnest. No longer simply tapping the instrument, the snack bar friend was slamming his fists into the drum with all his energy, while his face, suddenly drained of all color, stared, transfixed, at something behind the fishmonger, just to the east of the doorway.

The fishmonger, seeing the sincere fright, but iron will of his two friends as they increased their intensity, one reading while one drummed, slowly turned to face whatever had shocked his two, decades-long brethren.

As he turned, the fishmonger could feel a cold wind stir, blowing, not from the sea is it should, but from just beyond his doorway, heralding the arrival of the evening's unwelcome, but inevitable visitor.

Looking at his doorway and beyond, as if looking through a wavy lens of water, the fishmonger caught his breath at the sudden surge of inexplicable pain shooting through his chest. While his eyes began to water from the pain, the fishmonger took one step forward, ready to pay his debt, wondering if he'd actually see the debt collector through the pain and his watery eyes.

Suddenly, the shifting lens before him became clear and the fishmonger was able to see the shadow of the apparition standing at his doorway. Its long, near skeletal hands were flipping through the various talismans, with something like a low, guttural chuckle emanating from where the creature's face would be, were it visible.

Around the little shop, the world seemed to forget the fish shop was even there, with passerby ignoring, or simply not seeing, the shop, the shouts and banging of the two old men, the fishmonger's agony, and the strange visitor's deathly murmuring.

Chuckling continuing, the apparition glided closer to the fishmonger and his two friends and, although both friends faltered at the sudden interest by the visitor, they both, eyes wide open and hearts pounding in their throats, bravely continued their mission unabated and undeterred.

At first, the visitor seemed to just stand, as if it were a passing tax collector admiring a street concert, or watching over a couple of loud children playing in a park. It then seemed to lean in toward the two stand-in shamans, but the fishmonger, the pain etched on his face increasing, stepped in between the shadowy figure and his friends.

Although a red glaze was beginning to cover his eyes, and biting fingers of deathly cold were crawling up his legs and his arms, he challenged the visitor to honor their bargain, and demanded the wraith ignore his friends as harmless distractions.

"Old one...old one, you are here to settle our debt, not to toy with those who do not understand you," the fishmonger called to the figure, in a voice both strong and remarkably youthful. "Take my life's silver. Drag my beating heart into the black depths. My friends will understand one day why I do not fear you, but thank you and praise you for giving my dear one a few moments of freedom. An eternity of agony is a small sacrifice for her comfort and peaceful passing, old one. Leave these two to their superstitions. Leave them to their own lives, hopefully long."

The baker, reaching out with his free hand, attempted to drag the fishmonger away from the visitor, but found that the fishmonger's flesh was cold and rigid, immobile. Jerking his hand back, the baker started shouting the incantations at the top of his lungs, with the snack bar owner increasing his drumming to the point that his hands began bleeding at the edges.

The visitor, its grey and black, old style, tattered Hanbok billowing out to reveal grotesque shapes and twisted faces embedded in the ancient cloth's folds, grumbled something unintelligible in the old tongue and reached its left hand out to touch the fishmonger's face. Something like a smile formed in the dank emptiness of the visitor's blurred face as the creature appeared to relish its ultimate collector duties.

When the visitor's vile hand touched the face of the fishmonger, even that stoic, hardened man, who was resigned to his fate, uttered a desperate moan, a cry for redemption, for salvation, for…anything to cease the pain and have the visitor finish its mission.

The old fishmonger sucked in his breath and, steeling himself, let his eyes slowly close, his mind capturing the last images of his beloved fish shop, his Incheon street, the sounds of his friends, and the memories, the memories of his wife, his friends, his family, his old customers, his son, and, yes, even the old dowager.

"Devil!" screamed a raging banshee that suddenly appeared at the fishmonger's side. "How dare you come before a man's time!"

The banshee, who looked the world like the fishmonger's mother-in-law, threw herself between the visitor and its victim, breaking the hold the apparition had on the fishmonger.

The visitor, noticeably startled by the unexpected intrusion, threw its arms up and uttered a blood curdling scream to counter the high pitched yelling of the banshee.

"Yes, you poor excuse for a spirit, take me if you think you can handle me!" yelled the raving banshee, which was looking more and more like the mother-in-law, as the demanding figure even had a dinner napkin tucked into the collar of her blouse.

The apparition appeared to take a few steps back, as if to consider the situation, while continuing to utter its bloodcurdling shrieks.

"You haven't the guts to take me, you old bag of sewer gas!" the banshee-mother-in-law yelled at the visitor as she advanced, crowding the shadowy figure to the terrace wall. "Come on! Place your dainty hand against my face. The face of someone who does not fear you, or your master, Death!"

Suddenly, the visitor fell silent, its hood-draped head turning this way and that, seeming to be looking for something on the street or up on the rooftops.

"Yes, vile one, look for your master! You think I'd let you take my dear child's man? You think my bloodline has been dulled by years of soft living and modern life? You fool! I decide who dabbles in the fate of my son! My grandson's father! My dead daughter's good husband! Only I!"

The visitor, visibly disturbed, seemed to be losing bits of its garment to the winds. It reached out again to connect with the fishmonger, who was still standing, rigid as stone, evidently unaware of the full extent of the banshee's intervention.

However, the banshee-mother-in-law again stepped in front of the visitor and its hand found her cheek, causing her to shudder in pain, but not silencing her.

"What? Is that all you have, swamp snake that you are? Even the imugi laugh at you. Wait, what is that I hear? Yes! Your master calls. Calls us, he does!"

The shadowy apparition then jerked its hand back and, swirling its tattered robes, turned, for all intents, to flee the scene, but was blocked by a sudden darkening of not only the doorway, but of the entire block.

Abruptly, everything seemed to freeze in place around the shop. The few early evening stars out over the sea ceased to twinkle, while the salty breeze dropped off. Even the passerby, oblivious to the dark drama unfolding steps away, seemed to pause in mid-stride. The only actions or sounds that could be heard when the darkness descended was that of the baker and the snack bar owner continuing their brave efforts.

As the darkness crept closer to the fishmonger and his banshee-mother-in-law, the evening's first visitor let out a muffled wail and was gradually, bit by bit, rag and shadow by rag and shadow, absorbed into the all consuming darkness.

As its muffled shrieks were finally swallowed up by the nameless abyss, the visitor's skeletal hand reached out of the blackness and dragged its talon-like nails across the left side of the shop's doorway, leaving four deep, black gashes, just as it faded away, vanishing into a darker hole within the deeper blackness.

At the same time, another arm of the impenetrable blackness began to envelop the mother-in-law, as she smiled and turned to her son-in-law, who seemed to be coming out of his trance-like state and was seeing her for the first time.

"A moment…," the mother-in-law called to the darkness embracing her. "Just a moment…for a mother of the old blood."

The blackness then paused its advance and even receded a step or two away from the old woman as she reached out to her daughter's husband.

"Young husband, never make a deal when there is a bigger deal to be made," the mother-in-law said in a loving, surprisingly youthful voice.

Recognition slowly dawned on the fishmonger's weathered face, and he reached out to the blackness just behind his beloved wife's mother, and called in a strong, compelling voice.

"No! This is my debt. My honor! You have years of life remaining!" the fishmonger cried, again reaching for the blackness. "Stand to the side! I will meet my fate!"

"Hush, little one, your fate is to join my daughter in…in the decades to come. She loved you so. How could I let you squander that love and be in that other place for eternity? Or fated to wander these dying alleys slaved to…to who knows what?" the mother-in-law asked in her matter-of-fact way. "Hush, now, and play with your friends as I take the long walk. No need to fear. I will be with my parents and my sisters and my brothers who have gone before. There will be a dark place for a while, but my child's happiness and love eclipses all that."

"No, mother! You can't do this…!" the fishmonger called, his arms grasping at the darkness that had resumed its embrace of the old woman.

"Oh, but I can, and I have, young husband," the old woman called as the blackness seemed to fold around her, her voice fading. "Thank you, for being such a good husband. A good son…."

Falling to his knees, the fishmonger grabbed his mother-in-law's flowing dress and pulled with all his might to drag her from the clutches of her final sleep. Yet, his efforts were to no avail as the old woman smiled down on him, patted his shoulder and, with a long kiss, let the name of her daughter escape her lips one final time as the blackness and emptiness drew her beyond any mortal's grasp.

Gone.

The mother-in-law suddenly blinked away like a wisp of fog sliding away in the night.

Gone.

As the deep blackness receded beyond the doorway, and the darkness and the stillness gave way to the night sounds and movements again, the fishmonger found himself kneeling on the pavement, holding a bit of white cloth from his mother-in-law's dress. The distraught man stared at the bit of cloth in disbelief and then looked up and down the road for any sign of his brave and noble savior.

Nothing.

The street appeared to be normal. No apparitions. No cold blackness. Just couples and groups going about their evenings.

Even the old fisherman from that morning was hurriedly passing on the other side of the road and, with a knowing look, waved at the fishmonger, started to step across the road, but then signaled his haste with his watch and with a slap at the back of his assistant's head.

The fishmonger stared at his old friend hurrying along, and, without knowing what his hand was doing, returned the fisherman's wave.

The pain in his chest was also gone, but it would be hours before the fishmonger realized that.

Turning to his two friends, both of whom seemed to be in trances, chanting and drumming, but with less intensity, he grasped both of their shoulders. His actions seemed to snap them out of their dazes. They gradually ceased their actions as they looked around and saw their friend, still standing, with no frightening visitors, and with no mother-in-law.

The two men then smiled up at the fishmonger, who nodded his thanks to his friends, brothers for life. The three men briefly bowed, almost hugged, but then stepped back.

"Where is your...? I could have sworn I saw...," the baker started to ask, but was cut off by an abrupt wailing from nearby.

Suddenly, from the sushi parlor a few doors down, a long cry erupted. Then, without pause, multiple wailings could be heard from a number of women, coming from the direction of the sushi parlor.

After a few seconds, bursting out of the sushi shop's doorway, the mother-in-law's little lady friend appeared, her arms waving franticly, and ran over to the fishmonger.

"Come, sir, come! She has passed, sir! Lord save us! We were all eating and talking, and she was speaking of her daughter and what a good husband you were and how you've always been a good son-in-law all these years," the little lady rattled on, somewhat shattered by her older friend's unexpected passing. "So sudden! She was so strong, she was...!"

"There, there, grandmother," the snack bar owner, the first of the three friends to fully realize what was happening, said to comfort the little lady. "Let's go see if we can get the EMS here."

"Oh, they've already been called," the little lady replied, as she and the snack bar owner headed back to the sushi place, the drum still under the snack bar owner's arm. "She was so strong...!"

The baker, somewhat confused by all that had transpired and uncertain as to what might have been real and what might have been induced by his anxiety, hung back, and spoke to his friend.

"We...we didn't know, old cousin...didn't know that your mother-in-law...that she had made a deal...we didn't...," the baker stammered then gave up.

"Old friend, the longer I live, the longer I realize I will never truly understand her. Respect her, yes. Understand her, no," the fishmonger said as he looked back to his shop.

As the baker headed over to the sushi shop, the fishmonger started after him, his head still foggy. Pausing, he walked back to his shop's doorway and stared at all the bits of paper arrayed along the edges of the doorframe, and noticed two larger pieces he had not seen earlier.

Smiling he ran his fingers over the talismans his mother-in-law had been saving for years and had, somehow, without his seeing, placed on the doorway. He reached in, pulled the door closed, and clumsily found his keys. Just as he was about to lock it, a young couple walked up and asked about dinner. They said the shop had been highly recommended by a young American in the coffee shop that fronted the large fish market a couple of blocks away.

The old fishmonger thought for the briefest of moments, his mind finally clearing, aided by the faint sounds of an old love ballad trickling out of the terrace speakers, a song he remembered, but couldn't quite catch the lyrics. He then nodded to the waiting couple and pointed at the small terrace seating.

"Take the table in the corner, just there, you can see the sea, hear the night birds, and watch the evening," the fishmonger replied, putting the key in the lock. "I need to step away for a few minutes, but feel free to look over the selection."

"No worries, old friend," both the baker and snack bar owner said in unison, as they reappeared at their friend's elbow, having returned from the sushi parlor. "You see to your mother-in-law, we'll watch the store, and help this nice couple."

The old fishmonger, his head fully cleared, solemnly nodded his thanks, pushed the door back open, and, turning, put his keys back in his pocket, just as the little terrier, silent for a change, darted out the door, and, after pausing briefly to exchange a mental handshake with the old cat, dashed over to the sushi shop and disappeared inside.

Taking a deep breath of the sea air, the old fishmonger let his eyes follow the little beast, and then stared at the sushi shop.

Gazing at the shadows in the doorway of the sushi parlor, the fishmonger would swear in later years that his one true love had been standing there, waiting for him to attend to her mother's passing.

Although the moment had been brief, the old man smiled, turned to the young couple and his two friends, and called as he walked over to the restaurant, after reaching down to absently scratch the back of the old shop cat's ears, wondering, briefly, why the sleepy old fellow hadn't left the wall during all the commotion.

"Give them the best. All on the house this night. No protests. We must all encourage such young ones in love," the old, hard-bitten fishmonger said, surprising the young couple and nearly bringing tears to the aged eyes of his two long-time friends. "And, as a thanks to my long ago American friend, who was the one who encouraged me to woo my dear wife, these many decades ago, all the beer and soju that they can drink!"

Bowing elaborately to his two brave friends, the old fishmonger, destined to remain a constant fixture in the ever-changing landscape of modern Incheon for years to come, then disappeared into the sushi parlor to attend to his dear wife's mother, his true friend and final defender, his own beloved mother-in-law, one of the last, great heroines of old Inchon.

INTERLUDE IV

"Clever, you are, foolish human," the creature wheezed from the shadows, after the writer's last words. "And maybe daring? Having the dark scourge, the unnamed one, make a devil's deal with the old dowager to cheat the ghouls. Or, was her brat's visitor one of my nobler cousins? You did name the dark one, but your prattle was as the fog and no stirrings did I feel. Clever, boy."

"What...who do you think the collector was?" the writer countered, trying to read the unreadable creature's voice and body movements.

"Few are the old fishmongers who feed my cousins, few," the creature replied, tapping a long fingernail on the cold stone. "More the fishermen who ply the waves, without giving gifts to my coastal cousins. Those sad humans often pay the price to the more violent sea spirits."

"A tale I will tell you, scribbler," the creature continued, its tapping growing louder. "Of those old lanes and alleys from Incheon, to Busan, from old Jeju, to...to the smaller villages, away from prying eyes."

"Your tale of the fool boy from across the sea, that brought back to me the early days before my first trip to the sea, it did," the creature said, in a voice almost human-like. "Back when the great cannon were still lining the man-stone shoreline of Incheon, there was a place. Larger than your tale's puny shop. A grand shop it was, that eating place. Long it has stood. Russians, Japanese, Chinese, others. Many, many were its customers over countless cycles. That time the owner, he was...is Russian? Maybe still there, these many seasons on? Was our ally, my mother said, as we hid in the dank alley just beside, gorging on rotten fish piled high just behind, and a kitten or two when they tried to steal our food, since they are not yet strong enough to harm us at that age. But, we needed more, my mother said, before we sailed for many moons across the seas. She wanted me to have a few tasty human morsels to give me strength. I was young, I did not understand, but just listened."

"We waited a long time, as I remember sleeping and half waking to see other goblins and a few others. Strange, twisted ones I had never seen and have never seen since. My mother told me in whispers not to look at them, as some would even eat their own kind. From China were the thin ones, able to hide in the cracks in a door, or in the folds of a cloth or towel. Southern Japan ones who seemed to slither in and out of themselves, eating out their insides while they waited for some tasty morsel to fall their way. Cousins were there, too, but weak ones. Ones who had not proven themselves in the city, so roamed the edges trying to build strength and reputations. A motley group, that was, in that steaming alley."

"Finally, she tucked me into her belt, for I was a wee little one at that time, and, after a signal from one of the kitchen goblins, crept into the big, shiny room, with so many humans, and so many little oceans of fish, trapped behind the little oceans' glass walls. I was afraid, for I thought all that light and shiny metal would show us to the mean humans. Yet, we were able to walk freely among them, as my mother walked in the shadow of the owner as he made his rounds. Round, yes, he was very round. We stopped at a table with many foreigners, no locals. Several speaking as you do, human. The owner babbled to them, then reached back and, using his hidden left hand, pointed my mother's gaze to one of the fatter humans crunching, crunching, crunching shrimp or fish, and then we drifted back to the kitchen. After my mother stepped back into the alley and kicked away all the cats, she then stole over to the entrance, which the owner had purposely built next to the alley. Later, much later, after many humans came and went, I felt my mother tense up. The group of fools with the fat one, very juicy one, slowly passed through that door. The fat one complaining he had eaten too much, begged off, and stepped to the alley where he, yes, lost much of his earlier gorging. While he was in his weak state, for that brief moment when the head has not yet cleared and the body is not your own, that's when my mother struck. Softly, ever so softly, she reached in and dragged a large, heaping mass of the fat one's soul, with some of the steaming ooze he had lost. The fat one staggered back, seeming shocked, but then shook his head and joined his friends, loudly declaring he had left the owner of the eating house a little present."

"I watched the fat one stumble away as my mother and I tore at his greasy mass. To this day, still wonder if he ever suspected where he lost a few years in that dark, old Incheon alley?"

The writer, trying to avoid visualizing the creature's tale, but realizing the horror of what it was saying, tried to tie the creature's tale back to what little the writer knew at that point.

"So, the owner was in one of those leagues?" the writer asked.

"Leagues? The…oh, yes. He was the best kind of human. One without a soul," the creature said with a tone of almost human wistfulness. "Safe from us, but knew how to use us. My mother's cousins at the coast would scare humans from other places, and herd them toward his shiny place. The owner got fatter and he would throw a few humans our way as payment. Lived through many kings, wars, and names, that owner has. Supplied many seamen to rogue ships over the years, he did. Yes, maybe still there, he is."

"Amazing," the writer replied, then thought of another angle. "What happens to owners like that?"

"Human, there are worse things in the shadows of the coast than a few of my cousins nipping at the heels of the souls of the passerby," the creature's harsh voice oozed with relish. "Later. Much later, when they are no longer of use, humans like that are given over to the serpents who never fly…and not the ones from your fairy tales."

"Ah, so there are others whom you…other creatures that might be…?" the writer began, but was suddenly at a loss for words when he realized he had spoken too soon, in an attempt to challenge the creature's dominance of the shadow world.

Mentally kicking himself for being to eager, the writer only hoped the creature, with its mind clouded by old memories, had not noticed the veiled triumph that had been in the writer's voice.

Unfortunately, the writer soon realized, the creature had noticed.

"Fool! You are maybe trying to frighten me, stupid boy?" the creature hissed, its eyes seeming to spin in their black sockets. "Weak? You think we are weak? Are afraid of…are afraid? Are you so deluded that you dare think the lord of the reapers in your fish tale would frighten me?"

"No, clever one, I do not think you weak. Nor afraid. If I did, I would not tell tales of such disaster for your brethren…," the writer quickly replied, but was cut short.

"Our brethren? Our…?" the creature cried, waving its thin arms again in the air. "Such seaside trash? Such bargainers with your kind? These animals are lower than my cousins. These beasts of the dark seaside alleys are not our brethren. They are closer to you humans than you think. Yes, closer. Better the dark one take them, than they be allowed to make deals with our prey."

"But, you were there, dragging the fat one…?" the writer ventured, wondering if such a challenge might anger the beast.

Instead of replying, the creature fell silent, its eyes veiled and its movements stilled, as if the beast was thinking deeply, or had lapsed into some sort of slumber. Then, responding to scurrying in the trees just beyond the old firebox and stove, the creature stirred, and threw a few pebbles in the direction of the trees, emitting a low curse as it turned back to the writer.

"Yes, the seaside has changed, it has," the creature said, its voice carrying a tone almost nostalgic, while ignoring the writer's question. "Those old shops and alleys. Dark and vile many were. Later, once I was many more seasons older…easy for us, those older days. So few of those dwellings remain. So many of your stone and metal hive towers have crushed my cousins' old grazing grounds. Too high for even the bravest of goblins to haunt, some of them. I have memory of an uncle, when my sire was still here, who was a brave troll who dared to climb to a shiny steel, tall hive hut in old Gangnam. Fell to his early dust the first time he tried to spirit a child away in the night. The child was safe, as she would not fit through the thin window. Uncle, however, since he was a shifting spirit, did…."

"Hate them, we do," the creature continued to ramble. "Unfair to the natural balance. Forces my cousins to lurk in those carriage houses underneath. Nasty, dirty places, those carriage houses. Waiting for days, even full cycles, for a weak one to happen by. Why, some of my cousins have wasted away to mere splotches of rotted fat in some of those dark corners. Yes, hate those new dwellings, we do."

"You talk about 'weak' humans a good bit, vile stench of a beast," the writer called from his side of the enclave, hoping flattery would help keep the creature calmed. "What do you perceive as these weaknesses that make it easier for you and your cousins to attack and consume the less fortunate among us humans?"

"What is weak? You ask this, boy? Do you want to know our secrets?" the creature hissed, then bellowed at the top of its putrid lungs. "You are all weak, you humans! Some are weak one way, others weak other ways. We are strong! We were here first! We herded you in the earlier days, we did. Before you began to think for yourselves and began to devise ways to deceive us and then, as the world spun and spun, and the sun progressed countless times, to deny us our very...our very existence!"

Rising to its full height, the creature seemed to fill the entire enclave.

"How dare you ask what you are, human!" the creature bellowed as it slid across the forest floor to stand over the writer. "Shall I light the firebox now? Then you can see what your special weakness is...?"

The creature's gleaming, yellowed eyes, while terrifying to the writer, also revealed a new secret for the captured human.

The troll-goblin and its kin had increasing limitations in a modern, urban landscape, the writer realized in a flash.

Thinking quickly, the writer then flipped to a story that took place in a setting that had been undergoing a major building transition, from old Seoul to more modern, trapping some denizens in the past.

"Firebox? What? Before you've heard how human's look at their own weaknesses? Before I reveal more weaknesses for you to exploit?" the writer asked, trying to keep his voice from shaking.

"Weaknesses that we do not know? Bah! We know all your weaknesses, boy," the creature declared. "From fear of the dark, to running through tunnels so the wind spirits can't catch ahold of your coat and ride home with you. From the market demons who slip into your baskets when you cheat the old woman out of her change or an extra orange, to the opening you give the house goblin when you turn away a friend who has fallen on hard times."

"Yes, we have endless cycles of knowledge of countless weaknesses we can use to slide just under your eyelids before you close them for the night, to give you those night terrors that wake you in a drenching sweat of guilt or shame, in the pitch black of your diseased souls," the creature continued, slowly moving back to its table. "Yes, we see it all, human. What new can this sad child tell me? You mix and confuse my cousins, the spirits, the under earth sliders, and the rest, fool. What can you tell me? Bah!"

"Well, cruel one, sit back and listen," the writer encouraged, keeping his voice steady. "Maybe have a cup of that…that moldy drink at your elbow, and listen to this next tale. This one is a bit of riddle, worthy of your earlier challenge to find the darker shadows poking at the humans' sad little worlds. You can listen and then, once the tale is over, can tell me what you think, where your cousins might dwell at the edges. Who are the weakest and who might be the one, or ones, that you or your cousins would haunt or inhabit?"

"Or consume?" the creature teased, stepping back to its chair as the half-clean little one scurried from the trees.

The little half-clean one, whom the writer had concluded was his assigned beasty, quietly placed a small bowl of what looked like roasted soybeans and sugared tteok, sweet rice cakes, near the earlier bowl of nuts. When the writer saw the abject fear in the tiny creature's face when he, or she, saw that the writer had not touched the earlier offering, the writer involuntarily grabbed a couple of bits from each bowl. Little half-clean then showed what the writer thought was a quick smile. Walking backwards, the little child-thing looked sideways at the back of the master of the enclave and then gave a quick bow to the writer before turning and racing back to the trees, passing a couple of other little ones who had emerged to stare at the writer.

The creature, once it had turned, looked sideways at the writer and, annoyed at the uninvited appearance of a couple of the hideous urchins, who looked all the world like they were licking their lips in anticipation of an early dinner of underdone writer, it shooed the child-things back into the dark recesses of the trees and, slowly, finally, took its seat.

"Boy, my little ones are restless. They tell me in their silence that they like your tales. However, they must eat, as we all must, so tell your story and we'll see if I can keep them from gnawing at your puny ankles while you read," the creature chuckled and waved its thin, tattered sleeve and bony arm for the writer to continue.

"Yes, let's look," the writer replied and hastily glanced at the next tale, letting out a small sigh of relief, which the creature heard, and snapped at the captive.

"I hear your life force escaping, telling me you think you have found something to truly interest me? Showing me you can fathom my cousins and the peninsula, have you, boy?" the creature asked in a tone closer to its earlier scholar voice.

"Deep in the older part of Seoul, there is a place of painters, potters, calligraphers. Artists of all types, musicians, small cafés, little alleyways," the writer began, but the creature again interrupted.

"Bah, this old, sprawling village has dozens of such places. Many I have haunted, many, many cycles ago. Why do you toy, human, when your time is so short?" the creature demanded.

"Yes, Seoul, even Korea writ large, has many small neighborhoods, with distinct and memorable attributes," the writer retorted, raising his voice to silence the creature's additional attempts to interrupt.

"Many are similar," the writer continued. "Yet, even in a city of millions, with each group or clique claiming the latest trendy area, there are some that retain their old school feel, even with massive complexes invading each year, thanks to post-IMF rationale. One such place, maybe one with some of the deepest traditions, of happier times and, surely, of sad, dismal times gone by, still holds onto much of the old ways."

The writer paused for dramatic effect, then revealed the locale of the next tale.

"Insa-dong," the writer almost sang. "Nestled in the oldest center of Seoul's Joseon heart, Insa-dong has a long, long history."

As soon as the writer had revealed Insa-dong as the location, the creature had abruptly sat up, leaned over toward one of the trees bordering the stone table and had retrieved a small object, not much larger than a postcard. The creature stared at the object, mostly hidden from the writer, for a long set of nervous breaths.

Behind the firebox, or stove, the little ones seemed to have become agitated, either at the mention of Insa-dong, or at the creature's actions, or both, and, while the writer could not decipher their high pitched squealing and gnashing of teeth in the shadows, he certainly knew fear when he heard it.

And, smelled it.

A raw stench of primordial terror was wafting across the enclave, coming, not from the creature, but, to the writer's horror, from the little ones.

Were they reacting to some signal from their master, the writer wondered? Were they, even now, sharping their knives and teeth, ready to pounce and dismember their guest?

Snapping himself out of his momentary distraction, the writer coughed, wondered why he was trying to be polite, and then called to the creature.

"You have something there? Something that seems to, to excite your young charges back in the shadows," the writer called, trying to use deferential language for a change, to see if such had any effect.

The creature slowly moved its gaze from the object, which allowed the writer to see that it was a small drawing or painting, possibly of a bird or some other animal. The creature then slowly returned the object to its previous resting place.

The beast then turned to click its tongue at the little ones in the shadows, who returned their master's clicking with shrieks of terror. The creature clicked again, while the writer decided to keep quiet and wait out whatever drama was unfolding.

Finally, the older little one emerged, holding what looked like a fat stick, and slowly advanced to the master of the enclave. As the child-thing stepped gingerly around the stove, the stick twisted around and buried its fangs and what, to the writer, looked like a set of tiny claws in the child-thing's rag-draped side. However, the child-thing did not call out nor wince, even though the gallery of little ones, their dirty faces poking out of the trees, emitted a cacophony of terror.

The child-thing eventually arrived at the stone table and the writer watched the pitiful creature carefully jam the writhing snake into the huge mead cup, even as the snake or lizard, since it had claws, the writer told himself, continued to lash out, to the point the child-thing's arm was streaked with red and black claw marks and puncture wounds from the angry creature.

Once the small beast was in the cup, the writer watched in fascination as the master grunted some sort of unintelligible command to the gallery in the trees. Without delay, two of the smallest child-things darted out carrying what appeared to be a boiling celadon pot of something rather foul.

The writer was immediately alarmed, for, if the little creatures were cooking up some sort of ghastly tea behind those trees, then they might have an entire kitchen back there, waiting for their master to fall asleep so that they could emerge, dismember the guest and throw his parts into their own hidden cook pot.

All this was going through the writer's mind while he watched the two minions struggle with the large, steaming pot, an ancient piece of heavy, Korean celadon. Finally, with only a bit spilled near the corner of the stove, the two managed to heft the pot up to the top of the mug, or stein, the writer corrected himself, and, with the assistance of the obviously weakened older little one, poured the foul mixture into the stein and, of course, over the snake-thing, to its ready objections as it shrieked a sound the writer had never heard before and hoped he would never hear again.

It was the sound of countless starving babies screaming for their lost mothers.

It was the sound of whales dying by the scores in the merciless drift nets.

It was the sound of multiple tsunamis crashing over endless civilizations.

It was…it was, the writer was certain, the sound of what the end of time must be.

Then, silence.

Deathly, unnerving, nearly impenetrable silence.

The writer felt as if he had suddenly gone deaf.

Looking up at the trees, the writer saw the breezes moving the leaves, but heard no sound. He then watched the three little ones retreat, walking backward and bowing, the two small ones helping the lethargic older one to walk. Yet, he heard no footsteps. No sounds, even though their lips spoke some sort of obedience words to their master as they withdrew.

The writer then looked down at his notebook and, turning to the blank note pages at the rear, he hurriedly tore a sheet. Once. Twice. Nothing. No sound.

Looking back to the creature, the writer then watched with a mix of revolting disgust and riveting fascination as the creature raised the stein to its festering lips, mumbled some sort of unheard, devil's toast, and tipped the still steaming witch's brew into its cavernous mouth.

"Ahhh! Long have I waited to hear of old Insa-dong, human," the creature loudly declared, slamming the stein onto the stone tabletop, without any contents spilling. "Another den of cursed cousins, where I only venture when on revenge!"

The writer, relieved that his hearing had returned, but quite confused by the whole brew ritual and the creature's disregard for whatever poor animal had to be sacrificed for his captor's satisfaction, simply nodded, and tucked the torn sheet in between a couple of pages.

"Long before those alleys and dirt streets were paved over with your black roads, killing the streams and the few animals that had still survived, by mother's people were the night rulers of Jongno, choosing Insa-dong as their main cave, haven," the beast revealed, its right hand still wrapped around the stein.

"Before the bells rang in that foreign temple, where the old pagoda survives, my mother's family roamed those small hills and quiet stream beds. Moved in with the royals, they did. Long, long ago. Before the old scribbles got all mixed up with the new. When the last of the old winged ones were few and weak," the creature continued, its voice back to the voice of the old scholar. "We, my forebears, were the top of the food chain. We owned that village!"

The creature took another swig of the brew, blackish and yellow droplets falling from its lips as it wiped them with the back of its left hand's sleeve.

"Care for a taste of eternity, scribbler?" the creature chuckled, seeing that the writer was staring in horror at the massive stein.

The writer shook his head in the negative, puzzled by the revelation, even if a complete fable, that the creature believed his family had been the royal house elves or castle goblins for centuries. After the earlier discussion of royal protectors, the writer had concluded the creature and its kin would have avoided such special places. Deciding it was more prudent to avoid pointing out the contradiction, the writer chose a different angle to pursue.

Why was the wretch holed up in a twisted copse on the side of Namsan, and not down in one of the restored palaces haunting the tourists, wondered the writer?

"Your family was part of the long line of, of your kind that haunted the old royals?" the writer finally asked outright, deciding he didn't have the time to dance around subjects with the creature, or man, or whatever the beast considered itself to be.

"Human. There are tales I could tell, but...," the creature began and then, seeming to realize it had said too much, rose up out of its stone chair and began to crash about the enclave, to the cries and screeches of the little ones behind the trees.

"Trickery! Trickery! Trickery! You have played this well, boy," the creature suddenly spat out, stopping on the other side of the cook pot, staring over the stove at the writer.

"Trickery? I don't understand?" the writer asked, genuinely alarmed.

"What son of a devil's cur sent you, human messenger?" the creature roared and, grabbing the immensely heavy lid of the cook pot, raised the bone-crushing thing over its head, menacing the writer.

"Messenger?"

"Messenger. From those leeches of the new order. Those vile ones. Who sent you, little human, to pry into my memories? To draw me out? To lure me back to those damned lanes of Jongno?" the creature called, positioning the hefty lid as if the beast would slam it into the writer's head at a wrong answer.

The writer, suddenly aware that he had gone far beyond hitting a nerve, realized he had awakened a deep paranoia that obviously festered inside his captor's mind. Feeling he had nothing to lose, the writer went with the simplest answer, the truth.

"Vile sir, hereditary haunter and terrorizer of the royal court, I am an observer of things. I am a writer of tales. I wander the city and the city speaks to me. I wander life and life speaks to me. Years ago, I was in Insa-dong for the first time, long after all those changes you lament. With my family. Our children's first visit to Korea. In those side streets and quaint alleys of the old days, I felt something. I felt, even though I was born far, far away, some strong connection to those art shops, cafés, and struggling artists and musicians of my wife's ancestral land. Wandering the old village area just north of there, later, I stepped into a small woodworking shop and, somehow, I felt I was looking back in time. Back to a time before. That's when the tale came to me. That's when I jotted down a few notes in our hotel room later. That's when, looking out the hotel room window at Namsan Tower, that I realized there were more stories to be told."

"No vile enemy of yours sent me here," the writer continued, keeping his voice steady. "No long ago, mysterious conflict that obviously separated you, your family, from your royal haunting, has conspired to corner you into flying off your mountain to wreak your hellish vengeance on some wretched cousin, whatever caused that long ago rift. I am what I am. You can smell lies, you boast of it. What lies am I telling?"

For a long moment, too long for the writer to control the sweat building up on his brow, under his arms, and in his groin, the beast simply stared, but the writer dared not move, lest the creature fling the massive iron lid and kill him on the spot. Feeling the beads running down his body and stinging his eyes, he fought even blinking, focused only on the creature's eyes.

Slowly, with hesitation, the creature stepped around the stove and seemed to float, rather than walk, over to the writer. It still held the iron lid high over its head, but was flicking its tongue, as it had done earlier, instead of demanding the writer answer.

After circling the writer and the stone bench several times, all the while flicking its tongue and sniffing the writer's sweaty body, the creature abruptly tossed the iron lid at the stove, where it clanged against the stove's stone sides and came to rest near the pile of ondol charcoal and kindling.

"No lies, human, do I taste. Fear, yes. Healthy, deep fear. You should fear me, boy. At least you are not a moron," the creature declared as it stood over the writer, its eyes seeming to look deep into its captive's soul.

"You are a strange human, human," the creature suddenly said. "You see beyond what you see. You see…you see, almost, as my kind see, but blurry, only hints, human. It is no wonder some of your tales just miss the mark for full truth."

The creature waved its long arms at the writer.

"Yet, there is a taste of our side there. Maybe your forebears hosted some of my cousins from across the Dokil, German, Sea?" the creature asked, its voice sounding more and more like a scholar to the writer, and, even though he knew it was lunacy, the writer could swear the creature had taken on a more normal look, that of the old man the writer had first seen.

"Return to your tales, human. Entertain me, and the little ones. They are too frightened at making the makgeolli, rice-wine mead to come out and nibble at you," the creature chuckled, flinging a few drops of the vile brew toward the trees after stepping back to the stone table.

"And, human, we have ways of making you forget the things you see and hear in my domain. Painful ways," the creature added, its voice cold and distant.

"Best you lose any expectation of hearing more on the old days, from my mother's side. But, I would like to hear of your tale of the old quarter, if only to point out where you get your tale all twisted and mistaken," the creature chuckled, yet again, as it slouched back into its massive stone chair, which was a relief for the writer.

"We can move on, to a different tale, if your memories of Jongno and Insa-dong...," the writer offered, wary of having the creature angered again.

"No, little man, continue as you were. I wish to hear your tale of old Insa-dong," the creature replied from under its cowl.

"Yes, right. On to the tale, then," the writer said without delay. "A small incident in the life of one of Insa-dong's long time residents and artists. But, an artist who had all but abandoned his craft, until he sees himself through the eyes of...well, let's just tell the tale."

Even though the little ones at the back of the enclave had calmed down, the writer knew he was not safe if the beast fell into a slumber. Still wondering what had spurred the creature's outrage, and what was the meaning of the little painting that had begun the incident with the snake and the stein, the writer tried to clear his mind and focus on the story. And what wild history did his deranged host believe in, the writer wondered?

The writer then shook off those distracting images and, as he quickly collected his storytelling thoughts, glanced at the first page of the next story and, taking a deep, long breath, the stench be damned, he began to weave another tale for his captor.

"Let's take a taxi, it's faster, to the top of that old neighborhood, hoping that we can still recognize where we are with all the change happening," the writer began, alternating between sitting on the bench and standing, to pace a bit as he spoke.

"As we pass the street musicians, the tourist stalls, and the noisier shops at the main plaza, we finally move into the quieter depths of the older section, with its quaint, beckoning alleyways, serious artists, and fading artisans of older, almost forgotten skills. Just at the corner of that alley, beyond the shiny new mall, around the corner from today, and just at the edge of our vision, a rare few of those old talents are on display, waiting quietly for us to wander by, discover their wares, and, if the mood is right...well, let's just see what transpires at an almost forgotten intersection of two of those bygone, creative alleyways of Insa-dong."

5

THE LETTER WRITER OF INSA-DONG

In one of the oldest dongs, or neighborhoods, of Seoul, due north of
Mount Namsan, about twenty minutes by taxi, if traffic cooperated, or
thirty minutes by train, the aged streets of Insa-dong, in the Jongno district,
house many an old memory of an almost forgotten Korea, a Korea before
the wars, the occupations, the other wars, and the various governments.
While hip cafés, trendy art galleries, stunning boutiques, and street
entertainers abound, a few of the older skills that once plied the former
village's older, dirt covered streets still managed to survive in one or two of
the alley corners where modernization had not yet absorbed, or, more
likely, discarded the old. Artists from many schools of technique still clung
to the less rent heavy store fronts, some mere alcoves, with a bit of cloth to
delineate the artist's domain from the bustling street. All manner of art
could be found, with painting and ceramics abundant, metalwork less so,
and textiles even less. Further down the list of bankable art, arguably not
even lofty enough to be included in the monetized view of the visual art
scene, was the position of the humble writer. Oh, not those of the
celebrated novelist, the clever short story writer, the sought after playwright,
the tragic poet, the popular song writer, nor high-paid screen writer, but
that nearly forgotten word artist of yesterday, one who was once
indispensible to both common society and elites of old, the letter writer.
Why, even the old kings and queens of Joseon employed dozens with that
special talent. As with many professions from the old days, the talents and
secrets were passed on from father to son and, in more recent years, also to
daughters, who, in turn, passed the skills on to their daughters, and sons.
One man, possessed of those rare and quickly disappearing writing talents,
was just setting up at his corner on a busy alley just off the main street, a

few meandering steps beyond the cluster of traditional artists shops, where serious collectors bought investments, and passing tourists purchased memories.

As the weekend lunch crowd began to arrive, the small, almost frail man set out his two folding chairs, one for himself and one for expected customers. He unfolded his wide, meter and a half worktable and then carefully arrayed all his writing instruments and accessories around the table in a specific, time-honored pattern. After the table array, he then unfolded a rather tall, lightweight, dark screen, with which he encircled the customer chair on three sides for better privacy for the customer, and, known only to the scribe, for him to better hear the whispered sentences his clients would utter at such low volume so that passerby would not hear. The screen was very tasteful, mostly black, with white markings that could be seen as birds, or clouds, or whatever the viewer might dream up as he or she passed by.

The scribe, a title from olden days, then used one side of his station's backdrop, a windowless wall, to prop up a weathered board with small brass nail heads just poking out of its ancient wood. On those nine small nails, he hung nine drawings, mostly of people's faces, with a couple of cat drawings and one or two of either a phoenix or a jay bird, depending on the angle of the viewer's gaze. His final placement was a small sign, so small as to almost be missed, but somehow was always seen by the few, the very few, who sought out his most marketable talent, the writing of letters.

Whether appeals to officials for the resolution of some perceived grievance, or simply a long missive for an older woman with hands so arthritic she could no longer hold a pen or type on a keyboard, the scribe would unravel the words and put them to paper. Sometimes it was a love letter, or a letter of goodbye where the sender wanted to remain anonymous. Sometimes the letters were just a way for a lonely soul to get something off a world-weary chest, taking the finished document, never to be mailed or presented to the intended recipient.

Occasionally, but truly only rarely, some new type of customer would sit down in the chair, peruse the small menu with the far too low prices, select the type of letter and basic length, discreetly place money, real money, not plastic, in the little tray, and begin to dictate an experience new to the scribe's ear. Yes, such were very rare as the scribe had seen, at least to him, entire epochs come and go, and he found the issues his clients wanted to cover in a letter were the same, whatever the era, or the date on whichever calendar you adhered to. Yet, not long ago, on that bright, late spring, nearly summer day, when the normally wretched humidity of the capital threatened to melt even his most careful handiwork, a new experience did indeed unfold, albeit after the first routine customer, in the little scribe's small domain, just off the pedestrian path, and left of yesterday.

"Do you think that is too harsh?" asked a dramatically distraught middle-aged lady, a repeat customer, who had just finished dictating an all too long 'moving on' letter to her most recent conquest.

The scribe, who, like the forebears of his kind, never made uninvited comments on the letter's intent, but only on form and style and, when asked, word choice, simply smiled at the woman, knowing that she had asked the same question the previous five times she had used his services. While the scribe would offer assistance with language when requested, for a small, additional fee, he would never allow himself to attempt to alter or otherwise influence the overall, original intent of a client. That was the client's duty alone.

The woman winked at the silent scribe, stared at the text for another moment, outwardly appearing to review the mini-epistle, but was really trying to catch the scribe's eye. Unsuccessful, she finally nodded, paid the small extra fee for special paper, and moved on to meet three of her similarly single lady friends at the two-story coffee house just up the broad pedestrian avenue. The scribe put the money away in his worn case and set about cleaning the pens and brushes he had just used.

During the in between times, when no client sat in the darkened chair, and his cleaning done, the scribe would sit quietly, watching the pedestrian street, allowing its sights, sounds, smells, and even vibrations drift into his small, specialized station.

All around the scribe, shoppers rushed about, driven by the desire to nab the next great trend before anyone else. Small groups of teen kids, sometimes more in the mode of gangs, moved in and out of shops, cafés, art studios, and the street carts, often driven by something on the phones that always seemed to be in front of their faces, or by whatever was coming over their earphones, or, for the ultra hip, their earbuds.

Workers from the larger shops and nearby offices would often meet at the small tea and coffee shop just down the alley, slightly across from the scribe. Many were budding romances from what the scribe could see of their body language and the few bits of conversation he could see on their lips, a talent he had built up over the years listening to the nearly inaudible, desperate whispers of the love sick, or inheritance angry. And, yes, a few were illicit affairs, often with one or the other of a couple juggling several affairs at the same time.

The tea shop owner, a savvy older lady from Gwangju, kept the volume turned high on an old television behind the counter to help cover the conversations of her guiltier patrons, who tended to buy the most expensive items. The old comedy 'Pasta' was playing, and the scribe briefly smiled at the antics of celebrated actress Gong Hyo-jin as she flawlessly tackled a kitchen scene.

Down the other alley, just beside the scribe, a music shop, run by a middle-aged violin teacher from Daegu, was a favorite haunt of the slightly older kids who had decided music and playing music were important parts of their mildly, as it was Korea after all, rebellious late teen years. The scribe enjoyed hearing the youths test out the various instruments, most, sadly, copies of old, often discontinued global brands. The scribe also enjoyed hearing the variety of new music the shop pumped out into the alley, while wondering which of the many young artists in the Korean pop scene would have staying power. As if to answer him, versatile singer and actress Bae Suzy's newest track drifted down the alley to engulf his station.

At the café just down the way, whose owners seemed to change with the seasons, the scribe could just see the second level balcony, with its high-end consumers driving those very trends that the shoppers below were rushing about for. He imagined the less kind of those trendsetters watching the masses surging beneath them in the pedestrian street and alleys and, on a whim, a dare, or a bet, decide to change the new desired items, picking up their ever-present phones and telling their paid influencers what to tell the buying masses.

To the scribe's right, an old artist, who specialized in water color and charcoal, entertained a steady stream of customers, both art collectors and the rare, discerning tourist who wanted to carry home, not a standard souvenir, but something from Seoul's very heart, which a piece of real art, regardless of the market price, ultimately satisfied. The old artist had moved to the city decades before, from the small village of Songtan-si, where he had originally owned a very successful ceramics shop near the American base. Consequently, while he did not work in ceramics himself, he did sell, on consignment, the work of a number of the better, up and coming ceramic artists from across the country.

At that moment, the old artist was bidding goodbye to a couple and their college age son, who was carefully carrying two flat bags, one small and one fairly large. The Korean appearing mother, using fair Korean in the classic American accent of a first generation child, was thanking the artist as they departed. The father, not Korean, then added his own goodbye in English, and the three moved on.

As the small family passed his spot, the son paused to look over the drawings hanging from the scribe's display board. He then smiled at the scribe, gave the scribe a nod of approval, and moved on to catch up with his parents, who seemed to be hurrying to the two level café, probably to meet someone, the scribe concluded from the mother's repeated looks at her Rolex Oyster watch. Real, not a knockoff, the scribe had noted. The mother was urging on the husband, who seemed to want to step into all the older looking shops, rather than rush to meet anyone at the well-known café.

The old artist caught the scribe's eye and bowed slightly as a way of a mid-morning greeting. The scribe quickly rose from his chair and returned the bow, bending a good bit lower than the old artist had, both from deep respect and from continuing gratitude that the old artist had allowed the scribe to set up for years in the old artist's unused, second doorway alcove.

It was a good relationship, as many of the patrons who used the scribe, after getting whatever issue off their chest at the end of their letter or document, would often decide they needed a congratulatory gift for themselves and, with the varied display of the old artist's window just over the scribe's shoulder, the shop was a natural outlet for spending that emotional money.

All the while he had been watching the world move around him, the scribe had been cleaning the nib of the pen the recently departed client had always preferred. Turning away from his friend to place the pen back in its open box with the others, he was startled, his surprise showing briefly with his eyes opening a little wider, to find a potential client, a new face, sitting in the customer chair, pressing back into it as if the potential client was trying to get as much benefit from the three-sided privacy screen as she could.

Looking at the new, potential client, the scribe's face was briefly covered by a sudden wave of dark shadows, probably cast by passerby interrupting the glare of several bright lights from the various ads of a face boutique at the opposite corner, which implied their potions would have you looking like the acclaimed actress Park Shin-hye within minutes. Maybe the potential client had tapped the screen when she had taken the seat, causing the lights to ripple? Yet, wondered the scribe, why were the shadows still dancing after she had been seated and no other shoppers were close by?

After the shadows finally dispersed, the scribe was able to get a better look at the potential client.

This one desperately needs to get something off her chest, the scribe decided, as he finished cleaning the nib while watching her face. With care, he placed the pen point back in its plain, bamboo box. He then looked up, into the soulful, beautiful eyes of the young lady, and spoke softly, with a kind tone that nevertheless said 'you'd best be a customer or move on.'

"Yes, miss, how might I help you?" the scribe asked, subconsciously gauging, from her expensive clothes and shoes, her pearl earrings, her demeanor, and, once she spoke, her perfect teeth and high brow accent, what her high personal value might be and how much she would probably be willing to spend on a letter.

"You write letters?" the young lady asked, with a certain assured manner well beyond her age, already evidenced by taking the client seat without invitation.

"Why, yes, that I do," the writer replied, being careful not to show his mild annoyance that the young lady had sat without invitation. "And you need…?"

"Do you write to anyone, regardless?" the young lady demanded, her eyes scanning the drawings on the board, instead of looking at the scribe. "Anyone at all?"

"Yes, miss, to anyone," the writer replied and motioned to the small menu of types of letters and documents he customarily prepared.

"I need to write to my halmoni," the young lady replied, turning her hard gaze back to the scribe to give him the same critical scrutiny she had just given his drawings. "My dear grandmother."

"Well, miss, isn't that something your beloved grandmother would love coming directly from you?" the writer suggested, stopping his reach for his paper when he heard the recipient. "After all, a letter to someone like that is a labor of love."

"Well, I do write to her. And take the letters to...," the young lady began, but then repeated her first question.

"But, you do write letters? That's what your tiny little sign says, which, by the way, is quite hard to see, so I don't know why anyone would stop if they can't see the sign," the young lady said without rancor.

"Yes, miss, yes. I write letters," the scribe reconfirmed, part of his mind wondering why the young client had a vague familiarity about her.

"Good. How long does it take to write a letter to my grandmother?" the young lady asked, her darting eyes betraying her concern that someone might step from the crowd and end her brief enquiry.

"How long?" the young lady repeated.

"However long you need it to be," the scribe answered, puzzling over the potential client's skittishness.

"I see you also draw. People," the young lady then stated, as her eyes, failing to display the typically deferential downcast look of nearly all young ladies her age, seemed to bore into the scribe so intensely that he actually looked away before answering.

"Yes, I draw. Yes, people, mostly," the scribe answered, rehearsing in his mind his standard answer when patrons asked why, if he had such artistic talent, was he wasting it taking small change for lovelorn letters and not focusing on his true talent.

"Good. Please draw me when we get to the end of my letter to halmoni," the lady asked, already presumptive in her guidance to the scribe. "She loves getting pictures of me."

For his part, the scribe sat quite still, using only the most necessary muscles to answer the lady, while he waited for the lady to notice the small 'payment in advance' sign. With his repeat customers, he always let them pay after he had finished, but, having been burnt by one too many tourists, he had added the small sign.

Eventually, the young lady did notice the sign and, scrunching up her smooth, pale forehead above naturally perfect, dark eyebrows, she extracted several folded bills from a trendy and very expensive Louis Vuitton cross shoulder bag. Real, not a copy. Placing the bills in the tray, she then looked up at the scribe, her striking eyes asking when she should begin dictating.

"As soon as I have the right pen, miss, or brush," the scribe replied.

"Would you prefer old kingdom style, transition style, modern style, random selection, or some other style," the scribe asked, relating the most popular styles of the previous few years. "Please note that the brush takes a bit longer."

"Well, since it's to my grandmother, can we make it Joseon?" the young client asked. "She is very traditional, she is."

"Certainly, miss. Joseon style it is," the scribe replied with enthusiasm as he drew out his various pens, brushes, ink, and paper, writing and blotting.

"Do I need to speak slowly?" the young client asked, as she watched the scribe lay out three brushes and three old-fashioned fountain pens.

"Won't those slow you down?" the young lady added, waving her slim, possibly pianist fingers, the scribe thought, at the brushes.

"You may speak at any speed you wish to, miss," the scribe replied. "And, you may choose brush or pen, for your aged grandmother."

"Pen. I think it will appear stronger to her, as I want to make arguments for my case, you see," the young client replied, absently pulling on the edge of her chair, her feet dangling below her, not quite touching the ground, which was normal for many younger Koreans.

"Right, pen it is," the scribe replied, returning the brushes to their box.

As he took up one of the pens, the scribe dipped its nib into the heavy crystal inkwell standing on a small, unobtrusive tray, and poised his hand over the heavy parchment paper that he assumed would please the lady as it was patterned after official paper used during the period the young client had specified.

Leaning toward the table, the young client spoke quietly, almost conspiratorially, her hazel-brown eyes darting over her slim shoulder, looking toward the end of the pedestrian avenue, north of the little scribe's station.

"Your sign says the utmost confidentiality," the young client whispered.

"Yes. Without reservation. Many generations of my father's and his father's line guarantee such," the scribe declared with sincerity.

"Also, no one can see you in the chair, miss, so you do not need to worry about prying eyes, or ears," the scribe said, pointing to the music shop just to the left which piped the latest music into the street, conveniently creating a sound shield for the scribe's clients.

"Oh. Well, then. Let's begin?" the young client replied, a hint of nervousness slipping into her voice, prompting her to add a question. "Oh, how does one usually begin?"

"Well, miss, usually with a salutation," the scribe replied, watching the client's lips carefully, wondering why he was having trouble reading her lips as she spoke. "Do you have an endearment name for your grandmother? Does she for you?"

At the scribe's question, the young lady leaned back in the chair, letting her eyes wander from the little station to the old artist's window, causing her to let out a small, wistful sigh.

"She loves bringing me here, grandmother does," the young client said, more to herself than the scribe. "She's always saying how it all looked before all the modern, shiny new buildings. Says it is a crime to cover up the tradition, even if it's crumbling into the street, I suppose."

Using her hands to motion for the scribe to look to the other side of the street, the young client continued.

"Over there, not too far, she brings me to ice cream, the western kind, nearly every Saturday. In the winter we buy hot cocoa and filled pastries. All manner of filled pastries," the young client said, that wistful tone still in her serene voice.

"Down that alley, with the noisy music shop, is our favorite little ramyeon shop, and they serve yummy mandu," the young client added, craning her neck to try to catch a glimpse of the shop.

The scribe knew the shop quite well. It was his usual stop for early dinner, or late dinner, depending on the night, and lunch if the place was not too busy. Odd, though, he thought, that such an obviously well to do young lady and her grandmother would patronize such a tiny hole in the wall and not make one of the more exclusive, hard to get into cafés along the main avenue their go-to place.

"Yes, a great little place, very small. But, you probably know it. For us, it's our secret spot," the young client said, breaking into her first smile that the scribe had seen. "Mother would not approve, so we never take her there. She always wants to go to the Vine or Bush or whatever it's called over by the new mall."

"Yes, every Saturday that she can, she brings me down here," the young client continued, but then shook her head to say 'no, not this week,' when the scribe's eyes looked out to the crowds expecting to see the grandmother.

"No, not this week," the young client added verbally. "But, that's part of why I need to write her a letter."

Nodding, the scribe continued to hold the pen, mentally counting off the seconds until he would have to renew the old pen's ink, or even switch to a fresh pen if the wait was a bit too long, resulting in gummy ink.

"Yes, right," the young client then said, shaking her short hair as if to shake off the memories that were weighing upon her. "A letter…?"

Taking in a long breath, the young client turned her gaze squarely on the scribe and spoke.

"Dearest and most loved and respected grandmother," the young client began, her lyrical voice effortlessly guiding the scribe's hand.

"I'm sorry, say 'very sorry,' that we missed our park outings these last few weeks...or has it been longer? I do think it is quite dear that you went around to all of our places over the weeks, and took pictures to share with me. That was very sweet."

"While I don't want to be a tattletale, I did want you to know why I missed the park visits and the ice cream shop and noodle spot. As you know, you and Mother do not see eye to eye on some matters, but you've always been a fair and balanced grandmother, and have always told me that Mother's word is the final word. So, instead of complaining to Mother about my missed visits with you, I let her finally realize that the visits with you are, in the end, far more important, both for her, and me, than any errand that might interrupt our visits. As you know, we took the train south, which seemed odd as most of our train trips are north, to see Father, or west to see you and auntie. After what seemed like hours and hours, we got off the train in.... Hmm, I'm not sure of the place, so just say a far suburb. A new one. Everything perfectly manicured. When the taxi...yes, we took a taxi from the station, not our driver. When the taxi pulled up to the tower complex, I felt we were entering a Lego village, where everything was in its place, everything was squared off and functional, with some artificial beauty, but lacking all the Lego colors. Mostly green grass that looked like it came from a golf course, a few grey benches, some brick inlay pathways, and the glass and concrete of the towers, with a few red bricks thrown in to break up all the concrete."

The young lady paused as she took a breath, which the scribe used for a long dip of his pen in the inkwell. They both then resumed, he a split second after she continued.

"We took a rather nice elevator up to a high floor, I don't remember which, and got off in a long, well appointed corridor. A nice girl was waiting outside the elevator to show us to the office door. (Don't write this, but I wondered to myself how many times that poor girl walked the ten or so meters between the elevator and the office door on a daily basis, imagining a furrow being worn into the carpet by her high heels.) At the office, we were greeted by another girl who, I swear, halmoni, could have been the elevator greeter's twin, at least in the face."

"Well, you know how the visit went, so I won't spend time on that. I just wanted to let you know that I was fully aware of what Mother wanted for me and, as you always say, Mother has the last word. After the visit, the follow on visits were scheduled over the phone. I could hear Mother in the next room making arrangements. Father came down one evening, on the way to the airport for yet another business trip, and the two of them had an awful argument. Yes, I know that they argue all the time, but this time I think it was about me. I was too shy to listen in, so stayed in my room and listened to the Chopin playlists you bought for me last winter. I couldn't play along on the piano, of course, but I did play a little bit, by feel, of course, after Father had left."

"Well, as you know, we went back to the towers two, maybe three weeks later, I'm fuzzy on exactly when, and you know the result. Not what anyone expected, least of all Mother. Although, without being too selfish, I certainly did not expect the outcome, either. I guess you can say we were all surprised."

"This letter, dearest grandmother, rather than a brief, fleeting visit, or a too short call…this little letter is a more tangible way for me to let you know how I feel, what I think, and how we can…what is it that you always say? Remember you told me that when you were a little girl and the occupation ended, only to have that terrible war a few years later, forcing all the Ewha girls to leave school? Oh, right. I remember now. As you've always said, 'we can't always control what happens to us, but, as thinking people, we can control how we respond.' Even though I am always a little confused by the lofty things you teach me, and, you are the best teacher, ever, grandmother, I do think I finally understand that one."

"At first, I was angry, of course. Who wouldn't be? Angry for a long time. Then, as things cleared over the previous few days, I began to take to heart your teaching me about all the amazing things from our past, our family's history, and the country's history. I decided I was not going to dwell on any sadness, or allow anything to disrupt our visits, even if those visits were going to be fewer and farther apart. While we may have missed our recent visits, I take deep comfort in knowing you were there, taking pictures, and thinking of me. Just today, as I passed all the places where we have had our adventures, I thought of you, as well, and locked those images in my mind's eye, so I can share them with you when we see each other, even if not today, or even next week."

"I know the artist alleys and quaint cafés of Insa-dong are some of your favorites, so I was able to nudge…nudge Mother to let me come down here today, even with all that's going on with her. She really didn't want to, but this was one time she did not argue with me. So, while she is taking a coffee…oh, no, not alone. Auntie is with her, I'm sure. While she is at that coffee shop with the balcony…where I used to pretend I was a pirate when I was little, remember? While she is there, I decided to sneak off and visit some of the places we love together."

"Let's see. I stopped at the sculptures at the end, down there, bowed to the violin man statue as we always do, and watched children playing, tourists taking pictures, and even saw a young couple of buskers playing guitar and violin, with the guitar player singing an old love song. I dropped a small bill in the guitar case, like we always do, but I'm afraid the two were looking away, so they did not see me leave it. But, I'm sure it will help them, right? I stopped and watched the old calligrapher in the derby hat impress the tourists. I then stopped in that ceramic shop. Yes, the one where I nearly knocked down an entire wall shelf when I was little, and where we bought several of the little glass animals, like the ones you brought back from Murano. That was the start of my little collection. After that, I stopped at the western ice cream shop, but the line was terribly long, it is almost summer, after all, so I decided to head to the ramyeon and mandu spot early, eat, and be back with Mother and my auntie before they left the coffee house."

"Walking over to the alley, I saw a lady get up and leave the little scribe's chair, the one I always said that I wanted to use one day? Remember? He's the one at the corner, in a small doorway attached to the old artist's place where we always stop after the ramyeon shop? The one we always said looked like he had the world on his thin shoulders? Yes, him, the one with the huge little table and the many, many pens and brushes and whatnot that he uses to write the love letters you told me about. Well, I decided to sit down and employ his services, before going to the ramyeon shop."

"An added advantage, grandmother, of stopping at the scribe's little shop, is that I can look in on the old artist, your life-long friend, and watch him talk to customers and, when he is in the back, watch him working on his next piece. He's quite busy now, so I don't think he's seen me. If he does look this way, I'll wave and let him know I'll stop by after the ramyeon shop, as we always do, grandmother."

"Oh, grandmother, did you know the scribe is an artist as well? Yes, he draws, maybe in charcoal, people's faces, mostly, and a few animals. Some from legends, others from the back garden. Well, as part of the business of writing this letter, he's going to do a simple sketch of me. I know it will look like me and you will love it. Should I make one for Mother as well, do you think? She is more of a fan of those modern art splotches of color and old junk, so maybe not. Yes, after he completes the letter, which is almost done, he's going to do a quick sketch. But, very quick, since I need to move on, soon."

"I think I came down here today, after such a long time being away, so that I could share in those places that have been important to me, and to you. Funny, I thought about stopping by school, but knew none of my friends would be there on the weekend. Father is out of the country, again, so will try to see him when he returns, whenever that will be. I'm glad I was able to see Auntie. She is so good for Mother. I think today is the first day that I feel Mother is in good hands with Auntie. So, I knew I'd be able to visit our places, think of you, and maybe get a trinket at the ceramics shop later. Something small, something that you would like, too."

"So, to bring this letter…you should see the scribe, he's on his third sheet, so I have been talking too much…to bring this letter to a close, I wanted to assure, is that the right word? Yes, I wanted to assure you that, whatever you think of Mother and the events of the previous few weeks, and maybe longer, I'm really not sure, please do not feel bad in any way. You should rest happy and, yes, be glad that we have had all these years before, and, one day, will have many, many more. So, please smile, grandmother, wherever you are, and, when you are looking over those places that we both love so much, look for the other grandmothers with their little darlings, and rejoice that your traditions will continue. Your traditions, our traditions and culture that you are always teaching me, will not be replaced by a shiny new tower, but will always be embraced by grandmothers and their granddaughters for years and years to come."

"Be well, grandmother. Your loving and always happy, very thankful for you, granddaughter, your dear one, Jinju," the young client finished, her voice dropping at the end.

After the young client's voice faded away, the only other sounds in the small alcove were the graceful scratches of the old pen on the heavy, mid-eighteenth century style paper. Eerily, the scribe heard none of the usual sounds from around them, only his pen's last few strokes.

After he had completed the last words of the letter, the scribe looked up, but only briefly, to see a happy, almost contagious glow on the young lady's gentle face.

"Do you, miss...? Miss, do you wish to sign this yourself?" the scribe asked, bending his head low over the last bits of the letter, while another thought, unvoiced as yet, had come to him.

"Sign? Oh, no, you go ahead and add a fancy signature. I think she will like that better, sir," the young client responded, and drew her name in the air for the scribe to know the symbols for her name spelled 'Pearl.'

For a long moment, while the scribe carefully finished the young client's letter, adding an appropriately tasteful flourish at the end, the young lady sat in silence, watching the reflected crowds moving about in the old artist's window. The scribe realized that the young lady must see much of what he had seen earlier in the day, but with different shadows, and, of course, since it was a reflection, the world around them in reverse.

Finally, the scribe, who had been mostly silent the entire time the client had been dictating, slowly, almost reverently, placed his pen on a bit of blotting paper, and picked up his head to stare into the client's almost mesmerizing eyes.

Breaking with his profession's decades-long tradition, the scribe bowed to the young client and mentally prepared himself to ask a personal question of her, hoping his departed father would not be turning over in his grave at his only son's momentary transgression, even if his son's heart was in the right place in asking the young client such a question.

"Miss, may I be so forward as to ask you a question? Possibly a sensitive question for you? You do not have to answer, of course, but I would be in your debt if you were to oblige me with an answer," the scribe asked, using high level language one reserved for more formal and elevated occasions.

"Certainly, sir, ask away," the young client responded, her eyes telling the scribe that no question he wished to ask would be too personal.

"Your…your grandmother, miss, how long? Again, you do not have to answer. How long, miss, has it been since she passed?" the scribe asked, his own voice faltering upon hearing himself speak, thereby committing a rare breech of a nearly one hundred year tradition in his family and profession, but his deep, urgent concern for the young client drove his question.

In reply, the young lady looked at the scribe in puzzlement, staring first at his solemn face and then down at the letter she had just dictated, as if she was thinking through what she had just related, trying to understand how the scribe had come to that conclusion.

"Why, sir, do you think she has passed?" the young client finally asked, and then, with a look of alarm, jerked her head up to try to catch the eye of the old artist in the back of his shop.

"Does he know something, the old artist? They've known each other for ages. If something has happened to her? What did he tell you?" the young lady, visibly distraught, asked, and urged the scribe with her hand motions to go inside and ask the old artist to confirm her question.

"Miss, my deepest apologies. Truly my trusted friend, just there, has said nothing about your grandmother. I inferred, from the tone of your letter, that something unfortunate had happened to her," the scribe replied, bowing low and mentally kicking himself for breaking with tradition.

Slowly, as if almost floating, the young client fell back in the chair, her momentary pallor fading away and color returning to her cheeks. She then sat up, leaned in, and whispered to the scribe.

"Sir, you did give me a fright, as my grandmother says. Surely she is still with us, sir. This is the day she brings me to Insa-dong, so she will be along shortly. Your money is there. Were you not also going to make a quick sketch?" the young client asked, her brilliant eyes pulling at the scribe's artistic hunger. "If not too much trouble, I'd like a small mugunghwa, rose of Sharon, blossom included, my dearest halmoni's favorite, which I'm afraid we will miss seeing together this summer."

The scribe, keeping his gaze on the young lady, while silently thanking her for being so understanding, reached under his table and dragged out a small box containing his drawing tools and tablet. He then returned the tablet and took out one of his better canvasses, the ones he reserved for the rare subject that demanded finer lines and more subtle shadows, and tighter texture.

Silently, the young client, a young lady of her grandmother's old Seoul, and the scribe, a man of indeterminate age of the same deep-rooted Seoul, sat opposite each other, as the scribe, the artist, hurriedly worked away.

The young client naturally knew, without prompting, when to turn, when to change her head's angle and, finally, as the artist was finishing, when to add her disarmingly stunning smile.

Sitting back after just a few short minutes, the scribe looked down at his work and back at the client.

A mirror. But, more than a mirror, the scribe thought.

Slowly, the scribe held the drawing up and turned it for the young lady to see.

As the drawing was slowly revealed, a strong, deep smile broke out on the young lady's face, radiating from her classic eyes, confirming to the scribe's artist side that he had captured the young client's inner being, even if only partially, and for a few minutes.

"Oh! Sir! She will be thrilled! And the petite flower is precious!" the young client finally uttered, almost with a tear in her eye, the scribe thought.

Fumbling in her purse, the young client said something about having to pay the scribe more for such an amazing work, but she soon stopped, persuaded by the scribe's calming voice that no payment was needed and, indeed, he asked the client to take all her money back. He told her that his creed did not allow personal questions, but, in his honest concern for her and her grandmother, he had broken that tradition and could not, in any way, now take the client's money.

The scribe then took the three sheets, no, he realized, the four sheets, and placed separating paper between them and then gently slid the sheets into a rigid envelope. He then took a separate, box-like envelope, or, rather, an envelope-like box and carefully placed the drawing inside, where its surface would be protected from being touched.

"You have been so kind, sir," the young client said quietly, as the scribe finished his packaging, in a voice that was as sweet as when she had been talking of her grandmother. "Even though I have passed this corner dozens of times, I now know why my grandmother always said that you had the face and the eyes of a person someone could trust. Thank you for sharing that trust with me. I'm truly sorry that I had a part in you breaking your vows. But, I think, yes, I think your ancestors know your heart is good and will not be angry. They are very proud of you, kind sir. For me, but more for my dearest, dearest grandmother, I thank you."

The scribe then stood, and even with his small stature, he was amazed at how he seemed to tower over the client, who suddenly appeared smaller and more distant as she bowed her head in thanks.

Feeling momentarily dizzy, the scribe let his gaze drop, thinking that he needed to eat something, as he extended the letter and the drawing to the client, bowing his own head in turn. Breaking tradition must have hit him harder than he had thought it would, he added to himself, as he waited for the client to take the packages.

"Hey! Aren't you going to make our ramyeon run?" the old artist suddenly called from the back of his shop, currently empty of patrons. "An old man could perish waiting around for his porridge!"

The scribe turned to his friend's laughter after the last quip and called back.

"Yes, grand master, artist to the current emperor, I will attend to your stomach's demand a soon as I have…," the scribe called to his friend, but then fell silent when he turned back to the young client.

Gone.

What? Where had she run off to?

The scribe stepped out of his station and looked left and right, and then down the alley that would have taken her to the ramyeon place she had spoken of.

Not that way, either.

"Hey, you okay? You look a little pale," the old artist asked as he stepped from his shop door to stand with the scribe.

"A client. Her documents," the scribe said, his eyes trying to penetrate the massive lunch crowds.

"What? She left them? Even after paying?" the scribe's friend asked, lifting a corner of the box-envelope to peek at the drawing.

The old artist let out a rare whistle when he saw the small drawing of the young client.

"What? Don't hang that one up, or I'll be out of business and working in your doorway," the old artist quipped, letting the top of the box drop as if he had burnt his fingers.

"Seriously, older brother, the girl was just here," the scribe replied. "And, no she didn't have to pay, but, she did. She got away, before I could give her these."

"What? Are you going soft?" the old artist snapped back.

"Long story. I'll tell you at lunch," the scribe replied, and turned back to the alcove and placed the documents in his portfolio case for safekeeping until the client returned to claim them.

"If she comes back, just take them out and give them to her, please," the scribe said, then saw the money she had left and, evidently, had refused to take back. "Oh, her name is 'Jinju,' Pearl, and give her back her money there as well. Watch the shop, okay?"

The old artist, shaking his head, collected the folded bills and put them in his top shirt pocket so as to not confuse the bills with his own. As he watched his obviously upset friend head down the narrow alley to their favorite ramyeon shop, he slid the client chair and the three-sided screen closer to the scribe's table to prevent anyone from thinking the scribe was there.

Stepping to his shop's door, the old artist turned and, looking as if he was arguing with himself, he finally resolved his inner conflict and stepped back over to the scribe's portfolio. He extracted the box-envelope and, for a full minute, stood stock still, his mind running through the possibilities.

Finally, the old artist opened the box, stared at the drawing for another long minute and, letting out a long sigh, reach over to the scribe's board display and, removing the top drawing hanging there, he substituted it with the drawing of the scribe's most recent client.

"It's okay," the old artist mumbled to himself. "She can take it with her when she returns. But, true art should never be hidden."

As he stepped back to his shop, the old artist kept mumbling the same thing.

"Never be hidden. True art, must see the light of day. The eyes and hearts of our dearest traditions, even this mob should be allowed to see."

About fifteen minutes later, the scribe returned with their late lunches, but was still feeling a bit off, especially when the old artist let him know that no one had returned to claim the documents, or the cash.

As the two were eating in the semi-privacy of the back of the old artist's shop, the scribe saw that the old artist had placed one of the scribe's paintings near several of the old man's own works for sale, and had added the scribe's name and a tag line of 'limited availability from local favorite.'

"What?" the old artist asked, feigning innocence when the scribe paused in his eating and gave the older man a questioning look. "I had to put your drawing somewhere. After I put...oops."

The scribe, realizing immediately what the old artist had done, dashed to the door and, to his amazement, saw a large group gathered around the edge of his station, looking up at the board display and the quick sketch of the recent client. He paused to listen.

"Sign says it's not for sale, though...."

"No matter, we can buy one of the others...."

"Maybe if we offered him the moon, he'd sell it...?"

The scribe stepped back into the shop and turned to stare at the old artist.

"What? So, you're good?" the old man laughed. "I can't keep milking you forever. I know your father and I argued for years that you should dump the whole scribe thing and follow your art."

"Really, that old argument?" the scribe countered.

"Yes, even if you starve to death. Lots of great artists starve. Nothing to be ashamed of," the old artist replied, huffing and puffing like an old coal boiler ready to explode.

"Older brother, you are, you are unbelievable. But, this will probably pass," the scribe replied.

"Good afternoon, sirs. How much for the phoenix and the bird? Is it a jay?" an older man, well-dressed and looking sincere, asked from the doorway.

"Why…," the scribe began, but was cut off by the old artist.

"Don't mind him, all these artists are shy and woefully inarticulate," the old artist said as he stepped across the room and followed the man outside. "The phoenix, being larger, with more detail, is, of course, much more than the little bird…."

The scribe forced himself to stop listening as the old artist managed to not only sell the two birds to the old gentleman, but the scribe's friend also remained at the display board until he had sold all, except for the young client's quick portrait. The old man then opened the scribe's portfolio, which the old artist knew well, and managed to sell three more small drawings for considerable sums.

Once back inside, the old artist made a bit of a show of taking a large envelope out of his desk, writing the scribe's name on it, shoving the massive wad of bills inside and plunking it down next to the smaller envelope of daily receipts that the scribe kept in his friend's office.

"Artist? Scribe?" the old friend chuckled.

The scribe was speechless.

"Now, I was only able to move a few of the ones in the portfolio. I know you have dozens squirreled away in that hovel you call an apartment, so go home and bring them here," the old artist commanded.

"What, now?" the scribe asked, shaking a little at the sudden turn of events. "This may just pass…."

"The day is young! Go!" the old artist commanded, hustling his friend out the door.

As he watched his life-long friend, and the son of his oldest, now long gone friend hurry away to his little apartment just a few streets over, in one of the few surviving artist colonies in old Seoul, the old man fought back a creeping doubt that maybe his younger friend was right. A fluke. A momentary surge of interest because of the amazing portrait that the public could only view, not have. A classic marketing gimmick, the old artist and shopkeeper knew well, but did not feel it applied here at all.

The drawing was true heart. True beauty. Art as art should be.

Looking back out his window toward the display board, the old artist was heartened to see several other potential patrons gathered at the display board where the old artist had hung a couple more from the portfolio, so that the client portrait didn't appear alone and out of context of his friend's additional works.

Suddenly, an older lady in the gathered crowd, her back to the old artist, appeared to swoon. She then staggered back into the scribe's station, knocking over the three-sided screen, and landing in the client chair, where the old artist discovered her after running from his shop to assist, and to avert any legal action. A younger couple was attending to the older woman.

"Oh, madam, may I...? Little sister? It's you...?" the old artist called, realizing he knew the woman, a long time friend of his who often stopped in his shop. "Are you hurt? Let's go inside where it's more comfortable?"

"Sir, big brother, please, let me just sit here, where I can see it better," the older woman, an elegant lady of the old school, said quietly, calmly.

"Oh, your eyes? Are you seeing double?" the young woman asked of the grand lady.

"No, no. I just want to sit and...and see it. I'm afraid if I move, or look away, it won't be there when I look back," the lady answered, her aged, but still sharp eyes riveted on the young client's portrait hanging at the top of the display board.

The old artist followed his friend's intense, almost tragic gaze to the scribe's recent drawing of the absent client, suddenly seeing the face in the portrait for the very first time. A face, he belatedly realized, that resembled someone he knew, but had not seen for some months.

Looking back to his friend, the old artist knelt down beside her and, taking her hand, spoke slowly, with care and with the deepest compassion. How he knew, the old artist could not fathom, but his sinking heart told him he needed to comfort his old friend, who seemed so distressed by the client's image.

"Dearest, how long?" the old man asked, not needing to add any details between strong friends.

"How long? Yesterday? Months ago? In my heart it never happened," the grieving grand dame said as she stared at the portrait, fighting back tears that she was afraid would blur her view.

"Almost a year, dear sir," the young woman replied, whispering so that the only the old artist heard. "I'm her daughter. One of her daughters. My sister...my sister is away, for now, recuperating. We don't discuss my sister around my mother. My mother wanted to come down here today. You don't know me, but she talks about you all the time, and how you used to let...used to let my niece draw while the two of you talked."

The old artist turned his eyes back to the scribe's chance portrait of a young girl, and briefly shook his head. The drawing of the random client was hanging there for anyone to see, but had struck a chord of painful familiarity with his distraught friend of many years.

Slowly, with steady reverence, the old artist, suddenly feeling his advanced years, stepped over to the display board and, taking care not to step in front of it and block his friend's view, he gently removed the portrait, turned, picked up the empty envelope box and, turning back to his grieving friend, he placed the portrait of the young client in the protective box, but did not close it. He then tenderly handed the box to the young woman, who held the treasure before the matriarch, so that she might go ahead and shed her tears, knowing that the portrait was real, and not something conjured from an old woman's unending pain and grief.

Quietly, the young man, the daughter's husband, took the old artist to the side and explained the history. A botched surgery, done far too young, but at the girl's mother's insistence, had resulted in irrevocable consequences. The child lingered for months, with the grandmother going out weekly to take pictures of the girl's favorite places. Places that they had loved together. It was only that day that the grandmother had called his wife, her daughter, and had suddenly pleaded that she wanted to walk the old streets of Insa-dong while she was still able. Maybe see if the places she and her dear one, as she called the child, were still there. She had been worried that, after so many months, some of the places would have changed hands, but, fortunately, all their favorite spots were as they had left them, nearly a year ago.

After a few minutes of subdued silence, where even the late lunch crowds around the little group seemed to sense something poignant was happening and fell silent as they passed, the matriarch allowed her practical side to take command of the situation.

"How much?" the aged lady bluntly asked her friend. "And, don't tell me some piddling little number because we know each other. That is art. That is my granddaughter. That is mine. Exchanging money for it seems unseemly, but, as I always taught my dear one, always pay a fair price. Any price, in my opinion, it too low. My son-in-law here is my lawyer. I can sign over my estates to you right now."

No one in the little group felt the grandmother was being dramatic. On the contrary, all knew she would do exactly what she said.

The old artist, loathe to disappoint his grieving friend, was racking his brain to quickly figure out how to address the obvious problem of a client that might return any moment to claim her property, and who happened to have an uncanny resemblance to the matriarch's departed granddaughter. Maybe the scribe could create a quick copy, the old artist wondered?

"How was he able to capture her true self so well?" the young woman mused.

"The artist must have seen her many times when we visited your shop, I would gather. Right, big brother?" the grandmother asked, her sharp eyes seeing hesitation in her old friend.

Just as the old artist felt he would have to make up some sort of story, the scribe appeared, carrying a thick portfolio of his drawings. Seeing the screen toppled and a group crowded around an older woman, he rushed the final half block, arriving at his friend's side, his eyes asking the questions.

"My dear friend, little sister, here is the artist," the old artist declared, presenting the scribe to the grandmother, without being able to warn him about what was coming.

However, the scribe, after years of representing people's deepest emotions in his work, both in documents and in his drawings, knew that something, no doubt his quick portrait of the young client that the young woman was holding for the old grandmother to see, had greatly moved the older woman. Choosing his words carefully, he bowed politely to the grandmother whom the old artist had just called his dear friend. It had been some time, but the scribe vaguely recognized the older woman as one of his friend's regulars over the years.

"Madam, I trust everything is fine with you? You are admiring one of my humble works, I see?" the scribe asked, his mind racing trying to understand what was going on.

"You are a modest one, you are," the grandmother replied, turning her eyes away from the portrait long enough to look up at the scribe and acknowledge his greeting. "Even my old friend here, your colleague, knows this is fine art. The finest. We were just negotiating a price and I refuse a low value for this, this masterpiece. Whatever ransom you demand, I will happily pay."

"Your drawing reminds her of her granddaughter," the old artist whispered to the scribe. "Her...departed...granddaughter."

"Silence, big brother. Son, do not let my emotional attachment to your drawing's uncanny resemblance of my lost dear one influence you. A fair price is a fair price," the grandmother declared.

For a long moment, the scribe stared at the old grandmother, imperious, proud, and ready to ensure she walked away with the simple drawing.

Then, almost like the flipping of a switch, the scribe abruptly realized the implications of what the old woman was saying, what his friend was telling him, and, at last, what the young client had been trying to tell him. In his mind's eye, he saw the young client, not sitting in the chair dictating a last letter to her beloved grandmother, but sitting in his old friend's shop, smiling away as she patiently doodled while her grandmother and his old artist friend chatted.

Some time ago, however.

Taking in a deep, long breath, the scribe nodded slowly, silently thanked his friend the old artist, and then, bowing deeply to the seated matriarch, spoke in the highest language of the old courts, their remnants just a few blocks away.

"Madam, if I may be so bold, might I asked if you stopped at the sculptures at the front of the neighborhood, and bowed to the one of the violin man?" the scribe asked, choosing his words carefully, and, at the matriarch's slow nodding, continued.

"Did you not also stop at the ice cream, western ice cream shop just down the way? Yes? And, did you also pause to look in the little ceramic and glass shop a few doors shy of the ice cream shop? Yes? And, did you not introduce your, yes, daughter and her husband? Introduce them to the small ramyeon and mandu spot just down this alley, where you then returned by way of your old friend's art studio, to stop in and say hello before…," the scribe asked, but was then interrupted by the matriarch.

"Uncanny. Absolutely uncanny," the grandmother declared, half rising out of her chair. "How can you remember my dear one's routine after so long a time? How? You're not one of those stalking people? You're not…?"

"No, no, little sister. Calm yourself," the old artist said quickly. "He's a good man. I've known him since he was a baby. Knew his father and mother for years. You can trust him."

"Trust him?" the old grandmother repeated, looking from the scribe to the portrait, and back again. "Trust him?"

"Yes, dearest grandmother," the scribe answered for the matriarch. "For as many years as you brought your dear one to Insa-dong for fun outings, you evidently told her, and I'm greatly humbled and immeasurably honored, you told your little dear one that the scribe on the corner was a man she could trust. That, madam, she did. Your words, madam, brought the young lady to me, to us, today."

"Dear one…? How…?" the grandmother repeated, her eyes wide, her right hand pressing her chest in disbelief.

After his brief speech, the scribe stepped over to his main portfolio and, extracting the letter he had written earlier for the curious young client, he turned and, finding the final sheet, held the sheet for the grandmother to see the closing, the name, and, yes, the date, which was that very day.

"This, madam, I think, is for you," the scribe added with the utmost tenderness and formality, bowing low as he held the precious document out to its intended recipient.

The young client's grandmother, her grief and pain slowly evaporating, let her eyes travel over the scribe's letter, taken down, word for word, from her dear one. How the scribe had done it, the grandmother did not need to ask. The letter was riddled with information, phrases, advice, and, above all, terms of endearment that only she and her little dear one would have known.

The scribe then turned to the old artist who drew the cash out of his pocket and handed it to the daughter, watching the eyes of the grandmother grow wide seeing the telltale triangular folds of the bills she had always given her granddaughter during their outings.

The old grandmother, against the protests of her daughter and her old friend, the old artist, stood up, shook off everyone's hands and, straightening her back, she bowed low several times to the scribe, shocking passerby, since an older, aristocratic woman would never bow to a lowly street artist.

The scribe, horrified that the old matriarch was going to debase herself bowing to him, bowed back, and insisted on helping her to stand tall.

The old woman then actually embraced the younger man and, for a long moment, held on tight to the last person who would probably see her dear one for a long time to come. She then stepped back, her eyes asking, but her voice afraid to ask.

"Yes, she was happy, dearest grandmother. Extraordinarily happy. Due, madam, in large part to your teachings, especially on how we, as humans, can choose how we respond to events, good, or less fortunate. You raised her well, dear halmoni," the scribe said, finally seeing the child in his mind's eye for who she really was.

"And, her...her eyes? You drew her eyes from memory...?" the matriarch, the loving grandmother, asked of the artist, even though to ask tore at her already tortured heart.

"Your dear one has the eyes of a princess of old Seoul, dearest grandmother. Yes, she has your eyes, still. I can see that now. The eyes in the drawing are the eyes she carries with her into...well, with her," the scribe artist replied, trying to be sensitive to the grandmother's pain.

The scribe then calmed the grandmother as she fumbled at her purse, the larger version of the same one the child had held, and tried to soothe her concerns.

"Madam, I have been paid well beyond what any earthly gold can represent, dearest halmoni. Your dear one, little Jinju, showed me my art after so many years of repressing it. She also gave me the gift of being able to pass her thoughts on to the one person she knew her thoughts, her words, her joys, her ultimate happiness, would bring peace to," the scribe and artist said in gracious tones to the matriarch.

"Sir, little brother, I thank you. I will cherish these. These are my heart," the grandmother said, unfazed at the surreal existence of the letter and the drawing. "Will you join us at the ramyeon shop? It's a small request, but I think she...I think little Jinju would like that."

The scribe, objecting that he would be intruding on a solemn family gathering, turned to ask the old artist, her friend, to take his place when he saw his friend waving the ceramics shop's assistant over, and telling the assistant to stay at the old artist's shop and watch things until they returned.

With that, the little group moved down the alley, but not before the old grandmother paused and placed her hands on the display board where she had discovered her dear one after so long and so painful a time.

"Looks sad, nearly empty, doesn't it?" the grandmother said quietly, to nods from the group.

"Draw her, sir!" the grandmother suddenly declared in a strong, bold voice, as she straightened to her full height.

"Madam?" the scribe, now artist, answered.

"Draw her, young man! Paint her! Sculpt her! Share her inspiring image with the world!" the matriarch of old Seoul commanded.

"Madam, I assure you, you will be the only one who would ever have your dear one's image," the artist, formerly scribe, replied.

"No! Share her spirit, sir. Use your gift. Use it! She would want that, I think. Yes, she would want that. I know!" the old grandmother declared, her tone accepting no rebuttals as the little group faded into the alley on the way to the little ramyeon shop, with excellent mandus.

That parting letter for the wisp of a young client to her dearest grandmother was the final letter in over a hundred years of the artist's family's tradition of being scribes, first in the high courts, and then in the side streets of Insa-dong.

The former scribe, fully turned artist, returned to his passion and, over the following years, produced many, many works, a number of which found their way to museums across the peninsula, and to salons and museums around the world. In all that time, during all that success, the little artist retained his humble little studio in the alcove of his friend's shop. He kept the client chair and the three-sided screen, held to one side at a small display shop where the artist showed his wares, in the building he and his old artist friend finally bought. Over time, the two artists opened a rotating gallery, to host a range of young artists, modeling on an old friend's artist design colony in Shibyua, just north of Harajuku Street, in Tokyo.

Next time you find yourself wandering the few remaining traditional alleys in Insa-dong, or Harajuku, or Greenwich Village, or Venice's Jewish Quarter, or London's Soho, or any other refuge for the talented among us, look closely for that charcoal portrait of a happy young client, calling to you across time and space, to inspire you to great things, all the while encouraging you to thank any devoted grandmother you see on a weekend outing with her own dear one, or ones.

Such is the legacy of the last letter writer of Insa-dong.

INTERLUDE V

For several minutes after he had finished the tale, the writer wondered to himself if he should have inserted a few ghouls or night demons into the Insa-dong alleyways to pad the story with characters the creature could more easily identify with, especially after the beast's outburst and ranting about revenge and royal haunting, as yet unexplained. However, the writer, having shaped the story from a tale he had heard from an artist friend in Insa-dong years before, had not felt he had the moral right to alter the tale into some grotesque parody of what was a humbling story. He also reminded himself that his challenge to his host was for his host to find the creature's brethren folded into the background of the writer's pages.

"What is your fascination with these human ghosts, boy? These wandering gwisin?" the creature finally asked, leaning forward in the stone chair, and staring at the writer. "Is it that all you weak flesh creatures fear, your own demise, so must conjure up fanciful tales of those who have gone over?"

"Such are common themes across all cultures and countries. No doubt your sire and his people had grand tales of spirits from the old country?" the writer rebutted, trying to recall what little he knew of Norse mythology.

"Yes, there were such tales told, when the wind was high, the food scarce, and the little ones anxious," the beast replied. "Foolish tales to scare the little ones into being strong. You merely confirm how weak you humans are, calling for this spirit or that to return after moving on. My cousins make great sport of it."

"Sport?" the writer quickly asked, wondering what new horror his captor was going to spring on him.

"Great sport, a phrase we learned long ago from ones across the sea," the creature replied. "My cousins, and some of the younger, less developed ghouls, will wriggle into the newly d—...passed, causing all manner of mayhem at your burial rites, or at the homes after. Careful, they must be, as the true wraiths can be vindictive. Dangerously so. One cousin was in old Busan. Had followed a juicy bit and was carried there on your iron carriage. Tried to wriggle into an old man's family, just after the rites. Was swallowed by the man's protector, a phantom that lingers about many of the old ones who made the Meredith journey."

"The Meredith journey?" the writer asked, trying to bring up an old memory with that name, but was just not able to.

"During your foolish war, where many fell and fed many of my cousins. The war that brought my sire's humans. They escaped over the sea, away from the clutches of their human enemies and the grasp of my mother's people," the creature replied, tapping his long fingers on the stone. "Many, many lived, riding that boat south. That's why few cousins haunt Busan and south. Protected, those old ones are. At least, until the last of them passes."

"During the war...? The evacuation? From Hungnam? The miracle ship?" the writer replied, the memory of where he had heard the name before finally coming to him.

"Miracle? You fools do like your fantasies, scribbler," the creature spat back at the writer. "Do you know the dark wraiths that haunt the fringes of Busan of old?"

"Haunt? No, I...another time, I was visiting a buddy in Washington," the writer answered, his mind far away. "He invited me along on a ranger's walking tour at the Korean War memorial, where my buddy volunteered.

The talk was on the Hungnam evacuation, that the ranger always gave close to Christmas. Was mesmerizing. After the tour, it was late, almost dark, and nearly all the visitors had moved on, when he told me to go back into the memorial. Alone. Said to walk with my head pointed straight and to not turn my head to look at the statues, or the wall, the one with the faces and military equipment. Said to stare straight ahead and walk at a steady pace, and to only see the statues and the wall out of the corners of my eyes, my periphery."

The writer fell silent for a moment, forgetting he was in the lair of a crazed hermit, his mind reliving that long ago walk in the cold air of a Washington dusk.

"What, fool? Has your mind finally broken?" the creature challenged when the writer's silence dragged on.

"No. I was lost, briefly, among those stoic souls," the writer replied, in a distant voice. "As I walked, I swear to this day I still believe it, those battered and worn, tough and dedicated men were walking along beside me. Moving. Not frozen statues, but moving, as if alive. Cautiously. Stepping gingerly. Forever living that nightmare, but looking ahead to hope. For themselves, their squad mates, their loved ones far away, Korea, and all those unable to defend themselves. Find those soldiers in that time between day and night, when the light is dying, and when some believe souls can pass between worlds. Find them, with respect, and those steely grey heroes may allow you to walk with them."

"Buried there, your war lost?" the creature asked. "Busan has such. Very large. Protected, it is, by the old ones."

"No. No one buried. That's across the river. In Arlington," the writer replied, forcing himself to refocus on the beast and his predicament, and turned the questioning back to the creature.

"Didn't you say you spent time in Busan? After Jeju?" the writer asked, wanting to keep the creature talking, while using the more modern, subtly different English pronunciations for the two southern regions.

"Time? A little. Enough to know it is not the place for proper goblins or troll-ogres. Too many phantoms lurking in the dark spaces between humans," the creature answered. "They want the humans for themselves. Rarely make deals. And, in league with she-who-is-not-named, if cousins try to drag one of the old Meredith humans."

"But, enough of your questions, scribbler," the creature suddenly declared. "You evade. I ask again. Why dwelling on the gwisin? Do you fear? Do you fear your passing, scribbler? Is there no one who will wail for you and tend to your rotting bones? Will anyone spill those tears that are so common in your kind, when you are no longer around to babble your silly tales?"

"I ask you how," the writer countered, having mentally prepared himself for the creature's verbal attacks. "How do you and your kind? How do you prepare? Your father's and your mother's kind. Where do you go after death?"

"Stay your foul words, human!" the creature roared. "Have I not warned you about summoning her? Have I not invited you to take an early swim in the oil and fatty remains of the late solicitor, if you try to open a gate for her?"

"My apologies. Of course, you can't see beyond, even with your other...abilities," the writer replied, thinly veiling a challenge to the creature's self-proclaimed powers.

"Beyond? What is beyond for one cast off by the family of the peninsula and lost to one's sire's side?" the creature asked, more to the surrounding trees than to the writer. "Do I look to the east, or do I look to the west, human? What do your 'mixed kid' spawn do? What do they see beyond?"

"They are more practical. Looking mostly at earthly issues," the writer replied, loath to reveal any details about his children or family to the sick mind of his captor. "I doubt they even think about the beyond."

"Part of me yearns for the unseen rivers and mountains of the northern lands, the lands of my sire's Norsemen and their brethren across the German Sea. My sire spoke of these with great fondness, in those few seasons we were together. That could be my beyond," the creature replied, and then waved his left hand in a sweeping motion that encompassed the enclave. "Or, mayhap these old mountain stones are my beyond, to absorb whatever remains of my essence at the end, to be forever trapped in these forlorn, nearly silent stones of my mother's peninsula."

The writer was immediately struck by the out of character humanity of the beast's reply, seeming to voice an internal struggle that may have been raging within its decaying chest for decades.

"Maybe, if I might venture a guess, you have both beyonds?" the writer suggested. "Your sire's rivers and mountains, and your mother's...?"

"Samgaksan, on the spirit road to Heaven Lake," the creature answered, without its usual reticence. "Yet, she was abandoning any chance of that when she tried to smuggle me to my sire."

"Heaven Lake? The crater lake?" the writer asked, hoping to get the creature to explain further.

"Crater? What? Yes, far to the north," the creature replied, annoyed at the writer's feigned ignorance. "Yet, you call yourself an observer and you don't know the numerous traditional refuges on the peninsula?"

"I am always learning," the writer replied, but without malice, then continued.

"These beyond places you speak of, are they where you, your kind go after...after you've met that being whose name you do not speak?" the writer asked.

"Some, human, some cousins and other night beasts go those paths. Some simply spiral down into...into the dust, I suppose. Others...," the creature squinted its eyes and looked hard at the captive. "Others, boy, cycle into the next here."

"The next here...? Like reincarnation?" the writer asked, absorbed in the creature's sudden intellectual discussion, but not foolish enough to completely drop his guard.

"Your religions have this, I'm told by the temple cousins. Many believe you come back as a better thing than before. We don't come back, we simply continue," the creature answered, waving its stein around.

"A few, now...this is not for human ears, but yours will be soup soon, so...a few never continue, never cease, just are," the creature teased, its already cloudy eyes seeming to cloud even more with the effects of another gulp of the grotesque stein of devil's mead.

"Immortal?" the writer asked, almost reflexively, then regretted being pulled further into the banter with the creature.

"Everyone is immortal, human. Isn't that what your temple masters tell you?" the creature threw out as if it were a professor challenging a group of students. "Even as you dissolve in our sturdy pot there on that ancient stove, you will believe, as your flesh boils off, as your eyes pop, unless the little ones are quicker than the heat and take them as prizes first, as your tripe sizzles, you will cling to your belief in immortality. For many of my cousins, it is the same. Even as they are captured by the mountains and slowly turned to stone, or are cursed by the witches bored with their antics, they believe their fate is only temporary and, one day, always just a few days on, they will return to the...to their hovels and haunts, whole again."

"Where do you...?" the writer began, wanting to find out just what the creature thought its fate might be, but his captor had had enough talk.

"Continue on, boy. No more secrets from me, you will extract," the creature barked, then softened its tone to one of humor. "I might be a night spirit, but a moron, I am not. Continue. The tale of the human child was, no, is interesting, as I have a certain fondness for the denizens of old Insa-dong."

"Yes, you had mentioned?" the writer suggested, leaving an opening for the creature to continue its reflective mood from earlier.

"Yes, some interest, but for my ears only, teller of woeful tales," the beast replied, taking a long draught of the stein. "The child was a waste. My cousins in your doctor houses would have starved waiting for her to awaken. She was sickly, this puny human? The wailing of the ugly aunt suggests the mother killed the child?"

"Killed? No. No," responded the writer. "The background is a veiled device, to carry the reader to the greater point of the story. The mother, maybe, the reader never really knows, maybe had a misguided sense of what was right for the child. In a society that demands perfection, the child had eyes of her ancestors. The eyes that spoke to the scribe, to the old artist, to strangers gazing at her image, and, most importantly, to her grieving halmoni, her dearest grandmother. The mother, well, as you heard the grandmother say, the mother had other thoughts…from what the aunt related."

"Yes, yes, the foolish mother. Do you think me a toadstool? A simpleton? Of course, the child's demise was caused by some misguided human mother's loony desire," the creature argued, his speech, yet again, returning to the more sane, the more, suspiciously, normal. "Yes, mother's milk can often be bitter, scribbler."

The creature made an odd suckling noise, to the writer's horror, imitating a child yearning for its mother's comfort.

"Yes, I know this, human. Many of my cousins thrive on the drippings alone from a single cutter's table. Allies in our thirst for morsels, these cutters are, boy," the creature boomed in its throaty, harsh voice, as it stood and walked around the enclave.

"Yes," said the writer, after a long stretch of silence. "There are no winners in this, except maybe your cousins. The ones who will, no doubt, consume the souls and morsels of the mistakes."

"What? Why would my cousins, as stupid as they are, eat the physicians' black hearts and rob themselves of the many others the fool pushes to the dark corners of your sad human lives?" the creature laughed, seemingly surprised that the writer would suggest such a thing. "No, fool boy, my cousins of the sick wards watch the even scarier shadows for those who would drag such a physician down. No, the longer she plies her tragic and glorious trade, any goblin, or even ghoul, will remain fat and greasy from her victims."

"Surely, you can't heap the blame on the doctor alone?" the writer countered. "Social pressures. Individual choice. Overbearing mothers. Marketing departments. Even real health concerns. These all contribute."

"Blame? Blame, silly human. Blame your sire's side. Yes, and the occupiers, for bringing such shallowness and contempt for the natural to these shores!" the creature yelled. "Great morsels for us, so we applaud such imports. Did you never wonder why so many of my cousins roam the lower reaches of Gangnam and the like? Yes, the cram schools are good targets, where dragging a fretting student, even a parent, is so routine that there is almost no sport. One of my little ones runs a small flock that infests the schools at suneung, the placement tests. They always return with enough fat to rest for half a cycle. Yet, far more filling are the armies of humans at the sick houses for those not sick. Teeming with goblins, exiled fairies, and older ghouls in the shadows and corners, all just waiting for the shavings from the knife and the droppings from the wandering souls. For some, yes, for some, there are quiet deals made in the night between the lesser talented cutters and the lazier goblins who drag the dregs down, all the while biding their time until they can drag the cutters as well."

Shuddering at the graphic imagery, the writer coughed and turned back to his notebook, looking at the remaining tales. Seeing the next one was somewhat tragic, but did not really appeal to the beast's more vicious side, and lacked a lot of what the creature called his cousins, he decided he'd just have to read it through, alter in spots, if possible, and see how the beast reacted, as he took a deep breath, only to be interrupted by his captor.

"Yet, that letter writer, boy, did take me back to my uncles' stories. Stories of the time before the constant wars. The time when a goblin or a spirit knew his place, knew the order of things. Your Hongdae tale showed a little of that old way. That order, old, decaying, rotting from within, was still our order. We knew where we stood. The chaos of the wars, the rebellions, even the occupying, all were good for my uncles and cousins. My uncles said we never wanted during those times. But, after, as you humans continued to wander in your own darkness, unsure as to what order was the right order, you drove many of my kind, both my sire's and my mother's, into home exile, into the alleys and dark undergrounds where only your waste and your machines live. Many, many of my cousins faded to dust, trapped in their old ways, thinking the humans would return to their proper order and all would be as before. No, human, the before is never more."

The writer had listened and watched the beast soliloquize while it wandered about the enclave. He was close to deciding that the beast was actually just a mentally troubled outcast, living out the end of a very disturbed life in a bubble of insanity on the slopes of Namsan. While the creature had talked, the writer also thought he had seen the creature's ghastly appearance soften. The skin seemed to have less pallor. The bone thin hands appeared to have gained some meager fat. Even the weeping lesions on the beast's face and neck had seemed to fade to scars.

As his captor fell into quiet reflection as it walked, the writer looked away from the wandering host to scan the dark trees behind the stove.

Silence.

Not even a rustle out of the little ones, the writer realized.

Looking back to the creature, the writer was shocked to see that even the beast's robes had ceased to be threadbare rags, but had hazily returned to those of the old scholar who had lured the writer into the enclave.

Wait, the writer said to himself, and quickly looked away, counted to three, and then looked back.

Just as grotesque as earlier, the writer saw, as the creature passed close to the bench, leaving a stench in its wake.

For some reason, probably sanity, the writer was relieved that he had just been hallucinating, lulled into thinking the beast more human due to its normal voice and demeanor, and that it had not suddenly morphed into some pleasant, older professor type.

Better to die in the pot of a deranged beast, the writer thought wryly, than at the hands of a pleasant intellectual.

"Now, grotesque beast," the writer spoke up in a commanding voice, switching out what he had called the creature to play on the beast's vanity, "let's move away from the ghosts of Insa-dong, and look just over that ridge, between the trees, beyond the old walls, and you can see the general location of the next tale."

After a moment, the writer's words piqued the creature's interest and it walked over to the trees to look out over the mountain toward the Han River. Waving its arm, several of the branches bent to the side so that it had a clear view of the sloping terrain down to the river, to include several of the bridges spanning the dark water.

"Noodle shops," the creature suddenly said as it looked out over southern Seoul.

"Noodle shops?" the writer repeated.

"In your tale, fool. Down that ghoul alley. Noodle shops," the creature retorted, its thin, yet wide shoulders blocking the writer's view of the river.

"Yes. You know that shop?" the writer asked.

"Yes. That shop, and countless others. From, yes, from my younger days, scribbler," the creature replied, looking back over its left shoulder. "Many a mid-day company man we plucked, as he slurped and slurped. That black, oozing sauce. That sound. So loud in those small shops that my cousins and I had free rein. Easy life, even if the morsels were a little dull and lacking spice, they were plentiful. My mouth still waters to think of those days."

"Those western coffee houses your tale seems to exalt, while the prey was plump, the morsels were thin," the creature continued, grumbling. "A cousin would waste several moons trying to fatten up on the thin gruel of those haughty patrons, boy. Better to haunt a grandmother's cart near the schools, where the morsels were bright and shiny, ready for plucking."

The creature then fell silent, while the writer wondered whether to nudge the beast to the next tale or to keep it talking.

The creature decided for the writer.

"You say over the ridge? Yongsan? Where so many of your kind used to dwell?" the creature asked, as if it had a bad taste in its mouth, turning back to look to the river.

"A little farther," the writer replied. "At the river."

"It is a long river, human," the creature snapped, clearly not in the mood for riddles.

"The bridges, vile one," the writer snapped back. "We turn to the bridges over that river."

"Which? No, don't tell me. I want to be surprised," the creature quipped and turned back to the writer as the beast waved its arm and the opening closed. "Many a cousin I have, and other, darker, ones-with-no-names, who lurk about those massive roads you humans have built over the water. The river itself has many water spirits. Not so many as before, but, certain places, especially near to the shore, where you fools gather. There go many a bloated goblin or ghoul. Yes, surprise me, scribbler!"

With that, the writer cleared his throat, and, deciding to stay seated for the story, at least initially, began, keeping one eye on the creature as it settled back in its chair, and one eye on the dark spaces between the trees behind the old stove.

"Let's head down to the river's edge. Where, unlike the marshy swamps of old, couples can stroll, children can play, artists and musicians can create, teens can dance, and romantics can dream along the much cleaned up and reimagined banks of the mighty Han," the writer called in a loud, crisp voice, so his captor would hear clearly. "Let's join one of those dreamers, as he heads off to meet...well, to find something precious along those winding paths, manicured parks, and floating dreams of Seoul's Han River."

6

MAPO, BRIDGE OF SIGHS

About thirty minutes west-southwest of Mount Namsan, straddling the boroughs of Mapo-dong and Yeouido-dong, stands one of the many bridge spans that carry Seoul's inhabitants to and from their daily, and nightly, routines across the Han River, that great waterway that has been so integral to the nation's history. For society's overworked and constantly on the move generation, the river and the many bridges spanning its normally tranquil waters are fleeting reminders of simpler, less hectic days of yore, when life was humbler, people were less stressed, and getting somewhere, outside of one's home village, was undertaken rarely, but with planning and care. A bridge enables that journey. A bridge carries hopes and dreams from one point to another. A bridge can also be a barrier, something for a child to fear to cross, thinking the waters beneath are too violent for the supports and the concrete spans. A bridge can also be, when the moon is just right, the waters a little swifter with snowmelt, and the air full of hints of spring, a place of reflection and discovery. Such a personal discovery, to be played out as a frenzied search with the ending yet unknown, was what one young man had undertaken one recent evening, while hoping the bridge, that vast, emotionless expanse of horizontal steel, concrete, and industrial polymers would not be on the menu once the young man had gone down to the river. Let's step out of our own comfortable shoes, for a few moments, and slip into that young man's bank account breaking Italian boots, finding him...oh yes, just there, after his father's company car had dropped him near one of the favorite haunts of today's youth, not far from a clever sign, 'I Seoul U,' along the Han River's southern shore. It's a cold evening, so we will also bundle up in the young man's tailored coat and, being careful not to disturb him, join his thoughts as he makes his way to the river's edge.

Call me...?

Call me a foolish man.

Call me a man in...maybe in love?

That inexplicable condition that doesn't present a structured, easy to understand framework.

The good.

The bad.

The happy.

The dark.

Avoided subjects. Quick changes to plans. Steering conversations to safer, less demanding topics.

Call me guilty.

Yes, that's a good name on such a blustery, dark night.

Guilty one.

Let the sleeping demons lie, just below the surface, keeping them just enough at bay to move through life without having to address them head on. Better to fake it until you make it, one of the counselors had said.

Fool!

Suddenly, the cold, western wind was biting at the back of my neck as I approached the river walk from where the car had dropped me off. A few other souls had braved the late evening weather, but none, I surmised, would have the same mission as I.

Or would they?

Was I so special that common things did not happen to me?

Mission?

Was that how I would describe my frantic dash from home? My quick, futile call to my best friend, my darling...who was offline? The mad ride, fueled by the promise of a hefty bonus to one of our younger drivers, across town to the Han River park spread out before me?

Wait! What's that sound?

A soulful, deep chested call rose from the rippling shadows of the water.

Looking across the water's silvery black expanse, I saw the source of the mournful sound, one of the brightly lit ferries, blasting its gloomy horn close to shore, near the terminal just to the south.

In spite of the forlorn sound, how many happy couples were on that night ferry, I wondered?

Shaking off the thoughts of ferries and strangers, I tried to remember which walk she had mentioned had been her favorite, the last time we had trod that part of the river paths....

Yes! She always said it reminded her of some song. Maybe from Italy...?

She.

My flawed perfection.

My…?

Yes, I was still being overly possessive. Yet another reason she….

Italy? What was that song?

My freezing brain battled to recall the lyrics of that old song she had hummed until I had, sadly, in retrospect, demanded she stop and learn another.

After I had passed the last stand of thick trees, the wind slapped at my face, as if to remind me of my earlier folly, and I stepped into the crossing to the park.

I had almost dredged up the elusive name of the song, but that blast of frigid air robbed me of all thoughts other than escaping the wind by getting lower, toward the river paths.

Rome?

Looking out over the ageless ruins of the Forum? Lingering on the Spanish Steps? Tossing coins in all those fountains?

No.

Florence?

Wandering the gold shops at the Ponte Vecchio? Getting lost in the grandeur of the Duomo? Pursuing the perfect pasta in those lanes and alleyways?

No.

Maybe…Venice?

Was that it?

Too long ago.

Too many missed opportunities.

Too many lost moments.

Where was I?

The sudden fear of being in the totally wrong area of the vast Han River parks system grabbed me by the throat. That fear, coupled with the merciless wind clawing at the exposed flesh of my face above my black clad body, drove me to pause, turn my back to the wind, and hunch over to check my phone.

An iPhone.

Which I no longer tried to hide from my more nationalistic friends.

Removing one of my puffy gloves, I tapped the maps icon and reviewed my location and the location of the walking paths and bridges nearby.

Wait. There were three or four within easy walking distance.

Which ones crossed any water?

That's it!

Crossing the water like the little bridges all over Venice!

Only three, my wind-numbed mind realized, fit the bill.

That should make it easier for me to find the right one, yes?

Standing at the edge of an unsheltered grove of nearly naked trees, tiny buds ready to welcome a frigid spring to Korea's capital, I wondered if I should turn left first or right?

What…? Who's there?

I involuntarily ducked my head at a sudden wide shadow that seemed to loom just above me.

Oh, just the trees leaning over from the wind, I then realized, and not some cunning night demon trying to steal into my frigid thoughts.

I again checked my find a friend app and saw that her phone was still turned off. Taking a deep gulp of the moist, cold air, I closed the phone and slid it back into my coat pocket next to the small backup battery.

As I tugged the glove back onto my hand, two young couples, huddled close as a group, hurried by, no doubt heading for one of the few open cafés near the river. Their low level chatter was muffled by their quick footsteps and the growing wind.

Young couples.

I smiled grimly at the thought. The four, even bundled up against the wind, looked like senior year students. Youngsters. Being a grad student allowed me to think of the undergrads as young.

Yet, why rush into getting older, I mused, as the small group faded into the evening. Better to be young when young.

Turning back to my quest, I mentally calculated the time to reach the three different paths, choosing first to turn right, to investigate the single bridge that spanned water in that direction. I'd then turn back and check the other two. It was a gamble, but the solitary bridge was closer, so should present the quickest option.

Rational, critical thinking.

I groaned inwardly at my thinking man's mantra, as I turned into the wind, and headed across the park toward the water's edge.

My philosopher's crutch.

What had rational thought done for me? For her?

I shook off such reflections as being unproductive, and tried to focus on the park around me.

The lights, which would have been cheerful any other night, danced across the bundled bodies and faces of a few brave couples and small groups who were, surprisingly, in the park. I watched them, absently, out of the corner of my eye, as most moved along quietly, not wanting to expose their faces to talk against the cold wind, with the taste of snow in the air.

I felt a wry smile bend my worried face for a moment.

Taste of snow.

My old grandmother, on my mother's side, used to say that to me. She had loved the snow, the accompanying cold, and the wintry wind. She had always said that the snowflakes were the tears of the family she had lost to the northern side, after the war. The snowflakes were the endless tears sent by her older siblings whom she had never forgotten, feeling warmth in the belief that the same snow storms would also fall on her lost family, giving them comfort from her own tears.

Funny, that I should think of my long passed grandmother now. Maybe I did have a something akin to a soul after all?

Wait!

Who was that? Just climbing the bridge's ramp not thirty meters in front of me?

The slimming black coat. The hesitantly confident stride, becoming more common among a new generation of independent Korean women. The height.

The woman's head and hair were hidden by a fur-lined hood, but....maybe?

I wiped the wind blasted water from my eyes and picked up speed. Yet, I didn't want to run for fear of spooking her, so simply extended my stride.

My eyes, blinking tears against the harsh wind, tried to follow the figure's progress up the footbridge's gently sloping ramp.

Just as the woman passed a small group of youths descending the ramp, she turned and, thanks to the light from the ornate carriage lamps lining the ramp, I caught a quick glimpse of a reddened left cheek and a perfect nose before the woman lowered her head again, against the wind.

Was it she?

Must get closer.

As I reached the base of the ramp, I hesitated.

Was it her face? Or, was she at one of the other bridges and this woman, this stranger, was simply a decoy, thrown in front of my anxious eyes by the laughing, cruelest of fates to delay my true rendezvous?

Not wanting to face the answer, I paused, momentarily, at the base of the ramp, and watched the woman turn onto the footbridge. I then immediately noticed she was slowing down.

She stopped.

While still over the park, not the water.

Not over the water.

I shook off my hesitancy and took a bold step forward.

The woman then turned and looked back down the ramp, forming a half-smile on her young, innocent face.

Had she seen me?

Through the blur of my wind tearing eyes, I saw a smile, and my heart jumped.

But, was it her face? Was the figure...was it she?

I silently cursed my blurry vision, taking care not to curse the wind, another legacy of my grandmother.

Suddenly, hurried footsteps came up behind me, which were quite loud, with the harsh, but solid sound made by expensive boots. The imported boots were attached to a fashionably dressed young man about my height and build, who continued past me, and rushed up the ramp.

I watched the young woman's smiling face follow the interloper up the ramp until she held out her welcoming arms for him.

Deflated, I abruptly turned away, not wanting to see the happy meeting between the young lovers.

Waste of valuable time.

Better to keep my focus and dismiss the lives of others.

'Dismiss the lives of others?'

Yes, that was my first thought. Something she had always tried to help me temper, while trying to gently guide me to caring about others. Rational me always thought she was being too sympathetic to others, weakening her own resolve.

Maybe she was right?

Of course, she was right, some baser part of my wind-addled mind yelled at the rational me.

Turning back, I stepped away from the ramp, having seen that there were no other single figures on the well-lighted bridge, and stole a quick look at the embracing happy couple.

That had been us.

Only a year ago.

Venice.

Lingering by the Academy Bridge, looking across the boat dotted water of the Grand Canal toward the sunset bathed dome of Santa Maria della Salute. Wandering the old Jewish Quarter in search of local breads, far from the tourists, and finding bakery heaven in an alley ironically called 'The Oven.' Chasing the perfect gelato all over the city, and finally finding the best candidate in the shadow of the Rialto Bridge.

During the spring break tour of Europe after senior year.

Finally, bits of that old song she loved, stole, with vague familiarity, into my consciousness as I hurried along to the other two bridges.

Something about the end of the day?

At the same time, her happy, laughing face came to me, bathed in the warm glow of the muted night lighting in Saint Mark's plaza, eating pastries with espresso and tea at the Café Florian.

Her mental image warmed me against the wind, strong even at my back, so I allowed the remnants of the song to stay with her image as I navigated an oddly empty section of river path to the second of the bridges.

What…?

My stride was suddenly, almost involuntarily, stopped.

A detour?

My progress had come to a screeching halt, within sight of the not too distant, second pedestrian bridge.

Construction.

Blocking my way forward.

A flimsy, but tall fence stretched from the water's edge across the park, to disappear somewhere in the naked trees I had passed earlier.

Forgetting my primary mission in the face of the unexpected distraction, my usual pomposity surfaced and demanded, from the unsympathetic night, what idiot city father had authorized construction on such a busy path just a week or two before the first spring blossoms were to burst forth?

Shaking off my indignation, I sized up the high fence barrier before me, and wondered if I needed to double-back to the road crossing?

A well-dressed young couple, unnoticed by me earlier, with possibly a nanny or a grandmother pushing a carriage, was just turning back from the barriers, having given up on finding a way through.

A baby carriage? In such harsh weather?

Part of me idly questioned what kind of people would do that to a little child.

The nanny, for she had the look of a nanny, and no Korean grandmother would have allowed a daughter or daughter-in-law to drag a young baby out in such cold, was happily cooing to the youngster, who was buried in several wraps, under a windshield lowered to protect the child.

The two parents were both chattering into phones, the mother looking back only once to the child and nanny as the group passed me, with no greeting, save from the obviously kind-hearted nanny.

Shaking my head slowly at the departing micro-family, I turned back to the barriers, thinking I might see a way through, but half wondering if I needed to follow the family group and look for a way around.

The muted lights from the construction site had laid out a pattern of alternating dark and light bands, somehow reminding me of the crosshatch shadows from the bars of a prison cell one sees in the movies.

Stepping closer to the barriers, a sudden movement to my right caught my eye.

Looking more closely, I spied a young boy, dressed in a bright orange snowsuit, weaving through the obstacles of the construction site to emerge on the other side of the inconvenience. The young boy was visible as he passed through the slanted bars of dark and light.

But, wait. How had he entered?

"Hey, little brother. Yes, you in the amazing persimmon suit. How did you enter this construction space?" I called to the boy, using my most authoritative voice, both from my obligatory stint in the armed forces and from running one of the larger hotel chains in my father's portfolio during the previous summer break.

The young boy, his head whipping around like a cornered Jindo pup at my call, and looking as if he might dash away, no doubt fearful of having been caught violating the law of the posted signs, broke into a relieved grin when he saw me standing at the fence, and not an officer. The child then pointed toward the river.

"There is a gap, just along the river there. You are skinny enough, old man," the cherubic child quipped, his face weighed down with the classic, overfed pudginess of a certain age of first sons in Korea.

Laughing at his little, but still disrespectful joke, the boy took off at a trot and disappeared beyond the trees at a curve in the path, giving the odd impression of a ripe persimmon trying to return to the bare trees just beyond.

I mentally dismissed the kid's cheekiness and looked over at the river's edge. Scanning the construction fence, I finally saw the gap the brat had pointed out.

Narrow, but I was slim, so should be able to squeeze through.

Without hesitation, which surprised me, since I would normally have dutifully doubled-back, looked for the proper detour, taken the other crosswalk, and would have avoided violating untold city ordinances, not to mention scoffing at the safety hazards by deliberately ignoring the signs and fencing.

However, a certain sense of growing desperation drove me. It was an alien feeling, something I had not experienced, not to the level that had addled my normally sensible, rational thinking.

Once at the river path's edge, I looked at the narrow strip of low wall and the long drop into the black, unforgiving waters below. Gripping the fence for a more secure passage, I sidled along the low wall for the meter or so to the gap in the fence and hopped through.

Inside the construction zone, the reason for the fence and the signs became acutely apparent.

Holes.

Very wide, spaced out all around.

Big holes.

Dangerous holes.

As I stood looking at the gaping, almost mouth-like obstacles before me, I had a flash back to my early childhood video games.

Grimly, I recalled I had always been squashed by the trucks when I had attempted to get too far across those crazy roads in that old game.

But, if a young boy could weave his way through, then I could, I told myself.

Wait! Hold still, part of my mind suddenly commanded, and I complied.

Security!

Fortunately, some part of me had seen the security guard before he had seen me, so I was able to freeze in place, well knowing most people would not see an immobile object, since the eyes are drawn to movement.

The guard, an older man, looking every bit like one of my uncles on my father's side who was a respected banker, paused to shine his light and rattle one of the locked gates on the opposite side of the construction. He then turned and looked down the path to where the boy had disappeared.

I remained still, hoping the guard would either pursue the child, or go back to whatever hidden hut he had been relaxing in, given that the guard was only in a sweater and not wearing a coat.

It was then that I belatedly noticed a small guard post just beyond where the guard was standing. No doubt he monitored a slew of cameras and had seen the orange clad kid as the kid had emerged.

What would he do now?

If he spotted me and I had to spend time explaining, my search would be dangerously delayed.

If he called the police or, worse, his own security bosses, then I'd be detained.

Wait. He's not going to want to point out to his bosses or to the police that he let some kid sneak into the construction zone. Why would he report another and be doubly embarrassed that he was not doing his job at keeping the public out?

Also, there was always bribery…?

Bribery? My mind really was slipping, I thought, as I tried to stay immobile. I had promised her I'd try to avoid such common, baser actions.

Finally, my concerns answered themselves when the guard turned and headed up the path to the lights of a lively looking snack bar, just beyond the entrance to the clump of trees into which the child had disappeared.

I allowed the guard time to get all the way to the snack bar entrance and step into the double door, built to keep the cold out, before I moved.

While I had been waiting, I had managed to map out a more or less safe route through the landmines of gaping holes, so I was able to hurry through the mess toward where the boy had found an exit gap earlier. One hole, exposed under a blown over tarp, did almost drag me down into the dark underbelly of the river's edge, but I steadied myself on the fence, making a bit of noise, but halting any fall into the merciless, sloshing black cauldron.

Grimly, I conceded that the barrier was a good idea, as anyone who fell into that abyss would never be found, except by maybe the nightmare creatures of scary childhood tales.

After I had skirted the dangerous drop-off, I then stepped through the gap the guard had either not known about or had just ignored, and hoped he was too involved with the little ajumma at the brightly lighted snack bar to have heard the rattle of the fence.

As I hurried to the same path as the boy, I had to pass fairly closely to the snack bar, its fried, spicy aromas breaking up the cold emptiness of the wind. Just as I passed, I saw the guard turn around in the chair he had taken, look through the large, fairly clear of steam, plastic windows and notice me. He watched me pass, scratching the back of his head and shrugging. I saw him turn back to the counter, probably thinking I had just come from the other direction, had seen the construction, and then turned back.

Mundane!

As I hurried along, my mind screamed at me for my worrying about such humdrum things.

She, in her unnervingly patient way, would often ask me why use up brain cells on such trivial issues?

Always the practical one, she would have called to the guard and asked him to open the gates, since she was in a hurry. She would have then bribed the guard with her soulful eyes or something from the snack window if he had balked. Evidently, a bribe of a pretty smile, or of a small food item, was not as evil as cold cash, in her mind, causing me to grin at her cheerfully twisted logic.

Shaking off the brief delay, I headed up the winding, tree lined path, while keeping a close eye on the distant bridge, which, due to the weaving of the path, seem to get farther away as I hurried toward it.

Since the trees were all still bare of leaves, with the slim branches sporting bumps of the soon to open buds, the trees did not block details of the second bridge.

No one was on the second bridge, which made sense, as it led to a small marina that had been closed for some time. Yet, the ramps were open there and, oddly, a few individuals and small groups were milling about near the closest ramp.

Why were they there, I wondered?

I pushed forward, deliberating if I should just hop over the low, winding wall, and make my way through the trees, in a more direct line to the bridge?

The earlier fear, set aside for the few minutes at the construction site, slammed back into my chest as my mind began to juggle the very few reasons a group of people would be milling about a deserted footbridge on a cold night by the river.

I then shut out the grim thoughts forcing their way into my mind and focused on my gait.

I hurried, nearly ran, and kept my eyes on the people to see if any broke away from the groups and headed up the bridge, or, worse, went over to the river's edge.

Finally, I emerged from the seemingly endless, tree-lined, serpentine path, and ran out into the open plaza, fearing the worse and convinced that the people were there, in the cold, braving the wind, wanting a ghoulish look. Maybe a gruesome photo for their social media accounts?

As I closed in on the base of the ramp, I felt my pulse quicken and my breath shorten, wondering....

I suddenly stopped dead in my tracks.

Then, thinking quickly, I continued at a more leisurely pace, turning to pass by the gaggle of several groups, and only casually looking in their direction, hoping to conceal my initial concern, and deflect the interest of the few people who had turned to see who had been running toward them.

Music.

The people who were milling about turned out to be teenage youths waiting for a group of musicians to start up again.

A truly odd sight, with the wind and threat of late season snow. Four young musicians stood with their backs to the underside of the second bridge's ramp, tuning their instruments, no doubt a losing battle.

The wind and cold must be playing havoc with keeping those instruments in tune, I mused, knowing from my early years of violin how impossible it was to tune during such cold. Happily, though, the small band had given me the answer to why a random group of youths would be milling about the base of a deserted and unused bridge.

Scanning the footbridge itself, the only people I then saw were small groups gathered to look over the side at the musicians. No lone figures could be seen, and both sides were visible due to the angle of the footbridge where it ended at the marina.

The death grip on my chest relaxed its hold a bit, but, with one bridge remaining, I realized I would not be able to truly calm such pressing fear until I had searched the final footbridge.

Would she be there? Was I in the right place?

Part of my mind simply refused to accept the possibility that she was not close by and was, instead, somewhere else along the vast stretches of the Han River. Somewhere inaccessible. Somewhere she thought I would know from her hints, but that I, in my self-serving, self-important reality, might very well not know.

My own selfishness would condemn her! She would think I had ignored her hints, or had missed the subtle meanings in her earlier texts.

Find her!

I have to find her, I screamed in my mind, letting my fist crash into my side as I turned away from the second footbridge.

The third footbridge appeared to be twice as far as the second bridge had been from the first, so I broke into a trot, ignoring the stares of the few strolling couples I passed.

About halfway to the third bridge, yet another landscaped path presented in front of me, like some ridiculous barrier in a K-drama thrown in at the end of an episode to artificially heighten the suspense and force viewers to tune in the following week.

Shaking my head in disgust at the unknown, artsy pathway designer, I plowed ahead into an even more serpentine and convoluted tree, shrubbery, bench, and artwork-lined path.

Just as I entered the path, the bratty persimmon boy emerged, with two fretting parents in tow behind him.

On seeing me, the boy looked alarmed and ducked behind his mother, who, whispering something to the boy, looked up at me and bowed a silent apology for her son's being so impolite as to be afraid of a stranger who was obviously well-bred, from my well-groomed, yangban demeanor, evidently successful, from the Italian boots and bespoke Barbour coat, and quite handsome, from my mother's side.

I politely nodded to the quiet wife in return, and winked at the worried kid.

The father, sadly, was typically clueless and simply grunted an age-old man-greeting as I passed.

The boy smiled.

Did he smile because I did not stop and berate him in front of his parents for being disrespectful in his addressing me in such a cavalier fashion earlier, when he had thought he'd never see me again? Or, was he smiling because I did not snitch on him and tell his parents of his daring exploits in the construction zone?

Part of me, but only a small part, smiled, thinking that the kid was actually thanking me, as I dove into the twisting path before me and dismissed the kid and his doting parents from my thoughts.

Interminable was the only word that came to mind as I fruitlessly searched for the third bridge through the barren trees and the endless twists of the all to artful path.

Too far away.

And, I wasn't exactly sure which side of the path it might be on, given that the insane path design seemed to move the visitor this way and that, at random.

And, the river curved back on the shore somewhere ahead, so that would add to the difficulty in spotting the....

"Sir?"

As I hurried on, I thought I had heard a voice calling out to me, but who would be calling out to me in the middle of a darkened, Han River park?

Dismiss it and move on.

"Sir?"

The voice was even louder.

Wait. Just there, on a curved bench, under a crazy lamp that must have been some sculptor's idea of modern art, an older couple was sitting looking out at the lights of the main bridge, and the skyline of endless sparkles of the city on the opposite bank.

Their age and something in the tone of the voice, the woman's voice, caused me to slow my progress as I neared the couple, yet, I had no intention of actually stopping.

"Yes, grandmother, is everything okay?"

I spoke with deep respect and bowed as I slowed my pace, but, again, did not intend to stop.

"Thank you, young man, yes, but my husband has made us a little lost in this confusing forest of modern treasures, so we stopped to look at the lights. However, with the taste of snow in the air, we now are not sure which way is back to the main road, we live just across there. We let our man off for the evening. Can you help us?"

The old grandmother's speech was non-stop, nearly without punctuation, common in some of the older, lower classes, which, of course, we don't call lower class any longer in our enlightened age. But, she was obviously kind and the old man did have the look of someone not only confused, but not all there. The last thing she offered was the name of a street and its cross street, not far away, and in a very upscale neighborhood.

Stopping, with part of me screaming in my mind at the delay, I took out my phone, found the street she had mentioned and, turning, pointed back the way I had just come.

"Take the first cross-walk at the end of this small section, to the right, of course. Go straight up that block on the other side and you will see a coffee shop, in green. That, I believe, is your street."

The old woman smiled, patted the old man, who suddenly looked up at me and, with a moment of clarity, nodded his thanks, his aged face showing a touch of embarrassment that he had gotten the two of them lost so close to their home.

Something kept me rooted to the path in front of the old couple.

Something she had said over and over.

'Don't dismiss others.'

I watched the little lady smooth over her full length, cashmere coat. I then spoke, using formal, high language.

"Grandmother, do you think you can make it? I could…I could call a car, or hail a taxi."

The kind little lady gently refused, and helped her husband stand up from the bench. The old man moved slowly, in that way the old do to ensure they are not going to break any brittle bones or pull an ancient muscle. His heavy coat, a male version of the expensive one his wife was wearing, also seemed to weigh down his movements.

Carefully, deliberately, the old man turned to address me, his shoulders pushed back, his speech strong, his words well thought out, betraying his highly educated life and well born station.

Instinctively, I bowed my head, thinking I must have offended the old man with my innocent offer, but then caught myself and watched his suddenly sharp eyes lock onto mine when I raised my head.

"Thank you, young man. You have warmed the hearts of a couple of old people by your undue kindness to us, strangers to you. I hope you find whatever or whomever you are rushing toward on this blustery and dark evening. If it, or she…yes, your eyes tell me your valiant quest is a she, is attainable in this wild wind and threatening night. I trust she, and you, are found in good health and high spirits. You have many years in front of you, but they fall away all too soon, so hold them dear while you can. Be well."

The loving wife then tugged at the elder husband, whose momentarily gleaming eyes then lost their fleeting, clear sheen.

Head turning away, shoulders drooping, the old scholar shuffled away with the devoted, formerly commoner, wife, back to the warmth of a nearby home fueled by their decades-long love.

Too long I stood and watched the old couple's progress until they had disappeared around a bend in the path.

What was that?

Just as the old couple had disappeared at the bend, a shadow, similar to a large bird crossing overhead, passed across where the two had just been.

I shook my head.

The cold, I said to myself, was beginning to make me see things.

'Hold them dear while you can.'

Oddly appropriate phrase for the old scholar to have said, I thought, as I moved back to my pursuit.

Turning, I could only just imagine I could hear her voice, the only voice, calling me forward and thanking me for showing a little kindness to strangers, so out of character for me.

But, I wondered, had I done it for the old couple? Or, for her? For me to impress her?

Shrugging off such strange, for me, thoughts, I focused on tilting my head away from the wind and continued on.

The third bridge remained elusive as I hurried around scattered benches, dodged clumps of artfully arranged trees in the middle of the twisting path, and passed all manner of sculptures conspiring to delay my progress. I appreciated art, but my patience was wearing thin at the endless turns, wishing the Daliesque landscaper had been simpler and had preferred straight, boring paths.

The one bright spot in the confused twists of the path was a lone tree just releasing the first bit of color, even in the frigid wind. Had I had more time, I might have stopped to investigate if there was some sort of heat vent or other source of warmth that gave the older tree an early start. Yet, the sight of the coming spring's bounty was comforting, spurring me to hurry onward.

When I finally escaped the clawing clutches of the artsy path, no bridge welcomed me across the open plaza.

Where was it?

I turned back, wondering if I had passed it, confused by the wandering lanes trapped in the forest of tree clumps and statues.

Nothing.

Had I read the map wrong? Had the bridge I thought I had seen been part of some other structure?

I had been on this stretch of the river before, right? Hadn't I?

Just as I was about to retrieve my phone to look up the map, walking forward as I pulled off my glove, the tell-tale curve of a concrete walk and steel railing came into view, magically suspended about fifty meters in front of me. Magically, as I could not see the rest of the footbridge for the curve in the river and another forest of bare trees extending almost to the water's edge.

Quickening my pace, I moved closer to the edge of the river path in order to reveal a fuller view of the footbridge and the larger traffic bridge beyond.

People.

Many more people than the first two bridges.

Too far to make out details, but at least there were no lone figures on the footbridge that I could see.

As the full footbridge finally came into view, another reason for its elusiveness became immediately evident.

The footbridge's land side origin began on the other side of the frontage road, so I would not have seen the beginning, as with the other two. Also, its origin was well beyond a simple stroll to reach it.

Stairs? Maybe there's another ramp, I decided, blinking at the bridge.

Blinking some more.

Blinking?

Snow!

A light snow, the kind that rests for the briefest of moments on your face, and then vanishes in an invisible vapor. Just enough snow to give the bridge, the park, the river, and the lights of the city an extra sparkle.

As the snow moved in, the wind abated a bit, but not entirely.

Looking up, the height of the bridge became apparent, and fear's powerful grip returned to my chest and added a second clasp on my throat.

Who would build such a high footbridge…?

The wind and light snow were forgotten as I strained to see any features on the faces of the people on the bridge. Most appeared to be walking toward the riverside, with only two groups heading toward the road.

Which way would she have gone, I asked myself?

Gauging the distances to the respective ramps and stairs of the footbridge was difficult, given the curved shape and the darkness covering the roundabout path to the riverside.

Finally, I chose the path that was the closest, arguing with myself that she would have taken the most obvious path, and would not have made her walk complicated.

Turning to walk up the sloping path to one of the ramps, I held my head up as I absently greeted the few couples passing me, and held my head down when I could to avoid the windy snow.

Finally, at the top of the ramp, with two choices, either head back down the second ramp just a stone's throw to the right, or go straight and end up on the main bridge's pedestrian path, which was, for the most part, well lighted. The occasional headlights whizzing by threw additional light, and shadows, into the mix.

Standing at the crossroads of the ramps, I anxiously looked back and forth at the footbridge and the main bridge, wondering which way to go, losing precious minutes as I debated with myself.

Take the logical route and stay on the pedestrian walkway that would carry me back to the river park? Or, take the less likely, more irrational path to the main bridge?

Looking at both options, I wondered what she would have done? If she were really…if she were actually nearby.

No, don't let those kinds of thoughts cloud your critical thinking!

Wait! What was that?

Suddenly, a group of a half dozen or so separated from a single slim figure as the larger group proceeded toward the second ramp from the main bridge.

The lone figure must have joined the group, then had split off where the two ramps diverged.

Watching closely, I saw that the lone figure was a slim woman, wearing a coat that might be…just might be hers, and, once she turned to walk up onto the main bridge pedestrian path, I saw that she had the elegant gait that I sought.

Wondering how to approach her without giving her a scare, or causing her to do something rash in her surprise, I decided to fall into step behind a group of two couples that seemed to be heading toward the main bridge's pedestrian lane.

Hoping I could get close to her before she saw me, I walked a few paces behind the quiet group, which appeared to be braving the wind and light snow to cross the bridge to the city's north side.

At the right moment, I stepped away from the small group and, as the four strangers passed the lone figure, only one of the men glanced over at where she was standing, silently, almost vigil-like.

The same young man looked at me when I stepped away from the group, but he said nothing to his friends as they headed across the bridge, their collective feet plowing a wide, if shallow, swath in the light touch of the freshly fallen snow.

Other than the group I had just left, the main bridge and the visible areas of the two ramps were deserted of other people. Not surprising, given the wind at that level, the start of the snow, and the lateness of the hour.

Sensing my presence, I saw her finally turn, and, I think, utter a short gasp of recognition, but the wind was hitting my ears at just the right angle, so I was not completely sure she had spoken. She then seemed to step close to the path's edge, resting her slim, bare right hand on the waterside barrier.

Taking in a deep breath, I simply stood as still as possible as I gauged the distance between us.

Too far for me to try to make a grab for her, I thought, especially in a well-fitted winter coat.

Finally, her immobility convinced me that I would be able to speak to her without frightening her.

"Good evening for a stroll."

Silly comment, but I wanted to lighten the tone as much as possible without being thought unsympathetic.

Silence.

Frowning, I took a small step toward her, noticing she did not move.

So, I took another quick step, then stopped, as she seemed to shrink back, leaning on the barrier.

"Please. Let's walk down to the park and get out of this wind," I called, feeling larger snowflakes on my face as I spoke.

In spite of the snow and damp air, my throat was dry, both from, hopefully, unfounded fear and from the unrelenting wind. Speaking was difficult, but the fire of my resolve warmed me as I tried to move closer with another small step, without spooking her.

Suddenly, she seemed to lean against a low spot in the railing, which was cordoned off by a set of road repair columns and some low, plastic barriers.

Barriers?

Must have been damaged by an auto or truck accident, and had been temporarily repaired, I decided, as I tried to figure out the best way to get through to her.

Even with warning flags, flashing lights, and wide barriers, the damage had resulted in the broken railing being too low to prevent someone from falling over, either by accident, or...?

No!

My mind, screaming at itself, forced away such thoughts as I raced to find words that would draw her to me, to safety.

Maybe piquing her curiosity would help?

"Bo-min won a prize."

Yes! I thought I saw an immediate, questioning look on her pale, oval face. A look that instantly seemed to reveal a true interest in our close friend's work.

"From the dean. For her translation of that American poet as one of her linguistics projects. Just came out on the board. I can show you...?"

What? I thought I saw her wrinkle her brow and realized she was not sure what I meant, so I drew out the story a little longer.

"The one who writes about her life as a minority woman in a world of white, male poetic giants? She writes about tragedy, and yet points out the beauty all around as those tragedies unfold."

I smiled at what I took as a spark of recognition crossing her face, and she also seemed to lean away from the edge.

A second questioning look appeared to want to know about the prize.

"For her not only translating, but bringing the poet to our country's attention. Because of Bo-min's series of interviews, the poet has agreed to visit the university soon. The department was so happy that the dean gave Bo-min special recognition. She gets to introduce...can't quite remember her name...at some event in a couple of months. Do you recall the name...?"

I felt her sudden smile at the good news for one of her closest friends was a good sign, but ignoring my attempt to get a response with a direct question was not, as she looked like she was leaning back against the weakened railing, while she just continued to stare at me with those perfect eyes.

Trying to maintain my calm while her continued silence picked at my already frayed nerves, I frantically tried to think of other things that might distract her long enough for me to lunge forward and grab her before...before she....

Damn! Where are all the people when you wanted them around, I asked myself?

Glancing quickly up and down the bridge path, I looked for anyone who might serve as a distraction, letting small curses escape my lips, but only in whispers.

No one in sight had appeared since a bicyclist had sped by earlier, focused on the weather and not on random strangers.

People. Any people. Any crowd or even a few, maybe even one other. That would give her pause, I was sure of it.

I concluded she would not want an audience of strangers watching her, judging her, gossiping about her.

Digging across recent memories that might prompt her to reply, I fell back on our last trip abroad, when we had escaped for a few hours from the organized tour during the Venice portion.

Yes! And that song she loves, I realized, might bring her over.

"Remember the trip to Italy? When we found that canal in Burano, and the ones in Murano? And sang along to the song Lee Ji-eun recorded there? And…and when those Italian shopkeepers came out and encouraged us, even with my horrid voice? And gave us wine, anyway? That Aperol Spritz? Remember?"

I inwardly smiled at what I saw as a wistful glow on her nearly frozen face. But, still no words.

I almost called out to her about our visit to the Doge's Palace and how we had paused on the ornate, yet sad bridge that crossed to the prison on the other side. The last view of so many condemned men who had looked out on the world for the final time from that ornate cage across the canal. Byron's title was apt.

I held my tongue, though, fearing the imagery was too…too dangerous.

Something else from the trip?

"Oh, remember how the pigeons at St. Mark's decided your handbag, the one with the small beads, was better than the corn we bought from the old lady?"

Even that happy memory only seemed to make her smile more wistfully, without replying.

"I see you are carrying that purse from Via Condotti, that we found after lunch near the Spanish Steps in Rome? Yes?"

I had taken a guess on the purse, which was mostly concealed behind her, but thought it might bring a cute response. The Rome portion of the trip had been less structured and we had found Fendi's flagship shop quite by accident.

Nothing. Not even a smile, that time. Maybe I had the wrong purse, I wondered, confirming, yet again, what she had always said, that I was self-centered and never really paid attention to those things that mattered to others.

"Do you think we should take Bo-min to dinner? Maybe to that Hanok place in Insa-dong that she raves about? Near the art museum?"

The thought of warm, traditional food suddenly made me shiver in the cold, as I tried to keep calm under her unresponsive, yet steady gaze.

Bracing against the creeping cold, unable to get her to reply, or to get her to move away from the edge, my mind raced to other thoughts. Of my own shortcomings, something I'd never admit out loud to anyone. Kiss of death in our academic and social circles.

All my life I had been independent. Not relying on anyone else for anything. Did things my way and be damned with the rest of society.

Now?

I'd give away my inheritance for a company man or a maid to walk by at that moment. Even a slowing cab driver would do. Anyone.

As my mind spun wildly, searching for a topic, any topic, to bring her away from the slippery edge, something soft and tantalizing murmured in the back of my mind.

What was it? Why wasn't it clear?

Or, was the cold, the snow, and the fear numbing my ability to think clearly?

'Dismiss others....'

What?

That makes no sense?

'Dismiss others....'

You've done it all your life. Why stop now?

Shaking my head violently, I tried to get the thought out of my mind.

My odd actions must have alarmed her, as she appeared to press her body against the broken railing, causing the damaged steel to groan in protest, even under her slim, fifty-kilo weight.

Fifty kilos!

What a screwed up society that makes women adhere to such artificial standards, I grumbled to myself.

But, I suddenly realized, that weight would, hopefully, make it harder to dislodge the seemingly haphazard repair. So, maybe the fifty-kilo target was a good idea, in an ironic way.

So much pressure on these kids. So little sense.

'Dismiss others....'

The little voice was back.

Did the voice want me to turn my back and walk away, leaving her to her own fate? Her own, independent decision?

Was I so callous and self-centered that, at the moment of crisis, I looked only at myself? And not those whom I cared for? And, those...who cared for...cared for...me?

'Cared...for...me!'

The little voice seemed to be screaming now, trying desperately to monopolize my attention.

What was the voice saying, I wondered, as I looked quickly up and down the bridge walk hoping to see other people?

Nothing. And, few cars.

Even if there had been a lot of cars, the broken railing, with the damaged lighting, made us almost impossible to see unless the onlooker was quite near. And, they would probably only see the repair flags and steer into the other lanes.

Nothing. Either direction.

"Dismiss others...."

What? What's in my head that's trying to grab my attention?

What?

Dismiss others?

Okay. Think about it.

Dismiss others. She's told me that since we were young.

She had always worried about me, saying that I callously dismissed others, and their feelings, in favor of whatever the hell I wanted at the moment.

The rest of the world be damned, she claimed, was the way I thought.

I used to laugh and tell her she was pretty cute when she was trying to save me from myself...

Trying...to save me...from...myself....

To save...me?

That's it!

Finally, the wind, the snow, the cold, the fear—all seemed to vanish with that one brilliant thought.

One who cares for me!

Not me for her, but her for me!

That had to be the answer.

Suddenly, my eyes were drawn by movement far down the bridge path.

Two uniformed figures, the street lamps dancing off the tell-tale reflective vests, were slowly making their way toward us on our side of the bridge.

Far. Maybe five minutes? More?

Would they frighten her? Would she be rash and act before they got to us? Does she even see them?

Were they police?

Were they just maintenance men?

Did it matter?

Police. Yes. They would want to take her in, check her into a hospital for observation. Put her delicate mind under a microscope.

Yes, professional help would be a good thing. But, only if it were the right kind. Her family, an old name, but with little financial independence, couldn't really afford the best.

But...mine could.

Sadly, tragically, I yelled inwardly, society still ostracized such troubled souls, even with the advances in the last few years.

Society could be unrelentingly cruel to those who showed any form of weakness. Imbalance, unresolved emotions, tragic life events, and more, all conspired to strip away society's embrace. Even to those who sought help, before something reached a point of no return, society would often turn a dark and disapproving cold shoulder.

But, society, and its perceptions, could be bought.

If one had the resources.

She did not.

But, I did.

What? Did she just drape her right arm over the weakened railing and shake her head at me? My eyes were blurred from the increasing snow, so wasn't sure, but I erred on the side of caution.

Don't come closer, I saw her doleful eyes saying to me, as I had unconsciously taken a step toward her while my mind screamed at the hollow future Seoul held for anyone foolish enough, yet brave enough to ask for help.

Wait! Should I try to use the two uniformed shapes to threaten her? Or, would that just drive her to act sooner?

'Dismiss others.'

The little voice and the earlier thoughts rushed back as the wind picked up.

Care for...me.

To...save...me.

Suddenly, some subtle change in her posture, or, maybe a new expression on her face, or some fleeting word the wind carried over to me, or, simply my pent up frustrations, abruptly caused me to fly into a fit of action.

Stepping over to the railing just opposite where I had been standing, about three meters from her perch at the damaged section, I grabbed the plastic light cover for leverage, even with the slickness from the snow, and, without hesitation, threw myself over to the other side, the side overhanging the river.

As I came down on the waterside of the railing, my feet landed on the narrow ledge I had seen and had been aiming for. My boots just fit on the sturdy ledge, which jutted about fifty centimeters out from the steel railing.

Securing my slippery footing, I gripped the railing with a bent elbow, as my puffy down gloves were too smooth to grip the damp steel or hold onto the plastic light covers.

From the dark side of the bridge railing, the choppy river below was dizzying, nearly hypnotic, so I forced myself to look away, and tried to focus on her as the snowy wind seemed to tease me with occasional gusts, causing my hands to slip, but just slightly.

Her face was hard to see at that angle, looking back over my shoulder.

Was that fear I saw in her face? Maybe mixed with disbelief?

I strained to hear her voice, given the wind and the low rumble of the dark, angry water below. Apparently weakened by wind and stress, she seemed to whisper softly, sweetly...as if from just by my ear.

"Why...?"

The word, if I had heard it right, might as well have been an entire play.

Such feeling.

Such concern.

Such caring.

Exactly what I needed.

But, she must not know. She must only know my desperation, I declared to myself, looking down toward the unforgiving river.

"Better I go over than you!" I called, my voice deep, torn with emotion.

I strained to see if my blunt words had caused her beautiful eyes to grow wider, with an even more confused and, yes, terrified look on her delicate face.

Her petite, but broad shoulders seemed to give a small shudder as I watched her lips form a second word.

"Over...?"

Part of me heard her speak, the word carried softly by the wind to my nearly numb ears.

'Dismiss others!'

Why did that little voice keep intruding, I grumbled to myself?

"Not complicated. You go. I go," I added, twisting my back to the right to get a better view of her, still standing by the broken railing.

My voice sounded odd. Cold and out of body. Blunt. Uncaring. Focused only on me.

Wait? Was her face sad?

I saw her head slowly move from side to side, as if she was in denial of what she saw before her. Puzzlement and, yes, dismay.

Suddenly, I thought she looked as if she was going to step toward me, but then stopped herself when she heard the sounds of running behind her.

As the two reflective vests had moved closer, they must have noticed us, and both had sprinted the last few dozen meters.

Damn! I had pushed those two out of my mind, I mumbled, while I shifted my hands for a better grip, part of my emotional side dreaming up all manner of nasty little night creatures waiting just below for the big buffoon to fall into their grisly clutches.

Grandmother, I called silently into the night, why did you tell me all those tales of water demons and ghostly heroes?

Looking back to the road, I saw, more than heard, the lead uniform, taller and with less bulk than the shorter one, calling out in a rough, streetwise voice.

"Hey, you there. What are you doing?"

The tall one then called to his partner.

"Man, another one. Call this in. We'll need help."

As the two men got cautiously closer, they slowed their pace to a crawl, and then stopped, leaving her equidistant between them and me, while she silently watched the encounter, as if she were simply watching two strangers meet as she sipped wine in that sedate restaurant on Namsan.

"Hey, fellow, let's talk. You can't do that. Not with her, you know, down there," tall uniform called, while the shorter fellow seemed to be struggling to get a signal on his work radio.

I wrinkled my brow at the tall uniform, but followed his gesture, not aimed at her, but at something below, and saw a small group of teens gathered for a night dance at the base of one of those mobile stages, where a petite young singer was belting out a tune lost to the winds. The stage was not too far from the ramp I had used, but on the opposite side, so I had seen nothing of that music gathering. I didn't think the kids could see me, but, if something did happen, they would no doubt witness it, and probably take some grisly videos to share.

I looked back to where she was standing, hoping the uniforms would ignore her, leave her alone.

I seemed to see confusion crossing her face as she turned to the two men, still in the shadows, so we could not tell if they were police or simply workers.

Before she could speak and draw the uniforms' attention and, probably, bullying response, I hastily called back to them.

"Hey, who are you country boys to tell me what to do?" I shouted over any words she might try to say, drowning her out, and causing her to turn back to me.

"Buddy. Just hold on. We're getting help. What's your name?" tall uniform shouted back, his hands on his belt with his elbows flared.

"Name? You want to know my name?" I shouted at the two with as much disdain as generations of haughty breeding would allow, shoving as much insult in my inflection as I could muster. "What...? Who do you think you are to disrespect me...?"

The tall one had begun to advance, but his partner held him back.

"Wait. No power. Have to use your phone," chubby uniform said, waving both his work radio and his phone at the tall one.

"What? Oh. Wait," tall uniform replied as he pulled his radio out of its cradle on his belt and checked it. "No juice, either. And my phone is back at the hut, charging, remember?"

"Then, how are we going to call this in...?" chubby uniform asked, his face beet red from the blowing wind.

The two men, uniformed, maybe workers, maybe security, then proceeded to bicker about who was responsible for the dead radios, while seeming to forget the stylish young man clinging to the wrong side of the bridge railing.

"Bra-ha-ha-ha...!"

I laughed, an almost maniacal laugh. A laugh so disturbing that the two men jerked around, stopped their bickering, and took a couple of steps backwards, knocking into one of the warning signs, nearly collapsing the fabric sign into a narrow strip, its little side flags flapping like arms in protest.

The chubby one mumbled something about hungry night demons while tugging at the tall one's elbow, seeming to want to leave the howling young man to himself.

Mentally dismissing the two guards or workers as irrelevant, I glanced sideways at her, to see if my artificial lunacy was having any effect.

Suddenly, through the snow and blinking at the wind, I saw her draw herself up to her full height, smile long and lovingly at me and then, moving like a dancer in the brisk wind, turn swiftly, and, with one graceful leap....

No!

I immediately turned my face away in horror, a visceral, numbing fear rushing into my every pore, tinged with an immediate rising guilt that I had been too cowardly to watch her shocking act.

And too slow witted to stop her.

I think I screamed.

Then, silence.

Dare I look at the water?

Should I jump in after her?

I was a strong swimmer.

I knew the math. Maybe five minutes in the frigid water, before it killed us.

If the fall didn't kill us first.

No time to think about it.

No time to delay.

Part of my mind could feel the dark, cold water of the Han River already clawing at my rapidly beating heart.

How long would it take to fall?

How far from her will I be when I hit the concrete-like surface, if I hit wrong?

Wait! I have to know where she fell. I have to fall close, but not so close as to hit her when I enter the water.

All these thoughts flashed through my mind in milliseconds.

Opening my eyes, I looked back at the now twisted, collapsed railing, where she had just...just made that ultimate decision.

I then let my eyes travel from the railing down to the water's dark surface, many, many meters below.

Some of the bridge's lamps sprinkled streaks of sporadic light into the black, unforgiving abyss that was the Han River that night.

Not enough light to see clearly, though.

Maybe the wind had blown her slight body into the pilings?

My stomach churned as horrific mental images burned into my soul, of her slim, dancer's body slamming into the unforgiving pilings, her perfect skin being scraped off against the rough concrete of the worn columns as she fell to the beckoning blackness below.

Would she be knocked unconscious? Would she remain aware until the…the ghastly end?

Would she scream?

Would she scream…my name…?

My stomach nearly delivered its contents at the bizarre thoughts rushing into my fear-fueled mind, almost seeing her young body and beautiful mind slamming into the rock hard, churning black water far below.

I swallowed my rising bile, trying to repress the urge to retch at the mental images of her merciless suffering.

My nearly paralyzing fear conjured up all manner of hellish night demons, probably courtesy of overhearing chubby uniform's skittish comment, coupled with memories of childhood nightmares.

Overhead, I imagined veiled demons flapping invisible wings, circling our discarded lives, calling to their minions to drag us under the brackish waves.

Below, my disturbed mind's eye saw a horror filled array of ghouls and goblins clawing at her delicate body from the dark corners of the bridge supports as she hit one, then another.

The grisly little fingers snatching…snatching bits of flesh, maybe a clump of bloodied hair, maybe a finger, her soft, loving fingers, broken and bent, like some caricature of a mountain witch….

"Aiyee!"

I cried out as loud as I could muster and then let her dear name silently escape my lips.

That's it!

Just as my legs were tensing up to follow her down into that dark, dark tunnel, I threw one last look at the two uniforms to ensure they had not advanced close enough to grab me, my eyes passing over the broken railing one final time, lingering for what seemed an eternity in that split second, at the last place I had seen her.

Mere seconds ago, but the time without her seemed stretched to eons in my scarred mind.

That spot should have a marker, I thought, irrationally, as I shifted my body to fully face the water and its gruesome, swirling soup of monsters from a distant childhood.

A marker to her sweet, giving life.

A marker and a small fence, I thought, as I leaned out over the vast emptiness below me, my wind-beaten, water filled eyes looking frantically for any sign of her pale, twisted and torn body in the choppy waters below.

A fence would be best, embracing that sad little section of weak railing, broken, and fallen into the bridge pedestrian path.

I irrationally lamented how people would forever have to walk around the bump out of that fallen railing and never know how such a petite young lady, pressured by a cruel and unrelenting society, had desperately pushed it down, even as slight as she was, and leapt to her....

Leapt...?

To...her...?

My mind froze on the image of the broken railing.

Fallen into the path?

Bumped out?

Toward the road?

As I felt my goose down gloves slipping off the smooth steel, my legs aching from holding the sprinter position so long, I heard that same little voice from earlier yelling at me to stop focusing on myself, my own grief, my self-sacrifice, my self-pity, and, for once in my miserable life, focus on the world around me.

'Focus on others...!'

The voice was insistent.

Rail...section...weakened...and...fallen...into...the...path.

Into the path?

Not...not...not into the river?

Suddenly, stark realization dawning like a blow to the back of the head, I shoved my gloved left hand into my teeth and, frantically chewing at the glove's fingers, pulled off the left glove just as my right hand slipped on the steel. As my body lurched forward with my aching legs finally giving way, my gloveless left hand, aided by the edge of my couple ring, found a solid grip on one of the vertical slats and, with some difficulty, I was able to pull myself back before both my feet left the narrow edge.

Hanging on for dear, miserable life to the slippery steel and concrete, I forced myself to look back.

Taking a deep breath, I looked over at the broken section and, holding that breath, confirmed that the section had fallen into the path.

Into the path, and not, not into the river!

Yes!

The section had fallen into the path!

Through a watery haze over my eyes, either from the snowy wind or from true tears, I saw that the two uniforms seemed to have not moved at all.

Blinking away what water I could, I was suddenly heartened beyond joy to see a small, third shape talking to the two uniforms.

With her back to me, she had not seen my near death plunge, I realized.

She appeared to be talking to the tall uniform, even though he was distracted by staring at me, the crazy guy on the ledge, and was not paying her any attention.

Chubby uniform, maybe still worried about night demons, I speculated, had obviously seen my antics and was staring, his large-lipped mouth agape, while he again tugged, dumfounded, at his partner's sleeve.

I strained to hear any snatches of her words, with mostly the wind reaching my ears as I slowly stood up straight on the narrow ledge.

What could she be...wait, a phone? Was that what was she saying?

"Phone...."

"Lost...."

"Looking...."

"Thought it was...on the ledge...?"

The jumbled words seemed to float over to me, giving me just enough of an idea to shape...to answer to the uniforms and any others that might appear as backup.

As I tried to listen, I also gauged how I would cross back over the railing. Awkward, as the railing was chest high and the wind was quite strong. And the narrow ledge was some centimeters below the level of the path.

Chubby uniform had finally managed to get the attention of the taller one, who then waved off any questions, so both simply stood with mouths wide open, looking at me, and, thankfully, ignoring her.

She then appeared to turn, saw what she must have thought was my being on the verge of falling, and tried to rush toward me, chubby uniform at her side.

The tall uniform called them back.

"Wait, he might go over if you get too close. You and I best wait for the negotiators to get here."

"Boss, we didn't call...," chubby uniform began, but was silenced by the tall one's withering look.

I tried to catch her eye, but she stood silently beside the two uniforms. Maybe she was making a call? Maybe friends or lawyers would be here by the time the two workers had summoned help, or superiors?

Whatever she was up to, I knew I needed to move, or those water nymphs from my childhood would have their battered meal.

My grip had been slipping, my legs were nearly frozen, and the dampness of the steel seemed to have gotten worse.

How to get back over without a running start on such slippery surfaces?

Look around you, I said to myself, mimicking the voice in my head from earlier.

The break?

Of course!

Smiling at the irony, I slowly shuffled along the slippery, narrow ledge until I had reached the weakened section that had given way just before my dynamic rescue attempt and, taking a deep breath, I stepped and crawled over the jumble of steel and plastic onto the path.

Catching my breath, I paused and looked toward my small audience.

I saw her eyes ask the question for me.

'Did you find it?' her eyes called to me.

Protecting me! She was putting on a brave act for the two workers.

"Yes, gentlemen. Yes, I was looking for my friend's phone. Went over the rail, we think, yes," I called out in a forced, but I hoped, most charming and convincing voice.

I let my nearly frozen left hand momentarily grip the backup battery to toss for effect, but then dropped it back in the pocket as unnecessary.

Her unblinking eyes asked the obvious follow on.

"What? No, I did not find it. So sorry. It slipped as I reached for it."

I felt her eyes were then smiling at me, almost singing to me that her heart was mine again…no, was still mine.

And, more importantly, I felt that she knew, beyond any doubt, that only she owned my wretched little heart.

"Listen here, young man," tall uniform said, keeping his distance as I had just been howling like a banshee from the war. "You can't just jump across like that looking for a lost item. There are procedures. There, just over there, is the call box for such things."

"Gentlemen, my apologies. I'm sorry I concerned you and you were inconvenienced by stopping," I called in my best executive voice, copying my father's, as my aching legs began to return to normal. "I trust my little indiscretion will not warrant further delay? I'll be sure to have my father let Commissioner L__ know how responsive you two men have been, and helpful."

At the mention of the construction commissioner's name, which I had thrown out on chance, the two men, whom I finally saw were not police, nor security, but workers, probably on their way home, both nodded quickly in reply.

"Boss, we going to call this…?" chubby uniform, a little slower to absorb things than tall uniform, started to ask, but was hushed by the older worker.

"Sir, thank you for your kind words. Be careful, however," tall uniform said as he waved his companion on, nearly pushing the confused looking chubby uniform toward the far ramp, where they paused, watching me.

Looking back toward where she stood, I smiled and, still wary about spooking her, especially with the broken railing so close, motioned for her to join me, to head back to the ramp to walk down to the park.

I detected hesitation, but, by the time I had stepped a meter or so away from the broken section, I found she had joined me, her face glowing from the wind and snow, and…dare I pray, from her heart?

As we walked, not quite holding hands, since her air was still somewhat distant, I decided to try to break our awkward silence, which was compounded by the two uniforms being so close as we approached the ramp.

"So sorry...," I offered. "I'm such a...."

I smiled at my lame attempt, and suggested she go first, hoping my failed gallantry had had some effect on her.

I watched as she turned her soft face toward mine, heedless of the snow, thicker now, laying down a crunching carpet under our feet.

Her face spoke volumes to me and said everything I needed to hear with what I saw as tears mixing with snowflakes on her porcelain face.

"Yes, I followed you. No, don't say anything, it was just the right thing to do," I replied to those doleful eyes.

Abruptly, through the cold and the roller coaster of emotions, the words of her favorite singer's Venice song finally broke into my full consciousness and, at last, after all the times hearing it and kidding her about it, the lyrics finally made sense to me.

"Well, at the end of the day...love. Love makes a man do odd things."

I felt that her pale cheeks reddened ever so slightly at a word she had never heard pass my lips before.

Love. Why was it such a hard word to actually say, I demanded of myself? And, why? Why had I waited so long? Too long, to let her hear me confess it?

I'm a fool.

I watched her faint smile, imagining her tears finally drying in the brisk wind, and, I almost, just almost, slipped her arm into mine, hoping to hear her silently whisper her own confirmation of my heartfelt confession.

I felt the strength returning to my legs and to my whole being, warmed by her radiant calmness, and her apparent resolve to face things together, as a couple.

I then gently voiced what we were both thinking.

"We'll see someone? Together?"

I thought I saw her head nod, slowly, in agreement, and her eyes again gave my aching heart a reassuring squeeze.

Passing the two workers at the entrance to the ramp, both doing a poor job of pretending to be inspecting a tilted light fixture, while actually watching our progress, I nodded to the two men, and gave them a small bow, which they both then returned with vigor.

"Sir, be careful on the ramp, there hasn't been time for the little miniplows to come by. It's ridged, so it's safe, just watch your step," tall uniform said as we started down.

Down the ramp we strolled, away from Seoul's own Bridge of Sighs, back to the park, back to our lives, and back to the city to work out our particular issues, to confront our demons head on.

Without the benefit of the river demons' help, I chuckled to myself, no doubt with a bit of leftover delirium from my adrenaline fueled antics at the bridge railing.

As we carefully descended the snow-covered ramp, the increasing snow laid down an even thicker, pristine white carpet before us, like in a fairy tale of old.

And, I, her honorable young knight, was escorting milady to safety, I mused, then smiled to myself, as I reached out to take her hand, but again drew my hand back, still deferring to her fragileness.

In the distance, the ferry blasted its deep-set horn, long and low, like the trumpeters of old in the long silent palaces of her forebears.

Water. We were still over the narrow bit of water.

Later, when we get to the park, I told myself, I'd offer my arm again, and tucked my hand back into my coat.

At a loud sound and passing shadow from above, maybe a car on the bridge, I turned to look over my shoulder as we walked, seeing no one else around to disturb our descent, as the two uniforms had given up their maintenance charade, and had continued along the main bridge, leaving a wide, dark swath of tamped down snow in their wake.

Turning back, my finally content heart suddenly bubbled up with a rare, long absent warmth at the beautiful sight of our own little trail in the snow. From the top of the ramp, leading down to where we walked, our boots were tapping out a clean, nearly pristine, single, narrow line in the white, crystalline carpet.

How thrilling, I rejoiced, but held back any outward joy for later, not wanting to stress her tenuous presence in any way.

A single, perfect, delicate line, guiding us gently on our descent.

Just as if we were walking so closely together, with our legs nearly intertwined, that anyone passing by might think only one set of boot prints had come off the Mapo Bridge that night.

Yes, I said to myself, with her eternal warmth radiating from within me, a white, whispering carpet of cleansing snow had let me gently, ever so delicately, carry home my silent, full of grace, forever princess.

INTERLUDE VI

The writer, caught up in the tale's action, had risen as he had narrated the last few paragraphs of the Mapo Bridge story, and had walked slowly around the bench, using his motions to emulate the narrator's journey. Pausing near the stove as the last words passed his lips, he was just able to see over the rim of the huge pot and into a swilling, beckoning blackness that almost engulfed him, causing him to jerk his eyes away as he finished the tale.

Standing only a about a meter from the creature, the writer let his voice fall silent, hoping the imagery of the bridge in the snow would intrigue his host, who appeared to be near sleep.

"No, boy, not so asleep that you can pounce and try to slit my throat," chuckled the creature from under closed eyes. "Your stench precedes you by at least two body lengths, human. Easy to follow you without eyes, or even ears."

The writer smiled at the creature's ironic accusation.

"No, not attempting murder, and rob you of that honor, vile one," the writer rebutted. "Simply trying to move the story more vividly by moving with the narrator."

"Yes, boy, I can smell the stench of she-who-is-not-named rising up from the waters under the Mapo Bridge, from the strange words you spin," the creature hissed, allowing its eyes to open to slits as it seemed to relish the tale more than some others. "So many of my lesser cousins linger there, in the dark spaces. When they still spoke to me, they boasted of hanging from bridge supports to grab at the falling humans. Mapo, Dongjak, others less known. My cousins at the river haunt them all. Tear a morsel here and there. Must stay above the soul eaters, those dirty of the dirtiest spawn of the lowest caste goblin-fairies, who leave only shells after they feast. They wait just at the water line to drag the fool human's tattered remnants of a soul out of him or her, just before they slam into the blackness of the unforgiving water, and, once there, out of reach, only to be battered about by the water spirits, like a gang of alley cats playing with a rat. No, a soft mouse in the case of the fool narrator's friend."

Shocked at the relish with which the creature spoke of the Mapo and other bridges and their sad histories, the writer kept silent, afraid his voice might betray the utter disdain he felt for the creature's callousness. He simply nodded, hoping the creature would continue and not refocus on the firebox.

"When I was younger, one of my cousins took me to another place. A dark place, with a double bridge," the creature continued. "No name. Just remember the smell was a delightful mix of night soil and rotting fish. We had to stay far away from the soul eaters. They are not that bright, so will often grab even our minds and drag them into the abyss. I only watched as one of my cousins caught the left eye and cheek of a young girl. Foolish human wailed of a lost love as she flew toward the black water. Lost love? Fool human. Didn't she know all love is lost?"

Seeing the creature turn to look in the direction of the cook pot, the writer cleared his throat, walked back to stand behind the bench to draw his host's eyes away from the stove, and spoke up, regaining the creature's wandering attention.

"That's…perceptive," the writer replied to the creature's ghastly comments. "The young do lead confused lives, at times."

"What do you…? How does 'love' work in your world, great beast of the night?" the writer then asked, keying on the brief comment by the creature.

The creature just grunted and then looked sideways at the writer, ignoring the direct question.

"This one pleases me. Not because you allowed the confused fool boy to live, but because you reminded me of the many who will not," the creature said with a level of glee in its voice. "You reminded me I have not slipped down to the Han in many, many seasons to catch morsels from the fallen. Tasty morsels they are."

"What? What do they…they taste of?" the writer asked, almost gagging on his words, but intensely curious as to how his deranged captor viewed the world, however depraved.

"Taste of?" the creature repeated, with more relish than the writer could stomach, causing the captive writer to conceal dry heaves as the creature spoke.

"Taste of? Fear. Always fear. Different fears. Sadness. Loneliness. Endless torment. Outsiders. Outcasts," the creature replied, letting its tongue slide back and forth on its top and bottom lips, as if remembering a tasty bit. "But, I always spit those out. Doesn't seem right for me to take morsels from fool humans who have been outcast. I do, however, take morsels from the ones who do the outcasting. When I taste an outcast, I can taste those who did the outcasting, through the anger and bile of the rejected human. Track them I do. Well, I did when I was younger. Sit and wait. Often at the most stylish bar, or the highest-end, exclusive restaurant. Oh, and under the popular kids' table in the lunchroom. Chew on their self-esteem and sometime the tips of their fingers under the table, I did. Some of those kids I'd haunt far into their adulthood. Fool humans."

The writer nodded, wondering how to respond to the beast's gleeful confession.

"So, boy, are you finished, so I can light my firebox and summon the tiny ones to prepare you…?" the creature then asked, stretching its arms as it spoke. "I think I'm getting hungry, finally."

"The popular kids are always growing up to be the bullies, do you think?" asked the writer.

"Bullies? Such an odd word. We prefer to call them ready-made-meals," the creature laughed, allowing itself to actually crack a smile on its rotting lips. "So easy to wriggle into their minds, whisper into their fool heads, cause mischief and, if away from prying teacher eyes, mayhem."

"All schools?" the writer asked.

"What? No, not all. Too few of us remain, boy. Haven't you heard my words of the demise and diaspora of our kind?" the creature barked, standing and wandering back to the edge of the trees, waving its left hand over its head at the sky. "I hear mostly whispers now, boy. Mostly whispers of our former numbers."

For a long moment, the creature was stock still, staring up into the evening sky, its left hand still suspended in mid-wave. The writer began to think the beast had passed out, or, in line with the insanity of the whole experience, maybe the beast was turning into stone?

"Whispers," the creatures suddenly repeated and turned to look at the writer. "Yes, your tale reminded me of those many, many cycles ago when my cousins hung from nearly every choice bridge spot, beside the most welcoming alleys, and in the shadows of your darkest passages. Itaewon, not far, had so many in the old days. From the more torrid of balconies, the longest of the tunnel carriages. Many, human, many were the haunts of my cousins and our brethren."

"Where do...where are your cousins? And, if you haven't spoken to them for some time, how do you know they are all almost gone?" the writer asked, welcoming the opportunity for the creature to continue talking.

"How do I...?" the creature began, then turned back to face the trees hiding the little ones, and let out a loud whistle, nearly ear piercing for the writer.

At the sound of the whistle, rarely heard in most of the peninsula's superstitious society, the little ones came crashing out of the trees, some literally falling from limbs where they had been hiding, others scurrying out from between dark spaces, pushing and shoving their comrades to be first to the line forming in front of the creature.

The writer was astonished, for the few little ones he had already seen suddenly multiplied into at least a dozen or so, and he could still hear more rustling back in the trees.

As the little ones lined up in front of the creature, unspeaking and staring straight ahead, the beast turned to the writer and motioned for him to join his host's review of the small squad of mini-demons.

The writer moved hesitantly over to stand just a bit behind and to the left of the beast, and looked into the array of distorted faces lining up. Some faces were confused, mashed things with only hints as to where eyes and mouths might reside. A few looked like the ones he had already seen, small child-things, dirty, hungry looking, rail thin.

"I just realized, chatty morsel, that I have been a terrible host," the creature declared with a bit of surprising pomp, eerily reminding the writer of Charles Dickens' child corruptor, Fagin. "Allow me to introduce my Namsan runners. Yes, these are Namsan, as there are others who gather in different, even more remote, quiet enclaves, tossing yut-sticks, awaiting my commands."

The writer nodded, absently pushed up his sleeves from the added heat of so many bodies, and even did a small bow to the line before he caught himself and, straightening, wondered if he'd be able to fight off such a horde, instead of the four or five he had wrongly guessed were hiding in the trees. Several looked more like small man-things, thick set, with numerous scars covering bulging muscles under tattered, old style clothing.

And, hideously ugly, the writer concluded, after a quick study of the new faces. Unlike several of the earlier child-things that were gender neutral, the pug like, squatty little men were definitely male.

"As I age, human, I find I need these little messengers more and more," the creature said with a clear tone of sadness, at least to the writer's ear. "The stones are not as talkative as in the old days. The trees, they still speak to me, but are slower now, conserving energy that you humans have foolishly sapped. My little friend of the wind flowers still speaks, even if weakly. So, yes, I have an array of gatherers who fan out, when needed, and bring me news and take my demands to...well, to those who need to hear."

"These are your messengers for...?" the writer asked, letting the creature fill in the blank. "And, what is a wind flower?"

"My...? My runners. Messengers. Spies. Ears and eyes for those places I can't always be," the creature replied, ignoring the writer's second question. "Each has particular uses. All are similar, but each has a talent. Yes, that's the word. A talent. This one, eyes a bit askew due to not being quick enough to evade one of your tunnel carriages long ago, can track a mole through the total darkness of Seoul's sewers, even the old style ditches down by...well, no place is too vile for this one's nose to sniff out prey."

"The skinny one there.... No, wait, what do you think the little skinny one has for a special talent?" the creature asked, turning to the writer. "You are the 'observer,' as you say. What do you observe?"

The writer was momentarily confused, as the remainder all looked emaciated to him, except for the already mentioned stocky, ugly beasts. Watching their master's movement, he managed to discern a small nod in the direction of a tallish, boy-girl looking waif, its face a study in sheer exhaustion, its clothes more skin-like, than cloth.

At a loss as to what the special talent might be, the writer simply randomly guessed.

"Sliding under the cracks under doorways?" the writer ventured.

"He can see those who are walking toward she-who-is-not-named," the creature replied. "Yes, doomed to forever know the end for so many, yet must sit by and let me, and, sometimes my colleagues, drag the sorry human just before...well, before that happens. When I was younger, such was great sport. Waiting at the very edge of the forbidden burial places. Fast. You had to be fast to cheat her of the entire soul, just before she pounced."

"Forbidden? Are there many places closed to you and your kind?" the writer quickly asked, hoping for additional hints of the creature's weaknesses.

"Tunnels under water are the worse," the creature replied without pause, but then looked down at the writer with a hard stare.

"Clever, scribbler, to play on such fears, of those who have no fears," the creature added, its voice flat, noncommittal.

The creature bypassed a couple of smaller little ones and stepped in front of one of the taller child-things, so thin that she, the writer felt, more than observed, that it was a she, seemed to blink in and out. There one minute, draped in shimmering black, and then gone the next. Notably, the creature seemed to lean back from the wavering tall one, almost as if the master was a bit unnerved being so close to its servant.

The creature then draped its long arm over the writer's shoulders and, pushing him closer to the wavering, tall little one, whispered odd questions.

"What is it you see, scribbler? What earthy smells do you smell? What depths does your worthless soul descend to when you look into and under those unblinking eyes before you?" the creature whispered in a voice so low that the writer felt the words were actually in his mind.

While staring at, or, more accurately, just as he finally was able to get a glimpse of the piercing eyes of the tall child-thing, since she wavered in and out, the writer suddenly felt he was falling, unable to catch himself. Abruptly, spread out before him was a small, yet grand cemetery, somewhere on a hill overlooking a river, maybe a lake. Down country, not Seoul, was all the writer could guess from the surroundings as the scene flew up almost into his face. The graves and markers were all of the old ways, before the routine cremations. The grass mounds over the graves were well tended. The rolling lawn surrounding was neatly trimmed, almost carpet-like.

The lush, green, tree-framed hillside was familiar, the writer vaguely realized. How? He had only seen a few such cemeteries during his times on the peninsula. Yanghawjin? No, not Seoul. Jeonju? Maybe…? Yet, how could it be, he wondered?

Suddenly, the writer, his gut churning, felt his face crawling with creatures from under the graves. No, from inside the graves! The death feeding, crawling and slithering creatures, sleeping for an eternity after having exhausted their long passed feast, had awakened at the writer's arrival, and had begun to gnaw and chew away at his face. The ungodly stench was beyond the experience of the writer, so that part of his mind simply shut down, rather than try to deal with it.

The writer, holding his mouth tight against the assault, then tried to shut his eyes, but, somehow, he could not. Small, unspeakable creatures, some he could see, many he could not, were attacking his flesh, slipping into his ears, exploring his nose, pushing at the undersides of his fingernails, and beginning to worm their way under his clothing, slithering up his legs in search of easier paths to his gut.

With the sheer terror of the onslaught of tiny death creatures tearing away at his mental resolve, the writer fought hard against a primordial urge to scream, which, of course, would open the gates for the tiny beasts to flood into his mouth.

Holding his breath until the last possible second, the writer's mind battled hard against the horror, and hastily made peace with his life, his family and friends, his colleagues, anyone he had wronged over the years, and anyone who might remember him. How long would his lungs hold out, the writer wondered, trying to shake something out of his left ear, while squeezing his legs together as tightly as he could?

"Umph!" the writer blurted out, after the long arm of his captor dragged him out of the nest of death creatures, the dirt and hillside falling away as his mind and body were dragged back across the peninsula to the creature's haven.

Smiling over the dazed captive, the beast then nodded at the wavering, tall little one, who bowed, turned, and faded away into the trees.

"Such is the fate of those who rob the graves of old, scribbler. She, I think she is still a she, is connected to what you call sacred places. Places that many of my cousins cannot go. I can stride across without fear, but I can sense little, as those places have many guardians, and much silver," the creature said to the writer, who was still breathing hard and trying his best not to reach up to his face to see if the gnawing little beasts were still there.

"No, fool human, there are no little ones nibbling at your pale cheeks. You only saw what she let you see. The fate of those who enter those sacred places to disrupt the long rest, and steal the sacred land from beneath those old, protected souls," the creature cooed.

"Steal the land?" the writer coughed, more to get his mind off the momentary horror of the grave, rather than from curiosity.

"Humans, fool human! You are your worst enemy. You plow up the old to build the new. You sell your ancestor's ancient homes and final beds in the earth so you can buy newer and shinier things, human. Those betrayers of their own or even others' ancestors, my little flickering flower can spot across a busy carriage house, across a mountain of change houses, across a hundred markets, across whatever expanse is placed before her. There is no refuge, scribbler, for those who trade in sacred places. Once she comes across one, guided by the ancestral screams of the long, long gone, she needs but one, gentle, light touch, and those lowest of humans…," the creature replied, as it moved to another little beast, where the master stopped in mid-sentence, leaving the writer to wonder what ultimate horror would befall modern day grave robbers, or more accurately, cemetery thieves.

The master then waved at a group of ragged little ones.

"Some of these wander the gambling houses, looking for the disaffected daughters-in-law who would trade their miserable lot for a brief run of luck, any luck. Or the company man who dreams of hitting it big and breaking his chains, only to toss his coin away, forging ever stronger chains," the creature laughed. "Those two there, the puny ones, climb into the cribs of the high-born and sing ancient songs of betrayal, avarice, blind ambition, and cold disdain into the minds of those malleable little ones. The round one there, and his kin, are those who haunt the halls of gluttony, feeding off those who eat more in one sitting than a wretched family might see in a moon."

The creature then poked one of the small, ugly ogres, causing the little beast to crouch, as if taking a wrestling stance, making the writer realize the small ogre and his counterparts probably represented traditional goblins.

"This one, the lovely beastie and his brothers, can crash through, what do you call them? Yes, your grooming places, your spas, stealing the cuttings from your weak little manes, from your puny talons, and even bits of the skin scraped off by your slaves," the creature said, laughing at the evident confusion on the little goblin's face.

"They and the lesser cousins use, often, those bath houses you humans seem to crave, for their spawning," the beast continued as it teased the ugly one. "The lesser ones then slip into the folds of the towels, the nooks in the egg crates, cling to the back of the straw, all to be carried home, to a workplace, or, to your carriages where they can latch onto other fools."

The confused ogre, its smashed face relaxing, abruptly reached out and, before the writer could withdraw his arm, ran its scaly little hand over the writer's forearm hair. Flinching from the little beast's touch, the writer dropped his hand, and pushed his sleeves back down, as the master shoved the little ogre back in line with a filthy stump.

"You have a lot of fur, scribbler. My little ones have not seen such," the creature chuckled. "Maybe they wonder if they need to singe your fur off, before the cook pot?"

"Well, blame my Scottish ancestors," the writer quipped, his mind not yet clear.

"Scottish…? Wait, fool. From across the German Sea?" the creature asked, genuine interest playing across its face. "My sire spoke of this place. Uncles there, the stories say. Maybe your old ones were haunted by my old ones, scribbler?"

"Stealing hair?" the writer asked, trying to keep far enough away from the line of small beasts so that they, when the creature's back was turned, could not quite reach the writer's legs.

The writer also wanted to move his captor away from thoughts that there might be some fatalistic connection between the writer and the beast, which would no doubt hasten the writer's trip to the cook pot as an ancestral rite of some bizarre sort by the creature.

"Steal? Yes, use for the potions. Use for trailing. Use for selling to the ghouls, those who have wronged my cousins, scribbler. Look closely, next time you, if you cut that thin fuzz on your crown, and you will see the little piles of cuttings shrink as my little ones harvest your castoffs," the creature answered, sniffing the air. "Some of the witches pay handsomely for certain locks from your mangy heads."

"Pay? You deal in money?" the writer asked, more to keep the beast talking than actually believing in goblin, or troll, to witch commerce.

"In kind, fool. They pay in kind," the creature answered, then suddenly waved its hands dismissively, cutting short the review.

The little horde skittered back to the trees, with several of them staring hungrily at the writer's various body parts as they passed him. One of the ugly little ogres even leaned over and tried to lick the writer's hand, to the chortles and grunts of the others.

"I tire of my own grandness, scribbler. I know you have another, or two, tales to tell. Why should I allow you to continue? Tell me, scribbler, why?" the creature asked after all the grotesque staff had slipped into the trees.

"Have all your cousins faded into nothing, or, as have so many of the people of the peninsula, have your cousins followed their humans, as your sire did returning to Europe, to the four corners of the globe? Are your kind also part of the diaspora of the peninsula's people?" the writer bluntly asked, hoping to focus his host away from the stove and on the writer's hints at an upcoming tale.

"Clever. Clever, you are, scribbler of tales. Yes, those who survive the crossings, I hear, do move about with their haunted families. At least, for a time. So many then fade away as the newer hosts are corrupted by their new lands, forsaking the traditions," the creature replied, its voice shifting to melancholy.

"Ah, as we discussed earlier in our…in our little chat," the writer added, avoiding sounding too triumphant.

"Why do you bring up such torture, scribbler? Maybe you have word of my far away cousins in those final pages?" the beast asked, its voice shifting back to menacing.

The writer ventured closer to the creature, finally immune to the stench, and looked the beast directly into the one eye the writer could see peering out from under the cowl.

"The next tale, my grand host, takes us away, for a bit, from the peninsula, to walk amongst a small group of those next generations your cousins would prey upon across the seas, as they grapple with…well, possibly your cousins or close associates of your cousins," the writer replied, trying to lure the creature's interest with what was almost a bold lie, but held enough truth that the creature would not detect any falsehoods.

"Away from my lands? Yes, that would be…that would be entertaining, foolish human. I hear only snatches from some of the returning cousins, weak from dragging so many soulless beings across the water, boy," the creature answered, reaching up and pushing the cowl halfway back, revealing its pale face and gleaming eyes.

"Yes, I imagine it's hard for anyone to begin a new life as strangers in a strange land," the writer replied, holding his eyes on the beast's stare.

"You may…wait, let me relax. This constant chatter has tired me, even with my, how do you say, enhanced rice-wine mead earlier. Let me sit, and then begin," the creature demanded, then moved back to its great stone chair. "Be wary, though, of the little ones just behind. The remainder have smelt your fragrance and, as you saw, a few of them are not as patient, nor as obedient as the smaller ones."

As the creature worked itself into a comfortable position in the great chair, the writer moved back to the bench and, flipping through the notebook, glanced over the last two stories.

Shocked that he only had two stories remaining, the writer wondered if he could simply make up more stories from his notes and from memory, or create brand new ones on the fly, if, when he came to the final tale, the beast wanted more.

The writer chuckled at a random thought that, if any of his bones survived the upcoming feast and were discovered years in the future, alongside his unpublished manuscript, then maybe one of his former students, grown and in his or her own professorship, would dedicate a storytelling day to the writer, holding such on the autumn slopes of Mount Namsan.

Shaking off the odd notion and thoughts of his imminent demise, the writer almost sighed, but caught himself and turned it into a short cough. He then began his tale of the Korean diaspora and the challenges for the follow on generations.

"While there are many, many places the peninsula's people have populated, we will turn to one on the other side of the globe," the writer began.

"California? I know many cousins are there," the creature called from its chair.

"No, not Los Angeles, although I do have a few outlandish tales from the 6th Street corridor, near Vermont, and elsewhere. Not San Francisco. East coast. Not Atlanta. Not the Washington, D.C. area, where I have loads of notes for a separate work, including a caterer in Annandale that harbors…well, that's another day. This particular collection of events unfolds in that mega-city, nearly unrivaled. New York. A western version of Seoul, if you will," the writer answered.

"New York. Yes, New York. Many dark, tall alleys. Many, many tall hive huts, too tall for most of my cousins," the creature added. "Begin, scribbler, your words of New York, and my brethren, who are doomed with the haunted peninsula people trapped there, as I am trapped here."

"Yes, let's begin," the writer answered and, settling in, dove right into the tale, with a silent prayer, deeply hidden in the back of his mind where he hoped the creature could not sense it, that he would walk those storied streets and avenues again, soon.

7

GOD KIMCHI OF NEW YORK

Far, far away from the wooded retreat of Mount Namsan, in the steel, glass, and concrete financial, cultural, and culinary world capital of New York, on a bustling Midtown Manhattan street, not far from the Great White Way to the north, and close to the chaos of Penn Station to the west, a thriving, indoor food hall was just rushing into the full, pre-lunch crush of frantic preparations to fuel much of the Korean diaspora populating the city. Competing, that windy, spring morning, with the many restaurants, high end bakeries, snack shops, food carts, and even a couple of full fledged grocers, the little food hall of endless crowd favorites harkened back to the days when many such quick bite joints of countless ethnic variety populated nearly every corner of Seoul's great sister city's beating heart, tucked between the Hudson and East Rivers. Over the years, the size of the small Korea-town had been reduced to a block and some change, as the diaspora had drifted into the mainstream and the need for such protective enclaves had diminished as prosperity lifted so many into higher rents and more family friendly neighborhoods. With the insane real estate prices in Manhattan, one always marveled at how such a hardscrabble little place as the food hall survived. But, survive it had, and, as one passed through its heavy glass doors and was immediately assailed by the symphony of smells, sounds, and sights, deep thanks were silently given by all to the real estate gods for allowing the little treasure to continue.

"Hey, dude, we don't have the time! Coffee. Just get the coffee!" Lee half-yelled at his buddy, Eddie, as the latter piled out of the double-parked car and dashed toward the faded orange marquee of the food hall. "Not again! Just coffee!"

"What? Where...? Hey, what's so critical we had to make a stop before heading to the track, gents?" Michael asked lazily from the backseat of the vintage BMW, mildly annoyed that he had been awakened early from his planned hour-long nap on the way to the practice track in New Jersey. "Saturday traffic is unbearable down here in the morning."

"Kimchi buns," Lee mumbled in reply, his eyes darting forward and back, looking for any meter maids ready to expand her, or his, kills for the morning. "He's suddenly addicted to some bad ass buns some old halmoni makes, in the food hall."

"Food? Hey, why wasn't I told?" Michael asked, perking up at the prospect of an early morning snack.

"Calm down, Friar Tuck," cautioned Jae, from behind his two phones in the opposite corner of the backseat. "The food hog never shares the things. Only lets us smell them."

"Hey, that's just not right!" Michael cried in mock affront. "And, that's not our Eddie. Maybe I need to investigate?"

"Don't worry, you won't starve. He always brings a box of those bungeo, red bean paste, fish pastries, with other stuffing, too," Lee replied.

"And, more coffee," Jae added.

"But, never, never, the sacred buns!" Lee sang out, chuckling.

"Never the bloody buns...," Jae chimed in, his voice falling upon returning his attention to his two business phones.

"Your fault, you know," Lee offered in a teasing voice, which he was careful with around Michael, even if from similar backgrounds.

"What? My fault? How is Eddie's trying to gorge on something my...?" Michael replied, trying to shake the sleep out of his eyes.

"Okay, 'fault' might be too harsh. Responsible adult?" Jae suggested, less crafty at concealing his own mirth.

"This better be good," Michael retorted, wondering if he should bother to hear the outlandish tale his friends would make up, or go after Eddie and try the buns for himself.

"Eddie says you guys were down here a few weeks ago on a donation pickup," Lee replied, and seeing Michael's slow nod, continued.

"Eddie had volunteered to drive the van, since parking, even for you, is crazy down here. Yet, he said he got lucky and plunked the van down just outside the food hall, there. You were headed over to the hotel to collect the donations and it occurred to you that a gift of food for the hotel front desk would be a nice gesture. Eddie was heading over with you when you told him to get something from the bakery. Just as you guys were parting, some kid, one of those eye candy types giving out samples to lure customers in, appeared near the van and offered you a sample. Eddie said you brushed off the kid, but politely, and she then asked if your friend, Eddie, would like to try. Knowing Eddie is nuts for new food, Eddie says you chuckled and, in your usual high minded fashion, waved him over to the girl, saying something like, 'please, take my worthy substitute, he will always cherish a handout,' or something like that."

Michael nodded, a memory forming, even though he was still half asleep.

"I do seem…yes, I think she was handing out samples of something steamed. Or, maybe fried," Michael slowly replied, trying to bring the fuzzy memory to the front of his sleepy head.

"So, it's true?" Jae asked, a thin smile creeping into his otherwise serious face. "You are the culprit?"

"True? Yes, I suppose I did throw my friend to the food dogs in my haste to get to the hotel. But, wait. When I came back to the van with the hotel guys, Eddie was there with the bakery boxes for them. No steam buns, kimchi or otherwise," Michael replied, wondering if his defense sounded as weak to his friends as it did to him.

Both Lee and Jae looked at Michael with the classic, suburban father face, mimicking looking over reading glasses, if the two had been wearing such, and made 'tsk, tsk' noises to their friend.

"Right, gentlemen! As your humbled, if infrequent, guest on these expeditions, it is my desire…nay, my very duty, given my hand in this…this obstacle to our progress, to secure those elusive morsels for such a deserved group. We must have the sacred buns!" Michael declared as he pulled his ample figure out of the car.

Ignoring the calls from his friends, Michael, still a bit sleepy, but letting his momentary eloquence, his slight confusion over his own role, and his forever empty stomach drive his reasoning, made his way to the orange canopy, opened the door, looked puzzled, and realized he was in the nearby bakery. Smiling at the wall of tempting pastries, he almost abandoned his original reason for his quest, but was jostled by a couple of kids, dressed in high-end, branded fashion with just the right accessories, trying to take selfies with the croissants, so he turned away, and finally made it to the food hall.

Stepping inside, Michael paused, his considerable bulk blocking others from entering as he allowed the dozens of amazing smells to drift into his nose and brain, accompanied by the symphony of sounds and sights of the many stalls, overlaid by the rhythmic throbbing of some K-pop boy band. Grumbling patrons, trapped by the big man's size at the doorway, finally nudged Michael's consciousness enough for him to move to the side.

At the bun station just at the door, Michael had expected to find his friend, but Eddie was nowhere to be seen.

Puzzled, Michael leaned around the stand's steam-streaked window, soaked from the constant production of a variety of buns, and called to the workers.

"Hey, did a tall, far too healthy looking guy just order a bunch of your kimchi buns?" Michael asked the masked kid filling metal display trays with steaming goodness.

The youth mumbled that the kimchi buns didn't come out until later, so no one had bought any. Seeing Michael's puzzled expression, the youth then motioned with his head to the back of the multilevel hall.

"Try the old bit…, the old grandmother. New place. Friend of owner, I guess," the kid mumbled, without missing a beat in his one-man assembly line.

Michael thanked the kid and headed toward the back of the food hall, letting his eyes, and his nose, inspect the various stands on the street level and, fleetingly, calculated if he had time to run up the stairs to check out the other levels which held a couple of his lunch favorites, and the bingsu, sweet shaved ice, stand. Shaking his head at the rash thought, he forged ahead through the crowds.

When he reached the back of the hall, the usual places that Michael and his stomach were very familiar with were all where they should be.

So, where would a new stand be…?

"Michael?"

Michael turned at hearing his name and, through the steamy fog of some rice cooker or other appliance, he saw the blurry form of his close friend standing in a narrow recess in the wall, relaying something to a pretty young teen or early twenties shop girl, who was even blurrier through the soupy steam than Eddie.

"Dude, even though we're already late, I have come for the elusive buns our comrades rave about, but, sadly, have never been graced with said buns passing their quivering lips," Michael called, still standing some distance from Eddie and the shop girl.

Suddenly, the blurry shop girl looked toward Michael and, after nodding once, backed away into what must have been a side opening, allowing Michael's eyes to finally be drawn to the new stand.

No different that the other dozen or so small, mom and pop stands sprinkled among the larger establishments in the food hall, the tiny stand was set back in a recess of the eastern wall, easily missed, unless a patron was looking specifically for it. Narrow and shallow, Michael wondered briefly how anyone could fit inside the stand, much less churn out tasty buns all day for a demanding public. For, if Eddie, with his reputation as a true foodie, had discovered the place and was in love with the product, then there should be a line out the door.

Strangely, there was no line. Only Eddie, and the now missing shop girl. And, no one was behind the small window, at least no one that Michael could see.

Just above the stand's small window, a grimy series of cheap, faded posters struggled to depict various constellations, or maybe ancient flyspecks, Michael mused. The two walls bracketing the stand into its manmade cavern were of various bright hues, as if a gang of graffiti taggers had snuck in under the cover of darkness and, fearing lights, had spray-painted the walls a confusing mix of unrecognizable images and geometries.

Michael found himself hesitating, not wanting to step from the light and bustle of the food hall's main area into the close, clammy, and somehow mildly disturbing, tiny niche holding the almost coffin-like kimchi bun stand, even if Eddie had raved about the place as Lee had said.

"Can you...can you make a second order?" Michael called, finally stepping toward Eddie, feeling the cloying moisture of the hot steam on his arms, face, and the back of his neck as he approached his friend. "To take to the guys?"

Michael glanced at the darkened window of the little stand and wondered if anyone was back there.

"Man, it's hot here," Michael said to Eddie, wiping the sudden, stinging sweat from his eyes. "Hey, why aren't you sweating buckets like I am?"

Eddie just smiled at his friend and, turning back to the small window, held up his right hand to indicate a second order and, speaking in high level Korean instead of the usual street Korean, asked the unseen cook or cashier for a second, but smaller order.

Michael, surprised at the out of character deference Eddie was paying to a presumably common shop keeper, leaned one way and then the other, but, either due to the stand's glass being fogged up, or just the angle, he could not see anyone manning the little booth. He then looked for a door or other exit that the shop girl would have taken, but only saw the painted, multi-colored plywood that separated the stall from its neighbors, a quiet ramyeon place and a closed soup stall.

After what seemed mere seconds, Michael heard the crinkle of a bag and turned back to see two orders sitting on the small, faded yellow plastic counter fronting the stand.

Now, how had that happened so quickly, Michael wondered? But, only briefly, as Eddie was waving at his friend to precede him into the main food hall, and to the coffee counter.

Michael complied, still wondering who was behind the small window, and, once the two were out of the steam-filled enclave, he looked at Eddie and wondered if the shop girl was the same one from the street a couple of weeks ago, and why she and his friend had seemed a little too chummy. Maybe a little too...familiar?

Maybe a...?

No way! Michael immediately scolded himself under his breath. Eddie was a man's man and a true family man. He would no sooner play around than Michael would ever dream of sleeping with a parishioner.

After getting the coffees, the two friends, who had known each other from childhood, made their way through the increasing crush of people in the food hall toward the main door. As born and bred New Yorkers, both men moved seamlessly through such crowds, making quick time.

Michael did find himself glancing toward the little stand, and saw that a short line of older, middle-aged men had formed, somehow fitting a half dozen into that small, steamy space.

Michael saw that the pretty shop girl had reappeared and was probably taking orders, he surmised, before his view of the stand was blocked by more patrons heading to the back of the hall.

Outside, the two saw that the car had moved, so they both scanned the block, busy with delivery trucks, two hotel entrances, office workers, a few old guys simply staring, tourists, and workmen from the site around the corner.

"There they are," Eddie finally called, waving at Michael. "Near the BBQ joint."

As the two arrived at the car, Michael suddenly reached out and gently gripped Eddie's shoulder.

Eddie turned, knowing that the familiar gesture from his longtime friend signaled unobtrusive inquiry, which was also compounded by Michael's deeply questioning eyes.

"Look, Michael, it's just some kimchi buns. You'll love them," Eddie replied, trying to slowly wriggle from his friend's grasp.

Michael's eyes switched to frowning, then dropped to the sole package that Eddie was carrying, with the smaller, second package missing. Eddie also looked down and then, with a surprised gasp, turned to run back to the food hall.

"Man, I must have dropped it somewhere," Eddie said, but Michael's hand held him in place.

"It's okay. The guys will never let us back in the car if they see us turn around. Let's just go. If I can't convince you to let me try one of yours, then I'll just look at it as a personal lesson in fighting temptation…and gluttony," Michael replied, in his half joking way around his friends.

Eddie smiled and, after shoving the buns into a small cooler after Lee had popped the trunk, motioned for Michael to take his seat.

As Michael handed in the coffees and then slid into the backseat, the still open trunk only partially blocked his view of Eddie abruptly ripping open the white plastic bag and, hands shaking, take a large bite out of one of the steaming buns, causing Eddie to momentarily shudder.

The sheer, carnal energy of his friend's frantic gorging caused Michael to quickly turn his eyes away, somehow deeply embarrassed that he had seen his friend in…in what? Michael held his half-formed thought at a distance, making a note to keep a closer eye on Eddie.

Slamming the trunk shut, Eddie stepped around the car, took a deep breath and, avoiding the eyes of his friends, especially Michael's, got quickly back into the front passenger seat. He then jovially endured everyone's taunts all the way to the practice track in New Jersey, where three of the friends all had stored their various weekend racers under a deal with one of Jae's business associates. Michael, due to his vows, did not, of course, own a track car, but was one of the better drivers. Even though Michael rarely went to the practice track, due to his heavy schedule, Eddie, playing on his friend's true need to take a break once in a while, had convinced Michael to accompany them that day.

Michael, thankful to his friend for the nagging, was equally glad he had witnessed the odd, wholly out of character behavior of Eddie, and repeated his silent resolve to keep an eye on his childhood friend over the next few weeks.

As spring marched toward summer, Eddie's quick visits to the little bun shop became almost a regimented part of his routine, although he always feigned it was simply accidental that he ended up in the area. Every Saturday morning, at the height of the busy morning rush, no matter what was on Eddie's, the family's, or his friends' schedules, he had to first collect his medium order of addictive morsels.

Initially, his wife and friends laughed at Eddie's unimaginative antics to ensure he was the only one who ate the treats. But, as the visits continued, the missed phone text excuses, the forgotten bag excuses, and the assortment of other half-hearted explanations all wore so thin that everyone in Eddie's circle simply wrote it off to some strange new food craze that would, hopefully, sooner than later, be replaced by something a little closer to the Upper East Side where he and his family lived.

Two people who did not keep quiet, however, were his two mothers, his own, and his mother-in-law. Both women, normally mortal enemy competitors for the attention and praise of their joint ownership in the son and son-in-law, were quite unhappy with Eddie's lackluster, nearly absent praise for their own dishes, kimchi included, after he had been frequenting the little stand at the food hall. Even with coaxing, neither woman could extract more than an obligatory nod out of the preoccupied devotee of the little food stand when he was at one or the other's home for dinner.

Silently declaring a temporary truce several weeks after Eddie's obsession had gone beyond their collective levels of patience, the two women joined forces one morning, bluntly lied to their respective families about their morning routines, and secretly met for a rare outing together to check out the little stand for themselves.

Arriving at the food hall mid-week, to ensure they did not bump into their son, son-in-law, the two made an inspection of the food hall after entering. Both their body languages and their noses let the proprietors of the stands they deigned to linger over know whether the two older matriarchs approved or disapproved of the offered fare. Neither women, both of good families and traditional roles, had ever actually been inside the food hall, leaving such errands to the younger generation and their maids, so they were somewhat intrigued by all the sights, the sounds, the choices, and the obviously devoted patrons.

By the time the two had found the odd little hole-in-the-wall, kimchi bun stand, a line of middle-aged men had formed. Shocked that none of the men, silently labeled rude and country-folk by both women, had had the decency to offer their obvious betters the front of the queue, the two matriarchs had to cool their expensive heels for a number of minutes in line.

After they had given their order and cash, taken by a rather odd little man, twisted nearly sideways from some distant, childhood malady, and had been quickly served by some unseen hand behind the small, overly dark window, the two ladies quickly retreated to the upstairs tables, hoping they had not been in the steam long enough for their two-hundred dollar perms to dissolve. In that less crowded sanctuary, they also felt they would be less likely to be seen by anyone they knew, on the remote chance that anyone in their golfing or bridge circles would frequent such a place during the week.

Opening the steaming boxes, each of the ladies invited the other to be the first to try. However, since that tactic might have gone on for some time, the two silently agreed to sample the buns at the same time, using the supplied wooden chopsticks to retrieve them.

After their first decisive bites, each of the women in turn searched the face of the other to try to discern the other's reaction, before making any commitment on the acceptability of the buns and their contents.

However, neither woman would allow her stone face exterior to reveal anything, until the second and third bites, when the overwhelmingly tragic nature of the buns hit home like a punch in the gut.

Nothing.

Bland, nearly devoid of flavor.

Nothing remotely special.

Both women, their tight eyes silently signaling their similar conclusions, were abjectly mortified that their darling Eddie had thrown over their own cooking and catering favorites for such tasteless and unbelievingly boring fare.

For a few moments, the two women simply sat, staring at the little paper boxes, wondering what to do next. Since neither wanted to vent to the other, they both hit on a joint solution without speaking, and, taking up the boxes with a flourish, the two descended the stairs like a couple of angry royals.

Indignant, the two momentary allies returned to the stand to complain, and to soundly put the owner in her, or his, place.

'Closed until tomorrow.'

A small, handwritten sign, in English and Korean, declared the kimchi bun stand closed until the next day, clearly mocking the two older women, in their minds, who huffed and puffed for several seconds, and then considered tracking down the food hall's owner, who was the second son of Eddie's mother's long time golf partner's sister's accountant.

Finally, after feeling their perms would not survive another minute in the steamy food hall, the two angry mothers just threw up their hands, deposited the partially eaten boxes of buns on the tiny counter to warn off others, and retired to the bakery and coffee shop just up the street, where two respectable younger men did move to give the upset ladies a table in the crowded pastry shop.

After coffee, the two women, again, with very little actual talking, agreed to forget the excursion and to never reveal their private disappointments that their darling boy had gone off on their cooking, and their own favorite caterers, for some cheap imitation of kimchi. Neither of the women let on to each other, or to themselves, the small suspicion that something else must be drawing Eddie's attention, and not the food.

Parting ways at the taxi stand, the two women feigned interest in getting together again, and sulked off separately to the suburbs, one to New Jersey, and one to Long Island City.

Other than the two ladies, who would never admit to such interest, especially after the devastating visit to the little stand, no one really paid much attention to Eddie's obsession, except for his closest friend, Michael.

Michael, even with his crazy schedule of multiple services, weddings, funerals, baptisms, and routine counseling, had made it a point to spend as many Saturdays as he could with Eddie and the car group. Unfortunately, his schedule only allowed every other week or so, so there were long stretches when Michael did not see Eddie.

However, those long stretches allowed Michael to better detect the changes in Eddie over time. Even his close buddies in the car group, either because they were less demanding or they simply wrote off Eddie's obsession to a passing fad, did not seem to be aware or concerned about the changes in Eddie, after Michael had made discreet inquiries.

Thinner, paler, less energetic, and more prone to emotional highs and lows was the Eddie that Michael saw some four or five weeks after Michael's introduction to the kimchi bun stand. Even Eddie's speech began to slur, albeit only Michael seemed to take note.

Michael had invited himself to Eddie's home on a couple of occasions over those weeks to see what Eddie's wife thought. Haejin, a lead investment banker at a new firm, did tease Eddie about the bun place, but did not seem to notice any changes in her husband. Even when Michael outlined, in confidence, Eddie's symptoms, Haejin had simply shaken her head and had said she just did not see it.

Puzzled, Michael initially wrote off Eddie's wife and friends as simply being too busy to notice any changes. Consequently, Michael resolved to do whatever necessary to pull Eddie out of his slump, even if it meant an argument or other conflict. The two had grown up together and were closer than brothers. However, the grip the kimchi bun place had on Eddie was unprecedented in their relationship and was therefore hard for Michael to address.

Even if Michael simply hinted that it was time to find another favorite spot, Eddie would become withdrawn and sullen. Only when Michael would acquiesce would Eddie perk up and, when alone, head for the little stand.

One Friday afternoon, Michael had been on a counseling visit in Tribeca, which ended early. So, he decided, on the spur of the moment, to swing by the food hall on the way home to try to get to the little kimchi bun stand before closing and finally sample Eddie's obsession.

After finding parking a block or so away, Michael made his way to the food hall, effortlessly gliding around others.

At the food hall, Michael made a beeline for the little stand, ignoring everything else around him.

Closed.

Glancing at his watch, Michael uttered an uncharacteristic expletive, quietly, then begged forgiveness to anyone who might have heard his momentary transgression. Shrugging, he turned to leave, not even thinking about the bingsu place upstairs, when he heard a loud creaking sound and turned back to the stand.

Stepping from the gaudily painted right hand wall, a small person, shielded from full view by a sign from the ramyeon stand, appeared. The person seemed to fiddle with something and then stood up in view.

For the briefest of moments, Michael thought he had seen a small, older man at the hidden door, but then realized he was staring into the wide, inviting eyes of the young woman who had been serving Eddie the time Eddie had forgotten the second bag.

The young woman's enchanting eyes held Michael as he stammered out a short greeting and then let his eyes ask about the stand and if there was any chance of buying some late afternoon buns.

The shop girl turned slightly, but held her gaze on Michael, and seemed to be listening, her head cocked slightly to her right.

"Sir, you've just missed us. All gone, I'm afraid," the shop girl finally said in clear, nearly academic English, surprising Michael, who had expected to hear the typical mix of street Korean and half-English college kids her age tended to use.

"Oh," was all Michael could utter, given that he was still preoccupied with the young woman's overly captivating eyes.

"Oh, but you are more than welcome to have these, sir," the young lady added, stepping closer, a little too close, to Michael.

Where had that bag come from, Michael wondered? Was it there when he...she stepped out of the wall?

"What? No, I can't take your own food. Here, maybe I can pay you for it?" Michael offered, trying to keep his eyes on the young woman's face and not letting his gaze stray below her neck, where he knew her curves and loose blouse resided.

"No. We wouldn't hear of such, sir. You've obviously rushed here at this late hour," the shop girl cooed her reply. "Let these be our...gift?"

Her eyes were finally too much for Michael and he forced himself to look down at his wallet.

No cash. Only cards.

Looking up at the young woman, she shook her head at Michael's unspoken question.

"Already locked up the register, sir. Please, just accept this small gift," the shop girl repeated, pressing the warm, slightly steaming package into his hands.

"No...no. Please, miss, I can't take this," Michael replied, finally finding his professional voice and recovering his wavering decorum. "I'll just come back again another day."

Frowning, the shop girl allowed herself to pout a bit, like a K-pop star in a K-drama rom-com, then opened the little paper box without warning, took the chopsticks and grabbed a bun, fully intending, Michael realized, to stuff it into his unsuspecting, but gaping mouth.

Stepping back at the young woman's persistent advance, Michael bumped into an older lady with her son or grandson, bowed and apologized profusely to the old woman as he reddened at the old woman's knowing nod upon seeing a young man being pursued by a young girl of such...such publicly observable attractions.

Shocked at the suspicion on the old woman's face and the slightly leering grin of the young man, Michael turned back to the shop girl to fend off any further attempts to feed him.

Without fanfare, the shop girl smiled, tore off part of the top of the paper box and plopped the bun she had been tempting him with onto it and shoved it into Michael's right hand, while resting her elbow on his arm.

"Try one, on us. Or, if you insist, on account and pay us another day...," the shop girl called as she released the box top, removed her soft, warm arm, and turning slowly, playfully, stepped into the crowd, and was gone.

Standing at the front of the small stand's two colorful walls, Michael let his mind relax and his heart rate return to normal, as his eyes scanned the food hall for the vanished apparition of the temptress shop girl.

How had she dissolved into the crowd so quickly, Michael wondered? He then chuckled when he saw that nearly two thirds of the young people in the place were wearing black, with white shirts, blouses, or accents.

Finally turning his attention to the little bun, Michael sniffed it, looked around and realized munching on it while standing in the middle of the crowd was too much even for someone as enlightened as he was. Folding the paper top around the small morsel, he then turned away from the little stand, pausing briefly to gaze at the soiled posters of the stars over the now barred window. Heading back to his van, he could have sworn the pictures had changed, or moved around, yet were still as grubby as when he had first seen them.

Back in the van, Michael sat quietly, thinking he might take one small bite of the bun before he headed out, but another car beeped him, nudging him to go ahead and pull out of the coveted parking spot and head back to Brooklyn.

Once he had arrived at the rectory, Michael parked the van and slowly made his way to his quarters, waving at the groundskeeper across the parking lot. Another denizen of the grounds, an ancient, far too fat, half-Persian cat greeted Michael at the door.

Michael then stopped. For some reason he could not place, the cat had reminded him of the sultry shop girl, which then reminded him that he had left the kimchi bun in the van. Turning back with a quick 'hello' to the cat, he retrieved the bun and, as he walked, took a small, tentative bite.

"Wow…," Michael blurted out to no one in particular as the tiny bite made its way down his throat. "Wow."

At the door, the cat sat up to accept her usual hug, head bobbing as she sniffed, no doubt smelling the bun and expecting a taste as a toll for allowing the tall human to pet her luxurious mane.

Michael grinned at the clever cat and, taking a small bit, ensuring he didn't give her any of the spicy insides, he leaned down and offered the cat a good chunk of the bun's oily exterior.

The cat perked up, looked at the piece with careful inspection, as cats do, unlike the groundskeeper's hound who would have gobbled it without looking, and then licked the bun with her pink tongue.

"Hiss!" the cat spat at the bun and then Michael, backing up, her usually flowing hair standing straight out like a grey porcupine.

"Hey, it's okay. It's good…," Michael called to the cat, who replied with an even louder 'cris-hiss' sound and bolted behind the building.

Shaking his head, Michael tossed the little piece of bun to the edge of the building where he assumed the cat would return and eat it later, once she had gotten over her fright of the spices or whatever had upset her.

Michael then popped the rest of the bun into his mouth, stepped into the rectory, and forgot about the cat, the bun, and even the shop girl as his evening duties kicked in.

Later that night, when the cook brought him a late dinner, as he had been unable to eat with the rest of the staff, he thanked her, but didn't touch his dinner. At her questioning, he replied that it was certainly not her cooking, but that he had been weak and had had a snack later in the day after returning.

The cook, suspicious of any outside food that she had not personally checked out, told Michael she'd leave the tray by him in the library so that he could eat something before turning in. However, upon her return that evening, none of the food had been touched. The cook did take a small bit of pride in the two empty glasses, one that had held milk and one Michael's favorite ice tea.

That night, Michael's sleep was fitful, full of images of worldly temptation and personal confusion. Long ago, deeply buried memories tried to surface, only to be washed over by his later years and rigid training. None of the images were lasting, however, and fled his exhausted mind before he awoke.

As was his custom, Michael rose well before dawn, but found himself drenched in a cold sweat, with a raging, almost painful hunger in his gut.

Before he realized what he was doing, Michael stole into the still quiet kitchen and, finding his uneaten dinner on a covered dish in the fridge, he stood with the door open to the cooling air and wolfed down the cold meal.

Later, after dressing and attending morning prayers, Michael sat down to breakfast and ate everything the cook had to offer, and more. The cook beamed at her charge's appetite and decided to whip up some blueberry pancakes, which was normally a Wednesday dish, not Saturday.

Saturday?

Saturday!

Michael suddenly realized that Eddie would be returning to the little stand that morning, if his routine held. Grabbing his phone, Michael tried calling Eddie, but kept getting sent directly to voicemail. He then tried Lee, and finally got his friend on the phone.

"Lee, are you guys going to the track today? With Eddie?" Michael asked, forcing his voice to be steady.

"The track, yep. Eddie said he asked you but that you…," Lee began, but was cut off by Michael.

"I can go. I mean, I have to work, but it's calls. I have to make a number of calls," Michael replied.

"Well, we're heading out soon, I don't think I can drive over to collect you and be back in time for…," Lee answered, but was again cut off.

"I'll meet you halfway," Michael snapped back, biting his lip that he had been so curt with his friend.

"Oh, okay. The museum parking lot?" Lee suggested.

"Right. See you in a few," Michael answered, and hung up before Lee could reply.

Gulping down several pancakes, Michael thanked the cook, palmed a bit of sausage, and then ran back to his room to change into street clothes.

As he dashed out of his room, Michael grabbed his most cherished rosary, a glass and silver graduation gift from his mother, which rested on his nightstand, instead of picking up what he called his 'work' rosary, which sat atop his dresser.

At the rectory door, Michael paused and puzzled on where the cat might have been since she was always waiting at the door for morning scraps, which the cook strongly objected to, but had always turned a blind eye. Shrugging, he looked for a good spot to drop the bit of sausage he had saved for her and was shocked to see the small chunk of bun, its oil having stained the pavement overnight, still resting where it had fallen.

Amazing, Michael thought, if New York rats won't eat the bun casing, no wonder the cat ran away. Must have something in it animals just don't like.

Michael then placed the bit of sausage next to a saucepan of water left for the cat, called back into the kitchen to the cook that he'd clean up the bun he had left for the cat, but had not been eaten, dashed to the van, and drove a little too aggressively to meet Lee and the others at the museum parking lot several miles away, just as the gang was about to drive away.

That morning was around the ninth or tenth week of bun madness, Michael figured, from his chats with Eddie and the car gang. He rode in mostly silence to Midtown, being careful to say nothing to Eddie or the others. He only broke his silence when he made a few counseling calls, where he primarily listened, after apologizing and letting the parishioner know that Michael was not alone and in a car. His explanation that he was on the way to a critical session was not untrue.

When the four friends became, once again, stuck in traffic several blocks from West 32nd Street, Eddie, growing more frantic by the moment with the delay, suddenly bolted out of the car, yelling back to his friends that he'd meet them at the corner after getting the treats and the coffee.

Michael, who, due to his trying to balance work with the last minute outing, was on the phone with an upset parishioner, and was caught off guard as he watched helplessly as Eddie faded into the crowds.

'Seriously?" Michael said under his breath as the parishioner's never ending saga continued to unfold, trapping Michael on the phone.

"Friar Tuck, you want I should hound dog our boy?" Jae whispered, showing a rare, empathetic side, then hopped out of the car at Michael's fevered nodding.

Just moments later, after the car had moved about twelve feet, the parishioner concluded the tale of woe, thanked Michael, and signed off.

Michael, slapping Lee on the back for encouragement in the nightmare traffic, climbed out of the car and dashed after Jae and Eddie, splashing through puddles from an overnight rainstorm.

The two blocks to the food hall, while more easily covered on foot than by car, were still crowded going, causing Michael to continually mumble apologies as he jostled his way through the New York street crowds.

Passing the bakery close to the food hall, Michael stopped cold, surprised to see Jae perusing the sticky buns.

Opening the glass door, Michael called to his friend.

"Jae, is he in here?" Michael asked, confused that Eddie would not go straight to the bun stand.

"Naw. Followed him to the sangyeo stand. There were a couple of others in front of him, with the old man taking orders. Don't worry, he'll be there a while," Jae called back, his eyes still studying the pastries.

"Thanks, Jae, I'll...," Michael began, but then halted in his tracks in the middle of closing the door, blocking patrons coming and going.

Suddenly, everything around Michael seemed to slow down, nearly to the point that he felt he had stepped out of his body and was looking down on the scene and was not really a part of it. The insatiable hunger that had been plaguing Michael since the early morning screamed into high gear and almost doubled him over in pain. Steeling himself, he forced his mind back to the bakery and spoke, slowly, distinctly.

"Jae, what did you just say?" Michael asked, ignoring the growing pain in his stomach and the distant pleas of the shoppers around him.

"What? That Eddie is at the bun joint...," Jae replied, but was abruptly cut off by Michael's unsettling outburst.

"No, dammit, what did you call the place?" Michael demanded, shocking Jae, who then turned and was shocked even more by the ghastly change in Michael from just a few minutes before.

"Call the...? Oh, you know. The coffin. Sangyeo. It's what everybody calls the little place. Probably from the murals, or maybe the size? Those little kokdu dolls lining the edges are pretty gruesome. A lot of them are headless. Look at it when you get there...," Jae called back, but went silent again as Michael crashed out of the bakery and plowed through the crowd like an entitled mom with a stroller on Fifth Avenue, oblivious to the passerby he had to push to the side in his frantic haste.

"Michael, are you okay?" Jae called half out the door when he realized he had pastries on his tray he had not yet paid for, so turned back into the shop.

"Am I too late...?" Michael asked himself, out loud, but not letting his mind form a full picture, fearing what that picture might be. "Too late...?"

Slamming into the heavy doors of the food hall, Michael's entrance alarmed shoppers, workers, and anyone close enough to see the juggernaut nearly take the heavy glass doors off their hinges.

Everyone got out of the big man's way as he dashed to the back of the food hall.

As he stormed through, Michael had to avoid tripping over several large tofu buckets that were catching falling water from the far ceiling, probably from new leaks caused by the previous night's storm.

Was he too late...?

No!

Michael silently screamed in his mind when he saw his friend just stepping to the front of the line, the lithe, seductive young shop girl nearly panting, her breasts heaving under the too tight white blouse, as she anticipated Eddie's order.

Eddie's final order, Michael shouted in his mind, his voice barely able to break out of a mix of fear and guilt, had he been too late to intervene.

"Stand!" bellowed Michael, not to Eddie, but to the slim young shop girl, her tongue darting along her pursed lips like the second hand of a clock ticking down.

At his friend's voice, Eddie turned, but could barely see Michael through the steam belching from the bun stand. Eddie then slowly turned back to the shop girl to complete his order, thinking he was hearing things.

Stopping a few feet from his friend and the far too alluring young woman, Michael slammed his fist into his chest to clear his throat and his mind.

"Stand, demon!" Michael called again, but calmer, in a voice that was not his, but welled up from his years of training and experience with both the good and bad sides of human nature, and with the darker things that preyed upon man.

"Today is not your day, vile creature. Stand!" Michael called in a mix of old and new Korean, adding whispered Latin passages at the end.

Michael felt other words, ancient words, coming to him, but forced himself to focus on his training and experience. The other words were faint, far back in his skull, from a different time in his life. In the here and now, he drew upon his faith, his brothers and sisters in faith, and his leaders in faith, as well as his unbreakable bond with his childhood friend.

Eddie paused and turned again, finally seeing his friend. He waved and beckoned to Michael to join him, wondering why Michael was mumbling some old song and waving his arms.

Turning back to the shop girl, Eddie flinched, and nearly jumped back.

Gone was the shapely little helper that he had met weeks before when she had offered him a sample at the front of the food hall and had drawn him away from the bun place at the front door to the little hole in the wall at the back.

Gone was the cute, perky shop girl who had cheerfully taken his order for weeks.

Gone were the shop girl's enticing smile and cute demeanor.

Gone were the cooing words and doleful, drowning eyes.

Gone was the girl.

In her place, to Eddie's astonishment, a twisted old man stood, his misshapen back, sideways head, and leering face revealing a complete stranger.

"Stand!" Michael called again, also visibly flinching when the young girl seemed to morph into an old man behind the blurry steam.

Not wanting to call to Eddie and break his chants, Michael stepped closer, into the swirling pit of scalding steam and flesh ripping heat, and reached for Eddie's back with his left hand as he gripped his mother's rosary with his right.

"Your chants are futile, blasphemer," the twisted little man hissed in the old tongue to Michael. "This one is long ours. Go save some other soul this day."

"Stand, old one. Receive your fate!" Michael called in return, dredging up his nearly forgotten lessons on the darker skills even the most benevolent of men must use when faced with man's inevitable adversaries.

"Fool. These new religions do not work on our kind. We've seen many come, and many go. Flee, before I bring you into the fold along with this one," the old man hissed, his face momentarily morphing into the shop girl's face from before, presenting a horrific image of the dainty face on the wretched, old twisted body.

"Demon, I am a man of the western cloth. Major orders…also taught in the ways of the minor orders. The Church is all knowing and all seeing," Michael retorted as he tried to grab Eddie's shoulder, while Eddie stood swaying, trancelike, seeming to almost fall back into the old man's clutches.

"Step back!" Michael yelled between chants.

"Run away, little boy, or I'll pull your memories out for all to see. Yes, even your little friend here will see behind that black curtain. Yes…yes, that broken promise so long ago…so long…," the twisted man began, but then clamped his thin mouth shut and stepped back, holding up his order book, which looked the world like a stone tablet to Michael.

When the odd little man suddenly fell back, Michael finally managed to get a grip on Eddie's shoulder, but was not able to pull his friend back. However, Michael, in spite of the intense strain on his arm, was just able to keep Eddie from falling forward.

Not foolish enough to think that the shrinking back of the old man meant victory, Michael continued to chant his verses, all the while holding onto Eddie. Out of the corner of his eye, Michael could see that the patrons in the food hall all seemed ridiculously oblivious to his friend's plight and to

Michael's chanting.

The odd little man continued to shrink back, his face a mass of fear and disbelief, appearing to flop between the twisted face of the old man and the horrific beauty of the young shop girl. Both faces were obviously racked with deadly fear, Michael surmised, but only briefly, as he didn't want any possible ruse on the part of the…of whatever the old man was, to distract him from his duty to bring Eddie back.

Yet, that was not what had shocked the twisted little man. No, it was what the bent little man had seen when he probed Michael's angry mind, looking for some weakness to use against the big man mumbling half wrong incantations that the twisted little man had assumed Michael had learned from some modern horror movie.

No, the bent little man had not bargained for what he had found inside Michael.

Nor was the twisted little man, messenger for other, darker beings, prepared for what had been unleashed in Michael's memories. His parents' memories. His grandparents' memories. His clan's memories. Stretching back, far back, before recorded time.

"No! I am just the messenger! I take the orders! I don't fill the orders!" the twisted little man suddenly screamed, contorting his grotesque face, as the steam around him began to turn a putrid, greenish yellow.

Michael continued to pull on Eddie's shoulder, but was making no progress in pulling him out of the unseen clutches of the old man.

Unseen!

That's it, Michael screamed in his mind.

Turning away from the old man, who, looking relieved that Michael had lifted his hardened stare, collapsed into a pile of his own soiling at the corner of the recess. The twisted little man then hid his face in his sunburned, nearly blackened hands, not from Michael, but from what was slowly emerging from the stand's darkened interior.

Old.

Older than the language the ancestors had groped for to describe the primordial horror of the flowing apparition.

Older than the bloodlines of the lesser demons man had battled down the centuries.

Older than man's first primordial screams.

Suddenly aware that some sort of apparition was forming from behind the stand, or possibly that the stand's owner was simply stepping through another unseen door, Michael managed to budge Eddie just enough to get his friend beside him, where Michael threw his left arm over Eddie and held him with all his physical might, while Michael turned his mental and spiritual energy to the apparition, or person, or whatever was coming toward them.

Through the dense, putrid, almost suffocating, sulfuric steam, Michael could just make out a shape. Tall, slim, but shifting to something larger as it moved abreast of the cowering, odd little man. There the figure lingered and seem to draw on the old man for…for something that Michael didn't have a word for, only that he saw the old man out of the corner of his eye grimacing in agony, flopping between the face and body of the old man and those of the young shop girl, all while the figure seemed to sway beside the old man.

Then the figure spoke.

At least, Michael thought he heard it speak.

What language or what the voice sounded like was lost to Michael's ears, but he did understand. Each time the voice was heard, Michael's hunger-riven stomach gave him a sharp, stabbing pain.

"Many, many cycles I have not tasted such power in the humans of this land," the figure's deep voice called from the putrid mist sliding off the stand's yellowed counter and pooling around the twisted old man, young girl. "You are of their priestly order? Yes?"

The figure seemed to lean, almost in an arc, over to Michael and Eddie and peered down at them, revealing deep, nearly bottomless eyes, surrounded by an oblong, almost too large head over thin, very thin shoulders.

Michael blinked back the sweat and the gagging steam, but continued to utter his Latin phrases.

"Boy, boy, did you not hear the old retainer? Your words are like gnats around my ears. Pesky. Annoying. But, inevitably, of little import," the figure said, maybe in old Korean, Michael thought, or maybe Chinese.

Stepping away from the old man, who seemed to then crumple into a pile of ragged clothes and limp flesh, the figure reached out and ran its pale hand along the multicolored wall, stopping just at the edge, as if its hand could go no farther. The figure then turned and, instead of stepping up to confront Michael face to face, simply leaned out in a shorter arc to peer into Michael's now bloodshot eyes, as they blinked back the foul stench coming from both the steam and the figure.

"Yes, there is something…something. The old fool felt it, but, alas, he is worthless to me in his current…state," the figure lamented, then blew into Michael's face and eyes, covering him with a veil of the sticky, yellowish air.

The figure then closed its dark eyes and breathed in deeply, drawing the putrid air back from Michael, tasting the air like an aged wine.

Seemingly frustrated, the figure, swaying slightly in some unseen breeze, as the steam hung limp in the close air, repeated the ritual several times. Each time, the figure would murmur something unintelligible that sounded like 'memory' or 'remember' to Michael.

Remember.

As the figure swayed over them, the food hall seemed to go about its routine around them, oblivious to Michael and Eddie's plight.

In his mind's eye, Michael, instead of seeing the seminary, his brothers in faith, and his teachers, as he expected to see during an encounter such as he had concluded was before him, he saw his far off childhood. An old man was standing over him, telling Michael something that Michael could not quite hear. As much as Michael strained to hear the old man, he heard only the wind and the water of some mountain retreat from some early memory.

Michael's clouded mind then recalled pieces of his delirious dreams the night before. Dreams of his summers in Korea. An old house. He was afraid of the strange animals that climbed all over the house. The old man was yelling. Always yelling, that old man did, Michael recalled. The old man had taught him in the old ways. The hard and harsh old ways. How not to be afraid of the scary animals. How to truly see them for what they were. How to walk beside them without...fear.

Suddenly, Michael's attention was back on the flowing figure as it stroked the twisted, crumpled old man, its tendrils...its fingers stroking the old man's hair, causing the shop girl to reappear, half in and half out of the old man, with the tendrils of yellow and green steam creeping into her clothes, both from above and below and, while there was a momentary look of beastly joy on the half-creature's face, that joy suddenly turned to agonizing terror as the tendril's color shifted from dirty, greenish yellow to blackish red.

"The grandfather!" the half-creature screamed in the old tongue to the swaying figure, then collapsed, half old man, half...half something that had once been a young girl.

Michael turned his eyes away from the pitiful half-creature and continued to focus on the stark figure shifting in and out of the putrid steam.

"Ah...that's it, then," the figure called to Michael, as it abandoned the wreck of the half-creature.

"What secrets do you hold, boy? May that I might touch your temple? Will you bite? No, I think not," the figure chuckled, its deep, rumbling laughter actually causing a few people near Michael and Eddie to turn and stare into the mist, then continue on their way.

As the vile figure extended its unnaturally long, thin arm toward Michael's brow, a sudden, darkened bulge in the steam caused the figure to pause, and leave its tendril-dripping hand a few inches from Michael's sweat and steam covered forehead.

"Gents! If you guys wanted a smelly sauna, I know a few cheap ones...," Jae blurted out as he stepped in close to his friends, one hand holding two clear bags, one that showed various pastries and one showing several water bottles, while holding a doughnut twist, cinnamon, in his other hand.

"Jae! Water!" Michael shouted, then continued with his chants.

"Water? Sure, here…," Jae began.

"No! The buckets. Find a rain bucket!" Michael bellowed, causing Jae to step back and bump his shoe against one of the tofu buckets.

Jae looked distastefully at the tofu bucket nearly full of drip water from the far off roof, looked back at his two friends standing like zombies talking to some old geezer, shrugged and picked up the bucket. He stepped back to Michael and started to hand it to him.

"Salt! Get the salt! There!" Michael screamed at Jae, using a shoulder to point to the closed soup stand that was being used as a condiment station. "Salt!"

Jae, starting to get angry, looked into Michael's eyes, and nearly fell over.

Something Jae has seen years before was just behind Michael's wide eyes. Far away in Afghanistan, in the stifling late nights, just as the inevitable surprise attacks on the convoys would kick off. The eyes of the ones who knew they wouldn't make it back.

Stumbling backwards, Jae dropped the pastry, and groped for the salt. He grabbed a large shaker and took one long step back to Michael.

"What is this? Another brother coming to your aid, boy? This one is hollow. Nothing there to siphon away. Nothing…oh, but he has seen. He has done…," the figure called to Michael, its words gibberish to Jae.

"Stand!" Michael yelled at the figure as it seemed to turn its attention to Jae, having completely forgotten Eddie, part of Michael's mind thought.

"What?" Jae asked, his feet welded to the floor, ready to do whatever his friend demanded in that moment.

"No. Not you. The salt. The bucket. Hold the bucket in front of me, but don't get between me and…and him," Michael replied, all the while uttering verses in between his words for Jae.

Jae then leaned in, and, avoiding getting between Michael and the babbling old geezer, he held the rain bucket about waist high and then waved the salt at Michael as a question as to what to do with it?

"Jae, take the top…off. Put the salt in my hand. As much as possible!" Michael called, his voice beginning to sound odd, as if in a tunnel, Jae thought.

Michael, his left hand still firmly holding back Eddie, who seemed to be in an unresponsive trance, extended his right hand to Jae and opened his large palm into a cup, his mother's rosary so tightly wrapped around the hand, the glass beads, forged by one of the top houses in Murano, were cutting into his hand.

"Michael, this salt's going to sting like hell," Jae said, hesitating with the shaker over his friend's bloody palm.

"Pour!" Michael shouted, then, taking a deep breath and steeling the screaming pains in his stomach, his head, his heart, his arm, and everywhere else, he repeated himself, but calmly, with ease, with control.

"Pour it, Jae, I won't feel a thing," Michael said to his friend, unnervingly calmly.

Jae did as instructed and, even though Jae winced when he saw the salt mix with Michael's blood, he was also astonished that the salt stayed pure white and did not absorb the blood.

Giving up on trying to understand, but knowing his friend needed him to do exactly as he had asked, Jae poured the entire shaker of salt into the big man's large palm, so large that none of the salt spilled.

During the entire minute or so of the bucket and salt activity, the swaying figure had stood off, as if amused by the antics of the people in front of it. It continued to mumble and, once or twice, would reach out and stoke the heads of passerby who veered, even a few inches, into the little enclave. The mist around the figure seemed to brighten up into a more yellowish hue when that happened, Michael noticed, but didn't have the ability to warn anyone off.

Finally, the figure seemed to tire of the delay and leaned back to reach out to Michael's forehead.

"Hey, grandfather, what do you think...?" Jae started to ask when he saw the skinny old man reach out to slap his friend head, causing Jae to step forward to stop the old man.

"Jae, it's okay," Michael said, his voice calm, almost peaceful. "Let him touch me. I think...I think I need him to touch me."

Jae calmed down, but watched the old man's hand like a hawk, while holding the bucket where Michael could grab it, or whatever he needed to do with it.

As the figure leaned in and its fingers, dripping rancid, oily steam, touched Michael's forehead, Michael's breath was suddenly cut short, and he felt himself nearly pass out.

Blackness.

Voices.

Old, old voices.

Grandfather?

Michael felt, more than heard his grandfather, in the large mountain home overlooking Seoul, years and years ago. Around his grandfather, other men were gathered. Other grandfathers. Ones Michael had only seen in old photographs or paintings.

All the old men were chanting.

Behind them, far down in the valley, Michael could hear his mother. His darling mother. The first in her family to convert.

The rosary.

The salt!

As the old men chanted, louder and louder, Michael steadied his hand, even in the blackness that was his mind, and, uttering the prayers of blessing, drained the pure salt into the rain bucket his friend held.

The salt flowed into the shape of a cross, slowly, with near machine precision in the blindness of Michael's faith as he spoke the words that had been spoken for two thousand years.

In Michael's mind, the old men chanted louder. Grandfather was standing on the mountain. The three mountains, waving his arms and a long…long something…something long…at the sky. At the stars.

The stars.

Michael, in his blackness, could see, no, feel the stars begin to take shape and swirl about his grandfather on the mountain.

Light!

Suddenly, the putrid figure jerked its hand away from Michael's forehead as if burned.

"What is this abomination?" wailed the figure, standing stock still in front of Michael, while the figure's putrid steam and flowing tendrils seemed to withdraw behind it toward the stand's little window.

As the flowing steam reached the window, however, the gritty old posters hanging above the window fell and lodged themselves in new configurations in front of the window's small opening, stopping the steam's retreat, leaving the tendrils and oily air to swirl in a small, lazy cyclone just behind the figure.

"Monster! Demon! You can not be both!" the figure wailed, wringing its thin hands over and over. "I am the master! I am the memory!"

Michael, his mind suddenly opening, crystal clear, began to mix in his grandfather's chants, as he had finished blessing the salt and then the water.

"Jae, can you hold Eddie? See that he doesn't fall," Michael directed, as he took the rain bucket, now with the blessed water, and stepped toward the rigid figure.

"Michael, wait," Jae replied as he stepped over to hold Eddie, who, though physically the strongest of all his friends, was nearly limp and weak. "I respect you, but maybe we should just leave the old buzzard here and head out?"

Michael, half turned his head to answer Jae, and, while keeping one eye on the rigid figure and one eye on the swirling steam, spoke to Jae, and Eddie, using the old, formal Korean that mostly only the old people still knew.

"Friend, you are not hollow. You are the mast to which Eddie will lash himself for these next…next moments. Stand ready," Michael declared in a voice that took Jae, and the subconscious of Eddie, back to their far childhoods.

"Jae, when you hear the words, first cover Eddie's eyes, then close your own," Michael called as he continued to walk toward what Jae saw as an old, very decrepit man.

"What words...?" Jae asked, reaching up to cover Eddie's blank eyes.

"You'll know, Jae. You'll know," Michael replied as he advanced on the figure, which seemed to be retreating.

Retreating?

Michael realized he had taken a number of steps toward the figure, wanting to ensure he was close enough, but the figure continued to be just out of reach. The more steps Michael took, the farther into the depths of the coffin-like enclave he seemed to be going, yet, his mind knew there was no more than five or six feet in depth to the little area.

Yet, the figure continued to retreat.

Pausing his steps, but not his words, Michael took a chance, and let himself see out of the periphery of one eye where Eddie and Jae stood.

So far away!

Michael almost forgot his verses and chants when he realized his two friends were nearly halfway across the food hall, or that distance from the back of the little stand, where Michael was standing just out of reach of the figure.

Letting his eyes trace his route back to where he was standing, Michael saw that the colorful walls of the little stand had stretched out and become elongated, revealing that the mishmash of confused shapes and colors were actually ancient symbols and talismans, with endless geometric shapes, figurines fanciful and grotesque, views of far hillsides, the sounds of surf on ancient coastlines, other worlds, stars, and....

No!

Too much to absorb, Michael shouted to his clouded mind.

Focus!

Focus!

As the walls beside Michael and the figure seemed to stretch to a breaking point, the figure, suddenly re-infused by the swirling, acrid steam, returned to its earlier fluid, flowing state, and leaned back over Michael, menacing words spewing from its thin lips.

"Blasphemer! Western stooge! You have no right to use the old words, worm!" the figure screamed, not in the wailing voice of fear from a moment before, but in the deep, age-old, unbreakable voice of the cavern gods and demons man had conjured up in the far recesses of prehistory.

The figure then began to enlarge, grow more concrete, more substantive, and seemed to press at the sides of the narrow enclave, threatening to burst the little stand asunder. Behind the grotesque figure, a small army of similar, but smaller figures appeared in the far distance, from the depths of the little stand's dark window.

Michael, his voice hoarse from the putrid steam and his continuous recitation of both the blessing verses and the ancient Korean and Chinese chants, felt his competing layers of belief slowly solidify into a unified front against the hellish figure. The ancient Latin verses, handed down by the church fathers, were aided and bolstered by his channeling, for lack of a better word, the mystic chants of his long dead grandfather and countless other generations, marching back into the far darkness of his family's long history of protecting man.

Protecting.

Sacrificing.

Giving of oneself to his own god to ensure the continuation of his own clan, his people, Michael grasped, through the haze of generations and different beliefs.

In the end, save them, Michael concluded.

The clouds fully lifted from his mind and the steam blew back from his eyes, revealing the massive figure of pure evil before him, close kin to those his grandfather and his grandfather's grandfathers had confronted in the old country, and that untold brethren of the church had battled over the millennia.

The old demons had traveled with the diaspora, leeching, as they always had, in the alleys, the shuttered homes, the corrupt back rooms, Michael suddenly realized, somehow, knew. The one before him had picked his friend. Why Eddie, Michael accepted that he would probably never know. But, he knew his friend, both his friends, would walk away, safe. He would not allow them to be dragged down by the writhing, scaly figure before him, materialized out of countless old country myths running from Asia to Europe.

"I cast you out, demon! Go from this place," Michael called calmly, using the old tongues.

The now huge figure, a mix of horrors that Michael's mind formed into a mountainous, shifting beast from some deep, collective memory, one moment an ancient, savage man-thing, the next moment a writhing, wingless serpent. Yet another moment, a screaming banshee more suited to Irish legend than Asia.

Then, the beast was suddenly a small child, weak and frightened, calling for its mother, trying to draw Michael to console it. Save it from the mean man.

Then, back to the screaming beast, wavering between hell and some deeper, more sinister place that man had never defined.

Finally backing the figure into the jumble of constellations that blocked the small window, Michael could see the army of smaller figures growing larger, deep within the background of the stand.

"Aiyee!" screamed the figure, futilely grabbing at its back, twisting one way and then the other, revealing to Michael singed, putrid flesh, burned in the star patterns that seemed to swirl about the figure's flaming back.

The figure leaned away from the star maps, but fell back at Michael's determined advance, screaming again in horrific, torturous agony.

In the background, Michael could just see the army of similar figures break into a fast trot, calling out with all manner of vulgar tongues and obscene shouts for the main figure to hold fast as they were nearly upon the blasphemer.

Now or never, Michael realized, as he slowly, painfully slowly, crossed himself, mentally ticking off the seconds to when he thought the vile army of terrifying allies would break through the back of the stand.

Stealing a last, long, in milliseconds, look at his childhood friend, held back by the powerful arms of his newer, but none the less stronger friend, Michael saw that Eddie seemed to awaken for the first time, saw Michael in the grips of some unspeakable torment, and surged forward, dragging Jae several feet as Jae fought to hold Eddie back.

Smiling at his friend, Michael nodded their secret head nod from childhood, turned his eyes back to the monster before him, and yelled over his shoulder in a clear, resonating, almost temple bell like manner.

"Now Jae!"

Jae hauled the struggling Eddie back to the edge of the enclave, and, slapping his right arm over Eddie's eyes, held his friend in a near death grip as he watched Michael drop his hand, with the rosary, into the bucket and toss the first of what would be multiple attacks of holy water on the beast that Jae could now see in all its horror and seductive magnificence.

Michael, sensing what he feared might happen, that Jae would cover Eddie's eyes, but not be quick enough to close his own, threw some of the precious holy water over his shoulder, squarely into Jae's face.

"Now Jae, close your eyes! Look away!" Michael commanded, his voice nearly disembodied, as he spoke the words from his faith, and chanted the old, ancient words handed down from his grandfather's faith.

Jae, part of him aching to jump to the aid of his friend, fought his instincts and, trusting in the whirlwind Michael had become, squeezed his eyes shut and held onto Eddie.

As the water landed on the monster's body, it screamed in brutal agony, even though the water seemed to simply slide down its scaly skin and battered clothes.

Michael could feel the bottom of the bucket as he dipped his hand in, tossed the water at the beast, while speaking the words for expelling the demon, and the words for destroying the beast, words that were having an impact on the figure, as it flashed between various incarnations.

Michael continued to press, hoping the small tofu bucket held enough rainwater.

Bizarre images of creatures from every legend, myth, and scripture seemed to flare up before Michael's eyes. Some, he recognized. A few he even felt he needed to turn away and not look upon, but held his steely gaze, the horrific images emblazoned on his mind. Some he could not even form an idea as to what they were or what sort of hell could have produced them.

The army!

Michael watched the blurs behind the shrieking beast and swirling vapor, wondering if time was going to run out.

Michael, reducing his flinging of the water to mere drops, tried to conserve the precious defense. He judged his last move to the split second, waiting until the hideous eyes of the first wave of the army of the damned appeared at the small window.

Now!

A voice in the back of Michael's battered head screamed at him.

Michael then took the remaining holy water and, pouring a few drops over his forehead, he walked into the slashing talons and claws of writhing beast. Without flinching at the pain, he quickly poured the remaining water, to its final drop, over the thrashing limbs, ripping talons, fanged teeth, and horned crown of the beast, ignoring the damage the beast was doing to Michael's own body.

Yet, Michael's head was protected. In spite of the blows and gashes to his chest and arms by the wailing, thrashing death throes of the beast, a cool breeze enveloped Michael's head, with a halo of grace surrounding his bloodied face and clear eyes.

Somewhere, far, far away, Michael could hear his old monsignor reciting the Prayer of Saint Michael, as if he were still a child at that old Brooklyn church.

Equally distant, but more in his gut than in his mind's eye, Michael could feel the blood of his ancestors fighting back, pushing him to his limits against the horror of a generation of nightmares.

Slowly, as the beast seemed to slip down, down into some far, hellish pit, beyond the sight of men, it struck out in a renewed frenzy at Michael, tearing long gashes, and futilely trying to gouge out Michael's unblinking eyes. Failing such, the beast again slashed at Michael's chest, then his waist, back, and legs. As the beast's lower parts disappeared into a puddle of black despair at Michael's feet, the screaming demon even slashed at the soles of Michael's shoes.

Lacerating Michael's shoe leather in one final gasp of defiance, the beast faded into its forever nothingness, while trying to drag Michael with it until the bitter end, all the while calling out in vulgar tongues to the hordes just beyond the small window to avenge their fallen leader.

Empty, the brave little tofu bucket that had served Michael so well, suddenly fell from his lacerated hands with a resounding peel, and bounced, once, twice, three times, sounding as Michael's voice had sounded earlier, like a sacred bell from before the fall of Solomon's Temple.

Bong…Bong…Bong!

The first wave of the grotesque army slammed into the jumble of swirling constellations, a few burning their gnarled, scaly hands, or paws, hissing in unison. There the swirling shapes seemed to freeze.

Whether it was the sound of the long peels of the far removed temple bell when the little bucket bounced at Michael's feet, over the oily spot where the creature had faded away, or whether the army of similar figures thought Michael had more of the holy water, or possible allies in the two soul mates standing at his back, the entire horde, the burned ones limping away at the rear, fell back, and retreated down that long, dark expanse to wherever such demons reside.

Silence.

Deathly silence.

For a long, long moment, Michael simply stood and stared into the bottomless void where he had seen his soul disappearing into, as he had repressed the vile energy of…whatever the beast had been.

Swaying from the strain of the horrific beating he had taken, Michael absently wondered if the undertaker would be able to hide the wounds from his mother and his friends.

His mind clouded with images and echoes of his chants and prayers, Michael felt his very core draining, slowly draining down into the pit that had swallowed his adversary moments before.

Draining, so slowly that Michael watched himself being born, loving his family, growing up, making lifelong friends, schools, entering into his vows, all to meet his end in the grip of a demon from the old country, in the little food hall on West 32nd Street.

For a long, long moment, as he felt his soul was being laid over the beast's oily patch, to act, his clouded mind assumed, as a seal against its returning, Michael whispered a prayer to his faith's teachers and mentors for getting him through…whatever the battle had been.

For that same long, long moment, Michael thanked his grandfather's harsh, but loving teachings from childhood that had helped him understand his foe, and meet that foe in its universe.

Finally, as his knees began to bend beneath him, Michael said a quiet prayer to his god and his savior, for being with him and believing in him.

Smiling at the jumble of stars before him, Michael closed his eyes and, with that deepest of faith that only few mortals ever know, accepted his fate, and waited for the end….

Suddenly, strong arms seemed to reach far down into the demon's pit and encircled Michael. Fearing the resurrection of the beast, he instinctively struck out with his rosary wrapped hand, just missing Eddie's face.

Eddie?

Michael looked up at his friend, wondering if the beast had killed Eddie as well. Then a second face came into view.

Jae?

"Eddie? I'm so sorry. Jae? You, too? I tried...I used the right verses. I...spoke the old words grandfather taught me so long ago...so long ago," Michael cried in agony to his lost friends, doomed to wander the beast's hell with Michael until the end of days.

"Sorry bro," Jae declared, and then emptied a bottle of water over Michael's head, the cooling water helping to clear the big man's momentary delirium.

"What...?" Michael began, finally seeing that Eddie, although still pale from his weeks of being under the influence of the figure and his minions, did not seem to be dead.

Neither did Jae, Michael realized, turning to face his other friend and then smiling at the second bottle of water Jae had at the ready.

"Thanks, buddy, but I think I'll take that one internally," Michael quipped, feeling his jaw ache as he spoke.

Suddenly, Eddie, after helping his friend to his feet, hugged Michael, which was quite a feat, given Michael's girth. Jae followed, and then the three stood back and just stared at each other.

Finally, Eddie spoke.

"Never let me be late again," Eddie said to Michael, helping his friend to a stool at the ramyeon stand.

"Late?" Michael asked as he slowly settled onto the stool, feeling all the wounds in his body complain in pain.

"To Mass, Michael. Mass," Eddie declared.

Michael smiled.

"Eddie, you carry it inside you. Even you Jae, confirmed heathen of the group," Michael quipped, the realization fully sinking in that his friends had survived and that he, banged up and in pain, was still breathing as well.

The three men then fell silent, young Korean Americans whose parents and grandparents had endured multiple wars, endless hardships, and some well-deserved successes, so that their children and children's children could prosper, either in Korea, if they chose to return, or anywhere the sun shone, and be proud wherever they landed.

"Friar T...Michael. You ever going to tell us what really happened here?" Jae asked, his eyes already signaling he suspected the answer.

"Yes, Michael, just why did you bash yourself again and again against that...that...whatever that was?" Eddie asked, color already returning to his face.

Michael looked back to the darkened enclave, walls bare white where they had stretched so far that the images and talismans had been expelled, and to the battered small window, its cracked, yellowed counter broken, with most of it lying on the oily floor. Nowhere did Michael see the constellations that had burned the beast and its friends, nor did he see the twisted old half-creature that had fallen at the back.

Had the half-creature crawled in after the beast? Or had the pitiful familiar found a hole to languish in until the next figure rose to challenge the light, Michael wondered?

"Boys, what do you say we forgo the usual and have some brain freezing bingsu and hot espresso upstairs?" Michael suggested, the searing pain in his stomach gradually subsiding. "Call Lee."

"I'll call him, but he'll never find a parking spot," Jae answered taking out his personal phone.

"Not to worry, I think there will be plenty of parking this day," Michael replied.

"Yes, plenty," Eddie added, realizing what his friend meant.

"Gents!" Lee called as he approached, just having entered the food hall.

"Man, that's weird, I was just calling you to tell you to join us for...," Jae replied, but was cut off by Lee's enthusiastic interjection.

"About five minutes ago, ten, twelve spots opened up. Guys were piling out of side doors, alleys...whatever. Even saw one creepy guy come down some scaffolding at the end of the street and grab a car. Funny, a lot of them seemed to just grab whatever car was closest when they hit the street. Must have been theirs, though. They all started. Strangest thing I ever saw on a New York street," Lee rattled off before anyone else could speak.

For a long moment, none of the friends spoke. Eddie then, helping Michael to stand, motioned to Jae to take the other side of the big man. Jae did so, and the three motioned for Lee to follow.

"Wait," Michael asked and turned to look back into the depths of the enclave. "The bucket."

"Bucket?" Lee asked.

"Lee, can you grab that little tofu bucket back there in the corner?" Jae asked, directing Lee's gaze with his free hand. "Just there, under the broken counter, with the stars."

Somehow, the gritty little mix of pictures of the stars had encircled the brave little bucket in the dark corner of the enclave.

"Seriously?" Lee asked as he picked up the container and then, seeing an old cleaning lady close by, walked over to hand the bucket to her.

"Lee!" all three friends called at once, startling Lee and causing him to pause in front of the old lady.

"Lee, give her one of those hundreds you carry for emergencies," Jae called, and then spoke politely to the cleaning lady. "For the bucket, grandmother."

Lee, totally bewildered, but trusting his close friends without question, dug out one of his several hundred dollar bills and gave it to the little lady, in spite of her vehement protests.

"Mother," called Michael to the little cleaning lady. "Keep half for yourself, for your placing of those buckets was a true godsend. Please feel free to give the other half to your church or a charity, mother."

The little lady acquiesced to Michael's soothing rationale and took the bill. She then offered a bigger, proper bucket with a metal handle, but the three friends waved Lee over. The little lady then shrugged, moved into the enclave with her mop and rolling bucket, and began to scrub the oily floor.

"Here's your golden bucket, Jae," Lee said, handing the battered, brave little container to his friend. "I'm sure there's a hell of a tale behind it, begging your pardon, Friar T…Michael."

"Not a bucket, Lee," Jae replied.

"Yes, even I saw that," Eddie added, his mind fully cleansed. "Not a bucket."

"Seriously? It's a tofu bucket. I bet my mom has three or four empty ones I can sell you cheap," Lee joked as the three made their way slowly up the stairs, where Lee finally realized Michael seemed to be in pain.

"Dude, are you okay? Did you fall?" Lee asked, true concern replacing his joking tone.

"He's fine, Lee. Fine," Jae answered. "Just had a run in with an ancient demon and its bloodcurdling minions intent on bringing hell on earth to Korea-town…."

Lee stared at his friend, and then looked at Michael and Eddie. Neither was smiling.

Lee simply nodded, and decided he would keep silent until someone started making sense.

"A healing bell," Michael added.

Lee's eyes asked 'what?'

"This dear little bucket, Lee. A proverbial Bell of Destiny," Michael replied, and then fell silent as he struggled up the stairs, clutching the little bucket with his rosary hand.

"Like he said, not a bucket," Jae repeated as the four close friends ascended the long stairs to the higher floors of the food hall in search of calmer seas and quieter nerves.

As the group made the turn at the halfway point on the stairs, Lee, in spite of his vow to remain silent until something made sense, spoke up.

"You know, there is an elevator at the back…," Lee started to suggest, but fell silent at the stares of his three friends.

"A dark, small enclosure that takes you down into the earth?" Jae offered, a wry grin on his face.

"Nah…," both Eddie and a slowly recovering Michael replied in unison.

"Fine. Okay, take the stairway all the way to the roof!" Lee replied, thoroughly confused.

"Lee," Michael called to his friend and, once Lee leaned in, grabbed Lee's collar and dragged him into the clutch.

As Michael and the group turned up the second flight of stairs, his view of the small, darkened enclave began to be blocked by the stairs themselves. He noticed the little cleaning lady bending over the grubby posters of the stars. She picked them up and, instead of shoving into the trash bin, he saw her smooth them over and carefully prop them up against the remaining section of the yellowed counter. He then saw her step back, stare at the old photos for a brief moment and, then, as if sensing Michael looking at her, the little lady turned, looked up, and smiled at the battle worn son of her old country.

Michael saw the beaming, nearly angelic smile of the kind little cleaning lady and, feeling the aches fade even further, smiled with a renewed warmth and nodded back to the little lady as his friends dragged him beyond the cleaning lady's view.

Only Jae, the self-professed disbeliever, saw the little lady turn back to her mop, flex her huge wings from under her classic ajumma vest, and then return to scrubbing, in earnest, the remains of the demons and familiars off her floor.

Her huge wings?

Jae blinked several times, then craned his neck beyond the railing until the last minute to stare at the old cleaning lady, wondering if he had lost his mind after all.

Then, all around the little lady, Jae saw a number of other figures who had also flexed their wings and were tucking them back under a waiter's jacket, a street worker's safety vest, and others scattered throughout the crowd. At the ramyeon stand, an old guy in a classic Hanbok was sliding a massive sword down a scabbard on his back. At the coffee counter, three colorfully clad old men were dropping what Jae would swear later were pitchforks or tridents into wooden boxes. Another, a powerfully built old man in a faded grey robe, was strapping an old bow to his back as he melted into the crowd.

At the closed soup shop, a small child, in what looked all the world like vestments, and Jae wasn't even sure what vestments were, was carefully gathering up the condiments and placing them into a gilded case. Behind the child, Jae saw fading outlines of several figures in brown robes, but they disappeared so quickly, he decided he must have imagined them.

Jae pulled his head back just before he would have choked on the railing, and looked at his friends. He then gave Michael's massive shoulders a small, manly, of course, squeeze. He managed to catch Eddie's eye and spoke softly, almost as if he didn't want to disturb the deep reflection and serene peace he suddenly saw on Michael's face.

"Guys. Hey, did you...? Guys, Michael...wasn't...alone," Jae said quietly, almost reverently for him, to Eddie, and to Lee, who still looked confused.

As the group struggled up the stairs, forcing patrons above to back up and patrons below to slow their hurried climb, Eddie, his mind fully cleansed, took a deep breath before answering.

"No, Jae, we never are," Eddie replied, seeing the color and glow slowly returning to Michael's battered face as the four bonded friends, and a brave little tofu bucket, ascended the food hall's stairs. "We never are."

INTERLUDE VII

"A tease, boy. Like your fallen gisaeng girlies luring soldiers into the alleys," the creature spat at its captive just as the final words of the diaspora story had left the writer's lips. "You promised me a glorious reunion with my cousins from across the seas, and this...this bastard mix of a monk and shaman grinds them to dust? Using the old ways?"

The creature's angry, blackened eyes drilled into the silenced writer.

"Bring me back to my homeland, scribbler! These foreign soils tire me, fool," the creature called from its chair. "Why must you humans wander the foreign lands, disrupting the natural order? Why must you forever seek that which is just beyond your puny reach? This...this confused shaman of the western cloth, what has he done for his own land, this peninsula?"

The creature grabbed at the loose soil covering the stone floor and threw a handful toward the cook pot, which caught its eye.

"Better the old one had dragged him into the dark underworld, so that the traitor shaman would suffer the agonies of his sires and grandsires before him!" the creature bellowed. "How can such a traitor to the peninsula triumph over that which he can never understand? How?"

The writer, bewildered by the creature's sudden spewing of nationalist diatribe, sat nodding, trying to neither disagree or agree with the beast, as it could simply be toying with the elements of the tale to see what the writer would do.

"Defend your work, weak one!" the creature snapped.

"There is no defense, vile one. I but put to paper what comes to me. There is no right or wrong, only the tale. The tale speaks for itself," the writer replied, trying to sound defiant.

"Bah! You invent these...these groveling bits of sad, weak flesh to do your selfish bidding," the creature retorted, slamming its fist on the table.

"Yes, but, they become their own, over time. I simply give them voice," the writer shot back.

"Excuses! Where is my fire-starter?" the creature demanded, and began to click its tongue, rousing the little ones behind the trees.

"Leaving these shores, or crossing the far mountains to the north, I've longed for, for many, many cycles," the creature howled, causing the emerging little ones to scurry back to the safety of the trees. "I have watched many children grow and turn old and into dust on this mountain, waiting, waiting, waiting. And your traitor to the western way skips merrily across the bitter, vengeful ocean, and tries to destroy an old one? One of my far cousins?"

"Yet, vile one, ask yourself why and how one of your cousins, or, as the tale outlines, many of your cousins, are wandering the dark corners of a Manhattan, or a London, or a...," the writer shouted back.

"Enough! Bring me back!" the creature demanded, holding its head in its yellowed, shaking hands, moaning for the tinderbox.

Three of the little ones appeared near the stove and, pushed forward by his larger comrades, one little one looked for the fire-starter, the tinderbox, and saw, to the minion's terror, that the tinderbox was just behind his master's huge stein, which blocked the beast's view. Dashing across the floor, the little one reached up, pushed the small tinderbox over to the creature, and then retreated, not daring to get too close to its disgruntled master.

Behind the frightened little ones, several of the slithering things could be seen just out of the corner of the writer's left eye, as if waiting to snatch a few bits of his flesh before he was consigned to the pot. He watched the retreat of the little ones and wondered if he could fit behind those trees, where there might be a way out of the devil trap, in spite of the snakes, which had also retreated with the little helpers.

The creature had become almost uncontrollably agitated and leapt out of its chair to glare at the writer, who stared back at the beast and held his ground.

"How can that wretched human follow two masters?" the creature yelled, yet in the voice of the earlier scholar, the writer realized. "Treachery, scribbler. Treachery! All you humans do is betray. It is your nature!"

The creature then jerked its greasy head around and leaned in to look into the writer's eyes.

"How can such a betrayer of the old ways defeat an old one, scribbler? Or, is this tale your clumsy way of warning me that there are powers that can defeat me? Fool, of course I know there are many...many avenues for me, and my kind to fall to dust! Fewer than the old days, though," the beast yelled, a look of even darker menace crossing its contorted face.

"I think you want me to send my little ones into the western temples, scribbler, to revenge the old one in your tale, yes?" the creature whispered, its tongue clicking in the writer's face. "Maybe your tale is a warning to my cousins and far cousins to cleanse those foreign houses, fool? From my own high pulpit I can send forth my own armies. Just there, below the mountain, I could began, yes, with that spire so many morsels flock to…?"

A look of sheer malevolence rippled across the twisted face of the creature, its long arm pointing toward the city below, adding to the writer's fears that the deranged hermit might actually act on its threats.

"It's a story, vile one. A fiction created to ask questions of cultural conflict, not a treatise on the merits of one over the other," the writer answered, knowing trying to argue with a crazed hermit or troll or whatever was probably pointless, but, on the outside chance the beast really would send his terrors after some local assembly, he felt he needed to steer the beast away from such thoughts. "Besides, the young man was still conflicted. The battle could have gone either way. And, how many untold morsels did the Manhattan beast consume before it picked the wrong victim?"

Swallowing the bile that had gurgled up while he was trying to appease his captor and deflect its thoughts, the writer watched as something like an evil grin flashed across the beast's face as it listened to the writer's words.

What have I done, the writer asked himself, hoping he had not given the creature yet another new idea for untapped targets of mayhem and terror. However, the creature seemed to just wag its head as it turned away from the writer without replying.

Stomping about the enclosure, the beast grabbed at its greasy hair and ran its bone-thin hands down its robe, mumbling more chants that the writer could not understand. Just beyond the far end of the stove, the creature paused near an old screen, which the writer would have sworn had not been there previously.

The writer leaned out to try to see what type of screen it might be, but could only see a few birds and clouds, white, against a black background, since his captor was blocking most of the view.

"So many of my kin have perished, scribbler, at the hands of greater beings than your sad mudang-monk," the creature called in a steady, unsettlingly calm voice after its initial anger.

Turning back to the writer, the creature's movement revealed more of the screen, its glossy black lacquer covered in an unusually sparse group of animals, flowers, and trees, and what looked like a large snake or dragon near the top, all done in mother-of-pearl inlay. As the writer watched, the creature, its eyes on the writer and not the screen, waved its left hand and the screen's images swirled about, to come to rest with even more black, empty space, and fewer birds.

"Gone, so many. Even our mythic foes, the great winged ones, have only remnants remaining. Weak, ineffective shadows of their former glory, human. You, your kind have banished them to the storybooks and flickering shadows of your big houses," the creature declared, its voice becoming even more menacing. "The mountain tigers, the palace lions, and other guardians of old have long abandoned their stations. Countless lesser nuisances have faded into memory. The balance is broken, human. No longer is there order. Order is dead. All now grab for whatever they please. Only a few do we still fear, though many fear us. Only a few still believe, as you, a foreigner, a despoiler of these shores, have already shown, weakening my brethren, my kin, and even my mortal enemies, pushing all to the shadows."

The writer, realizing he was looking into the face of not the deranged hermit, nor the multiple personality troll-goblin who had been toying with him, but into the pitiless face of an unapologetic murderer, felt the chill of death crawl up his spine for the first time. Somehow, the beast had decided to transfer all the wrongs it perceived had been done to it to the writer, spurring the writer to immediately respond.

"Wait, your enemies are gone? Other than she-who-isn't-named, you must have many, many enemies. Even you said your cousins made you an outcast!" the writer nearly yelled across the enclave, trying to remove the look of murder from the creature's horrid face. "There must be belief! Look at the roofs with the japsang figures. What of the guardians of the funeral rites? Why, look at all the winged ones. Look around you. Look at Seoul, Busan, anywhere. There are winged ones at every corner! Made from steel, bamboo, bronze, gold, and every material that is precious. On official seals. Even on my Korean service award medal! How can you say the humans don't believe?"

"Myths, fool. Stupid little children trying to save memories they no longer understand, scribbler. Long my adversaries have retreated beyond the grasp of your modern brethren. Only a few do I need to worry over," the creature replied and gestured toward the screen. "Even now, the southern coast serpent is fading. The little ones, they have all fled to the far fishing villages and farm pools in the southwest. Hard to capture them, now. The simpler humans protect them, unwittingly. They truly have shreds of belief, those few country and fishing folk. Many are safe from my cousins, as the little, wingless ones cluster there, fearing the modern world."

"Is that what was in that wretched rice-wine mead earlier?" the writer asked, realizing he might have witnessed the hideous death of a rare legend, as outlandish as it sounded to him.

"They prolong. The little ones. Too young to damage, but old enough to heal," the creature answered, its murderous stare shifting, but only slightly, to more of a learned gaze.

"The wavering one that took you to the graves, scribbler, is a lost one, herself," the creature added, walking back to its table, revealing that the black lacquer and mother of pearl screen had disappeared into the trees. "Her master faded many, many cycles ago, long before the last of the great beacons shone across these valleys. Her old master is barely able, if at all, to call on the reapers, as in the old days. As the old order fell, many of her kind were released and now roam without purpose, other than seeking out those who are soon to move on, with nowhere to send them. Many are the wandering spirits, scribbler, born screaming from the cycles and cycles of disbelief. She turned her wandering into reaping those who have robbed the reapers. She found me, not I her."

The creature then looked over at the writer and, shifting its thin shoulders, tapped on the stone table as it spoke, causing a deep ringing to ensue, which, in turn, caused the little ones in the darkness of the trees to begin to emit excited, if muffled, squeaks and grunts.

"You see, scribbler, your tales simply seal your fate. I knew from your first tale, of those grisly brothers, damned and separated by your wars, forever to dwell in that empty space between here and there. Your own tales confirmed that your kind and kin are slaved to the spirits, goblins, and trolls, whatever. But, confused and with many conflicts born of lost memory and stark disbelief. Yes. Order is gone. One lone foreigner's confused babble, using wretched mother tongue, will only confound the fools further," the creature called, its voice and body language, augmented by the last, dying ring of the stone, telling its captive the end was near.

Even with the heavy veil of an early funeral hanging over his head, the writer realized that the murderous creature had lapsed into one of its brief periods reflecting the scholar, versus the monster. As a result, he felt he might be able to use a ploy that was emotional enough to ensure the creature sensed no subterfuge, but also practical enough to get the creature to calm down, pause, and hear the final story.

Taking a deep breath and mentally saying his goodbyes to his family, the writer struck out, verbally, while he also acted out his pent up frustrations with wild hand gestures and movements.

"Then eat me, you cancerous blot on this otherwise glorious day!" the writer yelled into the creature's face, so boldly that the writer's own spittle splattered against the beast's left cheek, causing tiny little, whatever they were, to emerge from the creature's oozing sores to lick up the spit, almost causing the writer to vomit, but he held his own.

The creature stood in silence, its yellow-black eyes sizing up the writer. It then turned and stepped over to the firebox, and summoned one of the little ones from the shadows, who emerged carrying a small shovel of glowing embers. The little one dumped the embers into the firebox, bent over and waved air onto them, quickly igniting the kindling, and, seemingly far too quickly, the ondol charcoal.

"An act, all along," the writer cackled in a crazed voice, realizing the beast's toying with the old tinderbox had been a ruse to scare the writer. "Of course, the great goblin-ogre, or was it troll-goblin, of the Southern Mountain, the venerated Mount Namsan, and spawn of the great Norse legends and kitchen dramas, would never stoop to light something as mundane as the stove!"

The creature ignored the writer's outburst and simply stood watching the fire grow beneath the massive cook pot.

The thin smoke from the kindling was actually a welcome mix of scents to the writer after the stench of the creature and its lair. The smoke smelled of hickory wood, which reminded the writer of his youth in the American South, apple wood, which reminded him of his travels across the globe, and sandalwood, which reminded him of his travels in Asia. Even with the gruesome prospect of being dinner, at least he would make a fragrant meal, the writer chuckled behind his angry visage.

As the little ember bearer handed over the tending of the fire to a couple of the grislier child-things, the master of the enclave returned to its chair and table, and, sitting, continued to ignore the angry human. It turned its gaze to the stars that were beginning to emerge overhead.

Why had the beast not turned on him, or argued with him, the writer wondered? Was it truly the end, since he was being dismissed, and turned over to the little henchmen?

"Your tale of the old demons across the seas, scribbler, touches on many, how do you say, conflicts among my kind," the creature suddenly said, in a voice more distant. "I've lived a long time. Many times, human, and I have dragged many, many like you. I've had my taste of professors and kings. Of the lowest nobi and baekjeong, and the highest born yangban. Yet, here I sit. I am, for now, chained to these old singing stones. Why? You wonder? Why? I will leave that to just gnaw at you, at least until you are gnawed away."

The creature paused, waiting to hear a retort from the writer. Yet, the writer remained silent, trying to appear defiant, uncooperative.

"Yes, trapped here while my foolish cousins move about," the creature continued. "One day, when the right stars align and the right host passes by, and all the numbers fall into place, then I will go to my sire's land, beside the German Sea, as my sire's family has told me."

As the creature rambled, staring up at the unusually early night sky, the writer, presenting a stoic front, was even more desperate to escape, so let his mind race with all manner of plans.

Throw himself on the beast and fight it out?

Climb that old oak, just beside the firebox, and try to go over the trees?

Grab one of the child-things to use as a hostage?

Fall to his knees and plead for mercy from the mixed kid troll-goblin of Namsan?

The writer even considered rushing the huge gamasot and tipping it over, hoping it would crack on the stone floor of the enclave and maybe scald the beast.

Yet, try as he might, the writer knew none of his desperate schemes had any chance of success.

Then, forcing himself to focus only on the one thing that could get him out of the cage of trees and the clutches of the creature, the creature itself, the writer reviewed, in his mind, all the bits and pieces of what the creature had said or had alluded to during the previous few hours.

Something was there, the writer thought, as the creature continued to mumble of lost opportunities and missing cousins, even though, earlier, the beast had disowned its cousins after decrying they had abandoned it after its mother's demise.

The writer racked his brain to pull out something from the troll-goblin's chatter that would hit some nerve, no matter how far deeply buried in the creature's mind. Something that would appeal to whatever shred of former identity remained in that diseased mind. Maybe something earlier, possibly from childhood, before it had become an outcast to its mother's kin?

Maybe its mother?

No, decided the writer. The beast had shown zero empathy for any of the strong female leads in the stories, mothers or not.

Finally, the writer decided to try to draw something more out of the creature. Anything that might help the doomed man to craft a last-ditch effort.

Anything.

"The autumn stars are something, tonight, yes?" the writer called, stepping away from his bench to stand perilously close to the creature and the slowly simmering cook pot. "You seem entranced by them?"

For a long moment, almost too long for the writer, standing so close to the heat and the cook pot, his captor simply continued to stare up at the sky, almost as if it were oblivious to the man's presence.

As the creature stared, a lone leaf, curled into a narrow, brown and yellow half-moon shape, detached from the very oak the writer had considered climbing and, as it floated gently to earth, was suddenly caught up in the heat of the barely simmering cook pot, where several of the child-things had climbed up on the firebox to stir in what appeared to be rotting vegetables and chunks of unidentifiable fat.

The heat from the firebox and the pot caused the leaf to seesaw back and forth, and to rise and fall as it gradually descended. Its antics caught the eyes of the child-things, several of whom seemed to giggle like real children at the playful antics of the leaf.

The giggling, unusual in that den of depravity, drew the master creature's eye away from the stars to look over at the cook pot.

"Worthless beggars! Too scrawny to give me even a bite, what are you making such noise over?" the creature demanded.

"The leaf, master," one of the older child-things said in clear, old school Korean, shocking the writer that the pitiful things could speak. "The leaf looks like a ship on the waves, it does."

"A ship?" the creature repeated, then, glancing up at the stars above, it stood and, at the top of its lungs, shouted with such force that the trees shook, the visitors to Namsan were surprised by a cloudless thunderclap, and the child-things scampered out of the way of the creature's lumbering lunge at the leaf.

"Save it, you mealy bugs and pus filled worms! Save the ship!" the creature screamed, sending all manner of birds fluttering to the heavens all around.

The creature, so agitated as to be unstable on its feet, grabbed one of the older child-things and threw the small creature at the leaf, exhorting the little one to catch the ship.

For what seemed like many minutes to the writer, the creature and its minions attempted to grab the leaf, which, after each swipe at it, the air forced it up and over the cook pot itself, creating even more urgency in the troll-goblin, who continued to grab and throw its little creatures at the elusive leaf.

Suddenly, as the breeze from the antics died down, the leaf began to fall straight to the cook pot, which would no doubt instantly blanch the thing. The motley crew of would be rescuers was lying about the stone floor groaning from the many injuries and probably a few broken bones from their master's frantic efforts to throw them at the leaf.

The creature itself, in the face of the leaf's final dive, was frozen in place, its already hideous face twisted in abject horror.

Twisted in horror?

The writer looked quickly from the creature's face to the leaf and back again.

How can an embodiment of pure evil, of death and decay, of night terrors and day frights, be afraid? And, for something as inconsequential as a falling leaf, the writer wondered?

Then, with absolutely nothing left to lose, the writer, using the older child-thing, the one who had spoken, as a stepping stone, leapt to the top of the firebox, placed his boot on the edge of the huge lid resting just to the side, and thrust himself off the firebox and the lid, into the air, scooping the leaf out of the air just before it touched the bubbling water, which managed to scald the middle knuckle of the writer's right hand.

Once the writer had the leaf, his momentum carried him over the firebox and behind the cook pot, and into one of the dark spaces between the trees. He landed with a thump and, fortunately, had the presence of mind to roll when he hit, so he didn't think anything was broken when he came to stop just between the trees.

Feeling around in the partial darkness with his empty left hand, the writer felt a pile of sticks, no doubt extra kindling for the fire, and a number of bowls, no doubt to drink the ghastly soup stock from the meal later.

Climbing to his feet, the writer was greeted by the wounded, older child-thing, who held a burning stick in his one good hand to cast light into the darkened trees for the evening's dinner to be able to see his way out and back to the cook pot.

Rustlings and low level hissing from deeper in the trees convinced the writer that returning to the enclave, where he could at least see his coming assailants, was preferable to smashing about in the dark forest den of whatever horrors lurked there.

As the writer stepped over the sticks and bowls, the child-thing's torch dipped as the little creature turned, causing the light to shine on the floor of the dark place.

Not sticks for the fire.

Not bowls for the soup. Or, maybe they were used for the ghastly soup?

Bones and skulls, the writer guessed, with renewed terror, as he stepped out of the pitch dark of the trees into the repressive gloom of the enclave. Without looking back to the horror he had just crunched through, he stepped around the firebox and its boiling pot, and found himself staring up at the still transfixed troll-goblin.

Reaching up with his right hand, which was in some pain from the scalding water, the writer presented the still intact leaf to the creature.

For a long minute, the creature's eyes seemed to have trouble focusing on the writer's offering.

The writer shook his own head, not believing that the creature was incoherent and unresponsive. He realized, belatedly, that he could have used those precious few minutes to try to escape while the doomed leaf mesmerized the creature. Why the writer had chosen to rescue the leaf was, at that moment, beyond the writer's own sense of reason, so he simply stood and offered the leaf to the creature.

Finally, the creature's vision seemed to clear and it looked down at the hand holding the leaf. The creature then did an odd thing. It backed up, as if afraid of the leaf. Not of the writer, but of the leaf itself.

The writer stepped forward, following the backward sliding beast until the creature had backed all the way to its chair and, feeling it just behind, allowed its bony frame to collapse.

"No, scribbler, you hold it. I dare not touch...touch the ship," the creature mumbled and then pushed the writer to the side of the table.

For several minutes, the child-things picked themselves up from the ground and, with wounds untended, returned to the firebox and the cook pot, to continue to prepare for the evening's meal of American yugaejang, spicy beef stew.

The writer simply stood, waiting.

"Go back to your bench, boy, and eat what the little ones give you," the creature finally said, but in a severely weakened voice. "I need my meal to give me strength. So end this endless prattle and serve your role as the ages demand. I'm the goblin here. I demand my pay for allowing you to spew your scribbles."

The writer, noting the troll-goblin was confusing his rhetoric, remained silent and returned to the bench where he saw that the half-clean child-thing had evidently placed a dark tin of something else for him to eat.

Roasted garlic, the writer saw when he looked into the tin.

Grinning a little too hysterically, the writer finally realized that the child-things were feeding him to put various spices, flavors, and ingredients inside his stomach to help with the eventual flavoring once he was in the pot itself.

The grisly humor of it all hit the writer like a blow and, throwing all caution to the wind, he grabbed a handful of the powerful garlic and began munching and laughing at the same time.

The creature and his minions, who had all no doubt seen countless victims eventually lose their minds at the end, unable to cope with the coming terror, just watched silently as the writer began his own descent into madness.

The first step, playing the fool.

"Ho, ho! Too bad we don't have more time," the writer called to the creature and its tiny henchmen. "Why, a few weeks of this stuff and I'd add on ten more kilos! And, I'd be as fragrant as the pre-1980's Han River to boot! Maybe we should smear some of that moss from your coat over by chest for added texture? Hey, maybe you could jam some of those snakes in my ears. Too bad we don't have a shipload of some Jeju tangerines to stuff in my various orifices before you dunk me in my final bath?"

Shipload?

Suddenly, the writer fell silent, chunks of garlic hanging from his cheeks and lips, his left hand frozen above the tin and his right hand still holding the damned ship.

Ship?

Leaf?

Stars?

Slowly, the writer's mind pulled itself out of the black depths of resigned denial, and, with difficulty, began to form a thought.

An idea.

A path out of the darkness.

Silently thanking an unknown sea god for supplying him with a slim chance, while offering quick condolences to those lost, the writer fought back his emerging insanity.

Holding a mental image of his family in his mind, the writer shook the bits of garlic off of his hand, wiped the chunks from his face and, standing as tall as he could, he held up the creature's ship and called across the enclave.

"No, vile beast of the corners of a diseased mind, I will not go quietly into your pit of hell!" the writer called, his voice booming around the enclave.

Stepping toward the creature, with the child-things standing by with large, well-worn cleavers, the writer used as strong a voice as he could muster.

"I do have one last tale to spin. One more saga to relate. One more story on my own, lonely, dead-end road to Canterbury. And, you will listen, troll-goblin-ogre outcast of the Korean midlands! You pus riddled bane of decent folk everywhere. You bottom feeder of the worst river scum. You killer of innocents. You killer of your own mother! It's no wonder your mother's family threw you to the streets! No, the alleys! No, the sewer ditches of old Seoul! You are the ultimate disgrace! Impure blood. Goofy mixed looks. Why, even the priciest surgeons in Gangnam wouldn't have you as a patient if you were a son of the wealthiest of the chaebols! You call these sad little creatures, these slaves you have stolen from their homes so long ago they no longer know they used to be human, you call them bugs and mealy worms. Well, mister mixed kid, it is you who are the bug! No! Not even a bug! You are the impure, zombie parasite that feeds off the lowly bugs, you are!"

The writer paused to take a long breath, one eye watching the slowly approaching child-things who were looking to the master to give them the word to carve up the dinner entrée, and with one eye on the creature's diseased eyes, which had been veiled, but were slowly turning to look at the writer in puzzlement, as the beast responded.

"Human. If you are trying to anger me with your ranting to hasten your fate, or to make easier, the cook pot, dead as opposed to still breathing, since live ingredients make for a better taste, you are fooling yourself. My little charges are carrying those blades to appear menacing to get you to jump into the pot. Most do, more afraid of slow dismemberment and quartering, than what they think will be the immediate demise of jumping into the pot," the creature said with zero emotion. "You cannot be the master of your own fate. I do admit that you seem to be a little savvier than the average morsel, but you are still just that. A morsel. Go ahead and babble. Once the broth is just right, in you will go."

"And the ship? Your mother's ship? It goes, too, you vile worm, into this unforgiving ocean of swill?" the writer cried and leapt over one of the child-things to hold the leaf over the cook pot.

Looking at the seemingly crazed writer, the creature had a confused, 'where am I' look on its face. Then, recognition of the leaf and the recent antics reminded the creature of something else. Something outside of itself. Something of its own terrors.

"The ship? No. No, not the ship, the leaf," the creature said, rising from its chair to approach the writer. "It's too acidic. It will spoil all the effort to flavor you just right. Give! Give it to me…!"

The writer, sweating from the heat and feeling the back of his hand beginning to blister, shook his head vigorously and moved his hand even closer to the water.

The child-things, no doubt thinking it was time to throw the writer in the pot, began to close around him, causing the creature to sweep them away with a wide brush of its arm.

"Be gone, bugs. Leave me to reckon with this human devil!" the creature roared, sending the minions scurrying back to the dark spaces in the trees.

Yet, one little one was not so lucky. The creature's ragged sleeve entangled the squealing thing's legs and the beast lifted the pitiful wretch over its head, trying to shake it off.

The creature then smiled an evil smile and, with a quick flick of its wrist, hurled the little minion at its captive, narrowly missing the writer's head.

The writer, having realized just in time what the creature was about to do, had shifted his weight slightly and had moved just as the little child-thing had gone whizzing by.

Yet, the writer did not simply let the pitiful creature smash into the cook pot, or, worse, fall into the fast boiling broth. He used his free hand to snatch the little one out of the air and, with forced compassion, gently dropped the little bag of thin bones on the far side of the stove, where it stood stunned, looking up at the writer for the blink of an eye, and then ducked back into the trees. For the briefest of moments, the writer thought the little one was the half-clean minion who had been feeding him, but figured all the smaller ones looked alike.

Focusing on the writer, the creature's tongue flicked out, licking the pus from the sores on its chin, and then clicked in agitation at his captive's antics. For a number of long seconds, the creature swayed toward the writer, then back. It then jumped around its table, seeming lost and confused. Finally, the creature, showing signs of fatigue, its limbs hanging more listlessly and its speech a little slurred, backed up to its chair and sat, calling out to the writer.

"Boy, you say you have another tale. I can see by your hand that the broth is actually too hot now, due to all these distractions, so the little helpers will have to dampen the fire a bit, giving you a few more of those precious moments you humans seem to cherish above all else. While I tire of your tales, I will strike a bargain with you. If you release the ship, the leaf, and place it, carefully, mind you, in the crook of that tree there, where, over time, it will rot and return to the soil, and maybe cause a passing seed to sprout a wind flower or maybe some ingredient for my meal one day, I will let you tell your final tale, even though your book there has nearly exhausted its contents."

"Bah, to use your word!" the writer cried. "What assurance do I have that you will not have your vile children pounce once I have surrendered the ship to the tree's embrace?"

"None, human, I'm a goblin-troll, not a lawyer," the creature quipped, but its face betrayed abject fear that the writer would drop the leaf.

With the heat of the boiling water beginning to peel the skin off the back of the writer's hand, the pain was becoming unbearable, to the point the captive feared he might faint. So, looking deep into the frightened eyes of his captor, the writer nodded curtly to the creature and moved away from the cook pot. Stepping toward the old oak, none of the child-things appeared, apparently too afraid to return until their master expressly called for them.

At the old oak, the writer strained to reach the crook between the trunk and the lowest limb, but finally got the leaf placed and, with a small tuck for good luck, stepped back, hoping the leaf, the beast's ship, would stay put.

The writer then stepped over to the creature's table and, grabbing the festering drink offered earlier, took a large gulp of the awful liquid, and slammed the tankard back to the table.

For the blink of an eye, the writer felt his suddenly throbbing brain reel with fast moving images of his life, jumbled all about, screaming past the back of his forehead. Then, somewhere, in the mountains just to the north, he watched legions of men march to their death, while legions more marched into some distant sea. Deep, deep down inside some sort of black hole of an ancient Calcutta, he saw his own flesh melting into the walls, the iron bars, and the vanishing lives in desperate images of...of himself.

Pulling his mind out of the hellish mead's grip, the writer steadied his swaying body and forced himself to focus on his nightmarish host.

"Right, then. An ample swig of your 'mead of poetry' and let's proceed with this last story, without delay," the writer declared, hearing his voice as if he were speaking from far away.

The writer then stood by the bench, but at the end closest to the creature's chair and table. He turned his notebook over in his hands and tapped out a rhythm on the back of the book.

Under the cover of the notebook, the writer managed to wrap his burned hand with one of the surgical masks he kept in his coat pocket for riding the subway. The pain was minimal, but the writer knew he'd need treatment at some point, if he got out of that enclave in one piece.

"What? No build up? No more banter? No more clever wit to further deflect my thoughts from the cook pot?" the creature mocked, its grisly grin dripping yellow pus and flaky bits of skin as the beast rose again from its chair to grab the heavy tongs, too heavy for the minions, and poked at the broth, and then the ondol charcoal.

"What? Cleverness? No, just the tale, I'm afraid, my mythical nightmare," the writer replied, hoping his voice sounded defeatist as the man was trying to keep the creature off guard. "While I would have hoped these tales would live after me, I am content that I can, at least before I step over the precipice, tell the tales to this grand audience of one, with the gallery of trees, night animals, and your, uh, diminutive charges, that standing room only crowd of small wastrels gathered at the back of the firebox, no doubt eager for me to finish and thereby hasten their ghastly meal of my sad flesh and bones."

"No," the writer continued and turned his eyes away from the creature and the cook pot and back to the notebook. "No. No more banter. I'll let the final tale speak from its own words. Judge you then, foul troll-goblin, what you will."

Without waiting for a reply, the writer began to speak, his voice steady and with full alliteration of the words coming off the mental pages as he strived to ensure the tale, taken mostly from memory, was smooth and did not have long pauses where the creature could end things more readily.

As the captive human spoke, the creature scoffed, but then, as the writer moved deeper into the story setup, the creature put down the heavy iron tongs, stepped back to the stone chair and table, and, cocking its head, with stringy hair and vines dragging on the table top, leaned in and listened closely to what the beast knew were the final words of the strange writer of tales.

"Let us travel south, to that land of volcanic terror, majestic seas, hard working people, beautiful diving women, singular horses, and eternal optimism," the writer began, trying to think a few lines and paragraphs ahead as he recalled the draft of the final story and half-created new elements on the fly. "That land of vacation for many and, for a few, home. Jeju-do. Jeju Island."

"Jeju? Ah, another place I wish to haunt again before my days are few," the creature said, wiping a bit of greenish drool from its chin. "Snake cult goblins still wander under the earth there. Very few. The human shrines to your many warring gods have displaced so many of my cousins. But, the winds tell me that there are a few remaining."

"The winds tell you?" the writer asked, delaying the final tale as he worked out some of the elements in his head. "How does that work?"

"What work? The winds?" the creature repeated, suddenly giving the writer a suspicious look. "Your kind is deaf to the winds, human. You steal the wind's children and imprison them in your glass houses, forcing them to produce, over and over again. For what? The amusement of an old dowager? To hang from a sad bride's throwaway costume?"

"I don't understand," the writer replied. "How does the wind get captured?"

"Those aerial leeches! You fool. Those tree and cliff dwelling, life sapping gems of the plant world who are our brothers and sisters," the creature cried, seeming to wince in pain. "I don't, the human name escapes me. You steal them for their flowering, the hideous part, but not the part that sends the news out to the winds."

"Mistletoe? No? What else is a...? Wait. Orchids?" the writer asked in true bewilderment. "Orchids talk to you?"

"Talk? Is that all you humans understand, the prattle of speech? There are older, more certain ways to move messages and words, human. No, the wind flowers don't talk, they pass on news," the creature answered with disdain. "Many, however, have been silenced. So many, living near the balconies of your tall hive huts, send messages with no meaning, just a jumble of mixed words and senseless prattle. Your kidnapping them has scrambled their minds."

"Right. How do they...?" the writer began.

"Enough, human!" cried the creature. "The lovely leeches will turn one day. I've heard thoughts drifting up from Jeju Island and beyond these last seasons. If the wind flowers can finish forming their thoughts before all the kidnapped ones fully lose their minds, they will turn on their captors one day. It will take many seasons for my plant brethren, the 'orchids' you call them, to shift their scents to attack the humans, but, one day, they will. The fairies are helping, but there are so few left, even on the remote isles. Your helpers, when it suited them, the fairies were. Before you plowed under their forest homes to make your roads and vast cities. The fairies would nip at our own heels and send us down the wrong path, causing us to miss a particularly juicy morsel, they would. Happened to me leaving, well, leaving one of those iron carts that ride underground. A Jeju fairy, I think she was, from the scent of the sea and the ash from the earth there. Was helping some old one to find his way. She had lost hers and instead of wasting away as is the custom with the fairy folk, she chose to roam Seoul and help the lost, hoping, I think, someday to find one who might be traveling back to her lands and hitch a ride."

"What, uh, what became of her?" the writer asked, wondering why the creature rambled on so about something he claimed to loath.

"Became of? Oh, she found her human willing, at least she thought, to allow her to hitch a ride back to the south," the beast replied.

The creature abruptly stepped over to the writer and leaned in close to the writer's face, studying its captive's eyes. The beast then lifted a bit of rag from its left shoulder, revealing a squirming patch of diseased flesh, with, of all things, a tiny, pink and white orchid clinging to the edges of the lesion, its black-green tendrils embedded in the creature's yellowed flesh, with a cluster of stunted, yellow-green leaves spread to one side.

"She speaks to me, but rarely now, human," the creature whispered as it stepped back, gently placing the bit of filthy rag over the tiny flower. "Rarely, as she is weak these many seasons from so many of her kind being cruelly harvested to amuse you humans."

"Fascinating," the writer said, truly amazed at the odd companion to his demented captor. "Is that one of them? Is she the fairy you speak of?"

"The fairy?" the creature repeated, seeming to be confused. "What? No, fool human. A fairy's touch would burn and tear away my flesh. No, fool human, this is one of the few wind flowers who can still signal the winds and get signals back. Very weak, though. Very weak. The fairy did tell me, she did. Told me a few secrets. Secrets to keeping this little one alive. Secrets to keeping its fragile mind intact. Traded for the soul of the human who was taking her back to her lands, the fairy did."

"Maybe you could tell me about the fairy and her human?" the writer asked, trying anything to draw out helpful bits from the creature, especially about something that seemed to show an entirely different side to the beast, one of some level of compassion, even if self-serving.

"You delay, human. Tell you the tale? Maybe tell your boiled bones, if the little ones leave any intact in their hunger for your puny marrow," the creature retorted and then laughed a long, guttural laugh, staggering at the end.

The creature then stumbled back and settled into the large, stone chair, its hand gently stroking the small lump where the tiny flower resided on its shoulder. Coughing briefly from the laughing fit, and wiping black phlegm from its lips, the creature waved its free hand at the writer.

"So, begin, human, your tale of the far away land of this tiny one's parents. Let me close my tired eyes and listen to your words. To your not so hidden plea to escape the cook pot with this last tale," the creature said as it sank back into its chair. "Do not disappoint me, boy. And, look to the little ones as they scurry behind the firebox. If your tale bores me so, the little ones may emerge if I slip into sleep, to find their own morsels. Uncooked, of course, as they can't quite lift you into the pot. But, what they lack in brutal strength, they make up for in cunning. Were I to sleep too soundly and too long, I fear only your half-consumed, raw carcass would greet my awakening, human. So, yes, serve yourself well and keep your tale at the forefront of my weary mind, so that I might have that full meal at its end."

"Release, you mean, vile one. Not cook," the writer rebutted. "You will want me to carry your tale to the masses you despise, but sorely need. Thus 'release' for me, and 'survival' for you as you slumber. I fear not the little mouths attached to those misshapen creatures, but only pity their fate."

The creature, its eyes closed and its head fallen to the side holding the orchid, simply grunted and waved the writer to continue, while, in the darkened nooks and in-between spaces behind the stove and the huge cook pot, the little ones could be heard scuffling and scurrying, no doubt jockeying for the best position to attack the writer's legs and arms once the beast had fallen asleep.

With vivid mental images of being nibbled alive by the child-things, regardless of any ethereal deal the creature might decide to honor, the writer nodded, sat down, tucked his legs under the stone bench, backed onto the thick supports for added protection, and then flipped the notebook over. Allowing himself to look one last time at its dedication page, to a long lost loved one, he then began what he hoped was his final, decisive tale for the warped mind of the deranged hermit, or forest troll-goblin of Mount Namsan, and its tiny helpers.

Wanting to ensure the creature could hear every word, the writer leaned closer and, with his voice a little louder to penetrate the addled mind of the nearly snoozing beast, he began.

"Far south, either by train and then boat, or through the air bridges, Jeju Island rests in crystal waters, an inviting gem, beckoning to mainlanders to escape from their frenzied lives in Seoul, Busan, Daegu, and elsewhere, and spend time amongst the forests, the trails, the volcanic caves, the orange groves, the temples, and the other many wonders offered by Jeju, on land and on sea. Let's spend a little time there, not far from one of the favorite fishing spots of those heroic haenyeo, sea women, the lady divers of Jeju. Our destination lies somewhere on the southeast coast, where a jumble of rocks near a quiet beach serves as a momentary haven for one of Seoul's more famous citizens. However, for your consideration, the afternoon we are observing offers a strange interruption to her escape. Let's share a chance encounter she undergoes with the island's locals, and watch how snap judgments, preconceptions, and misinformed assumptions can cloud a person's view of the world, and, if unchecked, cause irrevocable damage. Yes, let's peek into what surprises fracture the solitude on that rocky, windswept, Jeju Island beach."

The writer looked hard at his captor, wondering if the words were getting through, and so added a little more enticement for the beast to remain awake.

"Recall that Jeju Island, the uncontested jewel of your southern seas, has many legends, many tragedies, and has hosted many of your cousins in the old days. Yes, you said yourself, that you have spent time on its shores and seas with some of the few remaining brethren. Others of your ilk no doubt still dwell there. Some unique to the island, trying to keep the old ways from slipping away, forced into the more remote reaches by the glare of the new and modern. Others stalking the tourists and the day-trippers for what you call morsels. Still others content to live out their own simple island lives in the shadows of the ones they haunt. Let's now allow ourselves to be transported with the visitor from Seoul to a small house, in the old, volcanic stone and thatched roof style, perched above a rocky, but quiet sea cove, just at the edge of the memory of those fairies, wind flowers, and goblin cousins of whom you speak."

8

JEJU ISLAND ENLIGHTENING

Far to the south of Seoul's Mount Namsan, the grey and black volcanic landscape, lush forests, and windswept shores of Jeju Island, that shimmering pearl of the Korea Strait, has served as a cherished refuge from the mainland for millennia. As human inhabitants had come and gone, the myriad rock formations, carved by the relentless sea, biting sand, and salty winds, had been christened with different names at different times, but all tended to be fanciful, mythical names, often testaments to mankind's preoccupation with its dark, unwritten past handed down by way of the telling of old tales and beliefs. Some piles of worn lava rocks were labeled dragons. Others were great birds of prey that had been absent from those shores many centuries. Still others were whimsical sea creatures, while others were more sinister snakes and night crawlers hidden from the light of day. One of those ancient stone giants had, so far, to the delight of a few quiet, sincere admirers, been missed by the social media hordes looking for little more than a spot for photo opportunities. One early afternoon, that secluded, volcanic seashore sculpture, possibly a half-carved dragon, or maybe a soaring seabird, was sheltering a young woman who had sought out a quiet place, away from the tourists, and away from prying eyes. From such a perch, she was able to see and hear the waves lapping at the shore, enjoy the birds skittering about or cruising overhead, feel the rise and fall of the drifting sea flotsam, and daydream of the promise of far sea voyages on the few distant ships. Albeit close to a popular park, the maze-like jumble of weathered rocks afforded the young woman just the right level of privacy, without the risk of losing herself in some remote wilderness area. As she leaned back against a smooth curve of an old, black and grey stone column that she had chosen as her perch, the young woman let out a

283

contented, long needed sigh, put her phone on 'do not disturb' for one hour, and dropped it in her purse, a boring little number she used when she wanted to blend in. She then pulled out a small, compact book that had been a gift some years before, but had lain unread for a long time, due to her crazy schedule. She hoped to at least start the book before she had to return to the controlled chaos of Seoul in less than a week. A smile formed as she looked at the title, kicked off her jandals, and let her toes mix with the slightly chilly, lapping water in a small pool at her feet.

As she opened her book, the young woman suddenly frowned and looked up. She glanced down to the main beach, only ten meters away, but could not find the sounds that had interrupted the beginning of her hour of solitude. She then cocked her head and stilled any movement, listening intensely until, over the normal sounds of the surf, the birds, and some distant traffic, she finally heard a distinct, melodious, man's voice from somewhere on the beach beyond the rocks.

Seriously, the young woman asked herself? Somebody had to pick the one secluded place she had found, to espouse on something? Now? Her solitude among the mythical creatures of stone disrupted, the young lady let out a long, disappointed sigh, and decided to seek out the source of ruin of her brief and rare escape.

English?

Puzzled at the realization that the voice was, indeed, clearly speaking English, and in a manner that a teacher would use with students, the young woman was even angrier that some rude, American tourist had invaded her private thoughts and brief escape.

While she understood English, the young lady of the shore rocks still had to strain to understand the man's soft words, given the distance and his rich accent, which she could not place.

Unable to hear clearly, the young lady slipped her wet feet back into her jandals, and moved closer to the edge of the rocks, allowing her to just see down to the beach and the small grassy area above, revealing the back of the speaker, who was looking away from her jumble of worn lava rocks. He appeared to be addressing an unseen audience.

Suddenly, several small voices could be heard talking all at once, startling the young lady, causing her to shrink back to the safety and anonymity of her secluded perch by the sea.

After the children's voices had died down, the young woman decided the audience was evidently a group of school children out on a mid-week field trip. From what she could hear, the teacher was telling the children a story, in English, to practice their listening and speaking skills.

Sliding back to the small gap in the lava rocks to listen more closely, the young lady found herself mouthing the answers to the teacher's questions as she secretly listened. For some minutes, she followed the story and the questions, and became caught up in the back and forth the teacher had devised to keep the children engaged and to help them progress through the lesson. She allowed her interest to temper her initial indignation.

Leaning back, the young lady closed her eyes and, after briefly wondering what the teacher's face might look like, turned her thoughts to her own concerns as she half listened to a series of replies from the students.

Regeneration.

That's what her dear mother had called their early visits to Jeju Island, the young woman smiled to herself. An ability to not only relax and escape the constant pressures of the stage, for all of her life was a stage, but also to spend a few days as a normal person, with no photographers, no overzealous fans, and no hangers-on. Just herself, with, of course, an omnipresent manager, an overprotective aunt, and a watchful security team that kept their distance, but was always nearby.

Suddenly, what sounded like a wrong answer tugged the young lady back to the teacher and his students, who were discussing an old farmer.

It's not a goat, silly, the young lady thought. It's a cow or a Jeju pony. That's what the teacher is talking about, she said to herself.

Smiling, the young lady leaned over and, pulling her long, black hair into a ponytail, she wrapped it and tucked it into her hood so that the hair would not blow around and expose her position to the teacher or his students. Satisfied she was still unseen, the young lady wiggled closer and began to listen in earnest to the story the teacher was weaving, allowing the American's calming accent to lull her into an even more relaxed state.

In between the gusts of wind and occasional crashes of waves just meters away, the young lady, by turning her head just so, was able to hear most of the teacher's new tale. She smiled as she listened, thinking back to stories her dear grandmother had told her years ago.

"We all know the celebrated sunrise crater at Seongsan Ilchulbong, where the morning meets the sea, and then the land," the teacher said, his voice a bit louder to carry over the wind, thereby reaching the ears of not only the children arrayed in the grass before him, but also to the rocks not too far away.

"How was that crater created? Who knows?"

Several of the children, after politely raising their hands and being called on, offered stammering answers in fairly proficient English. The young lady behind the rocks whispered the answer to herself, and smiled when the teacher confirmed her silent answer.

"Yes, old volcanoes. Very old. And, how many of you live in the old lava rock houses? What, no one? Well, there aren't many left, are there?"

The young lady sighed when the teacher mentioned the traditional homes that were rare in modern Jeju. On her visits to the island, she had always daydreamed of having a distant aunt who would live in one of those traditional stone houses, where she could visit during Seoul's frigid winters. Even though the old houses, with their thatched roofs and rounded lava stone walls, reminded even the most jaded observer of a fairy tale house, she had always thought they looked warm and inviting.

"Well, years and years ago, one of those houses on the southern Jeju coast had a cheerful front garden," the teacher continued. "The garden was full of bright flowers, well trimmed trees and shrubs, and even two small ponds, built generations before, one pond with carp and one full of frogs."

"As you all know, the birds love to snatch up the carp and the frogs from such ponds, but the ancestors who had built that house had constructed the ponds with ample hiding places in the submerged rocks and a few places along the edges where the fish and frogs, and any other small animal, could hide when needing a safe harbor or shelter."

"Over the years, the old man, a farmer, who lived in the house, tended to the ponds as he would a garden, ensuring they were clean, that the fish and frogs had ample hiding places, and that, when the great winds blew and dashed much of the water out of the ponds, that they were filled. One of his sons had constructed a small waterway, using hidden hoses, so such maintenance was less burdensome as the old man grew older."

"As the old man aged, to an even older age, he began to notice small items sitting on the edge of that little, double pond. Yes, it was a double pond, almost like a figure eight, or the infinity symbol, with one side for the carp and the other for the frogs. Near the middle of the two, where they shared a wall, a particularly spacious nook had been formed when the farmer...did I mention he was a farmer? When the farmer's great-great grandfather had built the ponds, he had placed several huge stones to shore up and support the top of the ponds, and to form part of the house's front garden wall. So, the little nook was actually more like a small cave."

"Well, as I said, the old man began to notice small things sitting on the ledge at the front of that little nook. At first, the man assumed some clever magpie or thieving raven had taken up residence and was leaving the items as some sort of decoration or declaration of ownership to other birds."

One of the children asked a quiet question about the items.

"Oh, small items. A small shell or two. Driftwood, or, drift twigs more likely. Smooth, ocean worn pebbles. Sometimes sea glass, worn smooth and looking like jewels in the midday sun."

The child who asked the question smiled and made a small, sitting bow to the teacher, who then continued.

"After some weeks, the old man decided to play a game with the bird that he thought was living in the small cave. And, no, he never saw the bird, as the nook or cave was quite deep and, since it was also part of the garden wall, he assumed there were other cracks and spaces where the bird might slip away unseen when the old man approached."

"So, the old man began to place small things on the ledge. At first, he would just place a button, a bit of string, or maybe an old coin, like the ones that no longer had value. He'd leave them and see what would happen."

"At first, nothing happened. Day after day, whatever he had left would be in the same place on the ledge, or, if the wind had been particularly strong, on the ground next to the pond wall. So, he decided to see if he did an exchange, what might happen."

'So, one day, very much like today, windy, but not too windy, he took up one of the bits of sea glass, a blue one, sitting on the ledge near the small cave, and placed a shiny, mother-of-pearl button in its exact spot."

"The next day, the old man was surprised to see the glossy white button gone and replaced with yet another bit of sea glass, green this time."

A murmur of anticipation rippled through the young audience.

"So, the old man, who, by the way, lived alone, as he had outlived his own family and his wife, and several of his children. One remaining son had moved away, to Seoul, of course, so the old man was alone. There was a cleaning lady who came to tend his house three days a week, but no family.

"The old man saw the new bit of glass and chuckled. He then placed two of the old coins, which he had scrubbed with sand to make them shiny. He took the blue bit of glass and added it to the other one sitting on his front window sill, just outside his small parlor at the front of his house, that looked out over the garden and the pond, and down to the sea."

"Over the following weeks and months, which turned into years, the old man and the bird exchanged many items. Sometimes the old man would return an item and the bird would replace the returned item with whatever the old man had left for it before, even if had been ages since the original exchange. Over time, the old man began to think of the bird as more of a human than a bird, for how could a bird, with such a tiny little brain, remember which item had been exchanged for which over months and months?"

One of the children blurted out the bird must be a raven, for his grandfather, who lived in Jeonju, had told him ravens were very smart.

"Thank you. Let's continue the story and see if the bird is a raven."

"After a number of years of the exchanging of items, the old man had quite a collection of the sea glass sitting on his windowsill. Even in the windy and rainy season, because the windowsills were so deep on those old stone houses, the glass never blew away or fell to the ground. Each time the old man saw the mosaic of colors, some frosty, some sparkling, outside his window, he did not feel alone. He felt warm and, in an odd way, loved by the small bird with whom he had a long term friendship, even though he had never actually seen the bird."

"One day, the old farmer, always awake before the dawn to care for his few cattle, which he would herd down to the pasture on a low hill by the sea to graze, was returning from the pasture to have his breakfast, when he encountered several young tourists admiring his front garden and the double ponds.

"'Hello,' they called to the old man, 'you have an amazing garden. May we take pictures?' This was from a polite young man who seemed to be the oldest in the group of young people. Probably college age, the old man thought, and who had probably come down for the festival honoring Grandmother Yeongdeung, Goddess of the Wind. 'Of course,' the old man replied, 'but can you do so from outside the gate? Some of the plantings are hard to see this time of year and I'd hate for you to step on them accidentally.' 'Certainly, grandfather. We will be most careful,' they said."

"So, the small group of three or four college students took a few pictures and then waved goodbye to the old man. One of the group, however, didn't wave and would not look the old farmer in the eye. The young man seemed to be harboring some sort of conflict, the old man thought, as the youth dashed by the old man with barely the minimal show of respect to an elder that most Korean youth do without thinking. Odd, the old man thought, as he went about getting his breakfast together."

"After eating, and before the rest of his morning chores, the old farmer liked to sit with a cup of tea and look out on his garden, wondering if that might be the morning when he would actually see the raven, or magpie, or whatever bird was playing the exchange game with him."

"As he looked out the window from his chair in the parlor, the old man detected something was different. He stared and stared at the pond, the ledge of the small cave and the garden as a whole, scratching his thinning head of hair in puzzlement. He knew something was different, but just couldn't put his hands on it."

The hidden young lady of the rocks smiled and leaned even closer, even risking possible discovery by the teacher, if he turned a certain way. But, she did not want to miss a word of the next part. She was eager to learn what had changed, with several ideas racing through her mind. Part of her wanted to shout out a guess or two, but she controlled her impulse by pinching her leg to remind herself she mustn't be discovered.

At first, the young woman didn't want to be discovered out of concerns over her own, selfish privacy. However, after listening to and becoming absorbed in the teacher's tale, even if his accented English was hard for her to completely understand, she didn't want to be discovered for fear of throwing the teacher off his spinning of the tale and ruining it for the children and, yes, for herself. So, she was even quieter and tried to squeeze herself into an even smaller ball, sitting among the ancient rocks.

"Upset at himself for not being able to figure out what had changed, the old man abandoned his tea and remaining breakfast, postponed his chores for a few minutes, and walked outside to the garden to see if he could discover what was wrong."

The smaller children in the group made muffled noises of concern for the old man in the story as the teacher continued.

"Wrong? Why would he think something was wrong, the old man had thought, giving himself even more of a worry. Wandering around the garden, the old man looked at his plants, his few little statues, for every Jeju house has a few statues, especially in the garden. He then looked to the ponds and the walls. He even carefully looked over the wee cave ledge to ensure nothing was amiss there."

The teacher leaned in and asked his audience if they thought they knew what might be amiss, as the teacher explained the word 'amiss' to the youths, and his hidden pupil. After a few energetic responses, with the hidden pupil remaining silent, of course, the teacher resumed.

"As the old man circled his garden a second time, scratching his thinning head with his left hand and stroking his thin beard with his right, he suddenly came to a dead halt at the windowsill outside of his parlor. For several minutes, he simply stared at the old window, its rough edges showing the ravages of time, weather, sun, and minor neglect, as he hadn't painted the house trim in decades. Slowly at first, then with a little more vigor, he extended his right hand and then his left, and drew them both across the worn paint of the windowsill, from side to side, his aged fingertips feeling the abrasiveness of the weathered grey paint. And, nothing else."

"The glass!"

A collective cry went up from the children, that the old man's sea glass was gone.

"What could have happened to it?"

The young lady was also perilously close to jumping out of her hiding place and shouting what she thought was the answer, but bit her lip and kept silent.

"What? What's that you say? The glass? What glass…oh, the beach glass, or, more accurately, sea glass, since it came from the ocean. Yes, he did have a considerable pile of polished glass adorning his window, didn't he? Whatever could have happened to it?"

Again, the cries from the students were so loud that even the hidden, accidental pupil heard them clearly over the sound of the lapping waves.

"The students? What, you all took the…? Oh, the college students. The one who was impolite? I see. He was impolite because he couldn't look the old man in the eye, nor speak to him without his guilt showing? But, should we condemn the students before trial? What other evidence is there?"

For a short minute, the students murmured among themselves and then shouted out ideas to the teacher. Some said to check for footprints in the garden path, to see if anyone other than the old man's feet were there. Others said to call the police and check for fingerprints. Others suggested all cameras in the area be checked, not realizing that the tale occurred before the ubiquitous camera culture had taken over the land.

Finally, one of the students, a young girl, near the front, suggested the old man hurry after the students and simply ask them.

"Right, that is a good strategy. The old man, upset more that his friend the bird had collected dozens of such shiny objects only to have them snatched, than he was of losing anything that was his. He did not think of the bits of glass as his, but only that he was their caretaker until the next occupants of the house and the cave moved in after he and the bird had passed on to the next life."

"Yet, he did not start off right away. He first reached into his jacket pocket, the cavernous one that all grandfathers and uncles have filled with treats and surprises for the children in their lives, and found two very shiny old coins. Sighing, as he sometimes did when he realized he did not have his grandchildren or grandnephews and grandnieces around him, as they lived in far away Seoul and visited only once a year, for just a few days to play on the beach, he turned to the little bird house at the pond wall and placed the coins there."

"Turning back, the old man stepped toward the house, prepared to grab his sturdiest walking stick and to dash, in his slow, old man way, after the students, who were probably just up the beach, when he was stopped in his tracks by the tiniest of voices."

"'Grandfather, what has happened? Have I angered you that you have thrown away all the treasures we have piled high these many years?' the tiny voice asked."

The children in the audience, suddenly surprised by the appearance of the voice and some unknown figure of what they thought was the bird, were all giggling with anticipation at finally finding out just who was living in the pond cave, more than worrying about the sea glass.

Even the young lady hiding in the rocks was hard pressed to remain in her hiding place. She leaned as far over as she could to look out of her left eye at the teacher and, through a space between the rocks, out of her right eye at the students, her own excited curiosity almost overpowering her resolve to stay hidden.

"The old man turned slowly, looking around for the source of the voice and, to his surprise, a small child, dressed in very old style clothing meant for girls or boys, called garot, persimmon-colored cotton, was sitting on the pond wall. Her little legs were dangling over the side of the wall, showing her equally old straw sandals on her small feet. Her? Yes, for some reason the old man assumed the little figure was a little girl, but was actually unsure, but needed to call the child something."

"The old man then stepped closer to the pond and the child held up her hand to stop him. 'Sorry, grandfather, but you can't come any closer. Curses and all that befall anyone, even you, if you happen to touch even the sleeve of my jacket or stub your toe on my sandal. Not my choosing, mind you. I'd rather not have such, but I don't make the rules. And, the rule makers have all gone the way of all old ones, so there is no one to change the rules. So, for your own safety, we must greet in the old way, with bows and ceremonial mumblings.'"

"With that, the tiny person bowed low at the waist, three times in a show of respect for her aged companion. The little child then retreated to the cave and immediately returned with a small pack."

Suddenly, several of the students began playfully shouting at the teacher. They seemed to be confused that, if the cave resident was a little girl or boy, then how could she, or he, fit into a small cave house that was only large enough for a raven at the largest?

"What? Oh, that's a good question. I wonder how this tiny child of Jeju, sitting on the old volcanic stone wall of the figure eight, infinity pond, could fit into such a tiny house. It's a puzzle all right. I know I have the story correct, for it was told to me…what? You think she is a what?"

Even the hidden pupil, the young lady in the rocks, was whispering what she thought the little person was, unable to control her own eagerness to be part of the story time with the students and the teacher. She considered standing and stepping out from behind the rocks, but was stopped by the teacher suddenly looking directly at the rock she was hiding behind, so she froze in place, hoping he would not see her and turn back to the students. He did not seem to see her, and then turned back to the youthful audience.

"A spirit? A sprite? How do you know what a wood sprite is? Oh, your uncle in Europe. An elf? Hmm. Are there elves in Korea? I thought that was a European thing, or maybe Russian?"

Quite boisterous, the students were guessing all manner of mythical beings that might explain the presence of the little person who could be child size and then fit with ease into the tiny cave house.

Suddenly, from the back of the group, a young girl, no bigger than one of the many small rocks that lie along the Jeju coast near their spot, raised her hand politely, instead of trying to shout over her friends. The teacher saw her and, after calling for silence from the group, asked her for her thoughts.

"Sir, teacher, sir," the young girl, standing up, said with serious formality and nearly perfect English pronunciation, "I'd like to suggest that we have encountered one of the Jeju Island fairies, sir. Or, at the outside, as my father likes to say, one that has wandered here from the mainland many years ago, sir."

Silence ensued. Whether from her fellow students' astonishment that one of the class's quietest students could speak complex English, with ease and with nearly no accent, or from the guess that had escaped everyone else, we will never know, as the teacher took that quiet moment to stand, step back and, again, look toward the rocks with the hidden spectator, then quickly look away, and step back to his post at the large boulder.

Several of the older students, puzzled at the teacher's interest in the jumble of large, weathered rocks just at the shoreline, craned their necks to see if something might be there, but saw nothing.

"A fairy? Why didn't I think of that? Yes, the little child from the garden rocks must have been a fairy. Why, let's continue the story and see if she will confirm she is a fairy? Yes? Okay."

The teacher took a deep breath and dove into the explanation.

"For a long moment, the old man simply stared at the small child, his eyes telling him he had just seen the child walk from the pond wall into the little cave house and reemerge with a small pack, which itself was nearly as big as the main stone covering the top of the little cave house. Shaking his head to get it clear of any morning drowsiness, the old man, heeding the girl's warning, squatted down to get a better look at her, but at a safe distance."

"As you know, the old man had lived a long, long life. He had been young once. Yes, even this old man had been your age. He had had loving parents, strict and traditional, but loving. He had gone off to school on the mainland in his youth, and had gone to war as well. He had traveled the world, and had seen and done many things. Later in life, he had returned and married a local haenyeo, a sea woman, and had several children, as we spoke of earlier. In all those years and during all those travels, the old man had seen his share of strange and wonderful things."

"He had seen the shadows of ancient warriors on the night shores of Crete, in old Greece, marching into the heavens to battle the old gods. Brightly dressed ancient ones in the temples of Kamakura south of Tokyo. Old knights, hearts heavy, dragging themselves back to the ruined castle above the festively draped Christmas market in old Heidelberg. Wraiths of crying winds in the closes and twisted streets of old Edinburgh on a foggy night. Yes, these and many more the old man had seen in his life, and, from his parents, he had heard the old stories of the ones who had come before. Yet, in all his life on Jeju, he had never met one, and, over the years, had assumed the stories from his parents had been just that, stories to keep a child wondering. Stories to help a child on his life's path. Just stories."

"So, looking at the little person before him, the old man was neither scared, nor all that surprised. What did surprise him was that it was so late in his life that he had finally come face to face with one of the ones who had come before, and, contrary to what his parents had told him, that the one sitting, well, no standing before him had not 'gone the way' of the old ones, at least not just yet."

"'What has taken you so long to say hello?' the old man then asked the little shape, which seemed to shift a bit in front of the old man's eyes. One minute the little person looked like a small girl, then a toddler little boy, then back to a girl, but a little older. Nearly as old as you all here."

"The little person smiled, giving the old man a warm feeling in the quiet places of his heart, and spoke again."

"'Sir, grandfather, you have never needed me to be me before. I've always been me. I've always, as far as I can remember, been here. Well, as long as the double pond your great-great-great-great-great...I'm sorry, I can't remember exactly how many great-grandfathers in the past there were before you. But, it's been a while.'"

"The little person bowed again and then hopped down off the wall. Pointing down the track toward the sea, she then waved her arm for the old man to remain at his home, telling him she would be retrieving the sea glass from the evil doers and teaching them a lesson as well."

"Alarmed, for the old man felt that only one of the students was to blame and, until he heard why the youth had taken the glass, if he had, he did not want any unfortunate fairy spells to befall the young man."

"'Wait, dear spirit of this old island. I must accompany you to ascertain the facts, and then determine the best course of action,' the old man said to the small person. As you might expect, the fairy, if that was what she was, but it's as easy a title as any at the moment, didn't understand the old man's insistence."

"'Grandfather, you need not trouble yourself. I may be in semi-retirement, but I still know how to cast a few runes and give that young man a few well-deserved bumps and wrong turns in life. You just go about your day as you normally do and leave the scary stuff to me.'"

"Such words coming from the tiny person partially amused the old man, but also alarmed him further. He then dashed to the garden gate to hold it so that the fairy could not leave. He hoped the fairy would listen to him. However, no sooner than he had laid his hand on the latch to hold the gate in place did the fairy address the old man from the other side of the wall."

"'Grandfather, maybe you don't know how this works. As long as something is natural, like trees, the sea, the earth underfoot, and, yes, stones...well, not all stones, but we won't go into that now...those of us who are, what did you used to call us? Hmm. Can't remember just now. But, those like me. We can pass through natural things. Made by the hand of man? Many we can't pass through. That's why you don't see many of my few brothers and sisters remaining living in your high-rise apartments or scooting about on the subway in Seoul. Although, I did hear of one of us falling into a subway train years ago and having to ride around for weeks, living off the groceries people were carrying and drinking hidden sips from water bottles and sodas. I bet you wondered why you didn't have a full water bottle sometimes? Easiest thing in the world to sneak from an overworked, too busy to notice his or her surroundings, human in the afternoon.'"

"'What was I talking about…? Oh, yes, I can find those evil doers much more quickly by my way of travel than if we walk together.'"

"'Can you fly?' the old man asked the fairy, who replied that she didn't exactly fly, more like wished herself from place to place. The old man then insisted that the two of them walk together, and that the fairy promise to not skip ahead and confront the college students without the old man."

"Before the old man stepped out the gate, he walked back to the windowsill to check if maybe, just maybe, the glass had fallen off to the ground. He was greeted by empty ground, save for a few leaves. However, tucked in the crack between the window and the sill a bit of paper attracted his eye. Extracting it, he saw that it was a large bank note, wrapped around an oval piece of lavender sea glass. It appeared that the robber had left behind payment for his deed, with one of the old man's favorite pieces. On the spur of the moment, the old man dropped the glass and the large bank note into his pocket. He then turned and joined the fairy on the other side of the garden wall."

"The fairy, always wary of promises, but quite fond of the old man who had been her companion for so long, nodded and, turning, picked up a small bit of driftwood lying by the wall, blown there eons ago from the bleached whiteness of the wood, and, holding it out to the old man, called for him to hold onto it. That way they could walk together, without the old man actually touching the fairy and then being subject to the old curses. The old man smiled and, grasping the other end of the stick, he stepped out smartly, with a surprisingly youthful vigor, forgetting the need of a walking stick, and the two hurried down the narrow coastal lane in search of the students."

"The path, as most ancient footpaths do, followed the contours of the land, at times sloping down to the shore and, at times, climbing into the dunes and small hills overlooking the low forests and then the beaches. Much like the path we took to this spot today, even with a number of places where large boulders littered the beach. Why, I wonder if there might be a fairy walking these paths later this evening? Using the seaside rock formations as hiding places?"

What? The young lady was suddenly alert, and no longer lulled to a near dream state by the teacher's rich voice. She sat perfectly still and tried to squeeze herself into the very rock, in fear that the teacher had actually seen her after all and was dropping hints to the students. If the student's took the hint and started to explore, they would find her in minutes. Once they had found her and, when more than a few would no doubt recognize one of the most famous young entertainers in the country, they would be like any other screaming fans and her illusion of sanctuary would be destroyed.

The young lady was slowly growing furious with the teacher for toying with her. She stole a look at his face, at least the side of his face she could see and, while initially angry, she suddenly saw what his students no doubt saw. A caring man, not old, but not young. One who had seen hardship in life, but had not let it define him. One who was a natural storyteller, and a natural teacher of men and women. And, of course, children. A man who could probably destroy someone with a well turned phrase, but a man who also understood the world and would not allow his students to badger a celebrity, or anyone for that matter. A good man was what the young lady saw and her anger began to melt away as she relaxed, settled back into her impromptu rock chair, and listened to the teacher continue the story.

"As the two odd companions walked, the old man wondered what his few neighbors might think when they saw him wandering the sea path with the strange child. He said as much to his little companion and she smiled as she answered. She told the old man that each neighbor or passerby would see what they expected to see. Some would see the old man heading down to the pasture to check on the herd, dragging a small stick along like a little boy, which would cause the old sisters just at the end of the road to chuckle about the old man's mind. The group of fisher ladies who were heading down to the rocks about fifty meters in front of them would see the old man leading a cow, for that's what the fisher ladies always saw and would always see."

"The old man nodded at the perfectly sensible answer, given that he was certain a fairy could appear as whatever the fairy desired."

"After several minutes of weaving through a particularly rocky section of the path, the two spied a small group of young men in the distance. The fairy, eager to exact her revenge and return to the comforts of her little cave house, began to drag harder on the driftwood to pull the old man to increase his pace. The old man, more reflective, resisted and spoke to the fairy about her intentions and the agreement that the old man would find out the facts before the fairy did any lasting harm."

"'Spirit one, why are you so eager to do ill to these strangers? Have you other grudges you wish to avenge?' the old man asked, slowing his pace and upsetting the fairy."

"'Sir, other grudges? No, not grudges, but justice must be served. He who does wrong should have wrong reflected back on him. What do you think we should do? Warts and boils? I had an uncle who loved to spread warts and boils on bad little children. Maybe love lost, for the rest of his life? I had a particularly severe aunt who would cast love lost potions on all manner of men and women whom she thought undeserving of some earnest companion. Maybe an infestation of…fleas?'"

"'Wait. Please, kind little princess of the garden, I hold you to your promise. I will ascertain the boy's guilt or innocence and then, and only then, we will discuss the consequences and agree to such, before you unleash your powers.'"

"The fairy paused her tugging at the driftwood and looked up at the old man. She scrunched up her little nose and spoke softly to the old man, almost in the voice of a angel."

"'Sir, grandfather, did the sea glass not please you? Did you not trade many shiny items, whether of real, human value is immaterial, they were wonderful to me. Did I not please you and bring some small happiness to your hard life, grandfather?' the little fairy asked, her large, mournful eyes tugging at the old man's heart."

"The little fairy's heartfelt words struck deep into the kind old man's own heart and he fought back the beginning of tears, nodding his head at the little companion as he collected himself enough to speak, which he finally did."

"'Yes, little saint of the sea grasses, you have, for many months and years now, brought me singular joy. For that, I am eternally grateful. I do puzzle as to why you allowed the small exchanges. And, of course, why you chose to be hidden all these years,' the old man replied."

"'Sir, hidden I was not. When you walked alone down to the sea to collect your herd in the evening, have you never wondered why you never stumbled on a stray rock blown into your path by the unforgiving winds? When you are lying asleep and, suddenly, an unexpected noise rouses you from slumber and, apprehensive, you begin to climb out of bed and reach for your sturdiest walking stick in case someone is poaching the chickens, or robbing the garden? Then, inexplicably, you have a sense of peace settle over your sturdy, but tired shoulders and you slide back under your covers and forget about the disturbance? Have you never wondered why your little grandchildren love to play at the double pond, even abandoning their toys to play hide and seek with the 'tiny bird' in the rock wall?' the small fairy asked, her voice quivering."

"'What? That was you? I always thought they had made all that up,' the old man interjected with surprise. 'And, those others? Does that mean all the hard work I've done over these years has really been just your powers?' the old man asked with shock."

"'No! Grandfather. No! I would never bring shame to you by using my limited abilities to do your work, or to shape your life. That is your doing. All of it. I've just been keeping an eye on the accidents and the fools who might do harm. Not all, mind you, as I can't be everywhere, all the time. But, I'm rather fond of this footpath to the sea and the rocks lying about. So, I didn't want to see you stumble, hit your head on a wall or a sea boulder, or have some of the old, not very nice goblins or other old ones sneak up on you, and then have to stand by you as you expired on this lovely coast, which would then be a sad coast due to your untimely loss.'"

"At that point, the little fairy was nearly crying as she spoke of the old man's possible demise. She was quite attached to her landlord and, over the years, had taken it upon herself to be his guardian and earthly angel. The old man, touched by the little person's emotions, leaned over to comfort her and reached out to drape his right arm over her shoulders....'"

Suddenly, the children in the audience began to shout a warning to the teacher, trying to will the old man's arm from touching the fairy, since they knew scary, unknown curses would result if anyone touched a fairy.

The teacher, waving his arms to regain control of the students, stood up from leaning on the large boulder and began to pace back and forth as he spoke. Because of the teacher's stride and because the flat area between his boulder lectern and the jumble of rocks where the young lady was hiding was only a few meters wide, the teacher came within an arm's length of her hiding place each time he turned and paced back toward the boulder.

The young lady, already intrigued by the tale and unable to tear herself away, was, for the first time in forever, actually turning off her phone since her manager had the ability to track her phone and she didn't want her manager, or her aunt, both of whom were on the trip with her, to wander into the teacher's story, interrupting and asking after the young lady. So, she had been distracted for a moment, but then heard the teacher's footsteps, throwing her hands to her throat at the risk of sudden discovery.

Scooting back deeper into the rocks so that the teacher would not see her if his stride took him closer to her hiding place, the young lady found another space between the rocks to listen to the story. Since she was a bit farther away, she realized she would no longer be able to hear the children's questions or comments clearly, but was still able to hear most of what the teacher was saying. To his credit, he paused when he turned during his pacing so that his voice was directed at the students so that they could hear him clearly. He had also begun to raise his voice, as the waves were getting closer to the small clearing and the rocks. Since the tide was coming in, making his voice harder to hear, he had compensated by talking quite loud.

The young lady was grateful for the sea's influence in getting the teacher to speak loudly, but she was also keeping a close eye on the water to ensure she did not get caught in the waves if they made it all the way to her hiding place. Turning her attention back to the teacher and the story, she tucked her scarf into her jacket and pulled her dark hoodie tighter over her wavy hair to silence some of the wind, which helped her to hear even better.

Joining the children's chorus of warning, but only in the lightest of whispers, the young lady secured yet a third, less comfortable perch, and turned her attention to wondering what the teacher would say next. Would the old man touch the fairy, thereby negating any good the fairy had done him, and releasing all manner of required curses? Or, would the fairy evade the old man's touch as before?

"What? Oh, yes, you are all worried about the old man touching the fairy. Maybe he forgot? No? Maybe he isn't afraid of fairy curses? Besides, how bad could a curse be from such an obviously nice little garden spirit? Let's continue and see what happens."

"As the old man's arm hovered just above the fairy's shoulders, a sudden shout from down the beach distracted the old man and the fairy alike. From what the old man could tell, the college students were in a circle and seemed to be yelling at the one who had avoided the old man's eyes, thereby incurring suspicion as the thieving culprit. Both the old man and the fairy then forgot their emotional sharing and hurried down the beach to see what was up."

"Arriving at the small group of youths, the old man scanned the beach and the hills above for anyone who might be watching, for he was quite worried that the little fairy, in her anger at catching the thief or thieves, might turn them all into goats or fish out of water, which would, of course, excite all manner of reactions from the humble island folk who lived nearby. At the least, they would spread rumors that the old man was in league with witches and demons. At the worst, they would storm the beach and attempt to mete out public justice to such a heinous criminal. Such is the life of unthinking mobs, the old man sighed to himself."

"Fortunately, other than the diving ladies who were far out in the surf and probably could not see them clearly, no other souls walked the beaches at that hour. So, clearing his throat, the old man called to the youths."

"'Young sirs, may my friend and I be of assistance?' was all the old man said, yet, when the youths stopped their bickering and turned to face the old man, they all stepped back in shock and fear, with two of the youth's even falling to the sand to plead forgiveness."

"Puzzled, the old man scratched his thinning head and, speaking softly so as only the fairy could hear him, spoke of the youths' odd behavior."

"'Can it be that we are so fearsome that strong lads grovel in fear at the sight of us?' the old man asked. The fairy smiled up at him and whispered back. 'Grandfather, it's not us they fear, it's their own guilty consciences that are causing them to seek forgiveness even before we have challenged them.'"

"'But how...?' the old man began, but the fairy silenced him with a wave and then pointed at the youths, which elicited even more mournful howls from three of the young men. However, the probable culprit, the one the old man suspected of taking the sea glass, was standing stock still, staring straight at the fairy, then glancing at the old man and then back at the fairy, as if he were a pillar of strength amongst his colleagues who were obviously overwrought with something."

"Finally, the howls and whimpering began to subside and only low murmuring could be heard as the old man and the fairy stepped closer to the group. As they got closer, the young, suspected culprit took several slow, steady steps to stand in front of his colleagues, head held high, as if he was fully aware that the executioner's song was soon to be heard, but he was starkly unafraid of his fate."

"As the old man and the fairy stood just at arm's length…what? No, the old man's arm length, not the little fairy's, yes. So, as they stood closer together, the young man bowed to the old man and spoke in a voice, respectful, but far, far away."

"'Grandfather, my apologies for my friends. They all counseled me to return to your house and make immediate reparations for my actions, saying that vulgar payment of money was more of an insult that a fair trade. They are blameless. Please do not unleash that fury,'…the young man nodded to the fairy…'on their innocent souls. For me, I welcome whatever your furious beast brings. I am at peace.'"

"The old man, both impressed by the youth's confession and willingness to pay for his crime, but thoroughly confused at the young man's description of the gentle little fairy as a fury and a beast, spoke softly to the student."

"'Son, young man, thank you for your candor and your unflinching willingness to sacrifice yourself, but I'm at a loss to understand why you took the glass and, now, why you look upon us as some avenging demons ready to tear you limb from limb.'"

The students in the teacher's audience let out a collective gasp at the vivid description, so the teacher paused and explained the idiom, 'limb from limb' was not literal as in the days of old, but more as a metaphor for severe, but just punishment. He then resumed.

"'Young man, I assure you I mean you no harm. I simply seek the why of all this.'"

"'Grandfather, it is not you I fear, but the talons and fangs of your hellhound beast of vengeance. Even with my admitted guilt and my being at peace with my actions, I am, after all, only human, and this flesh will no doubt feel the pain. So, in advance, I apologize for anything I say or do as your beast devours me alive.'"

"Now the old man was really puzzled. He looked at the little child of a fairy and then at the stoic young man and then leaned over to see around the youth to his friends still cowering in the sand, all three at that point, and grumbled that he was even more confused. The old man then took a step closer to the youth, which, of course, meant the fairy did as well, since the two were still holding onto the bit of driftwood."

"As the old man leaned over to look deep into the youth's eyes, the howls from his friends increased. The youth, however, did not flinch, nor utter even the smallest of cries as the old man's breath landed on the youth's cheek and the fairy's tiny breath landed on the student's left hand, hanging motionless at his side."

"Looking into the youth's face, the old man suddenly jerked his head back in shock at what he had seen reflected there in the depths of the student's dark eyes. Nearly losing his grip on the driftwood, as the old man's hand involuntarily recoiled from the beast he had seen in the student's eyes, a quick glance told the old man that the little fairy was still just a girl child. But, what the youth and his friends saw was a nearly indescribable hellhound, with eyes of flaming, blood red pits, teeth as long as those imagined on Dragon Rock, and fur a swirling mix of screaming faces of those who had been devoured by the devil's beast over the ages. Their twisted, agonized faces crawling about the fur and skin of the demon beast for all eternity. The horror! The horror!"

A loud shout went up from the collective voices of the both excited and frightened children. Even the young lady gasped out loud at the horrifying description of the demon beast, to the point she nearly fell off her perch into the nearby, encroaching water.

The children, who, unlike the young lady, were well acquainted with the teacher's clever tales, were more excited-scared, rather than frightened. They felt his stories were like the rollercoasters at the amusement parks, just with words. Unfortunately for the young lady, since that was her first time hearing the teacher, she felt he was far too graphic and was truly terrifying the students. Part of her was becoming angry and wanted to give the teacher a piece of her mind. But, both her curiosity at how the story resolved and her desire to selfishly protect her own privacy prevented her from jumping out and demanding the teacher stop scaring the children.

After a couple of minutes, the excited children quieted down and the teacher chuckled at some of the student's comments, which pleased the students, for the teacher was signaling that he was impressed with their use of English. However, the young lady was angered further, as she thought the American's laughter was being overly mean to the students, which, while not unusual for a Korean teacher, was rare in guest teachers. Maybe a westerner can be a mean teacher as well, she thought.

"Okay. Calm down now. Yes, the reflection in the student's eyes was a little scary, but you all have weathered scarier tales. Remember the one about the ghosts wandering the old Army post at Yongsan? That new park? What about those tales of Edgar Allen Poe we read and discussed earlier in the class? Yes, scary, so let's continue."

"The old man, feeling he might have imagined the image from the youth's eyes, gingerly held the driftwood with the tips of his fingers and spoke to the young man in a very grandfatherly voice."

"'Son, just what is it that you see and, pray, tell me true why you have taken the glass, such a small thing that has kept an old man happy through the years. Which, had you asked, I would have gladly shared with you. And, thank you for leaving the lavender piece, it was a particular favorite, and the large bank note, which I am returning to you.'"

"'Sir, grandfather, you are kind and understanding of such a wretch as I. No, I cannot say why I took those bits of…those tiny bits of broken glass. I left the pitiful payment and one bit of glass, as I knew you would be pained to have your little treasures gone, so could not bear taking them all, sir.'"

"'As to what I see, sir, standing in all its horrifying glory, sir, is the beast of man's evil and injustice to other men and the world around them. In the demon eyes of the beast, I see petty revenge and countless, endless conflicts, which have crushed much of the beauty in this world. In the face, I see the monsters of our sleep, those night terrors that children know so well and we tend to forget as we age and become dulled to the natural world around us. In the beast's paws, or are they hooves? I see the downtrodden crushed by those who rob men and women of their dignity, reducing so many to lives of misery and destitution. In the ears I see the temples of man built up and torn down over the centuries, each new god crushing the old. In the beast's coat…sorry, sir, this is the most painful to describe…in the coat I see the faces, at least, I think they are faces, of the most evil, wretched, doomed souls that no one should ever be allowed to witness and walk the earth freely. Tortured wraiths of a disturbed side of human nature, giving any decent man or woman pause to wonder if such nightmares may inhabit his or her own mind. Waiting in the shadows to manifest. Waiting just behind our morals and our religions, behind our decency, ready to devour not only our own short lives, but those loved ones around us. Madness, sir, I think I see in the beast, sir. Madness and a vengeful justice that is remorseless as it is vicious.'"

"'Your demon beast's anger, caused by my guilt, has brought forth his hellish brethren, no doubt sensing the coming carnage. From the rocks just there, twisted goblins are joined by nameless, lesser horrors, ready to snatch away any shreds or morsels that your hound tosses aside. The sea nymphs, usually happy and playful, smell the abject fear, sending the little nymphs to the very edge of a feeding frenzy, as they throw themselves up the beach to reach us.'"

"The farmer, looking to the areas where the young man had motioned with his head, only saw a few small crabs dodging some sea birds climbing about the rocks. At the water line, the old man only saw piles of seaweed, twisted up in bits of driftwood. Shaking his head, he refocused on the young man's next words."

"'Dear grandfather, unleash your dragon hound, your demon beast, your distant herald of the gods' and nature's unrelenting vengeance, and rend this flesh asunder on this white sand. And, fear not that my mortal remains will long stain nature's beauty, for, whatever your hound's horrific brethren miss, the birds and animals will carry away any fleshy remnants. The bones will bleach and become brittle with time, falling into beach dust. The sea, sand, and salt, aided by the time-honored winds, will scrub the blood stains clear, cleansing this island cove's nature and those who may bear witness of any stain I may have brought upon my friends and family. Tear away great beast! Call your little terrors! Do not toy with me any longer!'"

"With that last, shouted statement, the brave youth knelt down before the demon beast, as he saw the fairy, and, with eyes wide open, held out his arms to receive the vicious, gnashing teeth and flesh ripping talons of the huge, nightmarish, demonic…!"

"Stop it! Stop!" the young lady suddenly screamed from behind the rocks.

All heads jerked to look toward the screaming rocks, with the teacher falling silent and turning to look as well.

"I demand you cease this instant!" the young lady then yelled at the surprised teacher as she pounced from her hiding place onto the clearing to confront the storyteller, her hair flying out of her hood, with her scarf flapping like the wings of some crazed seabird.

"Cease this horrid tale immediately! I am going to call the school. I'm going to…!"

The young lady was abruptly silenced by the pandemonium that had broken out all around her at her abrupt appearance.

"Aiyee!"

"Manyeo!"

"Witch! Witch!"

"Hideous goblin!"

"No! Evil sea witch!"

"Sanyang-gae! Sasin!"

"Save us! The demon hound is nigh!"

Many of the students were shrieking at the top of their lungs, in a confusion of English and Korean, at the appearance of an apparent apparition at one of the tensest moments in the teacher's tale.

Others had actually fallen over themselves as they retreated to a group of weathered boulders on the opposite side of the small clearing.

Several of the smaller children had huddled together in the back and were reciting an old Korean nursery rhyme for warding off witches.

Looking around, the young lady was shocked speechless at the children's fear of her sudden appearance. She immediately turned to again yell at the teacher and blame him for the children's obvious fear of a little lady like herself, which was, in her angry mind, a direct result of the teacher's horrible antics in telling such stressful tales.

"Sir! You…you…!" the young lady began, but was silenced by the teacher's quiet smile, and then his calm voice, directed, not at her, but at his frightened charges.

Ignoring the stammering young lady, the teacher called to the students to calm down. He directed the older, less surprised students to gather up the more frightened, younger ones. He consoled many of the little ones himself, using both Korean and English. He walked among the students as a calming emissary, allaying fears, telling the children not to point at their uninvited, surprise guest, and not to blame her for scaring them.

Blame me? The young lady was both surprised and angry that the teacher was walking around, calming the students and telling them to not blame her, telling them that she was not familiar with the class and the series of mysteries they had been reading that term.

Gradually, as the young lady watched child after child lower his or her accusing fingers, which had been pointed at her as if to ward off whatever evil she had brought with her from her hiding place in the rocks, she began to realize that she had delivered real, non-literary fear to the children, jumping out of her hiding place like some movie witch bent on devouring the small children.

Suddenly, the young lady was horribly, almost tragically embarrassed, and immediately began to bow to the students close by, even though they were much younger than she, and begged their forgiveness for her thoughtlessness. She did so until the teacher returned to the front, one of the smaller children trailing behind him, holding the teacher's hand while hiding behind his legs.

Arriving at the apologizing apparition, the teacher whispered encouraging words to the small child, a little girl, and gently pushed her toward the bowing young woman.

The young lady turned to the young girl and, avoiding the searching eyes of the teacher, bowed to the little child and, head held low, asked her for forgiveness.

The young girl, emboldened by hushed encouragement from her classmates, stepped closer to the unexpected guest and, reaching out with her tiny hand, poked the young woman in her right side, several times. The child then carefully tugged on the apparition's scarf, but just for an instant. The young girl then smiled broadly, nodded to the teacher, and, turning triumphantly to her classmates, declared the feared, evil, ugly sea witch to be a human after all.

In English, the teacher encouraged the young girl, who then repeated, with help from her classmates, that the evil, hideous, black clad, wart covered, green-gill death witch from the sea rocks was just a big girl, or maybe a young lady after all, and not there to have them all for supper.

Shocked at the child's vivid description and still embarrassed, the young lady started to step backwards to the path to the rocks, clutching her bag for some level of mental support. She did not want to face the teacher after such an embarrassing turn of events, so had resolved to shout an apology to him and the class just before disappearing in shame into the rocks.

Unfortunately, the seawater had crept up to the path she had taken earlier and she was now trapped between the teacher and his class and the jumble of slippery rocks being covered in the tide, much of which held bits of slimy seaweed, which the young lady could have sworn looked like the flowing hair of sea nymphs depicted in the teacher's tale.

Shaking the random imagery out of her head, the surprised guest looked back and realized her only dry avenue of escape would be to walk up the clearing, through the jumble of students nervously resettling onto their towels and small blankets after their sudden scare.

Frozen in place, without a good solution to her escape, the young lady had totally forgotten about protecting her privacy and was mainly concerned with ensuring the students were calmed and that no ill effect resulted from her selfish appearance.

Turning to the teacher, who seemed twice as tall and much older up close, the young lady bowed low, raised herself, and asked for his forgiveness for her disrupting the class.

"And terrifying the little ones with your wraith-like descent from the 'demon rocks' to devour us…?" the teacher responded, his grin quite annoying to the young lady.

"My sincerest apologies, for everything, teacher," the young lady replied, in the best English she could muster, while muttering a couple of less pleasant words under her breath in Korean.

"We were not really scared, teacher," declared the little girl who had tested if the stranger was human or not. "We were just surprised by the scary lady, and the story was just getting to the good part."

"No, little sister, I'm sure you were not scared. And, I'm sure the young lady had good intentions. From what I could understand over the screaming when she appeared, I think she leapt from the demon rocks to protect you all from the scary tale. Which, I know you think is not as scary as some others you've read or heard this term, but she may have never read Poe or have even seen a scary movie. She may be one of those sheltered youth who do not go out in the world to experience life, but lurks about in the shadows of the coastal rocks, watching others, wondering what life is like with the humans."

"What? Yojeong! She's…she's a fairy…?" little sister asked, backing away from the young lady. "A good fairy, or…the other kind?"

"Well, miss?" the teacher asked, a smile behind his eyes.

"What? A spirit of the rocks? A sea fairy? Yes, I was listening. I just…just couldn't bear that the children were being frightened so," the young lady stated defiantly, forgetting to deny she was a fairy.

"No need to apologize, young miss. Even though you are not with the school, I think we can make an exception and allow you to join us. That is, if you wish to listen to the story with the rest of the students. Or, do you prefer to wade through the rising waters, and all those hidden sea creatures, to regain your perch by the cradle boulder to peek between the rocks at us as we finish our tale?"

Sudden red color crawled up the young lady's neck and cheeks at the teacher's comments, which revealed, but only to the young lady, that the teacher had seen her earlier and had probably played up the recent dramatic scene in the story to see if he could pique her interest. She was both angered and amused at the teacher's antics.

However, instead of getting angry and acting petulant, which was a routine trait for young people in the entertainment business, the young lady bowed again, turned, took little sister's hand and marched over to a low, smooth rock and, helping the little girl to sit, then sat down herself and smiled at the teacher as if to say, 'Please continue.'

Little sister, shivering a bit from her bold confrontation with the possible sea witch and from an uptick in the wind off the nearby water, pulled her jacket closer, causing the new arrival to pull off her scarf and offer it to the brave little warrior. Little sister objected at first, but then relented and cuddled up to the scarf and her new friend.

The teacher, amused at the young lady's harmless, but entertaining discomfort, and impressed with her obvious concern for the children's wellbeing, delayed the return to the story when he saw a couple of mobile phones appear and turn to take pictures of their guest.

"Class, remember the rule about phones? What is it?" the teacher called, looking directly at the teens who had slipped their phones out. "And…how do we treat our guests?"

"Never photograph without permission…always welcome and respect a guest's space," the students mumbled in unison, and all those who had phones out, stopped short of taking snaps and returned the phones to packs or pockets.

"Now, does anyone know where we were? Yes? At the beach? After the demon beast ate the…? What? Oh, before anything happened. Right, let's return to the beach and the encounter. That is, of course, if such meets with the approval of our new colleague?"

The young lady, her face still reddened from embarrassment, nodded and, after listening to something whispered to her by little sister, which was to answer the teacher in English, the young lady added a verbal response.

"Thank you again, sir, for inviting me to listen. Do your best, teacher, sir," the young lady said in very well spoken English, to the beaming approval of little sister.

The teacher bowed his head ever so slightly to the new listener, and then gave a couple of still excited older children a knowing eye, so that they would not again be tempted to take a quick picture of their guest, who, while vaguely familiar looking to the teacher, evidently had been recognized by several of the children.

"As I was saying, the youth was describing what he saw standing beside the old man, who only saw the sweet little fairy, and certainly did not see the other, darker island denizens stealthily approaching. To the young man, the fairy's image was both terrifying and fateful at the same time. The young man refused to cower or to run, preferring to stand, to both answer for his crime, and to protect his friends from the fiend and its brethren. However, the old man was not accepting of the young man's refusal to tell him why the youth had taken the glass, so the old man pressed his case."

"'Young sir, I must again beseech you to give your justification for making off with the bits of glass, whose value is truly only to me, and, in a way, my companion here.'"

"The youth then shook his head one more time and, with the same fatalistic politeness, asked the old man to not press the youth on his reasons. Suddenly, the fairy reached out and took the youth's hand in hers, nearly recoiling in shock at the images flooding into her fairy consciousness from the young man. The young man, who had seen the demon hound raising its talons to rip his arm off, also swayed at the sudden psyche connection with the tiny spirit of the garden."

"For the briefest of moments, the youth's deep, years-long pain that he had held inside him was revealed to the fairy, and, through the driftwood connection, for the old man to see. Deep, numbing pain. The pain of a lost hope. The pain of a life missing half of its very soul. The never-ending pain of a loved one lost. A sibling snatched away in early life, never to sing again. Never to play. Never to talk of dreams with her brother on the shores near their home. Never to again search the high tide line for...."

"'Your sister?' the old man asked quietly, leaning forward to gaze into the now tranquil eyes of the young man. Tranquil, as the touch of the fairy, instead of searing pain, had released the youth's years of pent up internal pain, survivor anger and remorse, and deep yearning to be at his sister's side. The young man had been at peace when he had stood his ground, so the old man, through the offices of the fairy's power, had felt the inner source of that young man's strength."

"No one spoke. The other college students had ceased their moaning and were all now staring at the demon hound who had somehow transformed into a small child. A gentle child. Even the youth saw the fairy child and no longer saw the hellhound. However, to the youth and his friends, the image of the child was brief, as she then transformed into a small, white, warm and loving Jindo pup, sitting patiently by the old man and the youth as if waiting to be petted.

"'Yes, grandfather, my sister,' the youth answered. The youth then opened his jacket and, reaching into a pocket, he extracted a few bits of the remaining sea glass. He held out his hand with the glass to the old man."

"'Sir, here is the rest. If your beast decides to return to its darker half, I wouldn't want your glass to be stained with my worthless blood. Please take it with my apologies.'"

The old man nodded and took the glass. He then asked the boy, for even a college student is a young boy to a very old man, what had happened to the bulk of the sea glass. The youth responded with a long look and then a plaintive tale.

"'Grandfather, my sister and I used to go down to the sea to play. She would always delight in finding unique shells, or any shells for that matter. Everything, no matter how beautiful and complex, or simple and plain, was a marvel to her young eyes. We spent hours playing among the slipping dunes, shore rocks, and waving reeds, devising games with our few friends and telling each other of our dreams for the coming years. Our dreams sir, will forever be just that. Just dreams....'"

"'She was lost...?'"

"'Yes, sir. Lost. She and many of her young friends, sir.'"

"At sea...?'"

"'Yes, grandfather. On her first, long, overnight, that is, school fieldtrip. Taking a ferry countless others had taken over the years. Was to be here, on Jeju Island. Never in anyone's worst nightmares would we have thought something would happen. It was sudden, sir. Oh, so sudden.'"

"'She was...?'"

"'No, grandfather, she was never...never recovered. She and many, too many, of her friends were never found. Lost to the sea forever. Doomed to wander between this life and the next, without her proper funeral rites. Without her little body being laid to rest in a proper grave. Without the words of her family around her and her ancestors guiding her, sir. Forever adrift. Forever...adrift.'"

"'And the glass? It reminds you of her...?'"

"'The glass? Sir, yes, the sea glass. We used to find it, collect it. Place it in the sun as you do, sir, on your windowsill by that charming double pond and enchanting garden. Yes, we did that, sir. For some time, I had forgotten the glass. I think...I think I might have been trying to mask the pain. I think. Well, I saw your sill full of that sea glass she loved so much and, something, sir, something took over my mind and I could only see that ship in my mind, sir. All those children, all those people, struggling to stay afloat as the ferry dragged them down to their watery graves. And the debris, sir. The debris is still, to this day, washing up on the southern shores and even over on Shandong. To this day, sir, all manner of debris washes ashore.'"

"'Yes, son,' the old man said quietly, as he slowly returned the few bits of smooth sea glass to the young man's hand, causing the young man to choke on his next words, so the old man finished for him."

"'Endless bits of newly broken glass…from the ferry?'"

"'Yes, grandfather, endless broken pieces. For months, I'd go down to the sea, looking for her, never finding her, but finding all manner of glass. Much of it was still jagged, not yet smoothed by time and the sea. At first, I left it, sad and full of self pity that I was suffering and they had stolen my sister. As time passed, I then began…I began….'"

"'To return it to the sea…?'"

"'Yes, grandfather. Return it to the sea. To my sister. For her to enjoy and, maybe, just maybe, for her to send it back to me one day. One day.'"

"'So, my little pile of sea glass reminded you…?'"

"'Sir, at your garden gate, I was gripped by something like a dark thief from the lowest gutter. I saw the glass and, suddenly, I just knew what to do with all the anger bottled up inside me. All I could think of was that ferry, and all those children, and all that debris, and how that glass, those very pieces at your window, might be a bottle one of those children had used, maybe for the last time. Maybe a cup a little boy had gotten as a souvenir at the Incheon ferry port. Maybe…maybe a flake of a mirror that my sister had looked into for the last time? Maybe….'"

"The youth, his energy spent, lapsed into silence as the old man took the young man's shoulders and held the youth for a long minute, allowing the young man to finally shed years of pent up tears. But, quietly, as a strong young man should. With dignity and deference to his sister's memory."

"After the old man stepped away, he realized he was holding the driftwood, but there was no fairy at the other end. Looking around, he saw the fairy walking among the youth's friends, touching each one in turn on the cheek with her hand, knowing that the young men were seeing a gracious white Jindo nuzzling each one to help calm their fears and cleanse their heavy hearts. For, while his friends had known of his loss, none of his friends had realized the depth of his despair. They had been trying to not only get him to return the glass, but to stop throwing it back into the sea like a madman. Now, they were content, as the fairy had absorbed most of their shock and guilt. But, not all, as humans needed a little to learn long term lessons."

"The old man then saw the little fairy, as a white Jindo, chase the birds and crabs back to the rocks, and then bark three times at the edge of water, before returning to the old man's side."

"Digging in his coat pocket, the old farmer found the lavender piece of roundish glass, that, turned the right way, looked a little like a fish, and, with the bank note, handed it to the protesting youth."

"'Sir, no, not your favorite piece. Please, sir, I've done enough damage. I will find more. Please use the money, sir. I can't just steal your treasures.'"

"'Son, take this as a gift of the sea, for the sea and your sister. Carry your bits of heart out to that spit of rocks there and throw those shards of memories into the surf to share with your sister. For, your sister may be there, waiting for your visits when you come down to the sea, but she is also there with you when you sit down to an exam. She is with you on those travels to other lands. When you are happy and when you are sad. She may not have a common grave on a hillside somewhere, but she is buried in the hearts of all who loved her and cared for her. She may not have sat with the ancestors at a formal funeral, but, know this, that those ancestors walk with her under the waves to comfort her and guide her to the next life when she is ready.'"

"'Take her bits of heart down to the sea, young man, and, do not despair. Rejoice in her life and in yours. That you were spared her tragic path, so that you might blaze an even brighter one on this earth for the both of you, and those who come after. Go down to the sea, young man, and share your love with your sister and her friends. Take the shards back to the sea so that your sister and her friends, and countless others can shape them, craft them with their own hearts and, someday, toss them out of the surf into the paths of other brothers and sisters wandering the sandy beaches in search of their next adventure and delighting in the finding of that elusive shell or bit of colorful sea glass.'"

"With that, the young man stood, bowed low to the old farmer, turned, and, quietly, with only the sounds of the waves, the wind, the birds, and the distant rumble of weather beyond the hills, walked slowly down to the spit of rocks and, with a silent prayer, tossed the bits of polished glass back into the blue-green waves and the pale arms of his little sister."

As the teacher spoke the last words, his student audience was serenely silent. Even the little ones, touched by the young college student's words, were doing a good job of holding back their own emotions and tears. However, their unexpected guest was not as accustomed to the twists and turns of the teacher's tales.

The young lady was nearly doubled over and trying to control her silent sobbing at the poignancy of the young man's tale, with little sister patting the young miss on the back to comfort her. The teacher, mildly alarmed at the effect of the story on the guest, kept one eye on the young lady as he concluded the tale.

"After a few minutes, the other young men, one by one, walked out to join their friend on the rocks and, with silent support, prepared to stay there as long as the youth needed. They formed a semicircle around the youth and, from time to time, would look back toward the old man and the Jindo on the beach, as if to let the old man know that there would be no more groveling and that they would protect their friend with their last ounce of strength and blood, while he spent time with his sister at the sea."

"The old man, touched by the young man's story and amazed at the fairy's transformation from an agent of revenge to one of mercy and healing, said as much to the fairy, who had, again, taken up the other end of the driftwood."

"'Not a contradiction, mind you, grandfather,' said the fairy as they watched the youth and his friends, and while the fairy kept an eye on the lesser spirits who had been denied a meal. 'I think those boys will think twice and thrice about entering some enchanted garden in the future. Nice of you to give away our last bit of sea glass....'"

"'What? Really, you would deny that tragic young man...?' the old man began, but then stopped and laughed at himself with he saw the fairy's grinning face. 'Yes, you are the clever one, aren't you? Well, what now?'"

"'Breakfast. I think we need to return home and find something to eat.'"

"'Right, we did rush off, didn't we? By the way, just what does your kind eat out there in that little cave house? I've never been missing any eggs or vegetables. Just what do you...?'"

"The little fairy, skipping along beside the old man, that bastion of all small villages beside all seas everywhere, smiled and winked as she replied."

"'I don't think you want to know,' the fairy replied, using her free hand to mimic crawling, hopping, and slithering bugs, while at the same time winking at the few lesser goblins still trailing behind them. At that deadly fairy wink, those last beasts dove for the rocks and stayed hidden."

"Eww....!"

A collective noise of disgust rose up out of the teacher's assembled class at the implied edibles of the little fairy. Even the unintentional guest laughed with little sister and made ridiculous faces at the imagined bugs, as she wiped the last of the tears from her face.

The break in the tension of the story gave the teacher the signal that it was time to return his charges to school. He began instructing the older students to gather up the groups they were each leading, count heads, pick up belongings, get in a line, of a sort, to answer roll call, and to return to the bus parked up the road, away from the beach itself.

The tide had turned and was slowly making its way toward the lower reaches of the little park by the sea, so they all knew that they had timed it right, and that it was time to return to school and the rest of the more mundane, late afternoon lessons.

As each of the leaders presented their complete groups, the teacher checked them off a list he had in a folder he had extracted from his pack. He then texted a note to the school chaperon, who had appeared at the top of the hill to lead the students to the bus.

The last group, to which the brave little sister belonged, waved goodbye and bowed to the teacher and to the young lady, who had insisted little sister keep the scarf to stave off the rising winds. The leader of the group, a teen boy, was suddenly unable to actually speak when the young woman took the boy's hand to give him the hand of little sister. The poor teen was so shocked that his hand went limp and little sister just grabbed on to the group leader's backpack straps. Of course, little sister, ever practical, did have one last question before she walked up to the bus, trailing behind her group leader, who did keep an eye on her and finally took her little hand in his as she spoke.

"Teacher, sir, what do we do with the not scary lady from the scary rocks? She's not in our class? Do we throw her back to the sea?" little sister asked, shrugged, and walked up the hill, and, turning just before she disappeared around the curve in the road, she revealed a huge grin and shouted back with unbridled glee, holding up one end of the scarf.

"Thank you, singer lady. You are nicer than your pictures. And, you have a pretty voice in person," the beaming child called to the young lady.

Smiling broadly, little sister then disappeared around the curve as the young lady stood slack jawed and surprised. She then turned to look at the teacher and saw that recognition had finally settled into his eyes as well. She immediately blushed again and, fearing a horde of fans might come screaming over the hill at any moment, since one never knew who such people might call, as her manager had always warned her, she quickly looked around for an avenue of escape.

Oh, god, and her phone was turned off, the young lady realized, so how could she call for the car without showing her hand to the teacher and, wait, why isn't the teacher going with the students? What, is he staying back with her? Alone? On the beach...?

"Miss, don't worry," the teacher suddenly offered. "Little sister, Ha-eun, knows you are her little secret. And, the others who recognized you will hold their tongues until they are back at school."

"I...I don't understand. You...you knew? They knew?" the young lady asked.

"Of course. Well, sorry, not a first, I admit, for me. For them, instantly. Even with the unbranded clothes, the lack of heavy makeup, and no trailing entourage, it's hard to hide the face that launched a thousand songs," the teacher replied, as he finished packing his small rucksack. "But, those kids live on an island, and everyone knows everyone's business on an island. And, it's an island where a lot of people with, well, with a certain level of fame like to disappear to for a few days. So, these Jeju kids, they have come to respect the privacy of those in your shoes. They remind me of Manhattan kids, who yawn at all the celebrities and divas they encounter on a daily basis. But, yes, they are kids, and will be squealing with disbelief when they talk to their friends, and with no pictures to prove anything."

"I must admit, that was odd, how they were so polite about phone cameras," the young lady replied, feeling the redness in her face finally fading.

"They were being respectful of my rules, miss, and did not want to disappoint me. Now, might there be one or two odd angle shots that two or three of the more savvy might have taken? Probably. But, you can rest assured those will never see social media. Too many of these kids have seen their own families damaged by social media, so, even a known stranger to the island is treated with respect."

"Sir, thank you for understanding, and allowing me to join in, even after I almost scared everyone away," the young lady said with sincerity.

"No worries. Besides, they all now have a great story of their own to tell. No doubt your surprise appearance will help them with their English exercises, and give them some additional themes to think about," the teacher replied. "Many of these kids, especially the ones with long histories on Jeju Island, know someone or have a relative who has been lost at sea. Usually in the past. So, I find the tale resonates with them."

"Yes, I would imagine. The story was very interesting, and quite touching. I know I'll never look at sea glass the same way, ever again," the young lady answered, looking up to the road, still half-expecting to see fans appear.

Suddenly, the throaty sounds of a bus starting up disturbed the tranquility of the little beach clearing.

"Wait, aren't you going to miss your bus?" the young lady asked, noting the name of the school posted in the large bus's front window as it passed on the road above them.

"What? Oh, me? No. I'm only the contract English conversation and exposition instructor. I only get this group twice a week. I have to head over to the eastern side for my next class. Their chaperon is on the bus."

The two accidental companions then walked up to the road, the one that circled the island and which was never far from the island's many beaches and cliffs. A number of cars were parked along the road. A few houses, some farms, others summer homes, were scattered about.

At the path beside the road, the young lady turned back and looked longingly at the beach and the rocks below.

"Hard to leave, isn't it?" the teacher asked quietly.

"Yes. And, hard to believe just a few moments ago I was lost in a tale of mystery and then sorrow and then…compassion. I had wanted to escape people by climbing around among the rocks. Drives my aunt crazy. The one who travels with me. But, then I heard your story and, well, after my foolish entrance, I wanted to be part of the group."

"Yes, miss, it's hard to join in when everyone has already formed an opinion about you. Judges you on the slightest movement, item of clothing, way you speak, and anyone you speak to. Must be a very lonely life, at times."

The young lady nodded, extracted her phone, turned it on, and sent a quick text to her aunt, without reading any of those that popped up on her screen, and then dropped the phone back into her purse. She then turned to scan the roadside for her aunt and the large hire car, which should have been fairly close by. The teacher simply stood, as if waiting for something. Finally, the young lady turned back to the teacher.

"What days do you teach? Down here, I mean? Is that normal, teaching on the beach?"

"When down here on Jeju, today and Thursday. And, yes, you are welcome anytime. I have to warn you though, Ha-eun can be a handful, but she seems to like you, so you can sit with her."

"She was such a little sweetie. And, she didn't say anything, until saying goodbye. I wish I could do something," the young lady exclaimed.

"No need. She is happy she made a new friend. Even if only for a few minutes," the teacher replied. "All the kids were thrilled, young miss, that you stayed and joined in."

Smiling, the young lady nodded her thanks and turned to look around again for her car. The teacher remained, so she turned back.

"You said 'when down here?'" the young lady asked.

"Oh, this is almost a vacation. My main gig is up in Seoul," the teacher replied, not volunteering any details.

"Do you tell tall tales there as well?" the young lady asked, trying not to seem too interested.

The teacher looked out over the cars toward the beach and the rocks, and seemed to think a little too long about answering, but finally did.

"Only once a week, given our crazy schedules, miss. A little different. Once a month, the students interview older folks, war veterans, retired politicians, aged divas, and the like, then tell short tales of their subjects' exploits. In English. Other days, I spin similar tales as today. Thursdays in Dosan Park, a pretty place, just at the edge of…," the teacher replied, with his last bit finished by his temporary companion.

"…the edge of Sinsa-dong. Yes, I know the park. Quite the oasis in an otherwise frantic area," the young lady replied, then continued, a note of wistfulness in her voice. "That's why I like coming down here, to Jeju. It's calm, the people are nice and don't press, even if they recognize someone. Jeju doesn't judge, teacher. Jeju just is. I can come here, wander the villages, wear whatever, make a mess of my bingsu, eat anything without fear, smudge my makeup, and even, well, let my hair down."

The young lady, beaming her signature pixie smile, then turned to the ocean and raised her voice almost to a shout.

"I can hum to the sea, or sing to the gulls. The sea just keeps being the sea. The gulls just fly by, going on their way. The world just goes about its business of being the world, without noticing me. Jeju doesn't judge, teacher. Jeju just is."

The teacher, smiling thoughtfully at the young lady's sudden joie de vivre, nodded in silence as she quieted down after several passing tourists looked toward the two. The young lady then turned back to the teacher, with a look of concern on her face as she spoke.

"Sir, don't you need to get to your next class? I know from my…my high school days, that headmasters get angry if contract teachers are late."

The teacher looked down at the worried eyes that had graced countless stages, screens, posters, and advertising over the years and, for only a few seconds, allowed himself to marvel that the young woman hadn't lost her inner grace in the torturous, unending mill of her business.

"Young miss, thank you for your sincere concern, but, as you might have expected, I'm not Korean," the teacher answered with a grin. "I'm from the South. Southern U.S. And we don't leave a young lady alone on the side of the road. We wait until her ride arrives. And, yes, I considered offering you a ride, but I think that would be mistaken for being too forward. And, my guess is that irate looking, steely-eyed lady who is rushing this way and probably wondering what sort of crazy you are talking to, with the large limo creeping along behind her, is your aunt, or manager, and your ride. So, I will ask your leave now, and, take care. And, don't worry. The fact that you jumped out of your hiding place ready to protect a bunch of children, strangers, from my overly colorful tale, shouts out that the human side is still quite strong in you. No chance of losing that. Good-bye."

"Good-bye! And, thank you!" the young lady called as the strange American teacher bowed to her, then to the arriving aunt, and, turning, walked along the road toward a group of cars.

"Dear, where have you been?" the overprotective aunt scolded, her suspicious eyes following the departing foreigner. "Did your mobile die again? I bought you that backup battery! Did it die as well? Really, you can't just disappear. What if the insurance guys heard about it? Your premiums would skyrocket. Really, what am I…? Dear, are you listening? Who was that foreigner? What did he want? Did he take pictures? Were you down on the beach? Did your feet get wet in the surf? Where is your scarf? Really, what am I to do with you…?"

Somewhere on the southern coast of Jeju, far from the screaming crowds of Seoul, Tokyo, or Hong Kong, a young singer smiled as the shadow of the quiet teacher from the seashore faded into the background of winding hills and coves of Jeju Island's southern shore. She vaguely heard her aunt and then, once the car door had been opened for her, she also heard her manager's distant voice calling for her to get out of the wind.

As she turned and looked down to the sea one last time before she had to depart, the young woman took a long mental image of the area, the beach, the rocks, the small clearing, the sea foam laced waves with enchanted seaweed and mythic creatures, and, to her right, the surprising sight of a far off cottage, just like the one the teacher had described. She strained to see if there was a front garden with a double pond, but the quaint little house was too far away to see details. Maybe next time, she smiled to herself.

Turning to climb into the car, as her driver stepped away and just before she ducked into her seat, the young singer also saw a long spit of rocks stretching out into the surf at a little secluded beach where several lady divers were heading out to work the sea. Along the stretch of rocks touching the beach, two youngsters were merrily playing with a small, tannish-white dog. Maybe a Jindo.

The young singer then smiled even more broadly at the local reminders of the teacher's tale of the old man, the fairy, the young man, and his sister, and how so many lives can be connected, even when no one expected it.

Yes, the young singer thought, and even when one is too blind to see.

After the door had closed, the young singer turned to her travel manager and asked for the itinerary. Looking it over, she then asked for a pen, made a couple of changes to the schedule, and then handed it back to the manager. The manager was wise, so said nothing, but the aunt was a little less passive, so took the sheet and scanned the changes just made.

"What? The mayor's lunch? How can you change that? What? Has your inner prima donna taken over? An English lesson? What English lesson? On Thursday? How do you have time for English lessons? And, what gift for what little sister? Who…? Really, what am I to do with you…?"

The sounds of her aunt's exasperated voice faded into the background as the young singer pressed the window button, and, as the window retracted, breathed in the rich, revitalizing sea air of Jeju Island.

English lessons on the beach? No one would believe her, which is exactly what the young singer needed. And, Dosan Park story time? We'll have to leave that to think about later, the young singer decided.

Jeju. A land of more complexities than the young singer, originally only seeking a momentary escape, had imagined, and, if she could survive her aunt's worrying, a land that she wanted to explore just a little more in depth. Maybe take the time to check out the lava tubes. Maybe get up early to climb the sunrise crater. Maybe return to that mountain grotto. Maybe wander that western beach where she had seen the hwangap party the other evening. Maybe try to ride one of the famous Jeju horses after a hike on Mt. Hallasan.

As the large, roomy car picked up speed, the young singer smiled at the retreating beach, musing further on her accidental encounter.

Perhaps take a long, slow walk down by those old stone and thatched houses and the windswept beach just beyond, the young singer thought. And, if she were fortunate and the stars aligned, maybe, just maybe, find a bit of colorful sea glass to marvel at, cherish for one fleeting moment, and then, carefully, oh so very carefully, toss the precious bit back to the sea, with a prayer for a loving brother and his brave little sister, and for all lost souls who have gone down to the sea, never to return.

INTERLUDE VIII

Once the Jeju Island tale was complete, the writer tried to read the creature's face for a long series of heartbeats, but was frustrated by the beast's stringy hair, and the fact that the beast shifted its gaze to stare at everything in the enclosure, except the captive writer.

Even the tiny ones were confused by their master's odd, silent and reflective behavior. Instead of emerging at the end of the tale, as the writer had assumed they would, they only lingered at the edges of the dark places, waiting for their master's instructions.

At one point, the writer considered demanding an unconditional release, but he also was wise enough to wait and allow the creature to open the conversation.

Finally, the creature took a deep breath, which, the writer had come to learn, was its prelude to a long speech.

"You are a clever and evil human, scribbler," the creature began, its eyes still looking away from the writer. "Tell me, did you embellish the tale to include the lost boat? Or, was that tale already written...? Be quick, and, don't lie, for human lies show as rents in your flesh to my kind, so I will know."

"The tale is as written. The ferry was central. I had to add a few changes, as the tale is not yet fully edited," the writer replied, his gaze steady, without fear. "As I told you when you dragged me into this hole hours ago, I'm on this mountain to finish the edit and to polish the tales. They all have small changes that need to be made."

"I remember the sea glass, human," the creature interrupted, its voice low and, surprising the writer, softer. "When I came ashore, after my first lost boat, my bruised hands dragged at the sand, the driftwood. Mixed in with the flotsam and scurrying creatures were little jewels that, in the moonlight, I mistook for beacons of...of something. Can't remember. I do remember giving one to my mother. Blue, like the frosted ice at the edge of a winter river, I think. She still had it when we took that last trip down to the sea, long ago."

"I remember Jeju, yes," the creature continued. "There were old, very old brethren there. Only a few, though. They had lost so many haunts during the purges that most just faded away. Many had become one with the rocks, hills, and old lava tubes. Their faces, crying out with their final, tortured breaths, can still be seen near the old sunrise crater and that southern temple, the one where 'those who must not be named' dwell now. One of the old ones showed me the way to a fishing village, with the old huts you humans had used for many, many cycles. I had to slave to a fishing goblin for a time, for several cycles, to get back to the mainland. Cold, hard lot, those fishing goblins, but what you humans call 'fair' to the ones they haunt. Others, though? I was told to avoid them, those that lurk beneath. Yes, I could tell you, fool human, tales of Jeju Island that would grow your hair long and white, those tales would."

"Really, I'd love to hear those, one day," the writer offered.

"Yes, there were the snake cult goblins who used to ride the grand Jeju Island horses across the misty meadows just before sunrise at Ilchubong," the creature said in a far off voice, closer to the scholar than the troll. "My...the fishing goblins, told me of surprising some...maybe some of your people, foreign, with pale skin they said, who were trekking up to the crater to see the great fire ball rise from the sea. The fishing ones said one of the fool humans stopped and watched a mare and her young stallion romping around the meadows, fading in and out of the fog...."

"That's...interesting," the writer said, not fully understanding why the beast was rambling, but better it rambled than stirred the cook pot.

"Interesting, scribbler, because the foreigner could see them," the creature added, watching the writer for any reaction. "As you know, some can see more than others. It was the first time, so say the fishing goblins, that the Jeju cousins realized someone from far away could know they were about. So shocked, they were, they fell off the horses, forgot to tease the human herder, and dashed back to one of their tubes under the ground, fearful that the foreign human might follow them and read the curses over them."

The creature grumbled a series of rhythmic chants in a strange tongue and then returned to using language the writer could understand.

"Yes, fool, many are the stories I could tell you of that island," the creature added, almost wistfully. "Of the old farmer, not unlike your tale, who moves his cows, yes, cows, each morning to the meadow just beyond a rise, and then back each evening."

"Sounds pretty normal," the writer replied.

"For hundreds of your cycles, human?" the creature barked in reply. "The old farmer, one with the earth, the sea, and the sky, had done his daily circuit so long, that when she-who-can-not-be-named claimed him, all she managed to drag away was an empty shell. The shadow of the human remained, and remains to this day, if you are on that part of the southeast coast in the wee hours of the morning, or as dusk settles, tricking the eyes.

Yes, scribbler, many, many tales of Jeju could be told. Many tales."

The writer decided to remain silent as the beast lapsed into unintelligible mumblings about the old days in Jeju and a few other islands that hugged the peninsula's southern coast. After a minute or so, the creature seemed to jerk fully awake, back to realizing where and when it was. It slowly turned to the writer.

"That boy, not the treacherous fairy, but the brother. He is strong, for a weakly human," the creature stated, surprising the writer with such an out of character pronouncement. "To endure his nightmares, fearlessly face the fairy hellhound, and still think he can...he can have impact, tossing those bits of glass back into the sea."

The creature then stared at the writer for a long minute, adding a surprising note, almost a concession, the writer felt as he listened.

"Mayhap, in some small way, that thieving boy is rare among you morsels," the creature whispered, its voice almost reflective. "Maybe, but, only a chance, he is one of your sad lot who can...influence his miserable few cycles. Maybe."

The creature swayed a bit in the stone chair and ran its right hand over the little orchid hidden under the shreds of cloth.

"She cries, human, for her lost home," the creature said softly, as if cooing to the delicate creature on its shoulder. "Your words have reached her. I feel her roots digging deep, drinking of my veins. She is calling to her sisters, far across Seoul. Far across the peninsula, down to Jeju, and beyond. She feeds on the tragedies carried by the winds. Human. Goblin. Fairy. Troll. Whatever. Her fate is to forever lament, like that boy for his sister. Like a troll-ogre-goblin, a mixed kid, for a mother barely grown."

The creature, its voice softened and almost human, let its head and shoulders sag under the weight of what the writer assumed were rising memories of the beast's long lost mother and the trauma of its subsequent ouster by her clan.

"Yes, clever, young human, to tell such a tale," the creature suddenly hissed through its mucus covered lips and took its hand away from its shoulder. "Is...is that the end, then?"

The writer nodded his answer, not trusting himself to speak, lest the creature hear the concern rising in the writer's chest. Not really fear, as the writer knew he was beyond that, but real concern that the creature would simply devour him anyway, regardless of any devil's agreement that they had parlayed.

"The end, is it, then?" the creature asked, leaning toward the writer. "The end...?"

The creature then stood and glided over to the cook pot, looked over the stove, and then glided back to its table and great, stone chair. There it simply stood, slowly turning the stained, vile tankard, allowing bits of mold and unspeakable debris to drop off the stein as the beast turned the hideous vessel side to side.

Slam!

The sudden sound of the creature crashing the vessel to the stone tabletop startled the writer to the point the writer emitted a low, involuntary exclamation, and then steeled himself for whatever the creature had decided.

"Yes, we must see what is next, shall we, young, fool scribbler?" the creature mused, its words dripping with bile as the beast glided back to the bench to stand beside the writer, its foul breath covering the writer like a black veil.

"Your fate?" the creature finally grumbled. "The path up to Mount Namsan? To mix with the lovelorn and the never loved. Or, the path to filling my, oh, and my little ones', empty guts?"

The troll-goblin of Namsan then let out a long, throaty laugh, shaking the enclave and causing the little ones to squeal with anticipation.

"Hah! Yes, scribbler, teller of woeful tales of haunted humans and fading goblin brethren," the creature shouted out, causing the trees to tremble. "Which shall it be? Which…shall…it…be?"

EPILOGUE

As the gnarled, ancient oaks and towering guardian pines of Mount Namsan seemed to press down upon him, the writer finally dropped the notebook, its contents and his imagination exhausted, onto the smooth, polished surface of the stone bench. He then stood, preferring to end it all standing, like a man, rather than trapped in a sitting position whenever the goblin-troll-ogre host decided to pounce. In fact, he was so far beyond worrying, the writer stepped past the brooding creature and stood near the heat of the fire, warming his arms and legs after so many hours confined to the cold, stone-furnished and tree-shrouded enclave.

"Scribbler, why do you do this?" the creature suddenly asked after a long silence. "You said words before, but my mind was…I want to hear your words again. Why do you come to my land, my peninsula, and rattle on about tales you can only know from life snatches stolen from others?"

The writer stood in silence, reflecting on the odd question from his deranged, yet often quite lucid captor. He then spoke slowly, using mostly English, with a little Korean added, and even a little Chinese in spots. He had concluded that the creature understood many more languages than it admitted to and could probably also read what it had called the foreign or odd squiggles in the notebook, and had simply been lying to test whether the writer would actually tell the tales in the notebook.

"Years, many cycles past, I was a young military man assigned to my first post, south of here," the writer began, with the creature interrupting.

"Ah! My memory is failing me. Of course, that scent. Osan, yes," the creature cooed. "The old turtle mountain. Tasted it on you. Faint. Long ago, but still a trace there."

"Yes, the American base at Osan. Really, Songtan," the writer replied, fully aware that the creature, through whatever extra sense it seemed to have, probably already knew what the writer was about to relate.

"It was after our Independence Day…," the writer resumed, but was again interrupted.

"Independence? Hah!" the creature boomed. "Which one, fool? The peninsula humans have had so many masters to be freed from. Which?"

"Sorry, the American day. What we call the Fourth. Fourth of July," the writer answered, and quickly continued.

"There was this Chinese joint, restaurant, not far from the main gate. After being introduced to it by our hapkido sabumnim, our teacher, I had struck up something of a friendship with the owner. Tall guy. From Shandong, or his parents were. Watched him build his new place, and heard about a long series of interesting real estate fees imposed by nearly every office he had to deal with for permits. His place was cozy, the food good, not too expensive, but not too cheap. Quality meats and such."

"When he was rebuilding, he kept one section of wall from the old place, which held an oddly situated door. Odd because it opened to the wall bordering the old rail tracks. Barely enough room outside for even a slicky boy, a second story thief, to squeeze through. He tired to laugh it off when I asked about it. Said his dad had made the door from the parts of the boat they had used to flee across the Bohai and the Yellow Sea, and settle there. He was a great guy. Years later, when I had returned after decades, I managed to find the place again. He was ill, so not there, but his son was, as I guessed when I met the younger version of the owner at the desk."

The writer shifted his stance so that his left side was facing the warm firebox, then continued.

"Years before, on that afternoon after the Fourth, a group of us had mostly recovered from too much soju and OB, so we were starving, and I convinced the group to head to my friend's place. We arrived and the lunch crowd had long left, but we were surprised to see the wife's cousin, who helped out, putting up the 'closed' sign. We knew each other, so I pretended to beg him to let us in for a snack, and challenged him on why the owner would close when he knew the post-celebration crowds would be descending later that evening? He finally relented, let us in, but told us to eat quickly. Only the second level cook was in the kitchen, smoking by the back door. He said hi, and then yelled at the cousin that the place was supposed to be closed for several hours. He tossed his cigarette and began working on our favorites, as we were pretty set in what we ate there."

"In the group was a New Yorker, from the Bronx, a tall blonde guy that school girls in Seoul used to follow around and giggle at. Another was a good kid from Ohio. She was the smartest one of the group. The last was an older guy from the hills of Tennessee, or maybe Virginia. And me."

"Just as our food came out, the cousin was all excited about something and was urging us to eat quickly and leave. Something about the clock on the counter being wrong."

"Suddenly, the loudest, deepest knock on a door I had ever heard came booming from that old door near the back. The sound shook the poor cousin to his core and he nearly fainted. Kept mumbling that they were too early. 'Not yet! Not yet!'"

The creature, sensing a key part of the tale was near, cocked its head and stared at the writer's eyes.

"We certainly didn't want to walk away if special guests had arrived and the cousin had lost it. Didn't want my friend to lose customers. So, I waved the old guy to a chair and walked back to the door. Looking at his father's handiwork, I seemed to recall my friend had said it was an old Shandong custom to appease some forgotten kitchen god."

"As I stood at the door, the booming knock came again, more like the sound of a far temple bell than a knock. It seemed to wash over me, and the room, like a wave. I reached down to pull on the latch, an ornate, heavy, wrought iron latch, and grabbed it, jerking my hand back from the cold iron. It was the middle of summer, but the latch was bitterly cold. I grabbed a cloth from the waiter stand just to the side and then pulled the latch, opening the door to a small group. But, I only had a glimpse, as the owner had suddenly appeared at the front of the place, had taken everything in with a glance and had rushed back to gently push me aside as he grabbed the latch and completed opening the door, with me just behind, his tall body blocking most of my view."

"As his special party was being shown to one of the private rooms by the wife, the owner called his momentary apologies, using the most honorific speech I'd ever heard him, a pretty gruff fellow, ever use. He then turned to me, and, instead of anger, he looked at my eyes with something like a kindred spirit and spoke. 'You saw them,' he stated. Not a question. A statement. I replied I had and wondered why he had a group of foreigners and some locals in a special room when he had closed to his regulars."

"Well, he just stared at me, asked me to return to my friends, and said he'd be back. I did. As we ate, we heard the low murmuring from the back, in a mix of American slang, older slang, and some Korean, a wide range, but mostly farm boys. And, unusual, but not unheard of, some Chinese. I told my friends what I had seen, but none of them had seen the group because, when I had opened the door, the cousin had abruptly recovered his senses and had grabbed the privacy screens from the side and had used them to block the view from the old door to the private rooms. The screens remained and continued to block our view, but not the sounds."

"We eventually lost interest in the odd private party after the wife had nervously taken our drink orders. The food had come out very quickly, which told us that the chef had already been working on dishes for his special group. We swapped tall tales about the various parties we had been to the night before, which girls and guys were...well, you know how military guys can get. After a bit, one of my friends, the older one from Tennessee, leaned over and said the strangest thing."

"He said the Korean he was overhearing was pretty dated. Almost archaic, some of it. Lacking any modern slang. And the Americans he had overheard seemed to be living in the Eisenhower era from how they spoke and the subjects they were discussing."

"I joked that he was just bringing the office to dinner, and that he should relax and ignore the group. He then got eerily serious and said the group was talking war tactics. I countered that we all talked about war and what might happen if it broke out again. It was the middle of the old Cold War, after all."

"My friend then silenced the entire table. 'They are talking about The War, as it's happening. Not as if it's in the past.'"

"Now, it was an odd coincidence, or, maybe not odd, that my friend came from a long line of those medicine women up in the Appalachian hills, eastern U.S. That is, women until he came along. His grandmother, as the skills were always passed to the grandchild, had chosen him to impart the gift. He had revealed this one evening months earlier when we had been swapping ghost stories from our youth. And, he was also the consummate professional military man. If he said that group was talking about the war as if it were happening, then that's what they were doing."

"One of my friends, the New Yorker, suggested re-enactors, like what some of the Civil War buffs do. No, not in Korea. So, we all got quiet and listened in as much as we could and, sure enough, Joe, my friend and mentor, was right. Weird, it was, hearing them go on about tactics, casualties, and such."

"Try as I might, I could not get the owner to discuss the group and why they were acting so odd. I didn't want to push it, not wanting to step all over my...not wanting to mess up some cultural thing. So, we dropped the issue and wrote it off to an amusing mystery."

"Later, of course, we noticed when the group was finished and began to prepare to leave. We heard some pretty strong language suggesting the group stay and not leave the place. In English, Korean, and, yes, even Chinese. But, an older, wise and seasoned voice, American, barked orders and the rest went silent."

"When the group trooped out a little before sunset, as we could see the shadows through the windows, we caught glimpses of the wide range of uniforms and the sheer fatigue on the few faces we saw when they passed from behind the screen to the door, and we smelled a mix of spoiled eggs and, strangely, fragrant herbs, of all things. They were in uniform, but we could not really make out which kind, mostly. After nearly all of the mixed group had disappeared into the gathering darkness, the last of them, two Americans, paused at the door, which the screens had not covered. The two looked over at us. One of them, a young, lanky guy, in an Army uniform, pretty beat up, smiled at us and waved. The other one, older, gruffer, and a lot meaner looking, barked at the younger one to stop delaying and to get back to the front. It was the same commanding voice from earlier. But, as the old sarge stepped to the door, he also turned and, giving us the thumbs up, called over to the table in a voice that sounded a million miles away. 'We'll make it work, boys. You keep it going.' His words were as clear as day and then he was gone. Out the door and into the dusk."

"The owner slowly closed the door and, instead of going back to the kitchen, or to the front counter, or even over to our table to chat as he always did, he sank into the closest chair and, letting out a huge sigh, dropped his head on his arms on the tabletop, alarming all of us. Since I knew him the best, I went over and sat down, not saying anything, but just sitting."

"After a bit, he spoke. Not raising his head, but just talking with his head on his arms."

"'When we emigrated, after the world war and the civil war, my father settled in this peaceful countryside to make a new life. The old door was made from the boat his family had used to cross over. The boat was a gift from some monks, who...well, they helped build it, but stayed behind. The iron and silver fixtures, yes, the ties and other trim of the door is tarnished silver, are from an old temple that my father had tried to save from some overzealous troops, which the monks had greatly admired him for. The monks, before...some of them Korean studying there...before they died, told my father to use the wood of the boat and temple fixtures to make a door, and to always welcome anyone who knocked. The monks said it was...it was like a vent. A safety valve between...between here and there.'"

"'My father did so and, for many years, there was never a knock. In fact, as you know, the door opens onto the old wall at the rail tracks, so there is barely enough room for a chicken to squeeze between the wall and the door. But, true to his promise to those brave monks, he built the door and, when he rebuilt his restaurant, yes, he had had one before my first one that you saw, before this one, he kept the door in. He was also the one who planted the orange trees around the place, even though they rarely ever bear fruit in this region, saying the monks had suggested it. After he passed, I considered removing the door, as it always confused customers.'"

"But, one night, years ago, during one of the dark times of heightened border tensions, around the time of the tree incident, a knock came. At first, I thought I was hearing things. Then it came again. A deep, resonating sound....' Like a temple bell, I said. My friend then raised his head. 'You heard it. And, you saw them.' I said yes."

"He then leaned back in the chair, his bulk causing the thing to groan, and stared at his hands as he spoke. 'The soldiers were there. It seemed like an endless line. Dozens and dozens. Americans. Koreans. British. Australian. Even Chinese. All mixed up.'"

"What…did they want? I asked. 'Simply a meal and a safe refuge, a few precious minutes of normality, before…before they had to return to that hell just beyond the old rail tracks,' my friend replied."

"All this time I had expected him to say something about a local brotherhood, or war enthusiast group. Korea, at that time, had a ton of American expats who had simply stayed on or returned after being posted here. I had not expected an outlandish, I thought at the time, tale of old ghosts from a long ago battlefield."

The writer then fell silent.

The creature, still staring, unblinking, let a knowing smile crease its rotting lips as it spoke.

"Yes, scribbler, that tale would bring even me back to the peninsula to seek out more haunts," the creature said, its voice quiet, yet teasing. "You wanted to follow, yes?"

"What? How did you know…?" the writer blurted out, then realized the creature had been sniffing the air again. "Yes. I had a wild idea to rush to the door, open it, and try to follow the…the men."

"Did you? Did you, weak human?" the creature goaded, knowing the answer.

"I stood. I stepped to the door. I even grasped the latch, no longer cold. But, something inside of me said to not walk through that doorway. It was only for those on the outside, wanting to come in from the hell of war. Not for curiosity seekers to look over their dying shoulders at the horrors of the past," the writer replied, his voice defiant. "They deserved respect, over curiosity, vile beast."

"Yes, human, good that you did not follow, or I would not have had this entertaining evening. And, you, scribbler, would not have spent a life looking for that missed door again and again, in your tales and sad stories," the creature added.

The writer, refusing to be baited by the creature at that late point in his captivity, simply nodded and waited for the creature to make its decision one way or the other.

After a number of minutes, while he listened to the increasingly noisy chatter of the little ones beyond the dark nooks in between the trees, the writer let his thoughts drift back to that long ago night in Osan…Songtan. He had learned later that it had been the anniversary of one of the first major battles. His mind continued to see, all those years ago, the trusting faces of that kid soldier and the old sarge, forever trapped in that in between space, that gaekgwi purgatory of the wayfarer ghosts who haunt nearly every corner of the peninsula. The words of the sarge echoed forever in the writer's mind, trusting that their endless sacrifice would be upheld by subsequent troops on the peninsula, and not forgotten to time.

"Yes, weak human, there are many who wander the empty places, forever lost to family," the creature finally added after sniffing the air again. "Yet, at times, when just the right family member visits a place, passes an alley, steps on a spot where an old, old bone might lie rotting in the earth. Then that rare gaekgwi has been known to move on, released by that ancestor's…what do you weakly humans call that which dwells in your hearts, but is not malice?"

"Devotion? Love? Compassion?" the writer answered, wondering if the beast had any understanding of such concepts. "I'm sure such are alien to your kind, vile host."

The creature turned its head to gaze for an unnervingly long time at the writer. It seemed to be calling up an old memory, from what the writer could see of the beast's face moving from one of murder, to one of thoughtfulness, and then to one of realization that an old memory had finally surfaced. Somehow, one or more of his words, the writer theorized, must have awakened another lost memory in the addled mind of the hermit-troll-goblin and caused it, suddenly, to relate that memory in a long, rambling speech.

"After slaving for the fishing goblins out of Jeju, one fiend selling my thrall to another, we landed at a quiet fishing hovel near old Busan. On those windy shores, I bought out my thrall with deeds that would burn your flimsy pages," the creature began, its voice slurring many of the words as if the memory was rebuilding itself as the beast spoke. "Once free, many were the cold, treacherous nights I froze on the road from Busan, all the time thinking my mother's cousins would take me in."

"Many were the small humans I dragged to survive that long trek. Hiding from the village guardians. Sneaking into hovels on the fringe. Many on the fringe were outcasts. This was before I was, myself, thrown away by my brethren, so I dragged many. One of those fringe places was for the small humans without families. Up a small hill on the road through Songtan of old. Yes, I think, maybe your Songtan. Wretched place. Cold, drafty, full of night spirits nipping at the small humans, terrorizing their overseers. I was so weak, so cold, so thin, that I stupidly stepped across a threshold that was protected. Strong protection. Luckily, because of my sire's side, it didn't kill me, but, in my weak state, I was trapped. I had to hide amongst the skinny little humans, while they were entertained by foreigners, ones who looked like you, scribbler. A long wait, but I endured. Found a place near the lone firebox, a smelly, but welcome blaze. The little ones suddenly fell silent. The foreigners had opened a huge basket. Gave each of those sniffling small ones little packages of rare foods. Each little one's eyes grew as big as their heads. They each waited until all had a little package, then opened. Saving the small ribbon, carefully winding it and putting it into ragged little pockets. Even the shiny wrapping, they saved in another sad little pocket. Each checked that the other had the same little morsels. One small one, very small, was given extra by the bigger ones, fools, from their own meager morsels. They were all so thin, rosy glowing cheeks, but thin. All but the smallest who had extra. She was round and plump. Then, and only after they had begged the foreigners to eat first, did the little beggars gobble up one of the morsels. But, only one did each eat. The remainder, each put back in the bit of shiny paper, retrieved the sad bit of ribbon, tied it up, then clutched the little morsels like they were gold filled Lunar New Year packets. Disgusted, I slid into the shadow of the little one who had the most morsels, thinking I could easily drag the child. As I stalked her, she suddenly turned and stared right at me. Instead of screaming, as you humans who can see us usually do, she smiled and chuckled. Astonished, I froze, thinking she must have seen a shadow that I had crossed, or maybe was laughing at one of her orphan mates. But, she was not smiling at me, she was smiling at the hell fairies who were floating above me. Yes, I had walked into a worse trap. A no-escape trap for my kind. I had only seen such demon fairies from afar, years before, when an unfortunate cousin fell into a long carriage. It had been a short fall, as the little demons made quick work of the cousin and tossed his empty shell into an old sewer ditch."

"Before I could run, the fairies had me. One breath before tearing my limbs asunder to use to beat me, the small, chubby one spoke. Garbled, spewing nonsense. But, whatever she said, the fairies paused, spewed nonsense back at her. Yet, the small one prevailed. She took out one of the small morsels, a sad little bag of spiced nuts, yes, like the ones there, and handed them to me. How she saw me, I'll never know. But, she did. Maybe her young mind was unclouded. Maybe her parents, whoever they were, had been shamans of old. The fairies, upset that they did not get their prize, poked at me a little too hard to accept the bag. I did, and quickly gave the hell fairies most of the nuts. The little human seemed to approve, then turned back to her brethren, her fellow orphans, and joined in some noisy singing, looking back at me from time to time. The fairies, still poking me with their sharp sticks, and clutching the spiced nuts the small one had offered them for me, pushed me to the threshold and, with two of them doing the honors, gave me a swift kick that shot me out the door, and beyond the danger of the talismans and the guardians."

The creature leaned forward, its dark eyes staring straight into the writer's soul as it continued without missing a beat.

"Scribbler, I never saw that small human again, and, to this day, do not know if she lived out her miserable life in that hovel of a human cave, or if she was bought by some farmer later, or if she went to schools, which, over time, I learned was how many of those of her kind moved beyond their imposed caste, or escaped my grip or my kin's. No, I never returned, but, later, after I was outcast, thrown away by my own, wretched kind, and had grown stronger from it, I sent lesser cousins to guard the place. No, not to be helpful, scribbler, but to lay claim against other cousins trying to drag the hovel, and, of course, to warn others of the powerful hell fairies guarding those abandoned, small humans."

The creature finally fell silent, its eyes still scanning the writer's face, as if searching for, of all things for a demonic hermit to desire, understanding.

The writer, fighting his own, renewed rush of memories, which pointed to a bizarre, remotely possible link to his demented captor, tried to look away from the beast's searching eyes, but found that he had to speak, compelled to answer the hermit-troll's piercing gaze.

"All these years later, and you are the fable those kids tell at that orphanage?" the writer declared, shocked beyond reason that the beast, his captor, his soon to be gourmand, might have been saved by one of the kids in the orphanage his unit had supported those many, many years before.

"They tell a fable?" the creature asked, its voice lowering into a more murderous tone as its eyes continued to stare, hungrily, at the writer.

"We, my unit and the supply squadron, supported the local kids. Not a hovel as you claim, but a happy place, if cramped and old-fashioned. And, yes, school was the ultimate escape. I can still see the two college kids who took a bus every weekend back to the place to tutor the younger ones," the writer replied, not believing the hideous beast before him could be the origin of the sweet tale he had heard and, frankly, had forgotten until the beast had related its story.

"The older kids told of a holiday dinner, years before my time, where some of the squadron had brought treats. Nothing much, but the kids were dazzled by the candy, the nuts, small cakes, and little trinkets. One of the little ones, then a two or three-year-old girl, was the darling of the place. The older ones always saw that she got extra food from their own plates, and gave her some of their treats. Later, when the matron asked her about some missing treat from her bag, the little girl said the 'dancing fireflies caught an elf and were going to eat the elf, but she stopped them and gave the skinny little elf a huge bag of nuts, which the skinny elf gave, all but one, to the angry fireflies, who then kicked the little elf out the door.' The older kids said she told that tale for years, never wavering," the writer said, shaking his head at the bizarre coincidence.

"And, to answer your unspoken question, I don't know what happened to the little girl, although I like to think she found a loving home," the writer replied to the questioning eyes of his captor. "I know several did from there during my time. Two young sisters, I recall, were adopted by a nice, middle-aged couple assigned to Seoul. American, I think. So, no, the children did not face such bleak futures as you describe, old one."

The creature, its gaze lingering on the writer, but with less intensity, seemed to be thinking about the odd coincidence that had been shared, reluctantly, by the writer. It then paced a bit, pausing several times in mid-stride to consult in whispers with its gruesome shoulder resident.

With the creature wandering about its lair, the writer returned to the bench, to get out of the beast's way and to be closer to his pack if he found a way to escape.

After several minutes of meandering pacing, the beast returned to the bench, sniffed the air around the writer, and, reaching out, ran its right hand over the writer's head and shoulders, lingering on the left shoulder, uncomfortably long for the writer, who had a wild thought that the creature was planting a cutting from its parasitic orchid on the writer's own shoulder.

Finally, the creature pulled back and slowly stood to its full, menacing height, speaking, as it did so, in a voice beyond old.

"Go forth, scribbler. I release you, with warning. Write more of your rambling confusion. One day, write of the 'mixed-kid' troll-goblin, with one leg in my sire's fjords and mountains, and one leg in the rivers, mountains, cities, and seas of my mother's peninsula. Write, you, and return here to tell the tale," the creature abruptly hissed at the writer, waving down a chorus of angry squeaks from the trees. "For, as you have hinted, I and my brethren will live long lives, full of tasty morsels, when the lowly hosts read your tales and the tales of old. Yes, go forth and scribble your ravings, for we will always be ready to catch, to embrace, to caress those weak humans who slip and slide into their own whirlpools of fear. Deceit. Envy. Treachery. Yes, we will catch them. Consume some. Drag the souls of others. Release a few. Only a few, to allow those, with the fear just behind their wide eyes, to tell of our terrors!"

"Yes," the writer began, with a growing suspicion that the entire encounter with the creature might have been engineered to use him as one of the demon's mouthpieces, yet he held his own tongue for fear of adding any doubts to the beast's mind on whether the writer would be released to write the tales, or not. "Yes, I can. I will write those stories."

"For this, young human, you must send a morsel or two my way," the creature chuckled. "Maybe one of those fat students I see passing by. Maybe a few children. I'll save one as a plaything for my tiny ones."

"Good god! I will not!" declared the writer, bile rising in his throat as he interrupted the chuckling beast. "We had a deal. Tales for time. Have you not even a shred of honor? You must release me! But, to…to condemn others for you? I'd rather boil!"

"Come, human, there must be those you'd like to see in the cook pot?" the creature slurred, leaning down and letting its long, diseased tongue run slowly over the writer's cheeks. "Yes, I taste…? I taste betrayal. So human a failing, trust. Yes, the girl. No. A woman now. What else? An old boss? A boss's boss? And, another woman? Why are there so many women you want to jump into the cook pot?"

"Rubbish," the writer replied, trying to hold his stomach from erupting at the gritty slime of the creature's tongue, which, somehow, allowed the beast to reach deep into the writer's subconscious. "I'd condemn no one to such a fate!"

"Ah! Suffer in silence, you do, boy. Suffering you have carried for many, many cycles. Well, don't let it eat at you too much. Makes you humans stringy and tasteless, all the self-doubt and suffering from those you have given your trust, and even shaped, in your own way," the creature chortled, its teasing voice giving way to something much darker. "Do you think they will ever know, or care, that they have scarred you? Given you that bit of darkness born from betrayal that allowed me to draw you into this pitiful lair? Torn away your veneer of civility to allow your black vengeance to send them to early dust to flavor my delightful stew? Do you think they will ever want to know? Do you?"

Alarmed at the more ominous turn of events, the writer swept up his notebook, clutched his pack, and, stepping to the area of the trees where he believed the doorway to be, turned his back on the beast, even though the tongue and now hands continued to explore his neck and his soul.

Suddenly, the writer felt a prick at the back of his left ear. Fearing the beast had taken a bite, as it had said the ghouls did to mark their future prey, he allowed his head to jerk away, but he hesitated reaching up to feel the damage.

"No bother, scribbler. No flesh for the ghouls this night, simply a, what did you call it? A treat? Yes, a treat for my darling, to help her remember Jeju Island through your time there," the creature cooed into the writer's ear.

Out of the corner of his eye, the writer watched in horror as, instead of the beast, the wavering shadow of the scholar wiped a few drops of red, the red of the writer's blood, onto the roots of the squirming wind flower.

"We…have…a…deal!" the writer uttered through clenched teeth, forcing his eyes away from the horror of the festering plant drinking his blood, its flower looking like a tiny death head, and away from his mind's delusion that the beast had transformed into the old professor.

The creature, no longer the writer's imagined scholar, then withdrew its tongue and hands, and, stepping beside the writer, held out its thin, rag-draped arms to wave at the seemingly solid wall of trees.

Slowly, as if some ancient, heavy oaken door was turning on tortured, rusted hinges, a space began to appear and gradually expand between two of the old trees. Too small to squeeze through, the writer realized, as he steeled his nerves waiting for the opening to widen, while listening to the creature's parting words. At least, he hoped they were parting words.

"When you do send them, I'll know, human," the creature gurgled in an even more unearthly voice. "You need only whisper their names when passing a dark alley in Hongdae, or crossing the Han River on a rainy night. Or when shopping that street in America in your tale. There are kimbap stands like your kimchi buns, where my cousins slide just under the kim, the seaweed, and wait for the right fool to buy from those hard luck purveyors of false hope. Or, you need to only call out their names from a nightmare's fevered sleep. You need to but scratch their names in the sand of the beaches of Jeju, Busan, Incheon, or anywhere that touches the seas, and the purging tides will bring them to me on the bare backs of the sea nymphs."

With the trees nearly wide enough for the writer to step through, he put his right foot forward, but felt a tug on his left foot. Looking down, he saw one of the child-things, a small one, the half-clean one that had fed him and that he had pitied and saved from the cook pot, clinging to his leg.

Looking up at the creature, the writer saw pure evil, primordial and without thought, staring back at him.

"Yes! The tiny one wants you to take it with you," the creature hissed. "Take him, her? Let him see his world. Knows the many tongues of his forebears. Take him…her? No bother. Will return. They always do."

"The others?" the writer asked, aware any talking could jeopardize his own escape. "What of the others?"

"No bother. They are too far removed from their former, wasted selves. They will live out their short lives here. Better than a dark alley, or a dank cellar," the creature replied, as it stroked the dirty hair of the tiny one, causing the writer to reach down and brush the creature's hand away.

"Already protective, you are, human," the creature chuckled, then waved at the trees one final time, which caused them to begin to close. "Such are your failings that lost another to you, yes?"

Startled, the writer grabbed the grubby hand of the small child-thing and jumped through the opening just before it closed even more. Yet, even as the writer felt the gloriously cleaner air outside his recent prison, he was stopped in his tracks by a long, twisted branch that had caught his coat. Struggling to free himself, he considered taking his coat off and abandoning it, when he realized the branch was the arm of the creature pulling at him.

"Remember, weaver of woeful tales. Remember. I, and my kind, will always be just outside your vision. That shadow you think you see on the underground carriage. That corner of the kitchen that never gets any light. That darkened toilet stall. That friend or colleague who never seems quite right in your eyes," the creature called, its voice fading away behind the writer. "You can't escape us, scribbler. You can only fool yourself to avoid us. Write my story. Return to me to tell it. The cook pot is always waiting if you wait too long, scribbler."

"How will I know?" the writer asked, forcing himself to not look back. "How will I know, when it's time to tell your tale, old vile one?"

"You will know, scribbler. You will know," called the creature in a voice far, far away, in space and in time.

Abruptly, the writer was back on the trail, just at the exit from the shortcut he had taken earlier, in what felt like days before, but, from the light and the sky, seemed to only have been an hour or so.

Stealing a look to the copse, the writer was surprised to see a normal stand of evenly spaced trees, none of which were like the old, gnarled trees of the creature's lair. No stone bench, no stove, nothing could be seen between the trees other than a section of the old city wall at some distance.

Vanished.

Had he imagined it all, the writer wondered? He then stood very still to try to hear anything from his recent host's wretched enclave.

Still nothing.

Looking up and down the trail, the writer saw a few groups passing the spot without a care, oblivious to the dangers of being so oblivious.

Swinging his pack to his shoulder, the writer shook his head and wondered, again, if he had just been daydreaming and had had a strange nap on the weathered bench not far from where he stood. However, a black smudge had appeared on his hand when he had dropped his notebook into his pack, and he immediately recognized it as the soot from the ondol charcoal.

No, the writer realized, he had not dreamed up the wretched meeting with the vile beast. The beast or deranged hermit, or whatever it was, was there, just beyond that innocent looking stand of peaceful trees, its death giving eyes secretly staring at its recent and, no doubt, future prey.

Reaching behind his left ear, the writer then found the small wound, no more than a scratch, which yielded no further blood, but did cause him to briefly shiver, and shove, far back in his mind, the image of the sad little flower writhing in his warm blood.

Carefully, as if in slow motion, the writer then turned away from the trees and looked ahead to the trail. Yet, something nagged at him, just at the back of his skull.

Something else was missing.

Something?

Wait, thought the writer, where's the child-thing? Little half-clean was just at his leg. What had become of it?

Frantically looking around, causing a group of college age young people to pause to ask the writer if they could help him find whatever the foreigner had lost. He thanked them in his broken Korean and then waved them on, lest the creature see them lingering and reach out for one of the 'tastier young ones.'

Finally abandoning the search for the tiny one, the writer scanned the trees one last time to burn the location into his mind. Satisfied he could find the spot again, he turned back to the trail, prepared to move on, but then paused.

Looking at the cleared stretch of the ill-fated shortcut through the fallen leaves and small brush, the writer walked backwards a couple of meters, quietly kicking leaves and debris onto the path in an attempt to conceal its obvious direction, so that at least one or two groups, that might have taken it, would stay on the main path and avoid his new acquaintance.

Turning back to head up to the tower, the writer felt the troll-ogre-goblin-hermit laughing at the sad attempt to save some stranger. Shaking that off, the writer found he was hiking much faster and with more vigor than he had done before his encounter.

By the time the writer arrived at the tower plaza, the sun was setting over Seoul, the day giving way to the nether time between day and night. Even before the encounter with the crazy hermit, or whatever his captor was, the writer admitted that dusk had often brought strange things, and so he hurried across the plaza and inside to take the lift to the café with lots of people, lights, laughter and, he hoped, loud K-pop, since he now knew the goblins couldn't stay around it very long. If such goblins existed, he added, as he stepped into the lobby and joined a small group on the lift.

Arriving at his usual café floor and finding a seat near a window, far away from the shadows lurking closer to the back wall, the writer silently thanked the dynamic young diva, Lee Ji-eun, or 'IU,' for belting out one of her signature tunes over the café's sound system. He felt the troll-goblin and his cousins would probably avoid the noisy, higher-level cafés, so the upbeat song helped the writer tell himself to calm down and try to relax.

Checking his hand, the writer was relieved to discover the bright red area looked more like severe sunburn than a partially cooked appetizer. He then took some hand sanitizer from his pack and rubbed the area thoroughly, before wrapping it with a clean, white, jogging headband from his pack.

Gazing around at the sheer normality of the café, the tower visitors, and the bustling staff, the writer wondered, yet again, if he had just had a wild dream down the western side of Mount Namsan. Southern Mountain, more correctly, Mount Nam, but English rendering invariably used Mount Namsan, or just Namsan, his mind's detail oriented side added.

Are there are equally bizarre colleagues of the troll-goblin at the other compass points, the writer wondered? Looking out the glass walls to the cityscape below, he let that thought float away and replaced it with more tangible ideas.

What had just happened?

If what had happened, really had happened, then what to make of it? Sanity finally slipping?

Maybe all the fictions the writer had created had coalesced into some psychotic manifestation?

Or, maybe, the beast, the troll-goblin-hermit of Mount Namsan was as real as the kids taking selfies against the backdrop of a Seoul nightscape a few meters away?

Maybe his brief host was simply some batty, misguided escapee from Seoul's less desirable side?

Or some long fallen stage performer, gone off the deep end?

Yet, try as he might to explain away the bizarre encounter, the writer always returned to the troubling possibility that the beast was what it said it was.

Better to count one's blessings and move on, the writer finally told himself, bringing his thoughts back to the café and his original evening plans.

When the very patient waiter returned for the third time, the writer finally pulled himself out of his mental exercises and ordered, telling himself he would have to address the curious reality of the beast later, along with whatever courses of action would satisfy his own very real concerns and any police or other official redress.

After the first espresso had arrived, been consumed, and the pastries eaten, the writer finally allowed himself to relax, but just a bit, and leaned back to look around the café at the mostly young people. He recognized a couple of the waiters and waitresses from earlier visits, and two students with whom he had a passing hello relationship. They nodded greetings and he returned the same.

No odd or inexplicably monstrous diners, or ghoul-laden tourists appeared, and no dirty little minions dashed between table legs, so the writer allowed himself to relax even further, and forced himself to think of things unassociated with the fellow of the dank enclave. Of course, as a creative writer, he had tried to dream up clever, and, if possible, alliterative titles for the creature of the copse. Hermit of the highlands? Grendel of the mountain gates? Troll-Goblin of Mount Namsan?

No, the writer admitted to himself, nothing he could dream up could ever convey the abject horror of his momentary captor.

Time seemed to creep along as the writer watched the people come and go, exchanged pleasantries with the waiters, watched a few frames of the older, but wildly popular 'Dream High' drama on a neighboring guest's tablet, and absently wondered how many budding romances had been born among the many young visitors in that Namsan Tower café.

The writer also marveled at the never disappointing views out the massive windows, with dancing reflections of the visitors in the glass mixing with the cityscapes. Smiling grimly, he silently hoped the shadows and reflections were all attached to the visible visitors. From time to time, in spite of his efforts to keep his mind off his experience, he would steal looks at either end of the bends in the curved space for any signs of...well, for anything out of the ordinary.

Other than a few loud tourists, not fellow Americans for a change, no goblins slid from the shadows, no trolls dropped from the rafters, no wood sprites banged on the glass windows, and no nine-tailed foxes tried to seduce the writer. He was, he realized, beginning to rationalize that he had imagined the episode, except that he could not explain away the soot on his jacket and on the cover of his manuscript and notes, nor the burn on his hand, nor the small nick on the back of his ear.

Notes!

That's it!

Suddenly, the writer realized that, while he had been trying to gloss over the experience with the odd fellow down the mountain, his creative side had finally kicked in with the caffeine, and he acknowledged that he needed to capture some of the experience while it was still fresh. So, calling for a second espresso, he took out his phone, which he was surprised to see still had a half-charge in spite of the issues in the enclave. Using the notes app, he sketched out a few of the more fleeting ideas from the encounter. After fleshing out a solid set of summaries, he emailed them to himself as a backup.

For the briefest of moments, the writer considered calling his family, but felt it would be better if he outlined his encounter in person. So, he then settled back in the chair and let himself actually enjoy his second espresso.

As he watched the crowds grow with the lateness of the evening, and listened to the wide variety of music being piped into the café area, the writer tried to match the other visitors and diners to the songs floating about, mainly to, again, move his mind off the afternoon's surreal encounter. It was a silly little exercise, the writer admitted to himself, and he was horrible at recognizing any but the most popular songs, but it helped relax his mind.

Eventually, without having done any editing on the manuscript that had saved him, the writer realized he needed to head back down to the city and rejoin his colleagues for a late dinner, which he had half-considered backing out of, but had then decided a couple of hours of normal, casual conversation would be most welcome. He mused that he might even offer his odd encounter to his friends for discussion, but would have to weigh that carefully. Both from his friends thinking he might have lost a screw or two, and from the remote, laughably outlandish possibility that the hermit, or troll-goblin, did have hidden listeners hanging from windowsills in the nicer neighborhoods.

Smiling at his future dinner dilemma, the writer called for and paid his bill, and, gathering up his pack and coat, headed for the exit that would lead him down to the open air and to the outside walkways.

Out in the crisp evening air, the writer ambled slowly along the boardwalk-like path that lined the edge of the complex and hosted an endless parade of lovers, would be lovers, and their thousands of friendship locks, with the city lights twinkling as far as one could see beyond Namsan's darker parkland.

As the writer passed a crooked bench where an older couple was sitting and admiring the avant-garde art of the locks against the growing darkness of the evening sky, he thought he saw a shadow dive behind the couple, just there!

No, the writer said to himself, as he hurried on. Don't fall victim to the creature's taunts. There is nothing in the shadows here. How could there be, with so many locks and other items proclaiming true love and caring between and among so many?

Passing a couple of college students, the writer overheard one of the young women speaking.

"No. I don't have the key," the student said, her perfect brow furrowed. "We tossed it over the side."

"Maybe you can break it off?" the second student suggested, glancing at an older, foreign guy, the writer, who seemed to be listening to them.

"Too hard. Guess I'll just have to live with it hanging over my head," the first student replied, adding a half-hearted laugh as she and her friend drifted away.

The writer froze in his footsteps after the young woman's comment about 'living with it hanging over her head.' A flash of bitter cold dragged at his chest, as if someone had just 'walked over his grave,' a superstition from his far childhood.

How many, wondered the writer? How many of those colorful locks represented failed loves? Betrayed friendships? Crushed souls of family members spurned? How many, just in that small area, represented the ageless fears of failure for so many?

And what creatures of the dark lurked in the shadows of Namsan Tower, waiting for those returning from the broken memories of those failed locks to lure the unsuspecting into even darker despair? The writer shuddered, again, at the thought that had instantly shattered his feelings of protection among the lovers' locks.

Looking back up the boardwalk toward the tower, the writer imagined he saw countless shapes weaving in and out of the locks and fences, seeking out those who were silently cursing someone they had once loved or cared for. Sniffing out the blunt scent of yet another victim.

"No!" shouted the writer, surprising the older couple and several youths who had just passed him.

Turning away from the locks and their scores and scores of shadows, the writer stumbled down the walk, not sure which way to turn. A growing part of him felt the fences, the artificial trees, the misshapen benches, and even the visitors were all in league with his recent captor, and were circling him, sniffing, waiting for the cover of deeper darkness to slip inside his coat, crawl into his mind, and toy with his sanity.

Suddenly, from out of one of the darker reaches, just behind one of the sculptures on the locks plaza, a thin, wispy youth stepped in front of the writer and, smiling, waved his, or maybe her arm, the writer couldn't see the youth clearly, and the shadows all seemed to scream and vanish as one.

At the same moment, the bright, outside lights of the tower and the plaza sprang to life, eliminating even the smallest pocket that might harbor a shadow and an unwelcome inhabitant.

The writer, shielding his eyes from a particularly bright lamppost behind the youth, called his thanks, even though he was not sure why he did so.

"Thank you, I think?" the writer said, his voice recovered from his earlier outburst. "Do I know you?"

The youth nodded, pointed to the jumble of locks just at one of the corners of the fence and called softly as she, the writer decided the youth was a she, faded back down the boardwalk.

"We're bound now, kind sir. As long as Mount Nam stands guard over the city of my fathers, and mothers. As long as there is caring in your world, and in my world again, however fleeting, you may walk with ease, sir, dear oppa," the voice called, as it faded into a rising evening mist. "And, yes, it helps to stay in the light, both outside and inside you."

"Wait! Please! How…? What? Wait! Who are you?" the writer yelled to the fading youth, both shocked and humbled by the youth's words, especially by her use of the age-old term for trusted older brother or cousin.

Standing alone, the mist moving around him, the writer felt, rather than heard, the wraiths, the ghouls, the goblins, and the other cousins of the creature down the mountain, and all manner of nightmare beasts just outside of his senses, avoiding him.

Avoiding the protected one.

The one who had taken pity on the damned and unsalvageable tiny ones in that wretched lair.

The one who would write the creature's tale, someday.

And, maybe, just maybe, write their stories as well.

The half-clean child-thing!

That's it!

The writer whirled around, straining to see into the folds of the fog, but to no avail. The little creature, the child, or teen or adult, or whatever it was, now walked free and had given him, a writer of fanciful tales, a possible gift of hope.

Where had she gone, the writer wondered? And, how would she survive in a world almost alien to her?

The writer then resolved to search her out.

Wandering amongst the promise-heavy fences silently bearing their burdens of endless locks, the writer peered through the mist, pausing as he passed young people to study their faces, then move on. After a number of fruitless minutes, he found that he had circled back to his starting point.

Nothing.

The youth had vanished.

Finally giving up his search, the writer bowed to a random spot in the mist and silently thanked the wee spirit for her curious goodwill.

Glancing at the mass of multi-colored locks where the child-thing turned protector had pointed, the writer saw, for the briefest of moments, as the mist and shadows parted, a small, yellow lock seeming to hang freely, without others crowding its spot. Small, worn scratches from a youthful hand had long faded on the visible side, losing whatever tender words had once graced the token's sides. Then, the shifting mist and shadows filled back in and the view of the lock was swallowed up by the many others crowding around it.

Turning, the writer then saw his own shadow fall into the mist and, smiling, he was randomly reminded of a long ago trip to London when he had taken his children to see the fanciful Peter Pan statue beside the swan laden waters of Kensington Gardens. The bronze figure of Barrie's most famous character had seemed to fill the air with upbeat energy. Coincidentally, the statue of the boy who never grew up was not far from the touching, yet cheerful sounds of children playing in and around the Princess Diana Memorial Fountain, where the Long Water blends into the Serpentine. Such solemn, yet cheerful places must be free of our gruesome friend's distant cousins, the writer declared to himself, walking toward the open plaza.

Of course!

The Peter Pan statue, the Princess Diana Memorial, and even the swans gliding across the water, all were mental sanctuaries, the writer realized, as were his children, his family. His own frightening experience, as he had finally admitted his fear to himself, had nudged his mind to go to happier times. Safer places.

Watching his shadow move about, first in front of him, then beside, and then split into multiples as he crossed under the array of lights in the darkening plaza, the writer whispered a smiling thanks to Barrie for the inspiration. He then held his head up, took in a deep breath of the autumn air, and decided to babble a bit.

"Where, Mr. Shadow, might you be off to this night?" the writer quipped in what he hoped was the happiest and most bereft of fright and worry voice he could muster.

"What's that you say? You're heading to the noisy streets and bright lights of Myeongdong? And, you're taking the cable car down?" the writer added as he made his way to the plaza exit, spooking a couple of teens who looked around for the object of the writer's questions. "An excellent idea. Much more cheerful than descending that long and winding road to the bottom. May I join you? Yes? Excellent!"

With that last shout, the writer, after another, yet brief interlude of on-the-fly, mental editing of the afternoon's bizarre encounter, hummed bits of every nursery rhyme, old ballad, Disney song, Raffi earworm, Studio Ghibli tune, K-pop melody, and buoyant rock anthem that he could remember, as he headed down to the cable car.

After all, the writer decided, glancing back over his shoulder for good measure, one could never have too many cheerful thoughts on a cold, misty fall night in the middle of old Seoul.

Turning forward to look out over the city through the nearly bare autumn trees of Mount Namsan, the writer wondered, in between tunes, how many of that great city's people, at that very moment of apparent tranquility, were hosting cousins of the crazed hermit troll-goblin of Mount Namsan, in the endless stretches of their 'tall hive-huts?' Were there truly unknown guests, half-seen, hidden in the shadows of those hurried lives? Were all the outlandish tales, to include his own, not the stuff of myths, legends, and fiction, but integral to the lives of the peninsula's people, and those beyond? If the troll-goblin was real and not simply a deranged, modern-day Fagin running hapless beggars in the darker alleys of Seoul, what did that say about other mythic creatures?

Pausing at the top of the massive stairway that would take him to the cable car station, and beyond, the writer took one last look at the plaza, the people, and the glowing tower. He let his eyes scan the crowds and wondered how the little half-clean child, now teen, would fair, alone in such an unforgiving city.

"Good luck, little one. Thank you, again," the writer uttered with a short bow toward the plaza, to the confusion of people wandering about him.

Looking back out over the city, the writer shook his head to dislodge his earlier thoughts about Seoul's 'tall hive-hut' dwellers, as his captor had called them. Instead, he allowed his mind to drift back to his first time in Korea, decades before. Great times. Sadly, with many old friends since lost. He reflected on the many returns to the country, the vast changes he had seen, and wondered how it might continue to evolve. Mostly, however, his mind lingered on the names and faces of so many who would not see the new Korea, somewhere out there on the horizon.

The writer then hurried down the wide, grey stone steps, picking one of his father's favorite melodies from a distant childhood. He was hoping such tunes would help to suppress rising worries in actually escaping the mountain before his new colleague of the 'cook pot lessons' changed its addled, vengeful, outcast mind and decided to send its ogres after him.

As he faded into the light mist, the writer's heartfelt humming of Burn's signature poem 'Auld Lang Syne' floated up behind him, bringing a knowing smile to a thin, waif-like, young teen, who, with a new lease on life, had set about figuring out how to use a borrowed cell phone, which she fully intended to return, to find her brothers and sisters, knowing her parents had probably long passed.

The slim teen, herself unsure if she was a boy or a girl, as the time with the troll-goblin had stripped away any such self-awareness, turned away from the disappearing, but eternally linked, foreign writer, and walked into the bustling evening crowd on Namsan Tower's plaza, quietly humming the writer's tune in an attempt to commit it to memory, vaguely aware that the pensive tune was one she had known in an earlier, far-removed life. Wearing borrowed, from a café worker's locker, clothes and slippers, which she fully intended to return, she then seamlessly blended into the twilight crowd of visitors.

The delicate youth, breathing deep the clean, crisp air of the open plaza, smiled at the innumerable sounds of people's voices, the percussion of their shoes tapping or sliding upon the paving stones, the swish of their clothes, and even the quieter jingle of their jewelry. She thrilled at the rustle of the trees, at the back and forth calls of the evening birds, and at the endless noises of the surrounding city stretching its night muscles.

Yet, just beneath the awareness of those strangers around her, the waif of Namsan's darker shadows steeled her gaze when she felt, more than heard, the barely perceptible clicks, shivers, and creaks of the troll-goblin's brethren sliding about the murkier spaces, waiting, watching.

Yes, the ethereal youth thought, with caution, free. For now.

At the same time, the hurrying writer, far down the steps from the plaza, spied the grey, yet always cheerful, cable car station, with the glimmering, modern city of Seoul calling to him from just beyond the darkened, guardian pines of Mount Namsan.

Stepping toward the station, a grim thought suddenly arose in the writer's mind, which, of course, he felt was solely of his own crafting.

Free.

For now.

#

ABOUT THE AUTHOR

A writer of both novels and short stories, Charles Mitchell is a retired U.S. Air Force intelligence officer and national security consultant, and has lived, worked, and traveled throughout the U.S. and the globe, to include living in South Korea and Crete, Greece. A native of South Carolina, he now calls the Washington, D.C. metro area home. Attuned to the many fables and legends of his southern U.S. past, he enriches his writing with tradition, myth, folklore, and superstition from many peoples and cultures. He holds a Bachelor of Arts in History, University of Maryland Global Campus, and a Masters of Science of Strategic Intelligence, U.S. National Intelligence University, Washington, DC. He is a member of the U.S. National Park Service's Volunteers in Parks program, volunteering as a guide and visitor experience interpreter at memorials and monuments on the National Mall in Washington, D.C. (to include the Korean War Veterans Memorial).

Other works:
- The God Song: Artificial Intelligence Meets American Appalachia (2019)
- Dark Sings a Distant Herald: A Christmas Story on Holding Back the British Twilight (C. Talmadge Mitchell) (2014)
- Beach Time: Tales from Several Shores (2005)
- Hues of Tokyo: Tales of Today's Japan (2003)